T0129233

YEARNINGS

A Collection of Short Stories

Armando J. Calonje M.

YEARNINGS
A COLLECTION OF SHORT STORIES

Copyright © 2019 Armando J. Calonje M.

All rights reserved. No part of this book may be used or reproduced by
any means, graphic, electronic, or mechanical, including photocopying,
recording, taping or by any information storage retrieval system
without the written permission of the author except in the case
of brief quotations embodied in critical articles and reviews.

iUniverse books may be ordered through booksellers or by contacting:

iUniverse
1663 Liberty Drive
Bloomington, IN 47403
www.iuniverse.com
1-800-Authors (1-800-288-4677)

Because of the dynamic nature of the Internet, any web addresses or
links contained in this book may have changed since publication and
may no longer be valid. The views expressed in this work are solely those
of the author and do not necessarily reflect the views of the publisher,
and the publisher hereby disclaims any responsibility for them.

Any people depicted in stock imagery provided by Getty Images are
models, and such images are being used for illustrative purposes only.
Certain stock imagery © Getty Images.

ISBN: 978-1-5320-7990-0 (sc)
ISBN: 978-1-5320-7991-7 (e)

Print information available on the last page.

iUniverse rev. date: 08/13/2019

Ↄ

... fictional stories are just tales which frolic and linger in the hallways of our mind ... they become real once they are written ...

The author

Ↄ

Contents

Foreword and Acknowledgements

...The novel is an ocean liner. The short story, a sailboat hugging the coast. An Olympic team is required to write a novel. Singular as he or she may seem, the novelist is a team of painters, city planners, gossip columnists, fashion experts, architects, and set designers; a justice of the peace; a real estate agent, midwife, undertaker; a witch and a high priest all in one. The short story writer, on the contrary, is a lonely navigator. Why this fidelity to solitude? Why this need to be in sight of the coast? Perhaps because the storytellers know that if they do not tell the tale this very night, near the shore, with no time to cross the ocean, there might be no tomorrow. Every storyteller is a child of Scheherazade, in a hurry to tell the tale so that death may be postponed one more time...

Carlos Fuentes, *The Storyteller*
The Vintage Book of Latin American Stories

Carlos Fuentes, a Mexican storyteller uses this beautiful metaphor to describe the writer of short stories, comparing the novelist to a transatlantic that ventures across the ocean and the storyteller to a small vessel that sails without going too far from the coast.

Fuentes continues with a detailed description of the subject citing some famous Latin American storytellers like Horacio Quiroga, Rómulo Gallegos, Juan Rulfo, Gabriel García Márquez, and Jorge Luis Borges among others, and finishes his description indicating that: *Yet, tender, angry or merciful, "realistic" or "fantastic," at the end of each story a question must hang over it, a perfume must linger, permitting the story to be complete, but remain open. After all, if a story is a declaration against death, its author is nothing but a perpetual convalescent...*

Isabel Allende writes that ... *fiction is something that comes from the womb and the heart, like all emotions* ... To write a short story in addition to requiring a certain technique the writer must feel it, as Allende says, it must come from his heart. The main objective is to attract the reader's interest fast and keep him engaged until the final outcome.

Chekhov had six principles as a guideline to write a good short story: "1. The absence of lengthy verbiage of a political-economic nature; 2. Total objectivity; 3. A truthful description of persons and objects; 4. Extreme brevity; 5. Audacity and originality: flee the stereotype; 6. Compassion."

I will add some of my own guidelines to Chekhov's list: 1. Minimize the number of characters to two or three; 2. Introduce a sense of time, be it an hour, a day, or a year; 3. Place the reader in the setting and situation being described, invite him to join you. (To me, the most challenging was the description of persons, namely their facial features.)

I do not pretend to be an expert in the art of writing short stories. I am an apprentice and an enthusiast of the art of storytelling.

My stories are simple and uncomplicated. I don't use fancy words; nor do I mention famous philosophers. They are based on memories; some have real nuances and others are simply a product of my imagination or my dreams. My main goal is to try to get the reader to enjoy that brief moment by putting a little salsa and flavor to his life.

If for some reason they resemble similar persons or real-life situations, it is just a simple coincidence. Regardless of how real they may seem; they are just fiction.

A few stories have been written inspired by real events or a genuine story. In these instances, the names of the characters were changed to protect the identity of their protagonists. The author has used "poetic license" to revive the dialogue and the situations and circumstances surrounding his narration.

I left Nicaragua at a very young age and since then, I have been telling stories to my friends and family, some believe these stories are real; others just look at me in disbelief by saying "what are you telling us?" I started writing short stories later in my life, I was too busy working and raising my family and I would not want to change those years. At this point in my life, my free time is spent reading and my spare time writing short stories.

"Why don't you write a story?" A friend asked me once.

"What do you mean?" I asked, "you just don't write something out of the blue, out of nothing."

"But that's what you do, you make up stories." Was his response.

For example, a specific request from a friend prompted me to write *The Quinceañeras*. The story of *The Blue Jay*, I wrote at the suggestion of my wife who — while we both were enjoying a glass of wine in our gazebo in Monterey, California — saw this chirping and noisy bird diving out of nowhere after a peanut that fell on the floor. She said: "it would be nice if you write a story about that Blue jay ..." In both instances, I obliged. A couple of anecdotes told to me by a good friend provoked me to write *Parade, Floats, Trinkets and Stuffed Animals* as well as *Yearnings* which I chose to title this book.

An annoying fly, who kept interrupting me while I was writing, prompted me to write *Discord Among the Insects*. *John* was conceived from a comment made by my aunt about a crime committed many years back at the Borg's Motel in Pacific Grove, California. Don't use the word "but" my wife would admonish me, use "nonetheless," "notwithstanding," "however." I like the word "but," I don't find anything wrong with it if you use it properly, such a friendly discord gave birth to *Analysis of a Story.* I could go on ...

In ... *I Guess I Am on My Own Now!* ... the reader will follow a memorable trip I took with my son from the east to the west coast. My stories also take you to places where I lived, visited and traveled. From my hometown of Granada, Nicaragua, to New Orleans, Louisiana, to Washington, DC, to Monterey, California, to Bend, Oregon, and to places I have not visited, such as Nantucket, Massachusetts. Funny as it may seem, with the exception of *The Streetcar,* I don't have more stories from the beautiful and mysterious southern city of New Orleans. But one is enough, which is one of my wife's favorites, perhaps for its romantic nature: a good-looking Chilean gentleman and a Venezuelan nun departing mysteriously.

"I read your story and I liked it but it had a sad ending ..." some readers would comment. I just shrug my shoulders in response. Like a great majority of storytellers, I write about life, or situations related to a myriad of experiences; such as the struggle of humans, immigrants attempting to get to El Norte, as well as the sad and debilitating disease of schizophrenia such as *The White Linen Dress.* I write about the abuse inflicted on a woman by a narcissist in *Lucila's Secret.* In *Parade, Floats, Trinkets and Stuffed Animals,* I relate about our memories and our superficial attachment to material things. Betrayal is depicted in *A Despicable Betrayal.* In *Abuelo, Can You Tell Me a Story?* I describe how an innocent young child asks his grandfather to narrate him a story, not one from a book.

Life is not always a party, a *fandango* ... we don't live in a continuous Mardi Gras. We have happy moments, and we have sad ones as well. We strive to strike a balance by trying to steal more of the happiest from the sad ones, but life is brutally cruel and unforgiving. We have afflictions, we struggle, we get ill, we dodge most of our illnesses, we move on until finally, life ends. That's what life is all about. However, my intention is to try to introduce some humor in most of my stories.

"I liked your story, but what's the punch line?" Other readers would question me. Although I try to introduce some humor into my stories, I don't write jokes, I'm not good at telling them, and least of all writing them. Having a "punch line" is not my style.

"Something is missing at the end ... if I were you, I would elaborate more ..." others would suggest. "You left me wondering what happened, what happens next...?" a few would ask. To elaborate or expand would be like going deeper and farther into the ocean.

After reading *Lola's Story* a good friend who never hesitates in giving me his comments, sent me his interpretation. *Lola's story is a sad story, but the one who reads it from upside down finds it jubilant; because in it he discovers the naivetes' of the human being who is harassed by the rottenness of evil. Of course, the inverted reader knows that the lowliness of evil, even if it does not seem like it, is always overcome by the sublimity of innocence and that is why he finds the story jubilant...*

Regarding the final tale, the one after which I titled this book: *Yearnings,* I must add a comment made by a loyal reader:

... Without neglecting other of your works. I loved this one. Very well achieved and with a structure and a descriptive method that abounds, distracts and above all helps the reader grasp the plot.

Very modern style. Involving several actors in the story ... making the description a kind of "collage" of personalities and interests was a very good idea. Taking as a point of reference the dialogue to a third party (Isamu) allowed the ruralist description to be much more fluid, the reference to the times that pass and want to return (the aspirations of Mrs. Smith). The element of surprise, wrapped in the localist tradition of characters in the shadows (the pair of cart drivers.) The reference to John Steinbeck's reading was also well placed, by way of a corollary, to express the need for closeness in friendship ...

I figured out after many similar comments, that what some readers expect is a conclusion, a climax ... or an ending, happy or sad, they just want to be led by the hand as you do with a small child. I decided against that. I want my readers to use their imagination to reach their own conclusions and to figure out on their own how the story ends. As Fuentes writes, *at the end of each story, a question must hang over it, a perfume must linger ...*

"Who is Baltasar?" Someone asked me a while back. Baltasar is a character I created. Baltasar was one of the biblical Magi also referred to as one of The Three Wise Men and the dedicated servant of Romeo (of Juliet.) There are many famous people who carry that name. *My* Baltasar, as I said, is just a fictional character, a small-town drunkard who likes to tell stories and shows up unexpectedly and uninvited in several places. I originally introduced him in the story *Playing Spinning Tops,* and whenever I feel it is appropriate, I bring in his character, as a player or as an observer. Another friend asked me: "is Baltasar 'Papa Fay'?" Could be. I recall the "borrachito" who roamed the streets of my hometown. But no, is not him.

I like to bring in to some of my tales the inexpensive Agua Florida cologne. A cologne used by many girls when I was growing up. I found it amusing that after so many years, I came across it at a pharmacy in Monterey, California and purchased a bottle to give to my wife as a joke. The store clerk did not know how it was used, so I told her that I used it to sprinkle it around the house to scare evil spirits. "Really!!!" was her reply.

When thinking of having a friend or relative to write the prologue to this selection of stories, I chose not to have one. I opted not to ask any of my friends or relatives to write the prologue. I wanted to spare them the agony!

Recently I read a book in which the author took the time to list more than one hundred persons who had in one way or another influenced him in his lifetime. Don't worry, I am not going to do that. However, I would like to thank all of those who took the time to read the Spanish version of my stories, but most importantly I want to thank those who were brave enough to provide me with their honest comments — not always positive — but constructive suggestions to improve either the story itself or its grammar. Thank you all!!

I want to thank Silvia, my wife, and writing collaborator, for her support and mostly for her honesty in providing me with her valuable comments, such as: "I don't understand what you are saying, please clarify it," in addition to the "'don't use 'buts'." She is as tough as they come and sharp as a tack. I thank my son Armando for designing the cover of the book, my daughter Silvia for her support in helping translate some of these tales, she wished she had more time to assist me. A special thanks to my daughter Carolina and my son-in-law Richard for assisting me with editing some of these tales. I also want to thank our good friend, the late Ada Martínez not only for helping me edit the Spanish versions but for her constant support in this literary adventure.

It is a pleasure to also thank my dear friends and classmates who took the time to read these tales in Spanish providing me their honest constructive opinions and those who helped me shape these stories into a book. Also, I thank my loyal readers Dr. Alberto Quiroga, Luis Gomez and José Antonio González for their honest comments. And especially I like to thank José Aburto, my good high school friend — with whom I reconnected after more than half a century — for taking his time to edit some of these stories and providing me his valuable comments. *Muchas gracias.*

And last but not least, I want to express my deepest gratitude to my good friend Barbara Darrah who, not only encouraged me to translate them into English but also for contributing her valuable time and linguistic abilities to edit a good number of them. Barbara, when you accepted my request to help me with this project, I not only felt honored, but lucky. *Ich Danke Dir.*

Juanocho

Granada, Nicaragua. Summer of 1951

L ike most summers in this strikingly beautiful colonial city, the temperature was unbearably hot and humid sending a large number of its inhabitants looking for a place to escape the heat. Some of its residents had gone swimming in the pool at the country club. Others had gone to cool off in the waters of the lake, or a nearby lagoon. Those who could afford a portable air conditioner had hunkered down inside their homes, while others sat under the shade of a tree to cool off drinking an iced tamarind drink and fanning themselves with a colorful straw fan made in Masaya, a city near Granada.

As usual, Gustavo Machado always tried to be present at his grandparents' house to enjoy the appetizing lunches his grandmother made. He was not always on time, and his excuses rarely managed to convince his strict and grouchy grandfather. Gustavo couldn't have been more than ten years old.

On a Saturday afternoon, Gustavo's family was gathered for lunch in the large dining room of the beautiful house of his maternal grandparents. In order to mitigate the overwhelming heat, they had turned on the electric ceiling fan. It was during these lunches that the family tried to be together at least once throughout the day. That particular Saturday, they had all been punctually seated at the dining table except for Gustavo who had not been able to make it on time and knew he had to listen to his grandfather's habitual sermon:

"This house is not a hotel! ... when are you ever going to be on time? One of these days you are not going to find anything to eat!"

Disregarding his grandfather's comments, Gustavo distracted himself by trying to cool off the crab soup he had just been served. It was then that his father surprised all those present by asking them:

"Who would like to go on a picnic tomorrow on the Ochomogo River?"

Everyone responded affirmatively, except the grumpy grandfather who answered that during the summer the river was usually dirty and it was not possible to swim in it... None of the diners paid attention to his negative observations. The whole family was ready to go on a trip, to spend the day somewhere outside the city and escape the scorching heat.

The Ochomogo River, compared to other waterways in Nicaragua, is a relatively narrow river and not very deep except in some places where the pools or backwaters reach a depth of anywhere between

1

six and ten feet. The river's smooth, grey stones, some covered in moss, were not large enough to slow down the flow of water, which sometimes ran faster on its way toward Lake Nicaragua. The Ochomogo River separates the Pan-American Highway, between the cities of Rivas and Nandaime. To cross the river an iron bridge, no more than a hundred or two hundred meters long had been built.

On the day of the picnic, the micro-bus that Gustavo's father had rented left them at the side of the road before crossing the bridge. Everyone helped unload the cardboard boxes and the plastic blue cooler with food and refreshments to be savored during the rest of the day.

Also known as the "bull rider," Tula the owner of a canteen-restaurant located near a mango grove by the river, was waiting for them. When she saw them, she hurried down and with a pleasant smile on her round light brown face, and greeted them with a warm and friendly welcome. Tula was nicknamed the "bull rider" because in her youth she had been caught naked in an open field on top of a man who was called "the bull." Although Tula was also known for other "gifts" — not deemed appropriate to describe in this narrative — it is fair to point out that she was famous for cooking the best *mondongo* or tripe soup in the whole region.

At the canteen-restaurant, the Machado family were also awaiting the arrival of two other families whom they had invited to join them for the Sunday picnic.

As impatient as he was, and eager to see how clean the river waters were on that day, Gustavo left the family gathering and headed toward the river. On the riverbank closest to the canteen-restaurant was an old man trying to fish. He sat on a large stone under the bridge with a manila rope tied to the end of a stick for a fishing rod. With the distinctive curiosity of a child his age, Gustavo approached him.

"There are no fish in this river." Gustavo heard the old man say to himself. With his left hand, the old man rubbed his stomach, which roared like a caged lion, and again he said to himself:

"Juanocho! Did you hear your stomach? Have mercy on it; it's asking for food, why do you think it roars? You have not eaten in the last two days! In what misery have you fallen?"

It was after his own conversation that the old gizzard noticed that Gustavo was looking at him. The old man could not have been more than sixty years old, but looked older. Although his face was hidden by a worn-out straw hat, you could still see his unshaven face burnished by the sun and the hunger that overwhelmed him. His arms, clearly weathered by the sun were black. His eyes were yellowish and the sad expression on his face was noticeable. Upon closer inspection, Gustavo noticed that the thumb of the man's left hand was missing. He was unable to detect the size of the old man because he did not make a move to get up when Gustavo approached him.

Gustavo was disgusted when he saw the man, who had been chewing tobacco, spit into the river.

"And what are looking at kid?" Asked the old man when he noticed Gustavo's presence. "What do you want, what are you doing here?" Did you come to fish, where is your fishing stick, what is your name?"

"My name is Gustavo. I came to spend the day with my family; they are in the canteen house. I only came to see how the river was," said Gustavo.

"Well, you saw it, now get the hell out of here, and tell your family to feed you, because you're thinner than a rocket's rod, the kind that they fire up at the processions of the Purísima, the Virgin Mary."

Gustavo was a thin adolescent child of medium height. The dark blue cap he wore partially covered his forehead and prevented anyone from clearly distinguishing the color of his hair or even his eyes which, appeared dark green with the reflection of the water. With a faint smile, Gustavo asked:

"What is your name?"

"Why do you want to know? What do you care?"

"I don't know ... I just wanted to know your name."

"My name is Juan Ochomogo, but people call me Juanocho."

After a brief pause, Gustavo asked:

"Why is your name the same as the river, why weren't you named after your father or with any other name?"

"Look, kid, don't ask so many stupid questions, what do you want to know? What do you care what my name is!"

"I'm only curious," answered Gustavo, "that your name is the same as the name of the river, and not your father's."

"You're too nosy kid," Juanocho muttered. "My grandfather was very religious and tried to raise my mother by giving her a Catholic education, but she ignored him, my mother was a *piruja* and chose the easy life."

"What's a *piruja*? Was she a witch?"

"No kid, a *piruja* is a whore. Do you know what a whore is?" Juanocho asked with some disgust.

"I think so, but why do you call her *piruja*?"

"Because that's what my grandfather called her when he ran her out of the house: *Piruja! Piruja! Piruja!* He shouted at her, and at the age of five that word stuck in my head like a sharp nail."

"But you still have not told me why you call yourself Ochomogo." Insisted Gustavo.

"After my grandfather ran her out of the house," Juanocho added, "she started wandering and going from one job to another. She earned her living that way, *pirujiando*, until she came to work

3

around here and among other things, washing clothes in the river. She became pregnant with me; do you know what it is to be pregnant?" He asked, frowning at him. "One day while washing clothes in the river I was born. Since she did not know who my father was, she gave me the first name that came to her mind, Juan and the surname was the name of the river where she had given birth."

"I understand," said Gustavo. "Do you live around here, how did you come to the river, where is your mother?" Asked Gustavo.

"I live upstream, in a straw hut that I built. I come here on Sundays because after the rich people like you leave, Tula gives me some leftovers to eat. You are asking too many questions! What do you care? My mother died in the *llena* of 1948."

"What's a *llena*?"

"You don't know shit, boy!" said Juanocho raising his left hand as if swatting a fly. "The *llena* is when the river rises because of the rains. After a drinking binge, she fell asleep near the river, and did not realize that the waters were rising; after two days they found her dead, floating in one of the river's pools. So that you don't ask me where I was, I'm telling you that I was in the hut asleep and did not notice when the waters rose up or when the current dragged her out."

While Juanocho was casting the baited line into the river, the music from the jukebox in the cantina started to play. They were playing the popular Bobby Capó song *Piel Canela* (Cinnamon Skin) as well as *En el Mar la Vida es mas Sabrosa* (Life is more fund by the Sea). Both songs were so popular at that time that the cantina customers did not stop playing them on the jukebox or the radio.

"The words of that *Piel Canela* song irritate me, they make me sick!" said Juanocho, looking toward the cantina. "Everyone spends their twenty-five cents to hear it, it is the falsest song I've heard: '*I care about you, and you and you and only you ...*'" Juanocho hummed some of its lyrics.

"Why do you think it's not true?" Asked Gustavo.

"Because it's a lie, no one cares about anyone, everyone is selfish, everyone is worried about themselves and nobody cares if you are hungry or thirsty, if you are sick, if you live or if you die. Look at my mother, those who saw her being dragged down by the river and didn't lift a finger to save her, they'd rather save a pig than save her. Look at my finger, it got cut off when I was cutting cane at the sugar mill. Nobody cared about my finger, the only thing that mattered to the owners of the mill was that I kept cutting cane, and I kept cutting cane until my finger fell off."

"What a shame about your mother and your finger!" Said Gustavo.

"Why do you feel sorry?" He replied, and in a contemptuous tone, Juanocho answered. "You didn't even know my mother; you wouldn't have cared about my finger either."

"Do you have other relatives, any brothers or sisters?" Asked Gustavo.

"I don't know, my mother told me I had a sister; who knows who her father was. I think she went to live in Guatemala, I never met her. Why do you want to know?"

"Why do you live here by the river, hoping that Doña Tula will give you the leftovers on Sundays?"

"Look, boy," he said. "After working at the San Miguel mill for several years, I became disenchanted with life. When I stopped working, they did not even say goodbye. I just left with my machete, the clothes I was wearing and a few cents."

"Why did you come to live by the river?"

"Because I do not bother anyone here, nor does anyone bother me; the river has no feelings, it's not envious, it has no hatred like humans. The river speaks to you in silence and you don't have to answer if you want. The river washes me, the river feeds me, the river can be violent but not like men. The river witnessed my birth and I bear its name, the name my mother gave me. This river that I love more than my own being will probably be the one who sees me die. And I will die happily, embracing it, and its stones, and its crystalline waters, green or filthy as the saliva I spit into it. I know that the river will forgive me, that it will not hold any grudges."

While Juanocho spoke he again cleared his throat, but this time he did not punish the river with his saliva.

"I cannot even spit," he told himself. "It must be hunger." He excused himself.

"Do you have a peso that you want to give me? I have not caught anything and I do not know if there is going to be any food leftover, I can buy one or two tortillas with a peso."

"I only have two pesos, which my parents give me for the rest of the week. I can give you just one." Answered Gustavo.

Looking at him with his deep eyes hid by his bony face, he said:

"Thank you!" and grabbed the peso with his left hand, the one missing the thumb.

On Sunday, — two months after the picnic that Gustavo shared with his family on the banks of the Río Ochomogo — as usual, Gustavo was late to the dining room. Before sitting at the table, and as he used to do, his grandfather repeated his sermon:

"This boy will never learn that this house is not a hotel, next time he will not find food ..."

This time Gustavo did not have to blow the beef soup that had been served to him, it was already cold, but he ate it anyway because his grandfather's strict and cranky demeanor would not allow him to set the plate aside. Without saying a word, the grandfather observed

5

Gustavo who played with the soup spoon. The grandfather left him alone and turned to Gustavo's father:

"Did you read today's newspaper? The rains of these last days have caused havoc, some rivers have overflown, and the damages have been disastrous. The Ochomogo River also overflowed, dragging everything in its path. It took along a few straw huts that were by the bridge, some dogs, five cows, and three calves. It also took Guillermina Fuentes, her husband Ignacio and an old man, a so-called Juanocho who lived near the bridge in a straw shack close by the cantina."

"They called him Juanocho." Gustavo interrupted his grandfather. "His real name was Juan Ochomogo, that's the name his mother gave him because he was born in the river, and I'm sure that instead of saving him, they tried to save an animal."

"Did you read the newspaper, too?" His grandfather asked. "How do you know so many details of what happened?"

"Because Juanocho told them to me," said Gustavo.

"This boy is delirious!" His grandfather said. "Stop playing with the spoon and finish eating your soup..."

Buddy

To Silvia and Ada

H is name was Brandon James but he liked to be called "Buddy." He was the son of Dorothy, a sweet and loving older lady who lived in the historical and picturesque city of Monterey, on the central coast of California.

Dorothy was a gentle and peaceful woman who, notwithstanding her slight dementia and the beginnings of Parkinson, liked to take strolls along nearby streets. She usually stopped by our house to admire our small garden and to exchange small talk. She enjoyed looking at the small neatly trimmed juniper pines. But most of all, Dorothy was a good mother.

She had endured her son's alcoholism and drug abuse for many years. Like a revolving door, Buddy had been in and out the state penitentiary until she could not tolerate him and finally threw him out. Buddy sought refuge in an abandoned empty lot close to the ocean where other homeless and drunkards roamed.

Monterey, California, July 5, 2011.

The fourth of July celebrations of the United States' independence had already taken place. The local high school band had marched along the most popular streets; all the instruments including the large drums and cymbals had been stored away. The colorful fireworks such as rockets and firecrackers that lit up the night sky with brilliant yellow, red, white and blue colors had also ended. All the music, explosions and celebrations of that memorable day, not to mention the several glasses of wine I had shared with my neighbors, had kept me awake. I believe it was more the wine than the noisy celebrations that had kept me up most of the night. It was about three-thirty in the morning when I finally fell deeply asleep.

On the morning of the fifth, I woke up earlier than normal. The clock on the night table showed eleven minutes before six in the morning. I did not want to make a sound nor wake up my wife Berta. I decided to silently slide out of our bed and made sure not to slam the door as I exited our house to start my daily walk. But, regardless of all the precautions I took, she woke up slightly and gazed at the red numbers of the clock on her night table.

"You definitely are crazy." She said while looking at me in disbelief. "Why are you going out at this hour of the morning? You are going to be the only one on the streets, but if you decide to go out, wear some extra clothes. It is cold outside." (It's always cold and misty in Monterey.)

The fog that daily covers the city during the summer months was thicker than normal. As I approached the corner of David and Junípero streets, instead of continuing on Junípero, as I always did when I went out for a walk, I decided to change the route and walk the three or five blocks down on David toward the ocean.

Next, I crossed Pine and Archer streets. I waited for the traffic light to turn green on Lighthouse Street before crossing. Suddenly, I heard the sound of a lonely seagull wailing at me over and over from her perch on one of the electric cables. It sounded more like a lament, or a warning about the danger that awaited me, but I disregarded it.

Four crows perched on the telephone wires which crisscrossed Central Avenue also yelled at me, their caws louder than those of the seagull. I did not pay attention to them either.

'After all,' I thought, 'They are just birds, what can one expect from these animals? I had encountered seagulls and crows before and nothing had happened to me.'

After crossing Fawn and Foam streets I passed by Nob Hill supermarket. It was closed. Everything was closed. There was no one on the streets, not even on Main Avenue. There were no cars either; the rush hour had not started.

I noticed that Coco's restaurant was just opening. Through the window of his pick-up truck, a lonely client waited at the side of the carryout window to buy something, perhaps a cup of coffee.

I continued down David Street until I reached the doors of the Monterey Bay Aquarium. They were also closed. On previous occasions, I walked on the dirt path bordering the ocean. I always liked to admire the harbor seals lazily resting on top of the rocks, the ones the ocean had not been able to drown. But that morning I opted to follow a different path, on one of the sidewalks of Cannery Row. The Row was also deserted. All of the July 4th revelers had left. The tourists who had come from as far as San Francisco; or from the nearby towns of San Juan Bautista, Gonzales and Soledad; and from cities east of Monterey were long gone. Everyone who had come seeking the marine breezes, those cool and soothing fresh breezes blowing from the Bay had also returned to their hometowns. All the surroundings were silent.

At this moment I could not help thinking about the way this street was during the 1930s, during the time of the sardine fishing bonanza. I thought about the smell, that penetrating stench of raw and cooked sardines; of the odor hundreds of women who labored in the packing and canning companies. This morning the odor was rancid and bitter, the stink of littered unwashed streets; the leftover smell of tourists all dressed in shorts, T-shirts, and flip-flops trying to capture all the stunning sights and images with their digital cameras just to be erased by pressing a button upon arriving at their homes.

As I continued with my walk, I approached a narrow passageway between the Aquarium and a recently built hotel. I distracted myself thinking about how the Pacific Ocean looked that early in the morning. I thought it had been named Pacific because of its calm and peaceful waters which at that time of the day would barely make an effort to caress the concrete pylons supporting the Aquarium. I was also admiring the dawning of the day and thought about what the famous writer John Steinbeck called *...the hour of the pearl; that interval between the day and night when time stops to examine himself...*

I passed by Ed Ricketts's laboratory, — Steinbeck's inseparable friend — and by the remnants of the homes occupied by the first Chinese who came to this city in search of marine otters. The figure of the one-eyed wooden pirate outside the souvenir store stared at me indifferently.

The wine tasting bar was also closed, as well as the Bubba Gump restaurant. The Bolivian Indian who entertained the tourists with his wooden flute by playing *El condor pasa* wasn't there either. I heard steps behind me as if someone was running in the same direction where I was headed; chills ran up my back. I looked back and it was just a soldier jogging at that early hour and as he went by, he saluted me with the usual greeting: *Good morning!* He continued jogging toward El Presidio military base.

I went by the locked doors of the souvenir earthquake store, built to mimic the damage inflicted by the many earthquakes which punish the state of California. Nor was there anyone at the Ghirardelli chocolate store.

The abandoned empty lot, next to the restaurant El Torito was also empty. However, I was able to see the figure of a man facing a concrete wall between the lot and the restaurant. That concrete wall which is witness to the anguishes, wishes, hostilities, and dreams of lots of dwellers, those homeless people who daily struggle to live and survive at least until the following day. These homeless, drunkards, drug addicts ... who roamed the surroundings and who spent the nights among the rocks near the ocean.

'He must be urinating,' I guessed because the thick fog did not allow me to identify who he was nor what he was doing.

"Perhaps is Buddy," I said to myself when I saw the head of the figure of the man covered with a ragged black leather hat. I knew it was him because I had seen him before seating on the sidewalk of the nearby CVS pharmacy. I also knew that he was fed leftovers by the waiters of El Torito. Dorothy, his mother who had not seen him in the last five years, had also told me that he used to hang around the empty lot. Regretfully she had imposed a restraining order so that he would stay away from her house. It had to be Buddy; I thought to myself, he always carries a black plastic bag where he carries all his belongings.

"Yes! It is Buddy," I assured myself.

Suddenly, with a rock in his right hand, another figure appeared from behind one of the rocks where he had been hiding. I did not know who he was. I had never seen him before.

I leaned against an electric post to prevent them from seeing me, but the post was not large enough to hide all of my body.

Both men started to argue heatedly; I could just hear the obscenities they were yelling at each other. Their figures became clearer to me; I was able to confirm that the one with ragged black leather hat and jacket was Buddy.

The man holding the stone in his right hand tried to hit Buddy while yelling obscenities. While dodging the blows, Buddy receded until his back was against the concrete wall; the wall of the dreams wishes and intrigues. I watched the fight but was unable to do anything, it did not even occur to me to make a move; I was only a spectator of the tragedy about to take place.

Buddy continued to dodge the blows of his aggressor but could only escape being hit on his face. One of the blows landed on his shoulder. He bent over to escape a second blow while putting his right hand inside the right pocket of his black leather jacket pulling a dagger and stabbed his aggressor in the lower part of his chest. The unidentified man retreated backward several steps while putting his left hand on the upper part of his stomach as if trying to close the wound inflicted by the weapon and contain the flow of blood which already had stained his soiled shirt. Lifeless he dropped over the sandy soil of the empty lot. The thirsty sand was already absorbing the dripping blood.

Regardless of which of the men had been right, I had witnessed a horrible crime. I felt dryness in my mouth; I did not have any water.

Buddy cleaned his weapon against the dark trousers of his assailant who lay motionless on the cold sand. The sun had not risen yet. It would still have to wait until the thick band of fog dissipated at around nine-thirty in the morning for the sun to launch its rays and warm up the empty lot and be a witness of the horrific scene.

I remained motionless behind the electrical post while Buddy searched the empty lot and its surroundings to make sure that no one had witnessed the crime he had just committed. But I could no longer hide; the cap covering my head had given me up. Buddy had seen me. I was a witness to his crime; he started to walk toward me and I felt the chills and the terror that my body was experiencing at that moment. He was going to kill me, he had to eliminate the only witness to his crime to prevent being captured, brought to justice and sentenced to jail till the last day of his life.

He hurriedly tried to catch up with me. I had abandoned the post where I was hiding and started to walk at a faster pace. I managed to cross the street and headed toward my home. In the distance, I could hear the sound of a siren of a police vehicle. Perhaps someone else had witnessed the murder and had notified the authorities. I was wrong; the siren was that of an ambulance racing to the nearby hospital; perhaps it was transporting an ill or a wounded patient.

Buddy's double-bladed knife shined as he brandished it under the light of the corner street lamp. I had been unable to shake off the terror that I was feeling; I felt it in the pit of my stomach. I was thirsty but I did not have water. The temperature was still cool but I felt the perspiration dripping from under my armpits.

Buddy was advancing quicker than I anticipated; he was closing in on me. I reached the corner and started to climb the steepest street in Monterey, Prescott Street. I doubted if I could reach the next street, the less steep one. There was no one around on the street, not even the McDonald's employees had arrived to start frying the bacon and cooking breakfast.

I continued advancing to the next street; the heavy sweat had already dampened my undershirt. I felt a cold chill on my neck as if Buddy's knife had already stroke it. I removed the sweatshirt, the heat I was feeling was exhausting me. Once again, I felt the dryness in the mouth but I could not alleviate the thirst due to the absence of water.

I heard Buddy's steps nearby; he was closing in on me. I also felt a pain running on my left arm and heavy pressure on my chest as if someone had laid a large stone on it. My breath was faltering. It was then that I thought and asked myself; "Is this how one feels when the heart can no longer take it?"

The palpitations were accelerating faster than the car that crossed the corner at a very high speed. I could feel the pounding of my heart strongly pressing both of my temples; I thought they were about to explode. I resigned myself to die of a heart attack in the middle of the street and not by the weapon Buddy's was hiding inside the left sleeve of his ragged black leather jacket. Panting and very short of breath I managed to go higher one more block.

I could no longer go on. I could not fathom how a drunkard, a drug addict, a sham of a man could gather so much energy. I was in better physical shape; 'why was I exhausted?', 'could it be the fear?' or 'the dreading feeling of the blade being buried in my stomach or my chest?' I wondered how many stabbings would be needed to end my life.

I looked back and Buddy was only five steps away; I saw him pulling the knife from the left sleeve of his jacket. I tripped on a rock and fell backward in the middle of the street. While resigned to die, I thought about my family, my wife whom I had not given a kiss before leaving that morning thus breaking the pact we had made to each other about giving one another a kiss when one of us went out as if bidding farewell. I thought about my children and grandchildren as well as my friends. My life started to go in front of me like a lightning rod, similar to the way it went through Jesus' mind while at the Mount of Olives.

Buddy came closer. I noticed his deep and shiny eyes full of vice, and his nicotine-stained whitish beard; his copper bronzed face looked like an iron rusted by the sea salt or by the sun to which had been unknowingly exposed for so many years. I could smell his filthy odor, and see his unwashed and trembling hands; those hands full of dirt and blood which had not been treated with water for a long time. His right hand raised the knife.

I tried to avoid him by going backward; I abruptly sat up, it must have been the adrenaline remaining in my body; I was panting and sweating profusely. I dogged his first stabbing attempt and I started throwing punches one right after the other but none was landing in Buddy's face as if I was hitting an empty space.

Suddenly, I felt someone pulling me from my sweaty T-shirt and saying; "you are truly loco, it is not enough for you to wake up early to go out and walk on the empty and solitary streets, now you are boxing while seating on the bed."

"What is wrong with you," asked my wife.

"Nothing," I replied while getting out of bed.

I looked at the red numbers on the clock on top of the night table. It was seven minutes before seven.

Two days later, with her back toward the street, my wife was absorbed tending her small garden when Buddy surprised her offering his personal card and very respectfully said; "excuse me, lady, I am sorry to interrupt you, I sometimes work in construction and often as a gardener. If you ever need help don't hesitate to call me. I am not going to charge you very much, just a couple of dollars will be sufficient."

What Did You Do Today?

*...this story pokes gentle fun at the preoccupations and sometimes
sad lack of meaningful content to the lives of retired friends...*
Barbara Darrah

The other night I went to dinner with a couple of friends at a restaurant nearby. I had not seen this duo in a long time, not since I stopped working a few years back. As usual, Don Vito, the Italian restaurant on Main Street was crowded and noisy at that time of day — seven-thirty to be exact. However, despite the noise, I could distinctively hear the model miniature train going about and around on the suspended rail line above us, puffing fake smoke, choo-chooing and chugging along. We sat in a quiet corner of the restaurant at a table covered with a bright-red checkered plastic tablecloth adorned with fake flowers in a glass vase and a lit red candle on an empty Chianti bottle. An accordionist was playing *O sole mio* close to the bar.

My friend Rudolph — Rudy as we call him — ordered a beer, Johnny wanted a shot of whiskey, I ordered a glass of merlot wine. Dinner would be served — according to our waitress — shortly.

Twenty minutes later, our impatience started to grow while we waited for our meal; and we decided to order another round of drinks.

Ever since Rudy went back to his native country in South America, we had only exchanged e-mails. He always had told us he enjoyed jogging, going to the beach, visiting with family and friends among other things. However, he only mentioned that he had finally divorced his wife of twenty plus years but did not elaborate on the reasons nor he offered any specific details. We sort of suspected he would sever his matrimonial ties. He always complained about his wife's expensive tastes and shopping habits, but we respected his silence and moved on with our conversation.

When it was my turn to share with my two friends how and with what I have kept me busy since my retirement, I told them I enjoyed working outside in the garden, chasing weeds, planting flowers, mowing and watering the lawn ... I also mentioned to them my favorite hobbies, writing stories, reading, and copying music CDs to give to my friends and relatives.

"How boring," said Johnny with a wide smile on his face.

"Do you do that every day?" asked Rudy.

"Of course not," I replied. "It depends on how I feel; I don't always do the same thing every day, not in that same order. Sometimes I write if I feel like it ..."

"When you feel inspired when the muse hits your brain," jokingly interrupted Johnny.

"Yes, you are right," I said. "Then is when I write."

"What about you Johnny?" I asked. "You seem to be interested in what I do and what Rudy has been doing. What do you do? How do you keep busy? Tell us what you do. What did you do today?"

"My life is very boring," replied Johnny. "I don't read, don't write, but I often go out to have dinner with friends. If my wife asks, I run errands for her, as well as other chores around the house, vacuuming, you know, stuff like that ..."

"All that is fine," I said. "But you have not told us exactly what you did today, before joining us for dinner."

"I don't think you guys really want to know, I almost got in trouble with one of my neighbors."

"How so?" asked Rudy. "Why don't you explain, and tell us what happened to you."

"Well," he said, "you are all aware it is autumn, and what falls from the trees during this time of the year? Leaves."

"So, what's with the leaves? You rake them, and if you don't bag them you put on the street, by the curve," said Rudy. "How would raking leaves get you in trouble with your neighbor?"

"Could you bring me another whiskey?" Johnny asked the waitress who had just walked by. "Dinner is taking too long."

Johnny had not changed one bit since the last time I saw him. He was always the impatient type, he was the type of person who would curse for nothing or at anything, but he never meant to offend anyone in particular. He was just a good guy; that was his personality, the way he was, 'good ol' Johnny.'

"As I was raking the leaves in my front yard," Johnny explained, "I saw Willy — my neighbor — approaching me with his black Labrador in tow."

"Oh!" I said, "you finally befriended Willy."

"Of course not," Johnny replied. "Not that asshole."

"It must have been bad ... your encounter with Willy," I added.

"Yes, it was pretty bad. He walked toward me slowly, wearing what appeared to be a brand-new jogging suit — I have never seen him walk fast let alone jog — and as I was raking the leaves to put them on the curve, he stopped to say hello."

"You know," added Johnny, "that's the only way you speak to your neighbors around here. Either over the fence or on the street, these people are incapable of sharing an invitation. I have invited Willy several times to have a couple of beers with me, but he always has an excuse. He is a cheap sonofabitch; he probably thinks he is going to pay for the drinks."

"Anyway," added Johnny "as I was pretending to be nice to him and start a friendly conversation, his dog peed on my leaves. You know! The leaves I had just finished raking on the curve."

"So, what?" What's wrong with his dog peeing on the leaves?" I asked.

"They are my leaves; I don't want his dog peeing on them, not in front of me. And do you know what he told me? He said that the leaves were no longer mine, once I put them on the curve they belonged to the county, so he concluded that his dog had peed on the county's leaves, not on my leaves."

Rudy and I laughed out loud at what our friend Johnny was telling us and decided to ask him how he had taken care of the "problem" he had with his neighbor. He said:

"The nerve of this guy, to tell me to my face that those were not my leaves, so I raked the damned leaves back onto the lawn and told him, 'OK Willy, now they are back on my lawn. Your dog just peed on my leaves.'"

"And what did he answer?" I asked.

"He told me I was crazy."

Our waitress interrupted this interesting conversation by putting a dish of ravioli on the table for Johnny, the chicken parmesan in front of Rudy and a bowl of fried calamari for me.

"So, what happened next?" asked Rudy.

"My wife came out holding a half-peeled banana — I eat a banana every morning for health reasons — and reminded me not to forget to take my blood pressure medication. Perhaps she thought I was fighting with Willy."

"But you were arguing with him, just because his dog peed on the leaves," said Rudy. "Perhaps your wife thought you were fighting with him."

"Nah! she was just curious," said Johnny.

"Silencio! Don't say a word," Johnny said, all of a sudden. "Tony and his wife Arleen just walked in; they are walking toward our table."

"Who is Tony, is he another of your neighbors?" asked Rudy.

"Yes," Johnny replied. "He is a nerd, a weirdo; I bet you he asks me about my muscles. Every time I see him, he tells me how muscular I look, he compliments my shoulders, how broad they are ... If he weren't married, I would start wondering about his sexual preferences ..."

"Perhaps he 'likes' you ..." said Rudy jokingly.

"Yeah, right ...!"

As Tony and his wife Arleen approached our table, he addressed Johnny.

"Hey, Johnny! It's good to see you, are these two good-looking gentlemen friends of yours?"

"Yes, they are my old friends from work. I had not seen them in a while." He introduced us to Tony and his wife.

"Say, Johnny, I have not seen you lately, are you still doing exercise to keep-in-shape? You look so good, so in-shape, have you been lifting weights to tone those muscles on your arms? Sorry, I have to go, our table is ready. Continue enjoying your meal, it looks pretty appetizing."

As Tony walked toward his table, he told us he was pleased to have made our acquaintance. We acknowledged him and said we were also pleased.

"I told you, he is weird, and I told you he was going to make a comment about my muscles, about my shape, about how good I look," Said Johnny. "I don't know how his wife puts up with him. I don't know what's with him and the way I look. He is so effeminate, look at the way he walks, he is dressed in a coat and tie, and nobody wears a coat and a tie anymore. Doesn't he look weird?"

"Sort of," said Rudy. "But who cares about how he dresses, forget about him. Let's concentrate on our meal."

"Besides arguing with your neighbor about the leaves, having your daily banana and bitching about your friend Tony, about how he admires your muscular body and how he dresses, what else did you do?" asked Rudy.

"Not a whole lot," replied Johnny. "My wife came out again and said it was time for lunch, and after lunch, it was time for my siesta."

"Wow! What an exciting day, Johnny," I said. "Who is going to pick up the tab?"

"I will," Johnny replied. "It's my turn to treat you guys; I hope you do the same for me next time, and would you please excuse me, I need to go to the restroom."

"Watch out!" said Rudy. "Tony could be in there as well, and he could admire something else besides your muscles."

Johnny just looked at us without saying one word. While he was away in the restroom Rudy asked me:

"Don't you think Johnny is losing it? He seems so obsessed with everything.

"I think he is a little crazy," I replied. "But he is a nice guy. He is paying the bill!"

"Yeah! You're right!"

John

It was a cloudy and gray Monday afternoon in the central coast of California. The sun rays had not yet penetrated the thick fog hovering over the waters of the Monterey Bay. Further up the northeastern side of the bay, near the city of Santa Cruz, the sun managed to puncture a wide band of fog and clouds floating over the water. The bay looked like a clear mirror over the calm waters. On that particular day, the Pacific Ocean was quieter and calmer than I had seen it on previous occasions.

A group of harbor seals rested on the rocks by the coast due to low tide. Seagulls and other marine birds frolicked over the rocky shoreline bordering the famous Lovers Point Park. The scenic rocky point protrudes into the ocean adjacent Pacific Grove, a town neighboring the city of Monterey.

The light breezes blowing from the ocean did not stop me from sitting on one of the wooden benches facing the Pacific. I noticed the water from the automatic watering system had turned off.

That Monday afternoon, the majority of visiting tourists from other nearby cities and towns had left. All was quiet and the surrounding tranquility was only interrupted by the murmuring waves. Walking by the park was a small group of Asians perhaps from nearby San Francisco or from other northern cities of California. While I heard them talking, they did not distract me from reading the book I had chosen to enjoy that afternoon. Making sure that there was no one too close to interrupt me, I rested my feet on top of the three-foot-high stone and cement wall built to prevent tourists from falling onto the slippery rocks by the shore.

A couple of young girls from the group of Asian tourists were photographing the scenery. They later stopped a man who was walking by and cordially asked him if he could take their photograph. He took the camera from one of the girls and scanned the landscape to make sure that the best angle of the scenic view would include both the ocean and the city of Monterey in the background. After taking a couple of pictures, he handed back the camera to the girls who thanked him and joined the rest of the group.

The man was lean and tall, not older than sixty-five. Because of the look of his dark tanned face, I could tell that he had been exposed to the sun. His straight looking nose was an extension of his ample forehead which he covered with a baseball cap with the letters *SF* embroidered on it. I figured he was a fan of one of the San Francisco sports teams. His graying hair was partially hidden by his cap, except for a ponytail tied with an elastic band.

I noticed a three-inch-long scar under his chin which he tried to conceal with the collar of his dark green flannel shirt covered with a blue vest. On his left hand, there was a smaller scar. The slightly faded cuffs of his blue jeans rested loosely on his bare feet and over a pair of worn Franciscan style sandals. They appeared to have traveled hundreds of miles. His eyes were hidden by dark sunglasses.

He lit a cigarette and threw the match on the sandy soil and stepped on it with his foot. Then he turned and looked at me and without hesitating, he headed toward where I was seated. After sitting next to me he said:

"My name is John. Do you mind if I sit next to you?"

I told him my name, and we exchanged hellos. I was hoping that he would not stay for too long so that I could proceed with reading and added that I did not mind if he sat next to me. But I soon realized that I was absolutely wrong! Obviously, John had not been able to talk with anyone that day who was willing to listen to him. He needed to talk and I was the one he had chosen.

"What are you reading?" He asked me, while curiously trying to see the title of the book.

"I am reading *The Long Valley,* its Steinbeck's book of short stories."

"His tales are amazingly beautiful; I read them many years ago. One of my favorites was the one titled 'The White Quail.' The story is somewhat sad because the husband of the heroine purchased a rifle to kill a treacherous raccoon spying on the quail and make it its meal ..."

"Please don't continue John," I interrupted. "It's a coincidence, but that the is the same story I am currently reading, and I would like to finish it myself and find out about the ending on my own."

"I am sorry, I was not aware that you were reading that same story." John apologized.

At this point I realized that John was a very persistent individual; he definitely wanted to talk, so I closed my book and I resigned myself to listen to him.

He said: "You are not a tourist. You don't have a camera. A large majority of the people who come here are tourists, and they never get tired of photographing the stunning and amazing views of the Pacific, the rocky ledges ... besides, I can tell you are not one of them because the way you are dressed. Your shoes are a very good example. Generally, tourists wear tennis shoes, T-shirts and shorts, as if they were going to encounter eighty-degree temperatures or higher. As soon as they feel the cool breezes of the ocean, they run to the nearby tourist shops searching for warmer clothing.

Did you know that the majority of Steinbeck's stories are based on personal experiences? The ones included in the book you are reading are some of his first tales. Where did you get the book? It's been a long time since I have seen a copy of it."

"Yes, it's true," I said "his stories were based on his personal experiences, namely those he wrote about the Salinas Valley and the city of Monterey. This book was given to me by a friend who has also read some of his stories."

"Did you know that the city of Monterey" added John, "is very historically rich? It's well known not just for being the first capital of the state of California but for the world-renowned novels of John Steinbeck and Robert J. Stevenson. In this area, the stories about ghosts, mysterious appearances and disappearances, suicides, romantic tales, hoodlums, vagrants, benefactors, and much more are abundant ..."

"Were you aware that during the gold rush and the construction of the railroad," John continued enthusiastically after noticing that he had grabbed my attention, "thousands of Chinese were brought over to work in the mines and the railroad? But that's not all; during the twenties, the human trafficking flourished and many ship owners lend themselves to the trade and smuggle them illegally. Local authorities persecuted those involved in the trade, but they couldn't control it, because they lacked the financial and human resources to do it. Some with knowledge about the trade, and who studied its background, say that when one of them got ill he would be thrown overboard into the sea to prevent him from contaminating others. Those traders were mean, heartless; they would not discriminate between men, women or children. The most inhumane and sad part about this practice was when a child was thrown overboard to drown or to be eaten by sharks."

"I was not aware of human trafficking."

"That was what originated all the tales of the disappeared and of the ones who managed to survive."

"After the Chinese" he continued, "came the Philippines; with the fishing bonanza of the sardines, the Portuguese and the Italians arrived and the human trafficking started to die, just like the industry and exploitation of the sardines. The agricultural development brought the Mexicans, with migrant workers settling in this area but mostly in the Salinas Valley. The population of this area is so diverse and so are its many tales."

At Pfeiffer Beach

"For example, further south of Monterey, you can find Pfeiffer Beach," he signaled. "It's a small but very beautiful and secluded beach with dangerous and treacherous waters. There is a tale that takes place at the beach from the 1950s. At that time, there was a family vacationing at Pfeiffer Beach in Big Sur. While the mother was spreading a blanket on the sand and the father gathered firewood to start a small fire, their two daughters, who were around nine or ten years old were playing nearby. One of the girls went near the edge of the ocean and was so distracted collecting shells of varied colors and sizes that she was unaware of the waves. All of a sudden one of those rogue waves violently carried her out the ocean. After hearing her desperate screams her parents frantically ran toward her, but it was too late. They were only able to see how her small arms extended above the water as she fought desperately to keep afloat but another bigger wave pulled her down."

"What a horrible scene to witness!"

"Her parents were not able to rescue her, they couldn't go in, because the current was too strong and the waves began to crest bigger and stronger, some reaching ten to fifteen feet high. But they did not give up. Hoping that a wave had pushed her back toward shore they started to walk hurriedly along the coast for a sign of their daughter. After going around a sandbank, they saw her. She was lying face down on the sand about three feet from the edge of the ocean. Her dress had been torn, she had several wounds and scrapes on her legs and arms and a deeper cut on her shoulder which was still bleeding. They desperately ran toward her asking her how she had managed to swim out of the water. But the girl would not answer, she was terrified, but finally, she composed herself and said:

"'The boy helped me out of the water; he rescued me, pushed me out the water but then quickly returned to the sea!'"

"'What boy? What's his name? What does he look like?'" Her mother insistently kept asking her.

The girl was so stunned and scared she could not answer. It was after making a great effort that she managed to say:

"'He was very young, about fourteen years old with dark eyes, like those of a Chinese. His hair was long, black and straight; I noticed that his hands and feet looked weird.'" The girl said.

"'What do mean they looked weird?'" The father asked impatiently.

"'His fingers and toes were joined together with a white membrane, like the ones you see on seagulls.'"

"'You are hallucinating dear; you have been through a horrendous and traumatic experience!' The mother told her while covering her bruised body with a gray blanket, and looking at her husband she said:"

"'I think we should leave; it's getting late' and whispered in his ear: 'I've heard of a very similar story which occurred at Monastery Beach. A boy very similar to the one our daughter is describing was spotted at that beach.'"

"What do think? John asked me. "Do you think he was an extraterrestrial?"

But John did not wait for my answer. He would not stop. He

was very enthusiastic about the tale he was narrating to me. He continued on:

"Do you think that the boy who rescued the girl was an extraterrestrial or a ghost of one of those Chinese children that were thrown overboard into the ocean?"

"I don't know! I doubt the existence of extraterrestrials, and I don't believe in ghosts either."

"I believe in both!" John said. "Those beings are always present all over and around us; they show themselves in many forms. We tend to identify them as they are shown in movies, with small bodies and large heads and eyes. Do you see that seagull standing on one leg over on the fence?" John added pointing toward the bird with his right hand. "She has been there very attentively observing us for more than ten minutes. How can you be sure that it's not an extraterrestrial in the form of a seagull?"

At the Del Monte Hotel

It became clear that John was not going to stop telling me more of his tales despite my efforts not to listen. In the end, I gave in and decided to continue listening.

"John," I asked him. "If you like to narrate all these tales why haven't you written them down and published a book?"

"I like to tell them to the tourists who I talk to at the park, at least those who are willing to listen to me. I don't like to write; I am not a writer. Besides, the majority of these stories have already been written. I am going to tell you one which occurred at the beginning of the century. Do you mind?"

"No, I don't, please go ahead."

"After the disastrous San Francisco earthquake in 1906, which leveled most of the city, lots of rich people, artists, painters, and others moved to this area. Some settled here permanently while many others would come during the summer and stay at the local hotels. One of the most well-known hotels at the time was the Hotel Del Monte. Everyone came for the weather and the cool breezes blowing in from the ocean. They would come on the train, by carriage and other means. Some would come looking for a good time, others came in search of a *paramour,* an affair ... and because of its privacy and exclusiveness, the hotel lent itself to guests interested in such amorous activities. The hotel is still standing; however, the land where it is located, including the building is currently occupied by the Naval Postgraduate School."

"I've heard that during that historic time some horrific crimes were committed as well as several suicides."

"Very true," John replied. "One of the most talked-about events was the suicide of a lady from San Francisco high society. She would frequently stay at the hotel in a discrete and luxurious room. Here she would meet her lover — another eccentric, belonging to one of the wealthiest families of San Francisco. I don't remember his name but he was one of the richest men during that time. Perhaps he was one of the Hearst or the Del Monte families."

"No one really knows what happened," John added. "Supposedly, the lady threw herself from one of the fourth-floor hallway balconies landing on the atrium floor. Can you imagine throwing yourself off the fourth floor? It was a very violent death. She must have been embittered and desperate about her affair being discovered and instead of facing scandalous news within her high society circle she felt she had no other option but to kill herself. It's rumored that after midnight the lady's ghost roams around the hallways of the hotel. Some have heard the ringing of a very small bell, like the one used to call for services … However, when the concierge opens the door of her room, the steps stop and so does the ringing of the bell. No one has been able to solve the mystery."

The fog had not yet dissipated, it was even thicker. Although some rays had gotten through, the sun was still stifled by the fog and the sky turned dark grey. John's sunglasses fogged up with humidity. From the left back pocket of his jeans, he pulled out a white handkerchief and very carefully started to dry them.

It was then, at that moment, when I was able to see John's eyes for the first time. They were black, sad-looking and mysterious. They vaguely gazed toward the ocean as if anxious to penetrate its depths. His eyebrows had been very carefully trimmed but some thick white hairs rose above the others. I don't really know why, but at that moment I felt somewhat concerned, afraid; as I had not seen his eyes before and his intense deep gaze was unsettling. My heart started beating faster than normal.

Masking my fear, I got the courage to ask him about his scars, the one under his chin and on his left hand. After drying his glasses, he put them back on while making sure they rested perfectly on the top of his nose below his forehead. Then he said:

"The scars on my neck and left hand as well as others I have on my chest were caused many years ago when I was in an automobile accident. I was traveling north toward the city of San José with my wife and my fifteen-year-old daughter when just before crossing the vicinity of Gilroy, a boy suddenly jumped into the road and I was unable to stop to avoid hitting him. The boy did not survive, and neither did my wife or my daughter. I was the only one who survived the horrific accident. I prefer not to speak about that episode; it brings me very bad and sad memories."

"I am very sorry about the loss of your family," I said.

He appreciated my words of condolence, and without hesitation, he pulled a pack of Camel cigarettes from the pocket of his vest. He tapped the pack to get one of the cigarettes out and offered to me; however, I declined.

"I don't smoke."

"Do you mind if I do?" He cordially asked me.

Since we were sitting in a public place and on a bench where we both were enjoying the ocean breeze, I told him that I had no objections. He lit the cigarette and said:

"I hope I haven't tired you with my stories, you are a very cordial person who has patiently listened to me. Most tourists who come to this city are not interested in learning about the city's history and legendary characters; and least of all about my tales and anecdotes. They are more interested in taking pictures with their digital cameras and capturing the beautiful landscape of this central coast of California."

John seemed genuinely pleased that, that afternoon he had managed to get somebody to listen to him. It became clear to me that he had no intention of stopping. Although the afternoon chill was creeping through my short sleeve shirt, I decided not to interrupt him.

At the Borg's Motel

I hope this is his last tale.' I thought to myself while watching him light another cigarette with a trembling hand. Then he continued:

"Do you know that at the motel right behind us, the Borg's Motel, a family was assassinated several years ago?"

"Yes! I've heard something about, but I never bothered to inquire."

"It happened about twenty-five years ago. A couple with their daughter was staying at the motel when an intruder broke into their room after midnight and killed the three of them. It's been said that the motive was to rob them ... I say supposedly," John paused, "because the killer was never found. It was a violent death. They were stabbed to death, but the weapon was never found either. It's not known what kind of a knife it was but was presumed to be a kitchen knife.

"I had heard about the crime; however, I was not aware of the gruesome details."

"As I said before," John added, "people around here like to add some romanticism to the story, they tend to mix reality with mystery. They also say that the ghost of the dead man still roams around this park; some people have gone as far as saying that they have spoken with him, but no one believes them. When they try to tell the story, no one is willing to listen, people believe that they are exaggerating and making things up."

Suddenly, a chill ran over my back as if someone had dropped an ice cube under my collar. I kept my composure and disregarded it.

'It can't be!' I thought to myself blaming the chill I had felt to the cool wind blowing from the ocean. 'Am I just imagining this?'

While those feelings of fear and dread crossed my mind, I noticed a couple of white limousines parking in the lot nearby. I watched as a group of photographers came out of one of the limousines and started to strategically position their cameras and tripods. Six couples then emerged from the other limousine. The girls were wearing long purple gowns and the boys were wearing white tuxedos. A bride and groom also came out of the long automobile; she was wearing a white wedding gown and the groom a black tuxedo.

It is very popular for newlyweds to come and have their pictures taken at the famous Lovers Point Park. It is, after all, a fantastic view of the bay. I was so absorbed with the commotion of the entourage that I did not notice when John had gotten up from the bench where we had been sitting. I saw him hurriedly walking toward the restrooms located at one of the corners of the park.

'He probably needed to go in a hurry and could not wait' I thought. 'He will be back'

However, after twenty minutes or so, John had not emerged from the restrooms. I curiosity decided to go to the restrooms myself and wait for him by the doors. There I waited for another fifteen minutes. I asked a man who had just come out if he had seen him? I described John to him. But his response was more mysterious.

"There is no one inside; all the stalls are empty," the man said.

"It can't be possible!" I exclaimed aloud. "He could not have disappeared like that. He would not just leave without saying goodbye or thanking me for listening to all of his tales."

Still not satisfied I decided to cross Ocean View Street and head to the Borg's Motel. A young man was standing behind the counter and cordially asked me if I needed a room to rent. I thanked him for his courteousness but told him that "I do not need a room; I was just inquiring about a crime which had taken place many years before at the motel."

"Oh yes." The young man answered, "but it happened many years ago, and don't have too much information to give you, I was very young then."

But the young man was abruptly interrupted by a hoarse voice coming from the back of the receiving room. It was the voice of an old man who was sitting on a worn-out recliner chair. His scruffy white beard had brown nicotine stains. In his hands, he held an old version of LIFE. In bold letters, the title read: CAPONE TO ALCATRAZ. Over his thick eyeglasses, he curiously looked at me. He slowly rose from the chair and walked toward the counter where the young man was standing. Disdainfully, he tossed the magazine on the counter as if he was tossing a dirty rag. He approached me and in a hoarse voice said:

"The boy does not remember what happened at the motel. He was very young at that time. I am his grandfather and the motel's owner. The crime took place in room number six. An intruder managed to break in into the room, apparently to rob the family staying in it. They were a very nice couple with their fifteen-year-old daughter. It was a very violent crime. The wife and her daughter were killed first, the husband tried to defend himself by avoiding the blows of the killer, but his efforts were unsuccessful. He was stabbed in his chest, his arms and hands. The forensics team who examined the scene of the crime concluded that the fatal blow, the one that killed him was a cut below his left chin which severed his jugular."

As the old man continued with the horrific and macabre description of the scene of the crime, without thinking I automatically raised my left hand to my neck, searching in vain for the wound I had seen on John's neck.

The old man continued: "The room was full of blood. The walls were stained with bloody handprints; perhaps from the fight they had with the assassin and the carpet and beds were covered in blood. After the murderers, I decided to close the room for good and convert it into a storage room. That's why there is no longer room number six. After five, it goes straight to seven. It was a tragedy and the city was impacted forever. They were a beautiful family from San José; they used to visit this area during the summer season. There are people who go around gossiping about the ghost of the dead man, that he roams around the park and speaks with tourists, but I don't believe in ghosts or ridiculous apparitions. That's the true story of the crime occurred at the Borg's Motel." The old man concluded.

"Thank you very much, Sir," I said to him. "It's an amazing yet very sad story. Do you by any chance remember the names of the family members?"

"Of course, I remember them. Gertrude was the name of the wife, Linda was their daughter, and the husband's name was John ... yes John Sesione. I will never forget those names," the old man added.

As I exited the motel, I once again thanked the old gizzard for all the information he had provided me. As I crossed the street toward the bench where I had been seated, I repeated aloud:

"John Sesione" And again, automatically my left hand went toward my neck.

"John Sesione" I repeated. "It's not possible!" I murmured.

As I approached the bench, I noticed the seagull that had been standing on the stone fence was no longer there. I gazed over toward the partially submerged rocks and the seagull. A pair of shiny black eyes were staring right back at me.

Then I asked myself: "John?"

Once again, I felt a chill in my bones.

Playing Spinning Tops

"**D**id you hear what happened to Baltasar?" Francisco asked his friends Felipe and Raúl.

"We haven't heard anything," replied Felipe and Raúl. "What happened to him?"

"He fell asleep behind the railway station, and at midnight a couple of riffraff tried to rob him. They beat him up, but they did not find a single dime on him. Poor Baltasar, he never has any money, he is always begging, he's a drunkard and a vagabond."

"Poor Baltasar," the boys agreed. "He is always getting into trouble; one of these days they will find him dead on a street. Maybe that's why he hasn't been roaming around in the alley to ask us for money."

"Don't worry about Baltasar, he's sure going to surprise us any day. Are we still going to play tops, that's what we came to the alley for, Felipe brought a brand-new top today?"

The three boys were just kids about eleven or twelve years of age. Although they differed in age, they were all good friends, some were school mates, others were neighborhood buddies, but the most important thing was that they were all friends. The three were going to play spinning tops in an alley adjacent to Calle la Calzada, one of the main streets in the city of Granada, which ran from the Central Park to Lake Nicaragua.

The place where they met was a narrow, unpaved dirt and gravel alley; a perfect location for neighborhood kids to have fun playing various youthful sports like softball, tops, marbles and the like. Most of the boys in the city and one or some other adults knew this popular venue simply as "the alley," others called it "Valle's alley" for the very simple reason that in the corner opposite of the alley and kitty-corner to it, coincidentally two families whose surname was Valle lived there, although they had no family ties.

There is not much to describe about the houses in this alley. I remember their tall and gloomy adobe facades painted with lime slurries and one or two large garage entrance gates leading into a somber vestibule or a courtyard. The alley served the young crowd as a place where they could play, exchange stories and concerns. It was like a youthful "social club."

The friends who frequented this popular alley were varied and numerous; however, the permanent members of the "club," or rather the most frequent ones, were José, Francisco, Raúl, Felipe and Alfredo. Their constant presence at this prestigious venue and distinguished "club" was probably due to the proximity of their homes to it, as they all adjoined the main or surrounding streets.

Raúl always played his top carefully. He avoided dirtying his loose-fitting khaki pants but considering his medium height, he couldn't avoid the cuffs rubbing the sole of his shoes. The dark blue cap that covered his straight brown hair had the letter "G" embroidered on the front, named after the baseball team of his hometown, Granada. His friends called him El Khaki because most his trousers were tailored with khaki fabric that his father bought in the black market from his acquaintances in the National Guard.

José was unable to meet with his buddies that scorching hot summer afternoon. Apparently, his parents had taken him to Managua, the capital city. Alfredo, for unknown reasons, could not join the group either. On that particular day, there were only three, the most assiduous members of that friendly gang; Francisco, Chico pelón (Chico, short for Francisco, the bald-headed one), Raúl El Khaki and Felipe, El Canelo, as he was nicknamed for his cinnamon complexion.

Whenever Felipe said to his mother: "I'll be right back, I am going to go play at the Valle's alley," she always replied, "You are like the old horses, they lie down always in the same place. I do not know what you do in that alley for so long. Before you go why don't you drink a glass of milk and eat some bread?" Felipe always avoided antagonizing or contradicting his mother; he just looked at her and smiled.

Felipe was tall and thin, with a short nose accentuated by his high cheekbones, and to hide his broad forehead he usually combed his black hair forward.

Francisco had earned the nickname of Chico pelón because he liked to cut his hair short, almost razor-cropped. Francisco was the shortest of the group of friends and it was obvious he was well fed because his plump cheeks and his round face made him look like a yellow cheese ball.

"What a great top you bought," Francisco said to Felipe. "It must have cost you more than one Córdoba[1]."

"Yes, it cost me more than one Córdoba!" said Felipe, who that very afternoon very haughtily had come to the alley with his wood turned spinning top of guaiacum[2]. "I just bought it for C$1.75," Felipe added.

"You've almost spent your entire weekly allowance," Raúl added with his mocking giggle. "You have told us that your parents just give you two Córdobas per week. Unlike your parents, mine are

---

[1] The Córdoba is the official currency of Nicaragua, US$~C$33.
[2] Guaiacum or Guayacán in Spanish is an evergreen tree found in tropical America, known for its hard and heavy wood.

more generous, they give me five Córdobas a week." Insinuating that Felipe's parents were cheap and stingy.

It was a bad habit for Raúl to laugh without a motive or about anything, and a mocking giggle was always ready to come out of his mouth.

"I've spent almost everything my parents gave me!" Felipe said. "I only have twenty-five cents left. And these I have to save so I can buy chewing gum or ball candy, at Miss Gutiérrez grocery store."

"The wood of the guaiacum tops is very hard," Raúl said. "But my top is better than yours even if it costs less, the screw that the top turner put on is very sharp. I'll bet you the only quarter you have left, that I will split it in half in the first game."

Seeing that Felipe did not like the ironic remarks of his friend Raúl, and anticipating that both could start throwing punches at each other, Francisco, who did not like controversies, intervened by saying:

"Felipe, don't listen to Raúl," he said, looking at Raúl with some disgust. "Raúl is very bothersome; he thinks his stuff is the best; he is always bragging that his parents are wealthy, that they give him more money than anyone else to spend during the week. He is nothing more than a phony, a charlatan and a mocker."

"And you're the goody-goody," Raúl told Francisco.

And so, the three boys finally started to play and began to hit each other's tops without one damaging the top of the other. At about the fifth or sixth game, Felipe still was not able to hit Francisco's top and had to put his prized top on the ground.

"Now it's my turn," Raúl said to Felipe with a mocking smile, "I'm going to split your top in half."

It was perhaps due to a flaw in the guaiacum hardwood that Raúl fulfilled his threat by breaking in half Felipe's top at that very play.

"Damn you, guaiacum top!" Felipe said, disgusted by the fate of his top and even worse because Raúl's threat had been fulfilled.

"The sharp screw and the reddish turned top were useless, Raúl broke it, it's split in half. It is as if my top was made of cheap wood or as if it had been carved in orangewood or some sort of softer wood. Now I have no choice but to remain as a looker-on," he complained, while Francisco and Raúl continued playing and hitting their respective tops.

Felipe was so embittered and absorbed watching as Raúl tried to break Francisco's top that he forgot about the loss of his expensive and precious guaiacum top. As Felipe watched how Raúl and Francisco were throwing and hitting their tops, wrapping the string under their top's belly and throwing them back against each other's, none of them noticed that the drunkard and ragged Baltasar had walked in the alley and was approaching them. Contrary to other occasions, none of the boys started to run away after seeing

Baltasar. This time they saw him walk up to them and sit on the edge of the two-foot-high sidewalk that bordered Alfredo's house.

"Hello kids," Baltasar said in his low coarse, trembling voice. "Do any of you have a penny to spare, I'm hungry and need to eat?"

"Hi Baltasar, I thought you were still recuperating from the blows you were given by ruffians after falling asleep behind the train station. That's what happens to you because you're always drunk," Francisco said. Felipe and Raúl nodded to Francisco's comment.

Baltasar was tall and skinny, his hair was long, dirty and uncombed, his black unwashed and unshaven face was also dirty and wrinkled, and a fresh cut was visible on his right cheek, perhaps someone had cut him in his face when he was beaten up behind the railroad station.

It is difficult to describe how Baltasar's clothes looked. It was not possible to identify the color of his shirt and his striped gabardine trousers perhaps given to him by someone wealthy who took pity on him. In addition to being dirty with traces of having slept on the floor — who knows for how many nights — his fine cloth pants were stained and showed signs of having been urinated in more than once. Notwithstanding his appearance, everyone in the city knew that Baltasar grew up in a good family, that he was well-read and studied, but that his parents had cast him out because he had given himself up to drugs and alcohol. No one knew where Baltasar lived, but some people said that they had seen him spend nights in a man-made hut by the mango grove near the lake.

In addition to his past, and living under the stupor of alcohol, Baltasar was also known as a good storyteller.

"Well, boys," Baltasar said again to the three boys. "I'm hungry; I have not eaten yet, please spare me a few coins. Why don't you give me something?"

Baltasar had not finished with his question when automatically and without warning, Felipe put his hand in the left pocket of his short pants to make sure that the only quarter he had left after buying his "deceased" top was still there. He needed to save it in case he wanted to buy chewing gum or ball candy at the Gutiérrez's grocery store. The other hand he put into the right pocket where he felt the Nestlé chocolate bar that his aunt had recently brought him from New York. Inadvertently, he took it out of his pocket and, after partially removing the wrapper, he bit a piece of the tasty chocolate. It was then that Felipe noticed the thread of drool that slipped from the left side of Baltasar's mouth. This made him think that perhaps Baltasar was right; that he was hungry, and that perhaps he had not eaten in a few days.

"What are you going to buy for a few cents?" Francisco said. "We do not have a dime. Who do you think we are, the National Bank?"

"I do not have any money, either," Raúl added. "But I can ask my grandfather, although I doubt that he will give me a penny."

Felipe was the next one Baltasar would ask if he happened to have a couple of cents. But Felipe did not wait for the anticipated question and willingly said to Baltasar:

"All I have is a quarter. It's my only quarter for the rest of the week. But I'll give it to you if you tell us a story. I know you like to make up stories; I'll give it to you if you tell us a good one." Felipe added as he made certain that his last quarter was in his left pocket.

"Yes, tell us a story," said Raúl and Francisco in unison. "Felipe will give you his quarter," offering Baltasar what was not theirs.

"Why don't you give me the quarter first?" Baltasar asked. "I'll tell you the story later."

"No, the story first!" Francisco said. "Because a paid musician never plays a good tune."

"All right," said Baltasar. "I guess you don't trust me, but I have no choice. I am very hungry."

"No matter what story you tell us," said Francisco. "Hurry up, you better start before we change our mind and give you nothing."

"Do you know the story about the little old lady Doña Atanasia?" Baltasar asked the three boys.

"No, we have not heard that one yet," said Felipe. "Why don't you start telling it?"

"Well, I don't remember exactly where it took place, I'm not sure if it happened in the town of Diriomo or in the town of Diriá," Baltasar began. "But I'm pretty certain it was in one those towns where Doña Atanasia lived. For all of us who knew her, she was a well-liked and admired generous lady. Doña Ata — as she was affectionately called in the neighborhood — was a charitable person always giving money to the poor and bringing food to the old people's home. After many years suffering from arthritis and an aching back, she walked with a turned cane made of guaiacum to prevent her from falling."

"Guaiacum?" Felipe asked aloud, seeing in his hand his spinning top split in half. "That no-good wood!"

"Yes!" Baltasar continued. "It was at a Mass celebrated during Holy Week when Padre Vicente, the parish priest, paused for a moment of silence to recall the path of Jesus Christ on his way to the Calvary. It was at that moment of sepulchral silence when Doña Atanasia farted ..., it was just a short one, discreet and almost inaudible, but when that silent air crashed against the wooden bench, it sounded louder than what Doña Atanasia would have wanted."

"You're a liar," Raúl said with his typical mocking smile. "I am not an expert in the matter of silent airs but I doubt that that was possible."

"Yes, it is possible," Felipe said. "Baltasar please continue."

"Then Padre Vincente raised his head," Baltasar continued. "And raising the challis with both hands, said to Doña Atanasia:

"'To your health, sister Atanasia!'" And very spontaneously he addressed the parishioners, saying: "'Poor Atanasia, may the Lord have mercy on her.'

Just as he preached the gospel, Padre Vincente went on to say to them: 'Let us pray for our sister Atanasia, who, even in the House of the Lord, could not control the forces of nature, and with great pretense, she had to dispatch that harmonious breeze.'"

Baltasar paused and said: "You can imagine, boys, what happened next; all the parishioners lowered their heads, and in between giggles and smiles began to make the sign of the cross."

"Afterwards," said Baltasar, "Padre Vincente asked all the present parishioners to say a prayer and ask the Lord to pity and forgive sister Atanasia for her misfortune, when in fact, the good Padre should have been the one asking the Lord for forgiveness, after he disrespectfully, in the sanctuary of the Holy Church and in front of all the parishioners made such a shameful remarks about sister Atanasia's misfortune."

Baltasar had not finished telling his story when Alfredo suddenly ran out of his home, alerting his three friends that his aunt Cristina was coming after learning of Baltasar's presence in the alley. She did not like Baltasar spending time with the boys. Baltasar was not her cup of tea.

"And what are you boys doing?" asked Cristina, who peeked out of the doorway of Alfredo's house.

"We're just hanging around, not doing anything wrong, Doña Cristina," answered Francisco, "we're just listening to a story Baltasar is telling us."

"Baltasar never tells decent stories," said Cristina. "He is vulgar, he is always saying obscenities, and surely you are listening to all of Baltasar's blasphemies. And you, Felipe," warned Cristina. "You know that your mother does not like you wandering around in this alley and least of all listening to Baltasar's dirty stories. Next time I see your mother I will tell her."

"You old gossip!" Felipe murmured to himself.

"And for you, Baltasar," Christina warned. "Leave the boys alone and don't ever come back down this alley. If I see you again, I'll call the police. You scoundrel drunk!"

Raúl did not wait for Cristina to finish threatening Felipe, he left in a hurry before she continued; Francisco like a bullet sped away on his bicycle, Felipe also started running like a flash towards his house, but on the way over he remembered the quarter he had promised Baltasar. Quickly, as if someone was chasing him, he returned to the alley and was able to see Baltasar before he turned the corner.

"Baltasar!" Felipe shouted while approaching him. "Take the quarter I offered you for telling us the story. It was a good one. And also, here is the rest of my chocolate bar."

"Thank you, Felipe," Baltasar said. "God bless you, boy!"

Realism

A fter a long and exhaustive search for a home where to intern Pedro, his aging and ailing father, Luis settled for La Familia Home for the Elderly. It had been highly recommended by his family and friends as a reliable and family-oriented institution. Luis trusted the La Familia Home and did not bother inspecting the room where his father would be housed.

Upon entering, Pedro Alito found himself in a dark room. The thin thread of light creeping through from the skylight was not bright enough to illuminate the face of the ninety-five-year-old man sitting in a wheelchair next to the bed of tanned bronze bars. Someone had taken care of folding the sheet and the gray blanket to the edge of the bed. Two pillow covers, spittle stained by the old man during his light sleep, had been replaced by two clean ones. For some reason, the four walls of the room had been painted a dull dark gray. The only window which would have allowed him to peer out to see the light of day was closed. That window, through which he could hear running water from the courtyard fountain, chirping sparrows flying through the corridors that edged the garden, the crowing of crows and a nurse cutting lemons from the lemon tree, had been taken away from him. To prevent him from leaving the room, the window was covered with a board of wood eaten by termites; also painted gray, a gray brighter than the walls. The old man did not know why they were being so cautious; his physical condition would not have allowed him to even go to the door, let alone leave.

His movements were slight, and the gaze of his cloudy black eyes embedded in the bony sockets of his face was vague, distracted; sometimes he looked at the window, sometimes at the door, sometimes toward the crucifix hanging on the wall of the room. The old man could not fix his teary eyes on something specific. Sometimes in order not to look into the void, and distract himself, his eyes wandered around the room that jailed him. His bony hands and his arms flaccid dried skin gave the impression that the flesh was anxious to abandon his body. His hands rested on the cold metal of the armrest of the chair. The only bulb hanging from the ceiling of the room had stopped working several days ago, it just flickered intermittently. All of this was a depressing sight, and heartbreaking, to see a man who in the past was a vigorous man in such a state of abandonment.

The rusty hinges of the door, in need of oil or grease, with the sound of iron against iron, creaked with the movement of the door opening.

Luis had not visited his father in more than two months. He entered the room where his father was followed by a woman dressed in a white robe, who appeared to be the nurse or administrator of the disarrayed enclosure. Luis's surprise could not have been greater when he saw the dilapidation of the room and the physical condition and abandonment of his father. He could not figure out the reasons for the deplorable conditions of the room, or why they were treating his father as a prisoner.

In a low, quivering voice, Luis asked his father:

"Papá, what happened to you, why haven't you bathed or shaved?"

Pedro, his father, did not answer him. With the meager forces that his body still had, he shrugged. With a smile on his dry, cracked lips he looked at his son with an empty look; his gaze lost as he usually used to see the crucifix hanging on the wall.

Luis sat on the edge of the bed and again asked his father:

"Papá answer me. Why do you just look at me, do you feel well?"

But the old man did not answer; he simply looked persistently at his son. Luis, touched by the silence of his father, took his face in both hands and kissed his cheeks and forehead. The old man, still looking at his son, laid his trembling hand on Luis's left knee, as if wanting to say something, but his frail voice did not come out from his quivering lips. Making a superhuman effort he babbled five words:

"Son, I was expecting you."

He lowered his head resting his unshaven chin onto his chest, emitted an unusual snore and fell asleep.

"Please, ma'am," Luis said to the woman in the white robe, who had quietly observed the sad scene, "prepare the coffin, my father has died."

The Mysterious Death of Juan Garuba

When Gustavo Borges arrived in Washington, DC, to attend college at the beginning of 1956, he rented a studio apartment in a building located on Sixteenth Street, one block from Columbia Road in the northwest section of the city. By being located on this street the building was known as the "16ᵗʰ Street," although to some of its occupants was known as *El Perejil* or the parsley; however, none of the tenants could tell him with certainty why the building had been baptized with such aromatic nickname. The sixteenth is a high-traffic, two-way street and one of the most important streets in this capital city. It extends from Silver Spring in the state of Maryland to one or two blocks from the White House.

Initially, Gustavo didn't have very many friends nor did he own a car to get around in this beautiful city, he had to rely on public transportation. To prepare his meals, as he didn't like cooking, he only had the basic cooking utensils. Out of necessity, he learned to cook white rice which he often mixed with canned black beans in a frying pan charitably given to him by a lady who lived on the fourth floor. The few pieces of furniture — a table and a couple of chairs of the armchair type — acquired from thrift shops, and a sofa bed purchased on sale at PJ Nee furniture store in a neighborhood of Rockville in the state of Maryland.

On a sunny spring day, in the lobby of the building, Gustavo met Pablo, a young man from Central America, also newly arrived in the city, who told him about a Nicaraguan couple who cooked tasty meals at their home for a reasonable price. Pablo warned him that it was nothing like a restaurant but rather a private home where he could enjoy a typical home-style meal in a family environment. Following his suggestion, one day that summer Gustavo decided to go up to the home and try the native dishes instead of warming up the reliable black beans and rice. It was at that house where, on a hot day in August 1956, he met Juan Garuba.

The dwelling of Feliciano and Elvira Torrentes was located one block and a half from Sixteenth Street and Florida Street, NW, close to the Carter Baron Amphitheater. The home was not a mansion or anything of that sort but a wooden, modest two-story house painted in light grey, with large multipaned glass windows decorated with black shutters on each side. The first time Gustavo visited their house he noticed that all the rooms, including the bathrooms, were decorated with a tacky and outdated floral motif wallpaper. The Torrentes rented one of the upstairs rooms to a girl who was taking secretarial courses at a local school. The yard was noticeably unkept and on each side of the lawn, there were two laurel bushes and a few stunted azaleas. In the front of the house, there was a large porch which was adorned by a dark red swinging bench hung in a corner. At the other end, two wooden rocking chairs, brought by the Torrentes from Nicaragua, were placed next to a small white wicker table decorated with artificial flowers and a glass ashtray with the logo of a local hotel.

Feliciano Torrentes rocked back and forth in one of the chairs and to mitigate the unbearable scorching August heat, he fanned himself with a woven straw fan while he smoked a Camel cigarette. Feliciano complained about everything: the unbearable heat, the flies and mosquitoes, the lack of rain, having to mow the lawn, making repairs in the house and vacuuming, among many other house chores. He also complained about never having to work so hard since he left his native city where he happily spent his time — hardly ever working — sleeping his daily siesta lying in a multicolored hammock.

Juan Garuba, dressed in immaculately ironed white linen pants and a pink cotton shirt was slowly swinging on the porch swing, as he listened patiently to Feliciano Torrentes many complaints, who on that summer day wore a Hawaiian red and blue flowery guayabera and light color pants, a little darker than those worn by Garuba.

Besides the exquisite look of his clothing, the mannerisms of Juan Garuba were highly noticeable. His brownish complexion matched his slicked-back brown hair, his clear brown eyes and his black eyebrows were framed by gold-rimmed bifocal glasses which rested on his wide and ordinary nose. His face showed the signs of what must have been a severe case of acne during his youth. Juan was of medium height and trim build. If it had not been for his nose or the acne scars one could say that he was not bad-looking.

Seated at the table, his effeminate mannerisms were obvious and noticeable by the way he held the fork and knife to cut the fried steak with onions which Doña Elvira served that day. Among the diners were also a couple in their twenties and an older man in his sixties who left early after paying for the meal and politely excusing themselves. After savoring a delicious dessert, accompanied by a hot cup of coffee, and eager to help Doña Elvira, Gustavo removed the dirty dishes from the table and placed them in the kitchen sink. Taking advantage of this moment, while they were alone, Doña Elvira confided to him that Juan Garuba was homosexual.

After that first family-style meal, during the following months, Gustavo became a regular customer and continued enjoying Doña Elvira inexpensive dinners, including the conversations with her whining spouse Feliciano Torrentes and Juan Garuba.

At the end of October, with his few savings, Gustavo decided to buy some kitchen utensils to prepare his own meals and thus limit the expenses incurred by eating out so frequently. However, sporadically he would visit the Torrentes to savor their native dishes. During this period, Juan Garuba also visited the Torrentes and although somewhat reserved, his conversation was always entertaining.

During one of his visits, on December 28, 1956, after their meal, Juan and Gustavo held a pleasant and varied conversation. Juan portrayed himself as being a traveled and well-educated fellow. He knowledgeably talked about art, famous painters, classical music, and also his desire to move to New York City to pursue higher studies in interior design. Juan and Gustavo had established a close friendship which had gone beyond the casual, to the point of Juan confiding in him about his sexual preferences and how his parents had isolated and criticized him, which had led him to move out of his home and self-exile himself, not only from his hometown but also from his country.

That day in December 1956, was the last day he shared dinner with his friend Juan Garuba who, after that, had moved to New York in search of a job that would allow him to finance his studies in interior design. Elvira had mentioned that Juan was disillusioned and depressed to learn that his father had disinherited him because of his sexual preferences. It was a very hard blow to him, from which Juan never fully recovered. He suffered deeply from the scorn and rejection of his father.

Approximately six years later, toward the end of December of 1961, Gustavo moved to a larger one-bedroom apartment in the same building. It was then that he met an Ecuadorian couple who enjoyed cooking their native dishes and he became one of their frequent guests. Between the invitations from neighbors and his decision to cook his own food, plus the time spent at the university, the visits to the Torrentes home became more infrequent and at one point he stopped seeing them altogether.

The first day of January 1962, Gustavo was pleasantly surprised to find in the lobby of the "16th Street" building, *El Perejil*, none other than Elvira Torrentes, who although older by six more years, had kept her charming personality and was still a good-looking lady. After exchanging the habitual greetings plus a friendly embrace, Elvira informed him that her spouse Feliciano had died two years earlier and that it had been difficult for her to keep the house with her limited income, augmented only a little with her meals and room rentals. She wouldn't stop saying how much she missed the company of her husband, who — even though did not provide much financially and complained about everything — was always willing to help with the house chores. Elvira had sold the house at a good price and subsequently decided to rent an apartment at *El Perejil* after learning of a large number of Latin Americans living there.

A wedding invitation came a few months after Gustavo's encounter with Elvira Torrentes in the lobby of the apartment building "16th Street." The son of a prominent and wealthy cardiologist in the Washington metropolitan area had been engaged to Lorena Venecia, a very wealthy girl, native of Venezuela, with whom Gustavo had become very good friends at the university. He had not anticipated the invitation but accepted it with much enthusiasm. The Venecia-Smart wedding — Smart was the surname of the groom, John — would be held at St. Mathews Cathedral in Washington DC, followed by a reception in the exclusive and elegant River Road Country Club, on the outskirts of the city, on June 14, 1962.

To supplement his meager income and to cover the school tuition, Gustavo periodically drove a rental minivan to transport families and other passengers to the three airports, private homes, hotels, etc. His limited financial means wouldn't allow him to buy a tuxedo to wear to the wedding, instead, he decided to rent one. Although he did not have a steady girlfriend; during the recent Christmas celebrations, at a private dinner party, Gustavo had met Tatiana del Campo, a girl — also from a distinguished Venezuelan family — very beautiful to say the least, and decided to invite her to the wedding celebration. On June 12, two days before the wedding, to be able to rent a car to drive and impress Tatiana, he decided to work extra hours driving the minivan to make the needed money.

Union Station, the train station in Washington DC, at ten-thirty in the evening, was noticeably deserted. The majority of tourist stores had closed; workers responsible for cleaning the station had started their routine, and an older man sitting on one of the benches was having a hard time trying to keep awake. A young couple sharing a Coke also waited for the arrival of the last train from New York and Philadelphia. Resting against one of the columns of the station Gustavo distracted himself by browsing a sports magazine; he was waiting for the arrival of the train where two of his clients from New York were due to arrive. Despite the stormy weather that had been forecast for that evening on television and radio, the train arrived on time.

Without much difficulty, Gustavo was able to identify the two businessmen he was expecting, and as he was guiding them towards the minivan, he heard someone calling him by his name. When he turned to look back to where the call had come from, he was surprised to see that the person walking towards him, dressed in an elegant dark grey suit, was none other than Juan Garuba. In his left hand, he carried a tuxedo bag from a famous New York clothing department store, and in his right hand, a small black briefcase. During his years in New York, Juan had put on some weight; however, he had not changed much, he looked the same as Gustavo had known him years before. They briefly exchanged the usual greetings and Juan asked him to take him to his destination after dropping off the two businessmen at the Mayflower Hotel.

Coincidentally, Juan's destination was *El Perejil*, the "16th Street" building, where Gustavo still lived. During the drive, Juan told him that he was staying with some friends from South America who lived on the ninth floor. Gustavo knew the couple but had not befriended them as they were not well regarded by the rest of the tenants, not only because of their bustling parties but even more their dubious reputation. Some of the neighbors gossiped — without any evidence — that they were gay. He was not the least surprised that Juan Garuba would stay with them in their apartment.

Among the many things they talked about that same night while they were driving to their destination after dropping off the two businessmen at their hotel, Juan confided to Gustavo that his father had died and that he had fulfilled his promise of not leaving him a single penny of inheritance. He was disillusioned and very much disappointed after learning that his mother had not been able to convince him before dying to change his mind. His father stubbornness had depressed and affected him immensely. He also mentioned that the reason for his trip to Washington was to attend the wedding of a friend. Coincidentally, Juan Garuba had been invited to the same wedding as Gustavo, to be celebrated two days later: the Venecia-Smart wedding. What a small world! Garuba had met the father of the bridegroom in New York where he helped him with the decoration and selection of all the furnishings of the newlyweds' apartment. Juan had made a name for himself and had a large clientele of wealthy people in that great metropolis. He was very proud to have achieved his longed-for dream.

The day of the wedding celebration, Juan did not accept Gustavo's invitation to join him and his date, suggesting that he had made other arrangements and would go to the church and to the reception on his own.

When Gustavo arrived at the reception, at the famed country club, he realized what it was to be wealthy. The parents of the bride had not spared any money to celebrate the wedding of their daughter Lorena Venecia to John Smart. The money from oil revenues was being spent without reservation. The waiters all dressed in black tie were serving French champagnes as well as a large selection of the best wines. Beluga caviar imported from Russia was also served as one of the appetizers. The white roses and exquisite orchids that adorned the tables of the bride and groom, family members, and those of the rest of the guests, had been brought from Medellín, Colombia. The tables were adorned with finely embroidered tablecloths imported from Spain; the music was provided by the best Washington orchestra — *Ruy Le Mar* — which did not stop playing the favorite selections of the bride and groom as well as many other special requests of the guests.

At the newlywed's table, there was a truly spectacular ice figure of the Greek goddess Venus of Citeres emerging from a large shell, finely and invitingly decorated with prawns and oysters of many colors and sizes. Everything was truly splendid, and happiness and joy reigned. Everyone dined, danced and celebrated until past midnight. Juan Garuba danced with the bride, with Gustavo's date Tatiana, as well as with other girls. He was having the greatest fun — as if he had never had fun before — drinking and dancing as if that day was the last day of his life.

As guests were bidding farewell to the hosts and the bride and groom, at about one in the morning Juan — showing symptoms of being inebriated — asked Gustavo politely if he did not mind giving him a ride back to the apartment house on 16th Street. But Gustavo apologized to his friend since he had to take Tatiana to her home in the opposite direction, in the city of Alexandria in Virginia. Gustavo later learned that Juan had also asked others for a ride as they were leaving the party but nobody was able to take him. It was later known that he had boarded a taxi along with a couple of male strangers.

Phil Martínez did not want to answer the phone. The faded black phone on the left corner of his gray metal desk in the basement of the "16th Street" building maintenance office had not stopped ringing. The black numbers of the electric clock on one of the concrete walls of his cold and gloomy office showed six-thirty in the morning; it was the beginning of the day. At that time of the morning, Phil intended to lower the thermostat to regulate the temperature of the building's air conditioning system and he assumed that the numerous calls he was receiving were from Elvira Torrentes who occupied apartment number 505. Elvira Torrentes always complained of the heat and even more when the outside temperature rose above 75 degrees Fahrenheit. Her favorite temperature was sixty-eight degrees.

The leaves of the sycamores and the maple trees in the vicinity of the building and the adjacent streets, with the early rains in May, had acquired a bright green color rarely seen in previous years. Although his phone had rung many times in the past, this time Phil was wrong, it was not Elvira Torrentes insistently calling. The calls were coming from three or four tenants on the eighth and tenth floors. They were trying to use the elevator to go down but hadn't been able to reach the lobby. They were calling the maintenance office to complain about the malfunctioning of the elevator. Several other people from the fourth and sixth floors had also gone down to his office to inform him of the elevator malfunction. For some reason the elevator cab wouldn't go down all the way down, it remained trapped between the first and the second floor.

Gustavo's next-door neighbor, all intrigued and emotional,

knocked on the door and as he opened it, he told him of the commotion in the hallway of the second floor, but Gustavo opted not to go down to see what was happening.

Phil Martínez could not figure out what was wrong with the elevator which — although it had more than twenty years of service — was operating perfectly the day before, and it had been serviced only a few days ago without detecting any damages or malfunctioning. To try to solve the problem, he decided to make some adjustments to the electro-mechanic system, but the elevator was not responding. Unable to make it work, he decided to call the firefighters nearby who once had managed to make it work.

The station's captain, accompanied by four firefighters, arrived and Phil explained to them what was going on. They inspected the inside of the cabin, pressed different buttons, driving up the cabin to the eleventh floor and back down but unable to make the cab go all the way down. The cabin wouldn't go all the way down to the lobby, it seemed trapped between the first and the second floor. Then the captain raised the carpet covering the floor of the cab and opened a small door where he could see the bottom of the elevator shaft. It was then, that assisted with a flashlight, he discovered the reason why the elevator was not operating. Its descent was being obstructed by the body of a man that had fallen from one of the upper floors through the elevator ventilation shaft.

Alarmed by the unexpected and tragic discovery, the chief immediately called the police authorities of the District of Columbia — as the city of Washington is also known — who hastily made themselves present bringing the coroner and two detectives.

Gustavo's neighbor once again knocked on the door. This time, pale and with a shaky voice, he informed him that a body had been found in the elevator shaft. Gustavo rapidly went down the emergency staircase to the second floor where a large number of people had gathered, including Elvira Torrentes. Finally, after an hour of struggling to extract the body, they managed to remove it from the elevator, placing it gently on a stretcher on the floor of the hallway. It was the bare-chested corpse of Juan Garuba still wearing his tuxedo pants and his partly torn blood-stained white shirt. Before taking the body to the morgue, while the paramedics were covering him with a white sheet, Gustavo noticed two bites similar to the bite made by a human being. One was on Juan's left shoulder and the other on the neck next to his collarbone.

Elvira Torrentes looked at Gustavo and began to cry, telling him:

"What a horrible and tragic ending of Juan Garuba, such a good fellow!"

"Yes, he was also a good friend!" Gustavo answered.

The Quinceañeras

To my friend Carlos J. Chamorro,
who encouraged me to write this story

T his is a story of the innocent love of a fifteen-year-old girl for a young man, and how she declares her love by disguising it with a phrase and the prose of a popular song. The story unfolds in the city of Granada, Nicaragua in the magical atmosphere of the celebration of a Quinceañera.

In some Latin American countries, the Quinceañera is a special event when parents celebrate their daughter's reaching the age of fifteen. This party signals the girl's transition from adolescence to womanhood. The day often starts with a private Mass, followed by an elegant family lunch, culminating at sunset with a dancing party attended by immediate and extended family as well as family guests and friends of the honoree.

In Granada, as in other Nicaraguan cities, this celebration is one of the most important events in the life of a young girl and her proud parents. For some families, it is the way to officially introduce their daughters to society. When it is not celebrated in the parents' home, the affair takes place at a social club. The parents of the honoree often contact the local newspapers to make sure that the event is announced in the social section of the newspaper. A brief summary of the family will appear, and if a member of the family occupies a prominent position with the government a special mention will be added. Some families also strive to ensure that these elaborately planned feasts are the best and do not spare any expense, which in some instances can be astronomical.

The invitation was hand-delivered to Javier Navarrete by the messenger of the Tenembaum family. Javier excitedly opened the smooth ivory envelope on which his name had been delicately handwritten with gold letters and embellished with a pink ribbon.

Dr. Filadelfo Tenembaum and Doña Berta
Emilia González de Tenembaum
have the pleasure of inviting
Master Javier José Navarrete
to the celebration of the fifteen years of their beloved daughter
Teresita María
July 14, 1956, at 4:30 p.m.

Home of the Tenembaum family
Independence Street No. 40
Attire: Semi-formal.

This was the invitation he had been eagerly awaiting in order to attend the Quinceañera of Teresita, or Teté, as some of her relatives and friends called her. In the city of Granada, the festivities of Dr. Filadelfo Tenembaum — or better known as Don Fila — were famous, for they were the most sumptuous and splendid. He did not spare a single "peso." It was believed that he was of Polish or German origin.

"Were you invited to Teté's quince?" Domingo (The Dandy) Luna asked Javier, who was standing in one of the corridors of his high school talking to a group of classmates before Algebra class. Some of them already had the anticipated envelope in their hands.

"Yes!" Javier said, "I received my invitation yesterday."

"Do you have any idea who the guests are?" asked El Chino (The Chinese-looking one). His real name was Roger Espinoza. In Nicaragua, if you have almond-shaped eyes they will probably call you Chino, even if you are not Chinese or of Asian origin.

"Oh yes," said Javier. "They invited Carolina, Carlota, Indiana, and Damaris; also, they invited Katia and Liliana, Marina, Eduviges, and Laurita." And turning to Domingo he added: "I also know they invited Karlita because she is a good friend of Teté. The gossip has it that last Sunday they saw you in the movie theater, trying to give her a little kiss."

"Shut up, Javier. You are nothing but a blabbermouth. Now everyone will find out that Karlita and I are going out together" growled Domingo, who was starting to get annoyed with his friend Javier.

"You are a fool. Everybody already knows about your secret romance," Javier said to Domingo. "By the way, I don't know why they call her Karlita. She should be called Karlota instead because she seems to have a couple of cantaloupes on her rear," said Javier with a devilish smile.

"Besides being a blabbermouth you're an ass! I don't like you to talk like that about Karla!" hissed Domingo as the bell rang, quickly ending their conversation.

The Tenembaum family had a stately house with architecture typical of the colonial city, with wide corridors and well-tended gardens of palm trees, yellow and red rose bushes and other tropical flowers. On the morning of the fourteenth flowers abounded throughout the house. There were rumors that they had ordered carnations from Costa Rica and orchids from Colombia. The main table, covered with a white linen tablecloth exquisitely embroidered with festive motifs, had been strategically placed in one of the wide corridors that bordered the main courtyard of the house. Sweet pastries, sandwiches, and other treats were plentiful. The buffet and desserts had been bought from the restaurant El Águila and other pastries had been bought from El Canario Bakery. On the table, the buffet included ham and chicken sandwiches and other delicacies bought from El Huerto a well-known restaurant in Managua.

In the center of the table were two elegant rock crystal glass containers with their respective ladles; one contained sangría for the men and the other fruit punch for the ladies. One could appreciate the care with which these tasty drinks were prepared with local ingredients and others brought from abroad, such as canned fruits of tutti-frutti with their typical red cherries. Don Fila had gone out of his way to beautifully decorate his house for the occasion. The party was *a todo meter*, (everything in) although it would have been better to say that the party was *a todo sacar* (everything out) for surely Don Fila had taken many "pesos" out of his pockets.

At the end of the other corridor, the closest to the living room, was the band of Los Soneros, which was unfairly nicknamed *Chicheros* or cheap musicians, because some of its members played in religious processions and some burials of people of the lower class. Los Soneros was a local band and, despite its degrading nickname, they played all the popular music extremely well.

The spacious grand room had two tall doors of dark mahogany wood facing the street. From the ceiling hung a crystal chandelier that matched the crystal punch bowls, which had been brought from Italy. The white marble floor, imported from Georgia in the United States, shone like a mirror as if it had been polished by Lupe, the city's most popular shoe polisher. High on one wall were a couple of large oil paintings of Teté's ancestors, the first Tenembaum to arrive in Nicaragua. On the opposite wall were pictures of Teté's parents and other family members, plus an oil painting of a lush landscape, supposedly by a famous Italian painter.

Javier was not an Adonis, yet he was a good-looking young man. He was tall and lean, with a light brown complexion, dark brown eyes, and a pronounced aquiline nose made him look leaner than he really was. That day he had taken extra care to choose his outfit. He had chosen to wear his best white linen trousers. His brown shoes coordinated well with the belt of the same color adorned with a shiny silver buckle. To look even better, he was wearing a McGregor shirt given to him by his parents for his fifteenth birthday. All dressed up, Javier was ready to party at the Tenembaum's house. He had to look good as it was the first time he attended a Quinceañera.

Most of the female guests had already arrived and laughed as they surrounded Teté with congratulations and flattery. Domingo, elegantly dressed in gray trousers and wearing a white guayabera, nervously looked out the front doors anxiously waiting for his beloved Karlita's entrance. He was standing near El Chino Espinosa and El Turco Gustavo Manzur (if you had a surname from a Middle Eastern country, they would call you Turco even if you were not born in Turkey).

As the guests continued arriving, Javier approached Teté to congratulate her and to give her the gift his mother had carefully wrapped in tissue paper. It was at that moment that Javier noticed the little book Teté had in her hands. It was the famous *carnet* or dance card. The little book was the same color as the invitation and engraved with gold letters: "*Memento of my Fifteen Years*," her name, and the date of her birthday. A tiny gold pencil was attached to it with a thin gold chain. Teté handed the *carnet* to all the girls.

In this *carnet,* the girls were going to write who would be their dance partners for the rest of the afternoon or rather, which of the boys would be less likely to step on their toes. Since it was a courtesy to invite the honoree to dance at least once, Javier armed himself with courage. He timidly asked Teté to grant him the third dance since she had already promised the first dance to her father and the second to Manolo El Bitongo (The Pampered kid) Rodríguez, who was hoping to get Teté's attention and had shown up dressed in a coat and tie.

"Just wait," Domingo said to Javier. "With this unbearable heat Rodríguez will be soon taking off that coat and tie."

Agustín Chavez, El Popu (The Popular), as he was nicknamed, showed up all dressed in white baggy pants and two-tone black and white shoes. He looked rather like a "pachuco," referring to rebellious youth who wore zoot suits and flashy clothes at the time. However, that didn't matter since he was well-liked by the girls because he was a good dancer. With a peculiar jumpy little walk, El Popu approached the one girl that made his legs wobble, Marinita, and asked her to dance a selection with him.

Soon after the other male friends had started to arrive including, Pulgarcito (The Tom Thumb) José Sosa, La Hormiga (The Ant) Rodolfo Martínez who soon matched up with Katia; Fofo (The Fluffy) Alfredo Guerrero had filled up Liliana's *carnet.* Domingo had settled in the pergola in the middle of the garden with Karlita.

At the end of the second dance, Javier cautiously approached Teté and asked her to dance the popular "bolero" *La Hiedra* (The Ivy). Afraid to step on her feet, he didn't get as close as ivy to her like the song insinuated. Teté was a pretty blonde with light blue eyes. Today she wore a stylish light green dress brought from Paris and, despite being a little chubby, that day she looked like a beautiful Lladró doll. Nevertheless, she paled in comparison to Karlita, who had jet-black hair and emerald green eyes who earlier had made her triumphal entrance, in a tight dark blue dress and sparkling sapphire earrings.

After his turn dancing with the birthday girl, Javier quickly escaped to the adjacent corridor to have a glass of sangría and a pastry. He was approached by Eduviges, or Edu, as her friends called her. The boys called her La Garza (The Heron) for being tall and skinny with a large nose. Despite not being very attractive and having an even less attractive name, she had a reputation for being a good dancer. Edu who had not yet been able to dance a single selection, served herself a glass of fruit punch and with a half-ironic gesture asked Javier:

"So, Javier, who have you asked to dance?"

"I've invited several," Javier muttered.

"You're a liar," Edu huffed. "I have only seen you dance with Teté. No one else."

"Edu," replied Javier quietly, "I don't know how to dance. I am afraid I'll step on their feet."

"Well, don't be afraid anymore," Edu said, taking him by his arm. "With me, you're going to dance — or at least learn how to. You're going to be my partner for the rest of the party! You are going to fill my *carnet.*"

Faced with Edu's ultimatum Javier had no choice but to start dancing with La Garza. Edu was such a good dancer that Javier not only learned to dance but in later parties he only danced with her.

After dancing with her to the *Yerberito Moderno* (The Little Modern Herb-Man), *En el mar la Vida es mas Sabrosa* (Life is More Fun by the Sea), and the famous tango *La Comparsita* (Little Parade) Edu's white shoes were badly scuffed from the many times Javier had stepped on them. Javier's brand-new McGregor shirt was so drenched with sweat from dancing, that he had to venture outside to cool off because the ceiling fans in the ballroom were not enough to mitigate the warmth and humidity.

At the entrance of the house, some curious members of the less privileged class had started to crowd on the street and the sidewalk hoping to catch a glimpse of the dancing through the open mahogany doors, among them was the curious Baltasar, the city drunkard who never missed a chance to spy on a party hoping to get a free drink.

Javier stepped past them and started wiping his face with his handkerchief when he heard a young female voice from behind.

"Why don't you change partners? You only dance with the ugly skinny girl."

Javier turned around to see a teenage girl wearing a white blouse and tight black trousers. She was of medium height, with a dark complexion and fine features. Her brown hair, which hung freely at her shoulders, was held with a bright-colored band.

"I don't know how to dance. She's the only one who has risked dancing with me," said Javier, taking a step back. "Do I know you?"

"My name is Isabel. You don't have to tell me your name because

I know who you are. Your name is Javier and I've been watching you all afternoon," she replied.

"Why have you been spying on me? What do you want?" Javier asked.

"I don't want anything from you. I know I'm not of your social class. I just like to watch the way you dance, even though you are not one of the best."

"Thank you. I have to go back to the party. What did you say your name was?"

"Isabel."

"Isabel," Javier said, smiling. "It was nice meeting you."

"Nice meeting you too. By the way, I'll be celebrating my Quinceañera next Saturday. Would you like to come?" she asked.

"If I get an invitation, sure I will!" Javier said.

"You do not need an invitation, just come. My verbal invitation is enough."

"Where do you live?"

"I live at 28 Corral Street, near the Church of Guadalupe," explained Isabel. "See you on Saturday at five in the afternoon. Don't let me down!" said Isabel, wagging her finger playfully at him. She walked without giving Javier any more details.

"Thanks, I'll be there," Javier promised.

"I'm going to that party," Javier whispered aloud. Isabel was very pretty, unlike La Garza, thought Javier. "I'm so lucky to be able to see her next Saturday at her Quinceañera."

When Javier returned to the dance floor, Edu was waiting anxiously. With a jealous tone she asked:

"Who's the little bitch you were talking to? You should see how she looked at you as if she was madly in love with you."

"I don't know her," Javier said. "Her name is Isabel and she invited me to her Quinceañera next Saturday."

"Are you going?" Edu asked contemptuously.

"I don't know," Javier said. "Maybe."

Despite the jealous exchange with Edu, Javier danced two more musical sets with her before thanking Teté and her parents for their kind invitation and heading home.

"Where are you going so sharply dressed at this time of the afternoon? You are too well dressed to play spinning tops at the Valle's Alley," asked Javier's mother.

"I'm going to the movies with some friends," Javier lied to his mother, who was skeptical but had no choice but to accept his son's response.

Javier felt confident going to Isabel's Quinceañera, he felt at ease going to her party, although somewhat clumsily, he was sure that he would not embarrass himself or be afraid of not being able to dance.

He had danced with La Garza at Teté's party, he was going to dance with Isabel despite the social criticism he would be exposing himself later for having attended a party of the less privileged class.

With his meager allowance, Javier bought a bottle of Agua Florida cologne at the corner store near the bridge of the Dardanelos and wrapped it in pink tissue paper. He made his way past Valle's Alley. It was easy to identify Isabel's house. House number 28 was an adobe rowhouse with a narrow sidewalk similar to the houses on both sides of the unpaved street, it was also distinguishable as it had been painted dark red. Some of the guests were already taking the rented folding chairs to the sidewalk.

The house was not ostentatious nor was it in an exclusive neighborhood like Teté's house. It was a working-class neighborhood on the outskirts of the city. There were no tall mahogany doors, nor there was a crystal chandelier, ceiling fans or marble floors, the shiny concrete tiled floors of the living room had been carefully polished for the occasion. In the entryway welcoming the guests was Don Oscar Gómez, Isabel's father. Javier recognized Don Oscar. He worked as a plant supervisor at the cotton gin of El Fofo Guerrero's family.

"Good evening, Don Oscar. My name is Javier. I'm Isabel's guest," Javier said.

"Come on in, young man," said Don Oscar, firmly shaking Javier's hand. "Isabel told me that she had invited you. She is waiting for you in the living room. Thank you for coming," said Don Oscar.

The living room in Isabel's house was smaller than the Tenembaum's. There were no oil paintings of any ancestors. Instead, on one of the walls was an image of the Sacred Heart of Jesus. Underneath there was a shelf with a diminutive electric candle emitting a faint flickering orange-yellow light. On the other wall hung the image of the Virgin of the Immaculate Conception better known as La Purísima.

In the center of the room wearing a light-yellow dress was Isabel, talking with two of her friends. As soon as she saw Javier, she approached him and said:

"Javier, you dared to come! You shouldn't have bothered to buy me a present. Your presence is enough. I do not have *carnets*. I'm sure you know the first dance is reserved for my father. The second is with my brother Julián and the third is with you. And if you want we could dance more songs," said Isabel. Then she whispered, "I'm not afraid of you stepping on my shoes."

"I'll be happy to dance with you as often as you like," Javier said. "Your dress is very nice."

"Thanks!" she said, looking down for a moment and touching the fabric. It's made of taffeta. My grandmother Manuela made it, she is a good seamstress. She copied it from a Sears catalog," Isabel continued. "Go ahead and have a drink. We don't have punch or sangría. We have *chicha* (a drink made of corn). Have you had it before? It's very tasty. To eat we have *vigorón* (yucca with pork rinds) and tortillas with refried beans and *queso chontaleño*," (cheese from Chontales region in Nicaragua).

As he approached the table to pour a glass of soda, Javier could not have been more surprised. Already at the table were his friends, El Popu Chávez, Pulgarcito Sosa, La Hormiga Martínez and El Bitongo Rodríguez. Apparently, their families knew the Guerreros, the owners of the cotton gin, as well as Don Oscar.

When the band Los Soneros began to play, Don Oscar began the party by dancing with Isabel to the traditional birthday song called *Estas son Las Mañanitas.*

After the second dance, Isabel approached Javier with a mischievous smile. "This is our turn," she said.

Javier felt fortunate to have had impromptu dance lessons with Edu at Teté's party. He felt confident he would not be scuffing up Isabel's new shoes. They danced many more songs before stopping for refreshments.

She approached him to dance the last selection which she had specially requested of the musicians. It was a bolero titled *Como Fue* (How was it?) made famous by the popular Cuban singer Beni Moré. These are some of the lyrics:

> How was it?
> I can't tell you how it was,
> I can't explain what happened,
> But I fell in love with you...

This time Isabel drew Javier close to her. This was not one of the dance moves Edu had taught him. It was the first time Javier felt the warmth of a woman's body swaying lightly next to his to the rhythm of the music. It was the first time his hands had touched a girl's naked back.

Being very shy on the subject of love, especially at the age of fifteen, Javier had not noticed that the feelings Isabel had for him transcended beyond a simple friendship. It was an innocent love that he was not aware existed. As he listened to the words of the song, Javier suddenly realized that he had encountered her on several occasions around town before ever talking with her on the sidewalk outside Teté's Quinceañera. He began to remember seeing her near the lake while riding his bicycle, another time walking with her grandmother from the market, and again at the entrance to the movie theater.

'I'm an idiot!' Javier thought to himself.

"What are you thinking, Javier?" Isabel asked. She stepped back as Javier tried to hide his emotions but his flushed face betrayed him.

"Are you uncomfortable?" asked Isabel. "Don't worry about my father. He's with some friends in the kitchen."

"No, I'm not uncomfortable," Javier said with a shaky voice, but she devilishly smiled, pressed her body close to his again, and continued dancing and enjoying that moment for the rest of the song.

"Thank you for coming to my Quinceañera," Isabel said.

"Not at all," Javier said as he said good-bye, and that way, he ended the evening.

Days later, Javier purposely walked by Isabel's house on the way home from school. Her brother Julián was talking with friends in front of his house.

"Hi, Julián. Is Isabel here?"

"No," answered Julián.

"When will she be home?"

"Not for a while. My parents decided to send her to Costa Rica to continue her high school studies."

Javier was silent and felt his ears turning red.

"By the way, she asked me to tell you how happy you made her by coming to her Quinceañera," said Julián.

"Oh," said Javier. The back of his neck started to feel warm.

"Are you all right?" asked Julián.

"Yes. I'm fine. See you around."

After that brief exchange with Julián, Javier never heard from Isabel again.

Crossing the Cocibolca

To my parents, may they rest in peace

In the southwest part of Nicaragua lies one of the largest lakes of volcanic origin known as Lake Nicaragua. Lake Granada as its also called is not only the largest lake in Central America but one of the largest lakes in the world. It is also known by the indigenous name of Lake Cocibolca, meaning "Sweet Sea." Spanish conquistadors mistook it for an ocean until they saw their horses drinking its water. It is the only freshwater lake where bull sharks thrive. These sharks have migrated through the San Juan River which connects the lake to the Atlantic Ocean. The lake is also a popular tourist mecca for having more than three hundred islets with majestic views of the Mombacho volcano in the background.

During the fifty or more years Emilio Gutiérrez has lived in the United States, he has visited Nicaragua only a few times, not because of lack of interest but because of work-related and personal obligations. The last time Emilio visited his country was in the summer of 2003. This time he was proudly taking his wife Cristina to show her for the first time his country of origin.

The TACA flight (*Transportes Aéreos Centroamericanos*) from Miami, Florida landed at Managua airport without any delays. Lili, Emilio's cousin and her husband Alfredo joyously met him and his wife at the airport; they had not seen him in the last ten years. After going through customs and immigration, they drove to the city of Granada in their sleek, and impeccably clean Toyota Camry. As is customary, Sundays are the maid's day off and, to avoid having to prepare a meal, most people have lunch or dinner at restaurants or at private clubs. Before arriving home, they stopped for lunch at the most popular equestrian Polo Club on the outskirts of Granada. Alfredo wanted Emilio's wife to taste roasted venison, a delicacy recently added to the menu.

As they entered the main hall of the club, Emilio noticed a round table full of diners who smiled at him in a friendly and familiar way — they were old friends he had not seen for many years. Unable to recognize anyone by name anymore, and noticing they were approaching the table, he took his cousin by the arm and asked her to discretely help him identify the persons seated at the table in order to be able to greet them. He did not want them to judge him later as arrogant.

Fortunately, his cousin introduced the entire group to him and to his wife Cristina. Then someone rose up from an adjacent table and walked towards them. His cousin noticed that Emilio did not recognize this fellow and said:

"What's the matter, cousin? Don't you remember Germán, his nickname was 'Anguish Face'?"

Nicaraguans like to give their friends nicknames according to their physical characteristics, and the truth is that this fellow had a face that screamed "anguish." What a nickname! The one who baptized him with such a name deserved a reward.

As Germán got closer to Emilio he asked:

"Are you Emilio Gutiérrez?"

"Yes, it is me, Emilio Gutiérrez," Emilio answered.

He then hugged his old friend who invited him to join them for a drink, but he courteously declined.

After looking at Emilio's wife, Germán asked:

"Is she your wife? She is so beautiful!" Germán added. "She's not from around here, is she? You can tell she's foreign!"

"Yes, she is not Nicaraguan, but she speaks Spanish, and this is the first time she is visiting, she has been anxiously looking forward to spending time with my family and visit this beautiful country."

Although Emilio declined his invitation, Germán was the type of person who would not give up and kept insisting that they get together. He was not going to pass up the opportunity to treat his old friend. After some arm-twisting, Emilio decided to accept his lunch invitation for the next day at a small local restaurant recently opened, near the lakeshore.

Precisely at noon the following day, Emilio heard a deafening sound in front of his cousins' house. It was the deafening roar of a motorcycle. By the thunderous noise, one could easily guess that the muffler had been purposely removed. It was none other than Germán who showed up on a brand-new red Harley Davison with bright silver trim and two-tone tires. Obviously, Germán hadn't included Emilio's wife in his invitation for lunch. Emilio climbed on the back seat and after two accelerating roars, they both headed to the restaurant by the lakeshore.

After an abundant lunch of boneless deep-fried bass, rice with vegetables and the mandatory "half" bottle of Flor de Caña rum — which could not be avoided — they sat on two dark brown mahogany Adirondack style chairs overlooking the lake; that day, the water was crystal clear and particularly calm and not a single cloud obstructed the view of the magnificent light blue sky. The waitress served them each a cup of strong coffee.

It was after sipping some of his coffee that Germán started reminiscing. He began telling Emilio some of his adventures when he was young, about the trips he took to the many islets on the lake; to Asese, a privately-owned islet; to the larger islands of Ometepe and Zapatera, but that he had never crossed the lake. He paused, took another sip of the black drink and asked Emilio if he had ever traveled or crossed the Cocibolca. Emilio told him that he indeed had traveled to several of the privately-owned islets as well as the larger islands; however, he had only crossed the lake once with his father, when he was a teenager. After finishing the last drop in his cup, Germán called the waitress to bring two more coffees and asked Emilio to tell him about this adventurous trip when he crossed the lake with his father.

"Please tell me all the details," Germán added. "Don't be short on words, I have been told you have a reputation of being a good storyteller."

They both settled in their chairs and began to savor the second cup of the delicious Nicaraguan coffee.

"I don't know if you remember," Emilio said, "that my father was an avid hunter, he would never turn down an invitation to go hunting. He would leave everything and travel anywhere in the country in search of venison, a wild pig, something to hunt ..."

"My mother, always objected to his frequent travels," Emilio continued. "She feared that he would not eat healthy meals, and there was always the risk of drinking contaminated water, which was what eventually caused his deadly illness and his death. Not only did she disagree with his travels, but she strongly opposed to having me accompany him, and least of all on a hunting trip across the lake."

"Go on, go on, don't stop," Germán said, sitting comfortably on his chair.

"I was not more than seventeen," Emilio continued. "And I will never forget that memorable trip with my father, it was one of his last trips. Yes, I'm sure!" Emilio said. "It was his last trip. We were going to the ranch of a friend, but that's not all, the ranch was located on the other side of the lake, in the province of Chontales. We had to cross the widest part of the lake in a boat no bigger than thirty feet long. I did not pay attention to my mother's objections," said Emilio, "this was going to be one of my exciting adventures since I suspected that for the rest of my life, I would never have another similar opportunity. Imagine, I was going to cross Lake Nicaragua. In fact, it was the first and only time."

"What was your mother's reaction?" asked Germán curiously.

"Well," Emilio said. "She couldn't do anything to prevent it, after all, I was going to travel with my father. The day before the trip, we both packed two saddlebags, boots and leathers, a change of clothes for three or four days, some food for the night and, of course, the rifles, my father's Remington twelve-gauge shotgun and mine, a .22 Hornet."

"I also had a Hornet," Germán interrupted. "I let a friend borrow it and when it was time to return it, he told me it had been stolen. Such a scoundrel sonofabitch! I believe he was the one who stole it. At what time did you embark, what was the boat like?"

"It was not later than five-thirty in the afternoon," Emilio replied. "It had been cloudy all day long with the threat of rain, and night had started to fall. The boat was not very large; it was a motorized sailboat. We got our gear, out of the "coche" (horse-driven buggy) and walked on the pier to where the boat was anchored. I was so surprised when I saw the boat, I couldn't believe it! I asked myself aloud: 'Are we going to cross the lake in this boat...? In this piece of crap ...'? Maybe my father overheard me and noticing the surprised look on my face, tried to reassure me: 'Don't worry son, the captain knows the lake like the palm of his hand, he has made the crossing many times.'"

Emilio continued, "I had watched many films where the captain was a tall, slender man in a white or blue suit with a cap of the same color. I couldn't have been more wrong," Emilio said. "This so-called 'captain' was a man in his forties and of medium height. He wore a worn-out grease-stained shirt with the sleeves cut off, his trousers were half-torn at the knees with the cuffs rolled up showing his soiled and muddy bare feet. His mate was as raggedly dressed. There were no beds, not even a cot, only two hammocks, one hung in the back and another in the middle; a few unwashed aluminum plates were stacked on an improvised kitchen washer. The smell of gasoline was unbearable, the whole place smelled horrible and when the captain raised his arms the stench coming from his armpits was awful."

"Were there other passengers in the boat?" asked Germán.

"Yes," Emilio answered. "There were two other people, however, I did not pay much attention to them nor was I interested in finding out who they were; at that moment, all I could think off was where I was going to sleep that night. There was also a young woman, she was the only woman on board. She was indigenous looking, of dark complexion, with long straight black hair that came down to her waist, the captain called her Julita, I believe she was his girlfriend."

"And where did you sleep, on the floor?" asked Germán.

"No, I didn't sleep on the floor! My father suggested that I sleep in the hammock on the back of the boat, but I chose the one in the middle near a metal pole, I suppose the pole was the mast; I thought I would be safer in the middle of the boat rather than in the rear. That was a big mistake! It was stupid of me to choose the hammock next to the post, I should have listened to my father, I will explain later."

"After waiting for more than an hour," Emilio continued, "we lifted anchors. We sailed all night and fortunately, it did not rain. I found myself admiring the full moon playing hide-and-seek with the thick gray almost black clouds and listening to the captain's tall-tales, those of his mate, and of the other two passengers. They were all telling stories of many other adventures about crossing the lake; tales of when they had gone fishing and who caught the biggest fish ..."

"And what about Julita, was she pretty?" asked Germán.

"I don't know, I didn't care much about her," Emilio said. "I was more interested in the stories told by the captain, his mate, and the other passengers; which continued until after ten o'clock. The two passengers were drinking heavily, I feared that they would get rowdy with the drinks. Fortunately, they fell asleep next to two twine rolls stacked on the deck against one of the sides of the boat. That night the lake welcomed me with tremendous swells, the waves were so high that at one point they were almost reaching the edges of the boat."

"Good thing the two drunks fell asleep and did not cause problems," Germán commented.

"I feared that the boat was going to sink. As I said, I chose the hammock next to the mast, I shouldn't have! It bounced back and forth and I kept hitting myself against the metal pole, but also, the captain's loud flatulent discharges did not allow me to close my eyes all night, not for one minute. Not only did they stink, but after each fart, the captain said to himself, 'the first break,' and thus seven or eight 'breaks' passed ... The following morning after noticing I was awake, he asked me; 'How long have you been awake, young man?' To which I replied: 'ever since your 'first break.' In the end, I thought that perhaps I should have listened to my mother and not embark on this adventure, but it was too late to go back."

"How resourceful of the captain to manage his farts with such timely precision!" Germán chuckled. "Please continue, this story is getting so interesting."

"About five o'clock in the morning," Emilio continued. "The captain told us to get ready to disembark because we were about ten minutes from the port. The port!" Exclaimed Emilio. "You cannot imagine what the port was like!"

"I can't imagine," Germán replied.

"The so-called port was made of wooden planks tied with ropes to empty metal drums that floated fifteen or twenty yards offshore. My father and I carefully disembarked into a small dinghy and with the help of the captain's mate, we rowed to the shore where Nemesio, the person who was going take us to our final destination, was waiting for us with a canoe. The canoe was no more than ten or fifteen feet long; it was one of those canoes carved by hand with an ax, made out of a tree trunk.

"To satisfy our hunger, we bought a couple of tortillas, fried eggs and a bitter as bile cup of coffee from an old woman who lived in a thatched hut about twenty yards from the shore; and that was our breakfast. No comparison to my grandmother's pancakes, I had to settle for the tortilla and a couple of fried eggs," Emilio concluded.

"If life deals you lemons, make lemonade, you didn't have much of a choice," Germán said. "You were lucky that the old lady sold you something to eat."

"My father," Emilio continued. "Unloaded the saddlebags, the rifles, etc., and to my surprise, I saw Nemesio carry a sack of rice and a one-hundred-pound sack of beans into the canoe. I was worried about all that extra weight, I spontaneously said to Nemesio: 'This canoe is going to sink,' but neither he nor my father paid much attention to me, besides it was too late to go back; the ship had already taken off, I had no choice ..."

"My father suggested I sit in the front of the canoe, he sat in the middle and Nemesio in the back to be able to row. After ten minutes of rowing, we entered the mouth of a river; I didn't bother about the name of the river, I was dying of fear, and the peace and silence around us made it worse. I was afraid of the dangerous waters and also of what could happen to us. I had listened to tales of ferocious alligators living in the river and how they could launch toward their prey. I thought that the canoe would not withstand the attack of one of those gators; I thought I would need to jump in the water and rapidly swim to shore and what could happen if one of these hungry gators caught me and dragged me to the bottom of the river. I thought there might be also sharks lurking beneath. My main concern was all that extra weight of the sacks of rice and beans we were carrying in the damned canoe, all these thoughts worsened my fear. I was terrified."

"I would have been nervous too," Germán said. "Mainly with the weight of the sacks of bean and rice."

"In spite of all my fears," Emilio continued, "I could not help to admire the surroundings. I've never seen anything like it, I do not remember ever seeing such amazing sights before," Emilio added. "I was admiring the splendor and the dark green foliage of the jungle; the peacefulness of the river and the variety of colors reflecting on the water. In some places, it was bluish-gray, in others, it was emerald green and silvery in others where the sun filtered through the branches of the trees. We could see capuchin monkeys lazily hanging on tree branches from their tails."

"Your description is amazing!" Germán said. "I do not remember ever seeing so much beauty and so many colors at the same time; they say the jungle is beautiful."

"For some reason, none of us had started a conversation," Emilio continued. "The silence was sepulchral, only interrupted by a soft, humid morning breeze and the sound of the oar cutting the water, it was as if a double-edged dagger sliced through a soft gelatinous mass which heals as the weapon that cuts it leaves it."

"What a beautiful metaphor, comparing the oar with a knife," interrupted Germán.

"Suddenly the silence was interrupted by the chirping and the murmur of hundreds of birds, parrots, large and small, macaws of different colors and sizes," continued Emilio. "In the distance, I heard the howling of monkeys, they sounded much like prayers begging the heavens to open its faucets and release an early rain; the curious spider monkeys looking at us, intrigued as if we were from another planet."

"Awesome! Awesome! Beautiful! Beautiful!" repeated Germán.

"The wildflowers embracing and resting on both sides of the river were of all kinds of sizes and colors; mellow pink, yellow, blue and many other colors, the entire landscape looked like a floating water garden, it was a wonderful sight."

"I can imagine!" added Germán, taking another sip of coffee.

"I was so distracted, admiring so much beautiful nature, thinking that perhaps I would never see it again, that I didn't notice when we had reached a sandy shore on one of the banks of the river. Attached to a nearby bush were three horses and a mule. Nemesio tightened the saddle belt on the horses, loaded the sacks of beans and rice and our saddlebags on the back of the mule, and we headed toward the ranch of my father's friend, which, according to Nemesio's calculations was about half an hour away on horseback."

"Do you remember the name of the finca?" asked Germán.

"No, I do not remember it, but I remember Don Dionisio, as my father called his friend and owner of the finca. He welcomed us warmly and after we cleaned up, we were served charcoal-grilled plantains, slices of a crumbling dry cheese, accompanied by a warm mango fruit drink as there was no ice to cool it."

"That was lunch," Emilio told Germán. "The main house was made of wooden planks, reddish roof tiles covered with dark green moss. Nemesio, his wife and son lived in a smaller straw hut behind the main house. In the middle of the patio, there were three stones placed strategically on top of a solidified mud mound. That was the kitchen where Petrona, Nemesio's wife, boiled water for cooking and drinking, which she had brought in a small tin bucket from a nearby stream."

"Rudimentary!" Germán said.

"Yes, very rudimentary," said Emilio.

"I was so surprised when a naked boy of about seven years ran out from behind the hut to welcome us and introduce himself: 'My name is Pedro.' He was dark-skinned, just as his parents, with black and shiny eyes, uncombed straight bluish-black hair. However, what caught my attention was his extended stomach. I believe this is a sign of a worm infestation which affects children in the countryside after eating food mixed with dirt and worms. I doubt that's true. What do you think of that?"

"I don't know, man," Germán replied. "People here make up so many stories and you don't know what to believe, but what I've heard is that's what happens when they have worms, but I'm not sure, I'm not a doctor."

"When my father saw the boy naked, he took one of his shirts out of his saddlebag and gave it to him, who instantly, and very proudly put it on and thanked him for being so generous."

"'Don Julio,' "said the boy." 'With this shirt I look very elegant, but I don't have a penny in my pocket.' "My father smiled at him and handed him a fifty-cent coin. Pedro bit it to make sure it was real and ran off to the back of the house."

"What a smart kid!" commented Germán. "When did you go to bed, what did you have for dinner?"

"In the jungle or in the countryside, especially in such remote places, people are not guided by time nor do they have clocks, they wake up when the sun rises and go to bed when the sun goes down.

"At the end of the day, I felt so tired that I do not even remember what we ate that night. To prevent the persistent attack of the insatiably hungry mosquitoes I smeared myself with citronella oil, and like a monkey, I rolled up in one of the hammocks until it was time to wake up."

"You're making me thirsty again," Germán said. "Do you want another coffee?

"No, thanks, I'd rather continue with the story."

"Then go on," said Germán.

"My father and Don Dionisio, among other things, leisurely talked about the precious woods that thrived throughout the region, and how much money they would make if they were marketed. I was not that interested in the matter so I did not pay much attention to their conversation. After breakfast, they saddled the horses and went into the jungle in search of the famous trees and did not return until the end of the afternoon. I stayed lounging around the house and talking to Pedro, the naked boy, who was no longer naked after my father gave him one his shirts. It was then, during our conversation, that I asked him why he went around naked."

"'No patroncito,'" he answered. "'That's a trick of mine, especially when guests come to visit. When they see me naked, if they do not offer me clothes, they offer me money. I prefer when they give me money. I am saving for when I am a little older, I want to go live in the Gran Sultana, do you know that's how they call the city of 'Granada?' I want to go to school. I want to make something of myself.'"

"'Yes, I am aware of how Granada is also called, you're such a smart rascal'." I said to Pedro.

"Very intelligent kid!" said Germán.

"Yes, very intelligent," said Emilio, continuing his story.

"It seems that Nemesio had gone hunting during the night and on an improvised barbecue pit, he was about to grill our meal. I had no idea what he was marinating, but it looked like an animal larger than a cat. As I watched him, I thought to myself, 'hell, we are going to eat cat.' I had never eaten cat, but in the jungle, you cannot be too selective, you eat what you hunt. As I looked to the side of the hut, I could see the left-over skin of a tiger — a small tiger — that Nemesio had stretched and hung to dry. I do not know if nowadays there are restrictions to hunt these small tigers, but back then there was no law prohibiting hunting these animals, mainly these species that would later run the risk of being extinguished. That evening the menu was rice and beans, tortillas, the same dry cheese, and grilled tiger loins."

"I'm not going to lie to you," Emilio said, "that 'Tigrillo' tasted like chicken, as many people would say when they first eat something they have not tasted before. Actually, it did not taste like chicken at all, it tasted like roasted beef, a little sweet, but delicious."

"I've never eaten tiger meat," Germán added. "What happened when you returned home? Your mother must have been furious."

"No, she was not angry," Emilio said to Germán. "On our return, my mother was waiting for us to hear all the details about our trip. I told her about the natural beauty of the jungle which I had never seen before and the delicious food I had eaten. Of course, I did not tell her about the crossing and how crappy the ship was, nor did I tell her about the captain's flatulent 'serenade.' Although she wanted to listen to all my stories, she was more concerned about my father's health. He looked sickly and thinner than when we left. The progression of the hepatitis was noticeable."

"What a pity about your father," Germán said.

"My mother was hoping to hear how terrible my experience had been, finally she asked me if I regretted having made the trip. On the contrary, I told her, I would have regretted if I hadn't taken it, and to this day, I wonder how my father was able to make and endure all those harsh hunting expeditions."

Taking his last sip of coffee, Emilio noticed that Germán tried to wipe some tears that escaped from his eyes.

"Do you feel well, are you okay? Emilio asked him.

"Yes, Emilio, I feel fine. Nothing is wrong with me," Germán replied. "I was just thinking how lucky you are, not only because you crossed Lake Cocibolca, but because you had the opportunity to share with your father such a beautiful experience. I was not as lucky as you. Although I have everything in this life, the only thing I miss and long for is my father's presence. He passed away when I was very small. You do not know what it is not to have a father. Thank you, Emilio, for sharing such a memorable and beautiful story with me."

Parade, Floats, Trinkets and Stuffed Animals

If it hadn't been for a brief anecdote,
I wouldn't have written this tale ...

To José Aburto

On a cool day of January 2014, during one of my visits to the city of San Francisco, I was absorbed admiring the shop windows of Chong Lee — a store in the commercial district of Chinatown — when suddenly I felt a timid tap on my left shoulder. I felt cold chills running down my entire body wondering who it could be; I didn't know anyone in San Francisco. I turned around slowly to face the person who had tapped me. Right behind me stood an older man, slim, medium built with greying hair and light brown complexion with a warm smile on his face. His light brown and friendly eyes looked at me from behind a set of gold-framed eyeglasses. In his left hand, he was carrying a manila envelope and from his neck hung a crucifix. Noticing my surprise, he asked me:

"Don't you remember me? I am José Otruba, we haven't seen each other in so many years, perhaps fifty or more. I now live in San Francisco. What are you doing in this city?"

"My wife and I are visiting," I replied instinctively, without thinking.

Prying deeply into the archives of my memory, I managed to find him and in a flash of light, I started to remember. The last time I saw José was more than fifty years ago when we both shared anecdotes while sitting on a bench at the central park of Granada and savoring a delicious tamarind drink. In addition to the tasty drink, I also recalled the cool breeze blowing among tall coconut, almond and mango trees which helped mitigate the torrid dampness of that month of August of 1958.

As it so often occurs, when we haven't seen a person in a long time, we both stared at each other, examining one another from head to toe to make sure we weren't seeing a mirage, a ghost in a dream or a glimmer of one of those apparitions vaguely roaming in the hallways of our memory, which are revived and extracted from the aging and yellowing pages of the book of our remembrances.

Instead of just touching each other — to make sure we were not living a dream or seeing a shadow from a long-gone era

— we affectionately hugged, studying each other's wrinkles, looking carefully at the few strands of silver which adorned our heads. And, as we often say in those unexpected and unplanned circumstances: "You haven't changed one bit!" "You look exactly the same!" "The years have not passed you by!" In reality, all of these generous compliments are what we friends exchange with each other when we have nothing to say. They are just meaningless expressions because, in fact, we were not "exactly the same," on the contrary, we both had "changed" and time had definitely left its footprints all over the pathway of our lives.

After exchanging the usual hellos and familiar niceties, we inquired about our personal and professional achievements. José had taken courses in philosophy and theology, in addition to other spiritual studies, eventually obtaining a degree in electrical engineering. He mentioned that he also volunteered his services in a nearby school where he taught history and catechism. We talked about sports, baseball, basketball, but in particular about American football, and we exchanged the latest accomplishments or biggest defeats of our favorite teams.

Ever since that unexpected and fortunate encounter in San Francisco's Chinatown, José and I have kept in touch with each other, either via the telephone, or the Internet — by e-mail — and whenever I happened to be in the city again, we would share a lunch at Geppetto, our favorite Italian restaurant on Central Avenue. We have exchanged opinions about current events, politics and candidates aspiring to high-level posts in the country. Sometimes, we talked about poverty — monetary and spiritual — about philosophy and religious themes and, although we steer clear of speaking extensively about the last one, we sometimes cannot avoid the temptation of engaging and discussing this fascinating but difficult topic. My friend José is a very devout religious man.

On the subject of sports; in one of our latest exchanges of ideas, José shared with me a heartwarming and eye-opening event he had witnessed while watching the victory parade along Market Street in honor of the San Francisco's 49ers football team. That year, 1981, the 49ers won the Super Bowl. Joe Montana, the quarterback, who was then at the peak of his career, had been very successful and was now being honored in a special way. He was standing in a prominent place among the players, riding in a very colorful float surrounded by euphoric fans that had poured into the streets along with hundreds of revelers. Fans were wearing 49er colors, blowing horns and whistles, while others climbed atop lampposts and hung from street signs. It was quite a spectacle, a delirious city celebrating the victory of their favorite team. The streets were impassable, fans peered from office windows lining the parade route. They climbed atop of vehicles, they danced, they shouted.

Ahead of the float carrying the players, there were several other floats, crowded with revelers who were tossing candies and all sort of trinkets to children and grownups along the parade. José mentioned that right below from where he was standing, watching the parade, there was a group of children hoarding candies, 49er caps, toys as well as a variety of trinkets. Among the children was a little one, who could not have been more than three years old. That small child caught José's attention because he was standing there, loaded with stuff which he held against his chest with no more room for any more. José could not stop to wonder what would be the kid's reaction when the float tossing stuffed animals would pass by.

While confetti hailed down on the passing procession, it took only a twinkle of an eye. As soon as the boy saw the stuffed animals, without any hesitation, he dropped everything he had accumulated against his chest. In a flash, he ran toward the float, caught one of the stuffed animals that was almost as tall as he was, hugged it, kissed it, and could hardly contain himself from bursting with sheer joy.

Right from the start, I suspected that José had an ulterior motive for narrating to me the little boy's incident, and I curiously listened to the story of the parade, the floats, trinkets and stuffed animals. However, up to this point, I could not figure out what his motive was, and although I continued to listen, I decided not to think of it twice, not to pay more attention to it. After all, we had exchanged sports stories before, and I figured this one was just another one: a young child dropping his treasured possessions for a more attractive one. What was so meaningful about that?

A few days before he passed away — toward the end of June of 2015 — I was very fortunate to visit Félix Fuentes, a good friend from my childhood with whom I had shared a very long and close relationship. Félix was not only my good friend during my younger years, but he was also a friend to whom, because of his love for sports, I had given the nickname "el deportista," the sportsman. He loved baseball as well as American football. We would often get together at each other's home to watch ball games on television. Frequently — when we were lucky to secure tickets — we would attend the games being played in our hometown. Unfortunately, a few months earlier Félix was diagnosed with cancer of the colon which had metastasized to other vital organs of his body. Because of the rapid progress of the illness; he did not have many days to live on this earth. His weight loss was noticeable; and because of the frequent chemotherapy treatments, he had lost most of his hair and started to have a cadaveric appearance.

I knew my friend Félix was not going to be among us much longer and for that reason, I decided to make the most of what I suspected would be our last visit. I tried not to be solemn or pity him; instead,

I behaved normal and chose to distract him to lessen his pain. We talked about several topics such as daily events, local gossip, exchanged a joke or two ..., and, as we usually ended up in the past, we started talking about our favorite subject, American football. In spite of his physical condition, Félix — making a superhuman effort, and with that extraordinary strength that comes from deep inside of us — pulled himself up and rested his head against the bed's headboard cushioning his fragile back against a couple of soft pillows.

I started to tell Félix about my encounter with my other good friend José, whom I had not seen in more than half a century and how we had kept in touch virtually, via e-mail. Most importantly, I told him that José also followed American football and was a fan of the 49ers. When I mentioned football and the 49ers, Félix's eyes lit up like I hadn't seen them before, it was his favorite team. It was a magical moment, like in the good old days when we exchanged information about different teams, about the large sums of money players and quarterbacks were being paid we recalled the days when Joe Montana played for the San Francisco 49ers and how he led his team to several championships. I realized then that I had touched a vital chord, as if a flash of lightning had struck him, we were talking football. It was then when I decided to tell him the story my good friend José had told me, which at that time, seemed insignificant to me.

It was about the little boy, who during a parade honoring the 49ers, had dropped all the candies and trinkets he had captured before, to go after one of the stuffed animals tossed from a float.

Félix fell silent. Thoughtful and quiet, he gazed toward the window of his room which at that instant allowed a ray of radiant light through, giving brilliant life to his depressing and darkened room. Several minutes passed by — although they seemed interminably longer to me — then he looked straight into my eyes and said:

"Your dear friend José is brilliant! His story is translating a very meaningful event and, in the process, he is sending you a beautiful message. His message is all about our lives being interconnected with the parade and the reaction of the little boy ..."

"Sorry Félix, but I don't understand the message you are referring to. What's the meaning of a small boy euphorically watching a parade, people celebrating on the streets, throwing candy and trinkets and that young child dropping all just to get a stuffed animal? How is that related to our lives? You know how kids are; when they see a new toy, they drop everything they have in their hands just to get that new toy. In this case, it was not a toy, it was just a stuffed animal, a *peluche*."

"Very simple, my dear friend," Félix replied. "Perhaps you haven't had too much time to think, but I have. While lying on this bed I have thought and examined my life several times; I have scrutinized it. It's been a long process, and often it has been an ordeal to recall it, but I have time now. I have examined my achievements, my anguishes, my sacrifices and difficult times; how I overcame the obstacles and always moved forward. I have never stopped to look back, until now when I finally face this day, the day when I will die, that day for us human beings when we cease to exist in this world, when we prepare ourselves to be forgotten, even by those who love us the most."

I truly did not know how my friend Félix was able to overcome his pain with so much energy to talk, to reflect on an insignificant story and view it in light of his life and health condition; however, I respected his interpretation and decided not to interrupt his train of thought. He placed his pillows comfortably against his fragile back and continued, saying:

"In your friend Jose's story, *we* are the boy. The parade and the floats are a representation of *our* lives. Do you recall when our parents used to overwhelm us with lots of toys? I, like the young boy, was vehemently attached to my lead soldiers, the ones my parents gave me when I turned five years old; I played with them and simulated war games with my friends. I would be extremely hurt when one of those soldiers was damaged. Just like the young boy in the story, I cared for them and would hide them under my bed to prevent my sister from finding them and breaking some of them. I am sure you also did the same. You must have had favorite toys which you didn't want others to touch! Didn't you?"

"Yes, of course!" I replied.

"As time goes by, I should say, as all the floats start parading along, our toy soldiers turn into other more expensive toys — and just like the candies, the trinkets ... all those material things which we gradually acquire during our *parade,* through our lives, continue to fill our rooms, attics and garages. The revelers on the floats are no longer our parents who have relegated their role. Now there are others who are offering things for sale, many more ... and many more things until we reach a point when we no longer know what to do with them. And the more money we have, the more expensive those toys become, such as houses, automobiles, smart televisions and electronics ... we continue accumulating more and more material things, in other words, more *stuff* ... We often offer it to others, especially our children, but they don't want it, they already have started to accumulate their own things, their own *stuff* ... We spend half of our lives accumulating *stuff,* then spending much of our valuable time trying to get rid of it. No one wants it, we are often faced with the need to get rid of it, to give it away, to donate it. Some of those centers where we take it, accept it out of obligation or compromise, they don't even have enough space to process it all, 'others' who perhaps need it, don't even want it.

I recall a good friend of mine who invited his son to choose anything he wished from his house, such as paintings, furniture, decorations ... offering them for free, asking him to take them away to his own home. But after a while, after searching throughout the house, including the attic, his son came up to his father holding a shoebox filled with sports cards and telling him that it was all he was interested in. His son was not interested in taking any of his old man's *stuff*, which his father had accumulated over the course of his parade.

While we are participants of this parade, not for one instance do we stop to think that we are not invincible, that we are not going to live forever; we forget that we are mortal human beings, we forget about the spiritual meaning of our lives, and although we realize that our path, our parade, our floats will eventually come to an end, we continue acquiring and accumulating more and more things; it's very difficult to stop. We forget about the *peluche,* the stuffed animal for which the lad dropped everything he had accumulated; we forget about that insignificant toy the kid wants to hold and tightly embrace against his chest. How lucky was the kid who was able to give up and to free himself from all the trinkets he had accumulated during the parade! We should learn from that child, we should be like him ... and not be attached to material things, because at the end of our journeys, at the end of our parade, we don't take anything with us, everything stays. We need to search for that stuffed animal only!"

While Félix continued telling me his truthful reflections, I noticed that as he spoke, his breathing faltered and was not able to finish some words coherently. I suggested he should rest, not to continue making such an effort, but Félix wouldn't listen. Suddenly, Luisa, the nurse, interrupted our conversation. She was bringing painkillers to mitigate the pain which constantly afflicted him.

"When she is not drawing the last drop of blood left in me," Félix joked, "this young lady caring for me is poisoning me." He winked at me and said: "I am being poisoned in this place, they want to accelerate my death!" Then he swallowed all the medications at once.

I took advantage of that moment, and of Luisa's presence, to start leaving quietly. I said goodbye to my friend, promising him to come to visit him the following week.

"You won't find me here," Félix answered. He raised his right hand to his forehead and imitated a military salute, like a farewell or goodbye.

The following Sunday, as I promised my friend, I went to the hospice where Félix was being cared for. I started to walk toward his room hoping that his dreadful death diagnosis would be erroneous. In the hallway, I met Luisa, his nurse, who gave me the bad news. Félix passed away the day before. His family had decided that the funeral services would be private and they would not notify anyone. As I turned back to exit the hospice, Luisa stopped me.

"Excuse me, Sir, I don't mean to intrude into other people's business, especially in our patients' personal affairs," Luisa said, "but I couldn't help overhearing the conversation you had with Mr. Félix; I have not been able to erase it from my mind, all those reflections about his life of our lives ... Could I ask you a question?"

"Of course!" I answered.

"Do you think Mr. Félix found his *peluche,* his stuffed animal?"

"Perhaps ..." I replied.

The Funeral of Melquiades de Arquímides

... when we realize that life has only a forward trajectory,
it is then when we start missing it ...
Manuel Longares

The shovels in the hands of the two men crashed violently against the minuscule rocks in the scorching dry and thirsty earth. It scarcely rains in San Fernando; however, during the two or three weeks of winter rain, the water falls so heavily it feels as if the heavens were falling down in a deluge.

The two men had to hurry. It was getting late. In the darkness of the night, it was going to be harder for them to dig the eight feet deep grave. Melquiades de Arquímedes was a big man, more than six feet tall and they had to make sure that the casket fits loosely and without difficulty, otherwise, they would not be paid the twenty pesos that Agripina, his widow, had offered them for this work.

Their dirty and sweaty shirts clung to their black torsos as leeches cling to the flesh to suck up its blood, but their shirts only managed to absorb the copious sweat that trickled through their bodies. The stench that emanated from their bodies was unbearable; I was a sour smell like the juice of a green lemon.

Felipón was slim and wiry and the tallest of the men, but he compensated for his thinness with his muscular and agile body, his pleasant and honest looking face was lightly covered with an old straw hat. His companion, Goyito, was stout, smaller, *chaparrito* and bowled-legged; although of small stature, his strong body complemented with the one of Felipón in that they were both extremely strong. Without saying a word, they continued to dig the hole despite the resistance of the dusty, stony dry earth. They had to finish digging; the burial was as soon as the next day.

From the ground, with his left hand, Goyito grabbed a dirty, threadbare towel and with his right a green glass bottle. Wiping away the heavy sweat from his eyebrow he took a sip of the hot water and asked his companion:

"Listen, Felipón, why are we wasting time digging this hole to bury old Melquiades here, when all his family is buried in the marble mausoleum, the Roman looking one at the entrance to the pantheon?"

"Old Melquiades was a shameless scoundrel and a womanizer; his wife Doña Agripina does not want him nearby. If it was up to her, she would have left him where he was found lying on the other side of the hill, near the Las Lajas River with a bullet in his neck. If she had a choice, she would have preferred that his body is eaten by the vultures or the wild pigs who are always hungrily roaming by the river bank looking for something to eat. But these rich people are always pretending; they are all fakes and want you to believe that they are human and the most religious. They are those who go to church on Sundays, beat on their chest and no sooner they leave the church they begin to speak evil of their neighbors."

"The old man was also a murderer," Felipón added. "It's been rumored he killed more than two men."

"Who shot the old man?" Asked Goyito. "It must have been one of his enemies or some relative of the ones he killed," he answered to himself.

"People think Pilón Arquillas was the one who shot him," Felipón replied, plunging his shovel into the barren land. "Pilón was the son of Manuel Arquillas, the tailor who lived in the Redil neighborhood, that neighborhood at the end of town, that is near the hospital of the mentally ill."

"Are you sure it was Pilón? Here in this town you cannot trust or believe anyone."

"Look, Goyito, in life you can never be sure of anything; that's what people say. They have not seen Pilón since Melquiades was killed. Someone saw him boarding a train heading to El Norte. Hopefully, he gets lucky and makes it to El Norte. Such a trip is very dangerous; if they don't kill you on the way up there; you run the risk of being captured by the military. If he was the one who killed Melquiades, you can be sure that the military is already chasing him and they better not capture him because where they find him, they will kill him on the spot, these people don't care to find out if you are guilty or innocent. They put a bullet in your head and that's the end of it."

"Why do they suspect Pilón?"

"Because old Melquiades killed his father," replied Felipón.

"My mother told me that one day Melquiades went to yell at Manuel, Pilón's father, full of rage. He was complaining about the pair of slacks he had tailored for him which did not fit him, arguing that he had left them very baggy. Melquiades was so furious that he did not even wait for Manuel to lift his head to apologize. Melquiades snatched the needle — like three or four inches long with which Manuel was mending a twine sack to bring some hens to market — still with the thread hanging in the eye of the needle, Melquiades stuck it on Manuel's belly, a little above the navel. He saw him bend with his hands on his chest and it was not enough to stick him with the needle; when he fell to the ground, he brutally kicked him several times until he was sure he was dead. That old Melquiades was a savage and a despot. They say that Pilón witnessed everything from his room through a slit between one of the boards in the room."

"Why did Pilón not go to the sergeant to denounce Melquiades; to tell him what had happened?"

"You are so naïve, Goyito," answered Felipón. "At that time Pilón was just a small boy when he told the sergeant the story, he laughed ridiculing him saying that he was a liar; assuring him that Melquiades was an honorable man and incapable of committing such a crime."

Goyito shook his head from side to side without believing what his friend was saying, took another drink of water from the green bottle and continued to shovel the earth up from the eight feet deep of the pit. Unconsciously Goyito began to hum a song:

"... *ya el zopilote murió, que lo lleven a enterrar ...*" (... the buzzard is dead, someone take him to his grave ...)

"Goyito don't be such a dumb ass ...!" Felipón quickly interrupted as he heard Goyito humming the song. "If you keep humming that song, they are going to put a bullet in that hollow head or yours, the one you have embedded between your shoulders. Do you remember Tito, the shoe-shiner, who liked to sing idiotic songs mocking the military and the governor? One day they found him wrapped in a slipping mat lying in a stream with two bullets in his head. No one found out who had killed him. Someone said that he had been executed for singing the mocking bullshit of the military. So, shut the fuck up and don't hum that song again, which by the way you do not even know the lyrics. In this town, you cannot criticize the military and less the sergeant or the governor. Understood?"

"I'm sorry! I'm not going to do it again. I did it without thinking! Sometimes I like to sing," Goyito replied.

"Go someplace else to sing and don't do it when you're with me and less in the cemetery. Over here even the dead have ears."

"What are you going to do with the twenty pesos to be paid by Doña Agripina?" Asked Goyito.

"I'll save them all," said Felipón. "I am saving some pesos to leave this dry and arid town where even the grass dares not leave the earth. This town is full of envy. Here only the rich survive and the scoundrels that play to their whim; those who lie for them. I want to go to El Norte. That is what I have longed for since my mother died more than five years ago, but I could not because after she died I was an unbridled vagrant, driven to perdition. I got drunk, I did not work, I got arrested a couple of times. Fortunately, I did not get killed. What are you going to do with the twenty pesos?"

"I'm going to spend them all. I don't like to save money, the last time I put a few pesos in a cardboard box I found them all eaten up by termites. I was thinking of asking Panchita to pity me and let me give her some love. Do you think Panchita is willing for twenty pesos?"

"Goyito, you don't have brains in the head, I think not only you have it hollow but you have it full of termites. Panchita is a 'professional,' all her customers are soldiers who are good pay, I doubt that she is going to fool around with you for twenty pesos. You are so dumb!"

"One never knows," said Goyito. "What if she is not busy and wanting to earn twenty pesitos ...?"

"Listen to me, Felipón, when you leave town, do you think you can take me with you to El Norte? I would also like to leave this town ... I have heard that there is work in El Norte, that there is food in abundance, that the land is not so arid ... that the girls are white with hair the color of yellow corn; I would like to pair with one of them, who knows, I may have a light-skinned Goyito ...?"

"We shall see," answered Felipón.

"Felipón," Goyito said to his companion. "I would like to witness the wake and funeral of old Melquiades. I've never seen a burial of these rich people. The only ones I have witnessed are ours, those of poor people; they put you in a box of four badly nailed boards, mount the box on a mule and take you to the farthest place of the cemetery to make sure no one sees them, and they do not even dig a hole like this. If you are lucky they pray an Our Father and nothing else. They do not even say goodbye or fire a single rocket. I want to see the funeral of Melquiades ...!"

"Listen up Goyito, we do not need to go see the funeral or burial; I'll tell you what happens. I've seen a couple of them."

"Wow Felipón, you know so much!" said Goyito. "You seem to be well-read and studied; you even speak so well and intelligently ... with fancy words that I had never heard. Where did you learn to speak like that? Tell me about these burials!"

"Look, Goyito, tonight, for example, is the wake. It is when they put the dead man in a well-varnished box of oak wood, with brass handles; only the box costs a lot of money. The inside of the box is lined with a cloth of embroidered silk and with a small pillow of the same fabric they raise slightly the head of the dead so that people see him better. But before dressing the dead man in the best of his attires and with all his decorations they wash him with cold water so that he stiffens up faster; then they anoint it all over with ashes ..."

"With ashes?" Surprised asked Goyito. "Why do they smear it with ashes?"

"I don't know! Some people say the body is rubbed with ashes so that the maggots don't eat them so fast and to stop the termites from invading the body. It's very weird; what does it matter when the worms eat it? After all, he is already dead and under seven layers of earth."

"Yes! It's true, he's already dead," Goyito repeated.

"To prevent them from opening during the wake, the eyes of the dead," continued Felipón, "are sewn tightly with a fine thread. The nose sockets are filled with pieces of cotton, perhaps they put the cotton so that those blue-greenish flies don't get inside; they say that those are the ones that lay the eggs and from there the worms grow. So that he does not open his mouth and look like he is begging for water, his lips are glued with starch paste, then they put talcum powder on the face and often they put lip color so it does not look so yellow. There are people who perfumed them with Agua Florida cologne to hide that funny stench of death and to scare off evil spirits."

"So much work to put him in the ground," said Goyito.

"There is more, my friend," Felipón said. "There is always crying, it's common in funerals, to make sure there's really crying, criers are hired to do the crying during the wake. I am sure that Doña Agripina hired the Gutiérrez sisters. Those four do know how to cry; they cry and cry with tears rolling from their eyes and mucus from their noses ... Doña Agripina is going to dress all in black with a black veil covering her face. The pearl necklace positively will be hanging from her neck, with a few ounces of gold distributed all over her body. Her black hair is going to be embellished with a mother-of-pearl comb adorned with diamonds; to mitigate the heat she will fan herself with a black, hand-painted, fan imported from Spain made of sandalwood and in her black bag she will hang a hand-embroidered white linen handkerchief ..."

"You know so much Felipón!" Exclaimed Goyito surprised by all the details his friend knew. "Where did you learn about all this? Why don't we go up and assault the wake? With all that old Agripina's jewelry, we would have enough to go to El Norte."

"You're not only dumb, but you're also crazy," said Felipón, shaking his head from side to side.

"Doña Agripina will cry all night, especially in front of her relatives and those of the dead. Then come those who claim to be his friends, who by the way no one was friends with the old man, behind him everyone criticized and spoke horribly about him, even wanted his death. But that's the way those people are ...! Later the priest arrives to say prayers and sprinkle holy water around the coffin, to scare away the demons. What hypocrisy!"

"Yes! What hypocrisy?" Goyito repeated.

"Goyo! All you know is to repeat what I say? Is that the only thing you know how to say?"

"The only thing you know ..." Goyito started to repeat but checked himself.

"What time do they feed them?" Asked Goyito. "I heard they feed them and they also serve aguardiente."

"After midnight," answered Felipón. "To all those who endured all the weeping and the crocodile tears of the criers are served stuffed tamales, meat empanadas, strong coffee and also aguardiente, but of the cheapest kind; only the closest ones get the good rum and often serve them whiskey. Some of them get drunk and start telling dirty jokes. That shindig lasts until dawn but that depends on how many drunkards have stayed until the end when they come to collect all the chairs that were rented for the wake. No one is interested in the dead. But that's the way those people are ...!"

"The next day, or rather tomorrow, is the burial," Felipón added. "Listen to me, Goyito, don't forget to come tomorrow at about four-thirty in the afternoon, remember that just as we opened this hole, we have to cover it again with all this dry and stony earth. Don't go out and get drunk. Promise me you'll be here tomorrow!"

"I promise you, Felipón. I'm not going to let you down." Goyito answered.

"On the day of the burial, or rather tomorrow, they close the coffin at noon, and around two o'clock they take it to the cathedral where they celebrate a funeral mass."

"Felipón, what is a funeral mass?"

"I am more and more convinced that you are dumb Goyito. A funeral mass is a mass where the body of the deceased is present, that is still in the coffin."

"Forgive me, Felipón, don't be angry."

"During the mass, the priest recites a litany of praises about the dead man. He prays the Creed, God knows how many Our Fathers and Hail Mary's, as if with all those prayers are going to save him from hell. They give the blessing to the dead man and the widow; nobody dares to say that he was a scoundrel, a thief, and even a murderer. But that's the way those people are ...!

"What hypocrisy!" Added Goyito.

"I see you've learned something," Felipón told him.

"After Mass, they start walking toward the cemetery. Often, some relatives carry the coffin on their shoulders but usually it's carried in a hearse. The coffin is very heavy. The funeral carriage is a black car with crystals on the sides. It is driven by a coachman also dressed in black and the car is pulled by two white or greyish colored horses. It's here when things get interesting," added Felipón.

"There's music?" Asked Goyito.

"Sometimes," answered Felipón. "Sometimes they bring a band of mariachis from the capital but they are awful, really bad. The local band of musicians plays better. Those really know to play the drums, they are excellent players, and they know how to play a good tune!"

"As I was saying," Felipón added. "Now is when the speeches begin or rather this is the parade of the hypocrites, please do not interrupt me again." But no sooner Felipón has finished telling him not to interrupt, Goyito asked:

"Why do you say it's the parade of the hypocrites?"

"Because all those who talk are more hypocritical than the criers, at least they cry with tears, these people don't even pretend."

"Tell me more, Felipón."

"Look, the first to start is Benito the deputy, the politician. Like a good politician, he goes to all burials, even if he does not know the deceased. He stops the procession in the first corner, the closest to the social club. He always says the same thing: 'my dear coreligionists and friends, today we are here to say goodbye to our dear friend, to a great friend of our country ...' he repeats the same speech at every funeral even though he knows that he is not his friend, not a coreligionist and least of all a friend of the motherland. But so are the politicians ..., they say any lie to get the people's vote."

"What a liar!" Said Goyito.

"At the next corner, the socialist, Rogelio, La Culebra (The Snake), Rodriguez — they call him the snake because when he delivers his speeches he twists like a boa when it seizes its prey — and Bladimir, the communist, fight their way to stand on the steps of the Church of San Fernando. Both speak at the same time, one proclaiming the advantages of communism, the other wanting to convince the audience of how important it is to eliminate the differences of social classes, how to eliminate poverty by distributing capital ..."

"Distributing capital would be good," interrupted Goyito. "That way we wouldn't have to work and the government would give us a little money, so I could convince Panchita."

"You are so stupid!" Felipón answered. "Nothing is achieved in life by implementing such extreme measures. Look what has happened in other countries where they have implemented communism, now all are poor except the rulers and the elite who help themselves to the soup with the biggest spoon. It is also not good to depend on the government because if it maintains you will not want to work."

"Yes! That's true," added Goyito.

"Then it's the colonel's turn. All dressed in khaki in his well-groomed uniform with fifty or more medals hanging on his chest. He begins by praising the governor, enumerating everything he and the government have done for the benefit of the people, then goes to address the one who is perched on a bronze horse who only God knows for how long he's been there, he does not even remember his name, they say he is the hero of independence but I don't know who he is either. My mother told me that he was a general who had fought in many battles but he had won none. As usual, there is always someone in the crowd who plays the second banana to the colonel and makes a fool of himself and shouts: 'Yes, my Colonel!' 'Well said my Colonel!'"

"At the corner of the house of the señoritas Espinoza, like a madman Gabino España, the atheist, starts his speech. Gabino does not believe in anything, or his own shadow and so he preaches to all the members of the funeral procession. Then will follow Protágoras Asencio, the agnostic, who by the way I don't know who baptized him with that name ... I don't know what he believes in, but he competes with the atheist ... Not to be left behind in the atrium of the church Santa María Don Romualdo the poet is going to speak, or rather the one who thinks himself a poet ... he does not even know how to recite a poem and less write one, but he will try to recite one of the poems of the famous Nicaraguan poet Rubén Darío. Before arriving at the cemetery, you can be sure that the boxer, the circus clown, and Baltasar, the town drunkard will talk. By this time people don't want to know anything, and no one is paying attention to anything or anyone, they just want to reach the gate of the pantheon, to give the condolences to the widow, to go and drink aguardiente at the nearby cantina."

"What a sad end that of old Melquiades ...!" Exclaimed Goyito. "Do you think he repented of all the bad deeds he did in his life?"

"Listen to me Goyito and have this present in your future, life is like an alley where you always walk forward, there is no turning back; everything bad you did you cannot change it anymore. Many people regret and realizing that life is running out, they start appreciating what little they have left, but it is too late, what is done, is done and cannot be erased."

"Why are you trying to confuse me? You started to talk difficult Felipón. You know that I am a very simple man or very dumb as you call me, I do not understand all those things that you describe; but you must be right, it is very difficult to erase the bad deeds that we have committed in life."

"Listen to me, Goyito, we've talked a lot, it's getting late. Please don't get drunk, be here tomorrow. We have to bury old Melquiades. See you tomorrow at four-thirty."

Goyito fulfilled his promise. The next day, on the day of the burial, he punctually appeared in the cemetery, somewhat drunk but sober enough to grab a shovel and help Felipón to cover the pit where they would bury the coffin with the body of Melquiades de Arquímides.

At about six o'clock in the afternoon, accompanied by Doña Agripina, the six men carried the coffin of Melquiades on their shoulders. Each, holding a rope carefully lowered it to the bottom of the eight feet deep pit. Doña Agripina respectively paid Felipón and Goyito the twenty pesos she had offered them for the task of opening the pit and covering it after the coffin had been deposited in the dry and stony earth.

"Thank you, boys," said Doña Agripina. "Make sure that all the earth you dug out is shoveled back, later on, I will put a tombstone to let people know who is buried here ..." Agripina also paid the six men for completing their work.

Behind the nearby hills, the moon peaked with her round and light-yellow face in her effort to witness what was about to happen and shone a tenuous and fading light on the two men, Felipón and Goyito. They approached the edge of the pit, each with his shovel to finish the task they had started the day before.

"Felipón," Goyito called his friend. "Don't forget that I want to go with you to El Norte."

"You can be sure of that my friend," answered Felipón. "You're going to go with me to El Norte. But first, we have to throw all this earth into this grave. Please do not distract me anymore, it's getting dark and it gives me the chills to find myself in a cemetery at night!"

"Felipón," said Goyito. "I want to urinate."

"You Goyito have the weirdest needs at the most inopportune moments, go behind that mound of earth but make sure no one is watching you. Remember that even the dead have eyes here."

Felipón took his shovel and began to shovel the earth over the Melquiades' coffin. Suddenly, on the other side of the fence that bordered the cemetery, a brilliant flash of lightning illuminated the penumbra followed by the thundering of a high-caliber rifle, perhaps that of a Garand. Felipón dropped the shovel; with both hands grasped his bloody chest, his knees buckled, and slowly his lifeless body slid over the grave where the coffin of Melquiades de Arquímides lay partially covered with earth and stones. A cricket rubbed its hind legs to sing its nocturnal strident and irritating symphony. A dog barked twice; the eerie stillness of the cemetery was interrupted by the tenuous flickering light of fireflies which lightened the horrific tragedy.

Seeing that sad scene, Goyito looked around making sure no one was listening and sadly murmured:

"Oh, Felipón! Who would have told you that you would end up in the same grave with your father? I never had the guts to tell you, but your mother was once raped by old Melquiades!"

The Wolf and the Friar

To my wife

The following story unfolds in Bend, Oregon. It was in that picturesque city where I first saw the oil painting that prompted me to write this story to interpret the message the artist had tried to convey. When I saw this amazing work of art, it immediately reminded me of our visit to one of the museums in Italy where, for the first time in my life, I was able to admire the paintings of Caravaggio, the famous Italian painter whose characteristic theme was his view of humankind, depicting us in dark colors and with dramatic use of light.

Bend, Oregon, January 2011

The city of Bend is located in the central part of the state of Oregon. The clear and cool waters of the Deschutes River lazily cross it. The city is framed by the majestic and beautiful Cascades mountains that delight visitors and residents alike with their high peaks and snowy caps. During the winter season, the winter snows, which permanently crown the summits of these imposing mountains, also cover the surrounding paths and many walkways of reddish volcanic earth. Dark green forests of evergreen pine groves and other technicolored vegetation envelop the colorful highways and roadways leading to it. To drive the winding roads during this time of the year, chains must be installed on car tires, trucks and other means of motorized land transportation.

We had only once before, during the summer months, had the opportunity to visit Oregon. We were visiting our son, who at the time was living in the historic city of Astoria located at the mouth of the amazing and equally historic Columbia river.

Taking advantage of the weather forecast — no snow was anticipated during that last week of January — my wife had talked me into driving nine long hours to make the trip from Monterey, California to the captivating city of Bend. She wanted us to visit our son who had recently purchased a home and was taking up residency in that city.

Our ride was uneventful, without any major delays. We entertained ourselves admiring the beautiful landscape of peaks and ridges in the mountainous ranges along the highway, adorned with an array of conifers such as Douglas firs, ponderosa pines and spruces. We passed and soaked in the spectacular views of Klamath Lake. We were tempted to take a detour to admire the breathtaking sights of Crater Lake, but we needed to reach Bend before nightfall. We figured that since our son was living in Oregon, we could venture out again when we had more time and explore the many places that the picturesque northwestern state had to offer.

Two days after our arrival in Bend, while walking the downtown streets and its surroundings, our son informed us about a cultural event to be held the next day at the McMenamins Hotel in downtown Bend and invited us to accompany him. It was required of him to participate in the event due to work-related circumstances. It was a fundraiser for children afflicted with cancer and other life-threatening illness. He also told us that in order to raise funds and to make the event most profitable, there would be a silent auction offering works by local artists and artisans. Invitations had been sent to the city's art lovers, leaflets had been posted in schools and churches, and a special announcement had been printed in the local newspaper. A large attendance was anticipated and the organizers had rented the large ballroom of the historic McMenamins Hotel. The hotel is strategically located in the center of the city and is mostly frequented by tourists. Occasionally its beautiful and spacious halls are rented for cultural events, dances and other social activities.

When we arrived there, the main room was already filled with prospective art buyers, donors, friends, as well as representatives of the benefactor board. As we have done on similar occasions when visiting a new place, we took the usual tour and mingled with many of the other visitors, observing them and admiring the display of several works of art strategically placed on the walls and long wooden tables. Although it was not our intention, during our visit, to purchase any of the artworks, we decided to make a reasonable offer on one particular painting which impressed us for its medieval style and beauty. At the end of the silent auction, our bid had won. After the event, we would take the painting to our son's house. Since he had just moved into his new home, we decided to give it to him as a housewarming gift to decorate one of the living room walls.

At nightfall, after mingling for more than forty-five minutes, and not knowing any of the participants, my wife suggested taking a stroll around the hotel to check out and learn some more of its history.

During our tour, we observed that in addition to the large hall where the reception and the exhibit were being held, in the corridors surrounding the well-decorated and illuminated inner courtyard there were a lively bar, a busy restaurant, a theater and a gallery where artworks from a private collection were being exhibited. These were not part of the fund-raising event.

Outside of the hotel, we found another restaurant and a smaller bar. Both the restaurant and the bar were closed, due to the cruel

January cold. Our interesting walk took us to the entrance of an empty and dimly lit theater which we entered without any difficulty. The venue had been remodeled to show films and perform plays. Adjacent to the theater was what appeared to be a beer distillery.

Bend is not only the mecca of cyclists who travel from faraway places in search of the numerous trails, but it is also famous for a large number of distilleries and breweries and is the home of the Deschutes Brewery. Each year the city hosts many events celebrating its brewery culture. During our visit, our son invited us to taste some of the famous beers. One of the most memorable ones, because of its name, was the tasty blonde Red Chair beer.

Continuing our tour, along one of the wide corridors, we noticed several smaller rooms that appeared to have been used as classrooms. Our stroll led us to an indoor pool and Turkish thermal baths where couples soaked in its pools or, with their bodies wrapped in long white towels, were getting out. As we entered the area, some of the people enjoying the hot baths graciously asked us to join them; however, both my wife and I chose to courteously decline their invitation. We had never been to a Turkish bathhouse, and we were not prepared or excited to try it.

As we left the steamy Turkish room, we resumed our walk around the grounds of the building to get some fresh air. We then decided not to go inside any of the bars or restaurants of the hotel and, since we were running out of places to go, we proceeded towards the vestibule of the hotel, the Parish Center Entryway, which looked like an interesting place to relax and meet our son at the conclusion of the charitable event.

We decided to settle in one of the unoccupied vintage, dark red velvet sofas, which looked as if had been left unmoved since the thirties. An older couple sat across from us on another sofa, very similar to ours but of a lighter color. After exchanging the friendly "Hellos" and the mandatory "Where are you from?" we learned that they were also visiting Bend from a nearby city in California.

"Look at that interesting painting!" I said to my wife as I admired the oil painting hanging on the wall opposite to where we were seated.

"Beautiful ...! I wonder what's the meaning behind the wolf sitting next to the friar by the campfire," said, my wife.

"I don't know. You see, there is the friar with three other men and a woman, sitting around a campfire. Why would a wolf be seated attentively listening to the friar and also holding a cup, maybe of coffee?"

"It's very unusual and I am truly intrigued," my wife answered. "Let's ask if anyone knows what it means."

We started asking several people, including the couple across from us as well as others, coming out of the restaurant and the thermal baths, and also the hotel receptionist. They looked at the painting inquisitively, but nobody had information of its origin or knew the meaning of the painting, strategically hung on the wall of the main entrance of the lobby. All their responses were vague, some shrugged their shoulders. At the end of the event, and still curious about the possible significance of the picture, we asked our son, who told us he didn't really know but it probably had something to do with an old school previously located on those same premises.

Not being able to decipher the meaning of the beautiful oil painting, my wife — who always travels with her digital camera — decided to take a photo of the intriguing and beautiful work of art. Years later we were able to identify the name of the artist.

Monterey, California, July 2012

On that particular Sunday of the second week of July, we decided not to go out for our customary walk and chose to stay at home to read a new book recently purchased on the history of the sardine industry and the Monterey Bay. About three-thirty, in the afternoon someone rang the doorbell.

"Who could it be? I asked my wife. "We are not expecting visitors."

"I see it is our friend Inés," she replied. "How unusual, she is coming alone, without her husband!"

Inés and her husband, our good friends in Monterey, visited us frequently. They are close friends and we consider them as part of our family, and as such, they do not need to announce their visits, they are always welcome. Since Inés was alone, we assumed that her husband was attending Sunday services alone. Inés was carrying a bag filled with books.

"I bring you some books," Inés said, "they are by Borges, García Márquez, Donoso — all famous writers — as well as some Cuban short-story writers."

Inés was a Spanish professor who had recently retired from the Monterey Language School in Monterey, California.

On Sunday afternoons my wife and I enjoyed Inés' visits which we had named our "literary Sunday talks." They were habitual visits where we would exchange and share our ideas and listen to all of Inés' vast knowledge of literary history. This time, because she was visiting us without her husband, who was not a Spanish speaker, we were able to speak in Spanish about various authors, poets and other Latin American storytellers.

Both Inés and my wife started to recite the verses of a poem written by the Cuban poet, José Martí, *Los Zapaticos de Rosa,* the rose-colored little shoes. While my wife recited from memory the famous poem, Inés's eyes started to moist. To distract her, I mentioned our well-known poet Rubén Darío.

"Yes!" said Inés, "he was a contemporary of Martí, and I remember studying Darío's poems at the university. I love his poetry, but my favorite is *Los Motivos del Lobo,* The Wolf's Motives. Do you know it?"

"I remember reading it many years ago. My grandfather liked to read Darío's works, and before I left Nicaragua, he gave me a small leather-bound book titled *Complete Poems of Darío.* I treasure this book. Sometimes I open it and read in it at random."

Inés took the book from my hands, carefully looked for the poem we talked about, composed her breathing, and with a noble tone began to recite the first verses of the famous poem:

> *The man who has a heart of lily,*
> *Cherub soul, heavenly tongue*
> *The humble and sweet Francis of Assisi,*
> *Is with a rude and grim animal,*
>
> *Fearful beast of blood and theft*
> *The jaws of anger, the eyes of evil;*
> *The wolf of Gubbia, the terrible wolf!*

During her inspired reading, I listened attentively, but when she came to the phrase ... the wolf of Gubbia ... I could not help but remember the oil painting which we had admired only a few months earlier in the lobby of the Hotel McMenamins in Bend, on that cold day of January 2011. At that time nobody knew anything about the painting; a wolf sitting with a friar by a campfire. But through the words of the poem *Los Motivos del Lobo,* Rubén Darío — the Prince of Letters as he was also known — we had finally found an interpretation of that intriguing work of art.

The poem does not end here, but these stanzas are, in my opinion, the interpretation of the oil painting. The friar is St. Francis of Assisi, and the three men and the woman are the members of the village. The wolf explains to them that he acted so ferociously out of hunger.

The wolf goes to live in the convent with St. Francis of Assisi, but during one of his absences, the wolf returns to the mountain and again begins his misdeeds. When St. Francis finds him, he confronts him, and the wolf says:

> '*Brother Francisco, do not get too close ...*
> *I was calm, there in the convent;*
> *The people went out,*
> *And if they gave me something, I was happy*
> *And meek I ate.*

> *But I began to see that in all the houses*
> *There was Envy, Hurt, and Wrath,*
> *And all the faces burned*
> *Of hatred, of lust, of infamy, and of lies.*

> *Brothers to brothers made war,*
> *Lost the weak, won the evil,*
> *Female and male were like bitch and dog,*
> *And one fine day everyone hit me with sticks ...'*

> *'Leave me on the mountain, leave me at risk,*
> *Let me exist in my freedom,*
> *Go to your convent, Brother Francisco,*
> *Follow your way and your holiness ...'*

Not yet satisfied with such an alluring explanation and interpretation of the painting, my wife decided to continue researching and discovered that the famous McMenamins Hotel in Bend, had previously been the site of the Old St. Francis School. The school was founded in 1936 and, displayed in its main entrance, was the beautiful painting of St. Francis of Assisi.

This story confirms that the oil painting in the vestibule of the current McMenamins Hotel is the representation of St. Francis of Assisi who, while sitting around a bonfire with the wolf at his side, talks with the members of the village and explains the motives (The Wolf's Motives) for the hungry and cold wolf behaving with such ferociously out hunger.

The Streetcar

To my wife

N ew Orleans exudes the fragrances of cinnamon, magnolias, and blooming azaleas in spring; tastes like freshly boiled okra, beignets, gumbo and jambalaya. New Orleans swings to the sound of jazz, it rocks with Antoine "Fats" Domino's boogie-woogie piano, the rhythm of Louis Armstrong's trumpet and the clarinet of Pete Fountain; and then falls asleep with the romantic song of Irma Thomas, one of the Soul Queens of New Orleans.

In the summer of 1958, almost two years after arriving in that southern metropolis — that, like a crescent-shaped moon, curls up on the shores of the impetuous and dark Mississippi River, in that bustling city of many rhythms and flavors — Bernardo Valdez was going to start his university studies.

Bernardo had already become independent. He had come down from the hot, dank attic, and up from the gloomy cold basement where he had been forced to live due to his meager financial means. Bernardo had enrolled at Tulane University, and in order to support himself and pay for his legal studies, he had obtained a job at Ross Men's Clothing Store, a block away from Canal Street. Along with a friend, and with some of his few savings, they rented a room at a boarding house near the university on General Pershing Street. The guesthouse was a beautiful southern style, a two-story Victorian mansion with four large furnished rooms on the upper floor and two at the main entrance level past the wine-colored carpet that covered the elegant vestibule. Bernardo and his friend occupied a room on the upper floor.

After watching, at the beginning of the fifties, the film *A Streetcar Named Desire*, in his hometown of Santiago de Cuba, Bernardo could not remember how many times he had dreamed of riding on one of these streetcar "trains" of grayish-green color with their varnished wooden benches; those that ran from north to south on St. Charles Avenue, beginning their journey in the center of the city on Canal Street to the end of Carrollton Avenue and back. Bernardo also wanted to emulate Marlon Brando, the main protagonist of this film, but his pretentious imaginings only allowed him to achieve one of his wishes, to ride the streetcar.

One Sunday afternoon, on a hot and humid summer day, Bernardo walked three blocks to Napoleon Avenue, where, for twenty-five cents, he boarded the streetcar that headed north on St. Charles

Avenue. After about ten minutes, having comfortably settled on one of its brightly varnished wooden benches next to the conductor, Bernardo amused himself admiring the Victorian styled houses of the beautiful wide avenue as the streetcar approached the universities of Tulane, Loyola and Audubon Park before reaching the end of the route on Carrollton Avenue.

When the conductor saw that Bernardo was not exiting with the rest of the passengers, he asked him:

"Are you going to get off here, young man, or are you going to ride back on this car? If you wish to do that, you must pay another twenty-five cents."

"I'm going to do the entire route," replied Bernardo, depositing another quarter in the coin receiver near the conductor.

"Do you know that Canal Street is the end of the route?" Asked the conductor. "If you want to return in this car you will have to pay another twenty-five cents. The entire route takes about ninety minutes since it travels almost thirteen miles," again, the driver warned.

"It's all right, I understand. I will pay another quarter," answered Bernardo.

During the return journey, Bernardo entertained himself admiring the historical and beautiful mansions of the renowned Garden District as well as the other houses typical of that sector of the city. He admired the majestic monument dedicated to the famous southern General Robert E. Lee who, during the Civil War in the United States, had led the southern forces and fought in several battles against the northern forces, better known as the Union Army.

It was on the return trip of the streetcar, after making a short tour loop of Canal Street — at the stop between Canal and Poydras — that the elegant gentleman boarded the streetcar.

'He seems to come from church or a Sunday reception,' Bernardo thought to himself.

After depositing the required twenty-five cents, with the right hand, the man took off his grey plush hat and courteously greeted the five passengers who at that time were traveling on the streetcar.

"Good afternoon, Don Ricardo." The conductor greeted him in Spanish. "Do you come for your usual ride, your habitual route?" he asked.

"I come from the harbor," answered Ricardo. "You know I like to go for a walk and watch the steamships and the tourists' ships entering and leaving the river, but this time I will not take the usual ride, thanks just the same."

'He cannot be more than sixty-five,' Bernardo thought, looking at the elegantly dressed man.

Ricardo Mejía Blanco was a well-built man, tall, slender and good-looking. His dark gray suit matched his plush hat. Below the starched collar of his white shirt, a gray tie with red-wine colored stripes was neatly tied with a Windsor knot. A watch chain pinned from one of the buttonholes of his vest held a golden watch, which, after casually looking at the hour, he carefully placed in the right pocket of his vest. His tanned face was adorned with a well-trimmed mustache, which, like his well-groomed thick hair, already showed some silver threads. His small, unframed glasses allowed the afternoon light to shine on his bright black eyes. By his accent, Bernardo could guess that was from one of the countries of South America.

Before sitting next to him, Ricardo asked Bernardo:

"May I sit next to you, young man?" Bernardo nodded acquiescence and once seated while holding the hat with both hands over his knees Ricardo addressed Bernardo:

"Excuse me for being impertinent, but you do not seem to be American, even though your complexion is quite fair," added Ricardo.

Bernardo was of medium height, thin but not skinny, his somewhat curly black hair making his complexion look whiter than it was; his eyes, also black, complemented his pronounced eyebrows of the same color. He was a good-looking young man, not more than twenty-five or twenty-six years old.

"No," answered Bernardo, "I am Cuban. Are you, Don Ricardo, by any chance South American?" asked Bernardo.

"Yes, I am Chilean. I'm from Santiago, I lived there for a long time, and now I have lived only a couple of years in New Orleans. Young man, what's your name, have you lived here long?"

"My name is Bernardo, I have resided here just a couple of years, I study law at Tulane University, across from Audubon Park," Bernardo said. "What a coincidence! I am from Santiago, too. I was born in Santiago de Cuba, my parents left Cuba in the late fifties when the political reprisals began, they settled in Puerto Rico."

And so, Bernardo and Ricardo continued talking and exchanging personal and family information during the travel of the streetcar. Later Ricardo told Bernardo that Rogelio Pacheco — the conductor of the streetcar — was of Colombian origin.

"Rogelio was born in Medellín," Ricardo said. "where he worked as a train operator and also learned to be a machinist, he has many more years than the two of us living in New Orleans; he knows me well and we have become very good friends. I ride this streetcar a lot, I like to travel its route many times, I prefer to do it during weeknights when there are fewer people, between eight or nine. I prefer to ride on the streetcar and walk by the harbor to enduring my son's ill-treatment. Being a regular customer, Rogelio allows me sometimes to travel for free. Isn't it true, Rogelio?"

"Yes, Don Ricardo," replied Rogelio, the conductor, slowing down the car to guide it carefully around Lee's circle.

Noticing the question mark look on Bernardo's face, after what

Ricardo had confided in him about his son's abusive treatment, Ricardo went on to say:

"I'm sorry to bother you, young Bernardo, for confiding all my troubles even when we have just met, you seem to be a decent person I can trust. Can I call you just Bernardo? Since we're both from Santiago, we are both *Santiagueros*," Ricardo asked.

"Of course, Don Ricardo," answered Bernardo.

"I lived happily in Santiago until my wife died three years ago," Ricardo told Bernardo. "I worked as an accountant in an import/export company. On Sundays, we traveled to Valparaiso, you know, the harbor of Santiago, and although it was not a tourist attraction, my wife and I always liked to stroll on the pier; we entertained ourselves admiring the steamships that came from France, England and other European countries. We enjoyed listening to the raucous noise of the ship's whistle and dreamed of the day when we could embark on a trip to one of those European countries, but we never achieved it. However, I can't complain, we had a good life."

"Is that why you like to come and stroll along the harbor, Don Ricardo?" Asked Bernardo.

"Yes, it brings me many happy memories of those Sunday excursions with my wife."

"What kept you from realizing your dream?" Asked Bernardo.

"I had to save money for my son's schooling so that he could complete his university studies, something I was not able to do when I was young. I wanted him to be an engineer or a doctor. After many sacrifices, he successfully graduated with a degree in fluvial engineering. Now he has a job working for a department in charge of maintaining the levees that protect the city of New Orleans. He is doing very well. After my wife died, he asked me to come and live with him, but he doesn't treat me well, he humiliates me and blames me for many things that I prefer not to mention, Bernardo."

"How sad, Don Ricardo, but if your son treats you so badly, why don't you go back to Chile?" asked Bernardo.

"I cannot," said Ricardo. "When I moved here I sold my apartment, and Angélica, my only sister, died last year. I have only a few friends left and I cannot count on them, some of them are older, and although they have invited me to return, I cannot impose on them."

Ricardo continued to tell Bernardo that in New Orleans he had not been able to make new friends with whom he could at least share a glass of wine. Americans are very friendly but difficult to be friends with; his son's friends were very young and not interested in making friends with a person his age. He had resigned himself to endure the ill-treatment of his son, and to fill his days, he rides the streetcar and strolls through the harbor, admiring the ships full of tourists, dreaming of the past and his travels with his wife to Valparaíso, the harbor of Santiago.

"One of my favorite pastimes," said Ricardo, "is to ride on the streetcar, two, three or more times. I try to coordinate my outings with Rogelio's schedule, who sometimes allows me to do it without charging me. I am careful not to take advantage of his generosity as traffic inspectors unexpectedly appear from time to time. Rogelio is one of my best friends."

"Forgive me, Bernardo," Ricardo said. "I have to get off, we're on Louisiana Street, and this is my stop. See you on another occasion."

"See you later, Don Ricardo, it's been nice to have met you," answered Bernardo.

After this initial conversation, Ricardo's friendship with Bernardo and Rogelio, the streetcar conductor, had become closer; they had become very good friends. Also, the conversations in the streetcar were already very habitual; the three spent their ride talking and exchanging stories and mishaps, always being careful not to distract Rogelio and not draw much attention from the few passengers who at that time boarded the streetcar.

The rain had not let up on that day of mid-October of 1958. The trees that decorated both sides of the wide avenue of St. Charles had begun to change the colors of their leaves to brown, yellow and red; these were the signs of autumn approaching. It had started to get cold. The cool breezes blowing from the Mississippi could be felt as well. As usual, Ricardo, Bernardo and Rogelio, entertained themselves by talking and trading tales, of their visits to Santiago de Chile, the other as a child in Santiago de Cuba, and Rogelio about the time when he learned to be a machinist in the city of Medellin in Colombia.

After half turning around Lee's circle, at the Jackson Street stop, the car stopped to pick up a passenger. A religious sister, closing a black umbrella, climbed onto the streetcar. The clock, that hung close to the conductor stroke 10:20 pm.

The cuff of the sister's black habit was dripping with water, and her black boots were soaked as well. The black cloak that covered her head did not allow you to see her face and the white linen coif over half of her forehead made it even more difficult. However, it was possible to see the nun's white complexion, her sad look, pensive, deep as if gazing into an endless tunnel, where something was missing, but no one could figure out what. Her sky-blue eyes were accentuated by her silver-framed glasses. Despite her well-covered face, it was easy to see a couple of locks of her blond hair.

'She may be about forty-five,' Bernardo guessed.

"Good evening," said the sister, addressing the small group that was traveling on the streetcar at that hour.

Trying to open her small black leather wallet to get her twenty-five cents, one of the books that she held under her arm, slid to the wooden floor of the streetcar, also wet from her dripping habit. Both Bernardo and Ricardo were attentively following every move made by the nun. No sooner had the book hit the wet floor, that with his hat in his hand Ricardo got up from his seat and picked it up. With the chivalry that characterized him, Ricardo addressed the nun.

"Good evening, sister," he said, respectfully, and greeted her as he extended his arm to give her the book. "I hope you did not get all your habit wet. It has been raining all day very hard, and according to the weather forecast it will rain the rest of the night, but I doubt it will be another hurricane like the one which battered the city two years ago, it was a devastating storm."

"My name is Ricardo; this young man is my friend Bernardo and our conductor's name is Rogelio." As Ricardo introduced the trio, the sister acknowledged them and smiled discretely while sitting across the aisle on one of the empty benches.

"Forgive my indiscretion sister," continued Ricardo. "But I think it's dangerous to ride the streetcar at this hour. There have been some assaults in recent months, aren't you afraid of traveling alone at this time of night?" Ricardo asked the nun.

"My name is Sister Verónica María," responded the sister to Ricardo's questions and concerns. "I am aware of the recent assaults, but I'm not afraid; Jesus accompanies me, he guides me and protects me, he is my best companion. Besides," she added, "I have a short way to go, I finished teaching catechism at a children's center a block from this stop and I exit at the University of Loyola stop, where I currently live and study theology."

"I'm Chilean, from Santiago," said Ricardo. "Bernardo is Cuban from Santiago de Cuba, and Rogelio is from Medellín. Are you from Spain, sister Veronica? You have a Spanish accent," asked Ricardo.

Smiling, the nun addressed the curious Ricardo and said:

"Thanks for all the introduction, I am Venezuelan and as I told you I study theology at the University of Loyola; I recently started my second semester. It seems that the three of you are good friends already," added the nun.

"I am studying law at Tulane University," Bernardo said. "I have been almost two years in the city."

While the brief introductions were taking place, Ricardo could not take his eyes off the nun. Again, he insisted and with the courtesy that characterized him, he said to her:

"I'm sorry, but I will not have you take a risk walking alone at this late hour of the night, if you allow me, I will accompany you to the campus of the University or at least close to the building where you live."

"It's not necessary, but if you insist Don Ricardo, I accept your offer," replied Sister Verónica María, and they both got out of the streetcar.

After that rainy night, every time the nun traveled on the

streetcar, Ricardo's courteous offerings were not only anticipated but had become a routine. Ricardo not only offered to accompany her but also had discreetly found out the nun's schedule and wouldn't fail to be present on those days and share their journey on the streetcar. Sister Verónica María was already part of the friendly gang and their gatherings which took place on the streetcar, each sharing their stories. When some of the members of that informal club — whose membership had been only a coincidence — were absent, the others not only asked one another for the whereabouts of one of their members, but inquired with Rogelio who, as the conductor, was the most permanent and reliable member of the group and knew the reason for the absence of each one of them.

This was how the fun and animated gatherings on the streetcar continued throughout the autumn and most of the winter. The friendship between the four had almost become a brotherhood and the nun's sad and deep gaze had changed to a happy and brighter look.

It was at the beginning of April 1959, at the beginning of spring, when the azaleas and magnolias began to flower along the avenue that Ricardo and Sister Verónica María, for reasons unknown to Bernardo, had been absent for almost two weeks. Bernardo thought that perhaps they were sick or that Ricardo, tired of his son's ill-treatment, had decided to return to his native country, or that the sister had decided to abandon her studies and return to Venezuela. Bernardo had not thought to ask Rogelio for Ricardo or Sister Verónica María, he was concentrating on his studies and busy in the clothing store where they had increased his working hours. He figured that they would eventually show up again.

The absence of Ricardo and the nun had become so noticeable and suspicious that on a Monday night when Bernardo boarded the streetcar, he finally decided to ask Rogelio for them.

"Rogelio," Bernardo said to the conductor. "Do you have any idea what happened to Don Ricardo and the nun? I have not seen them for a while. Could they be sick, have they returned to their countries?"

"I don't know exactly what happened, I cannot imagine what happened to them," said Rogelio. "The only thing I can tell you is that on Sunday, two weeks ago, they both got off the streetcar at Canal Street."

"Did they tell you where they were going?" asked Bernardo, somewhat intrigued.

"I don't know," said Rogelio. "They just said goodbye and told me that they were going for a walk in the harbor to see a steamship that was leaving for Europe that afternoon."

After that walk to the harbor, they were never seen again ...

The White Linen Dress

Schizophrenia is a devastating brain disease ...
Usually, the one who suffers from this
tormenting evil does not realize it.
Those who suffer are those who are around the sick, the closest ...
The author

Inspired by a true story

Today, ten years ago, the Canuto twins, the children of Clemente and Consuelo Canuto were born. For the Canuto the birth of the twins had been a blessing from God because they had been trying to start a family since they came from Sicily fifteen years ago. The celebration of the baptism of the twins, Antonio and Luciano, had been overwhelming. Their proud parents had invited a large number of their friends and the party they later held at the elegant and sumptuous Hotel Marco Polo, one of the best hotels in the city of Coronado. The Canuto had spared no expense.

Among the distinguished guests were their neighbors and good friends Celestino, a professional roofer, and Sebastiana Montenegro, a housewife, whom they had known since their arrival from Sicily. With them, they shared their best dishes and some pastries like their delicious eclairs filled with cream of cacao and vanilla that Consuelo proudly prepared with her Sicilian recipes.

The twins were always ready to take to Sebastiana and Celestino their mothers' delicious eclairs and deserts. They liked to listen to Sebastiana who entertained them by telling her stories of when she was a child. Sebastiana also liked to see them walk towards the church on Sundays and enjoyed their cordial greetings. When Sebastiana spoke of the twins with her husband, she always said:

"Those children are a couple of fine gentlemen. How well they have been brought up by the Canuto; it is a pity that the only son we fathered was lost because of the pernicious fever, and with the unneeded surgical intervention I had to have I could not bear any more children."

As she used to do every Sunday, Sebastiana Montenegro had put on her best seamstress-made bone-white linen dress, and her pretty bright red shoes. She had pulled one of the wicker armchairs from her living room to the door that led to the street to sit and watch the people pass by at five-thirty in the afternoon as they headed towards the church of San Ignacio.

"Good afternoon, Doña Sebastiana," Luciano said graciously to Sebastiana.

"Good afternoon, ma'am." Antonio greeted her.

"Good afternoon to you too boys," Sebastiana said in disgust.

"I don't know when those brats will learn not to call me Sebastiana; I do not like that name that unfortunately gave me my adoptive parents. I do not know why they do not call me *china*, that name is more befitting of me since I look like a Chinese woman." Grumbled Sebastiana to herself.

The clock of the cathedral of San Jacinto stroked twelve-fifteen at night. It was the dawn of the Monday following the celebration of the tenth anniversary of the birth of the Canuto twins. Sebastiana very lightly slipped from the bed she shared with Celestino, her husband of twenty years. She did not want to wake him up. She picked up the white linen dress she had carefully hung on a coatrack on the hook of her closet door, and lightly adjusted her black shiny hair that she had mussed up when she put on the elegant dress. She took the doorknob from the door of the room and silently with her right hand closed the door of the street. Sitting on one of the steps leading to the cement sidewalk, she put on the red leather shoes she had carried with her left hand as she left her room.

Sebastiana did not have to wait long for the bus after walking the three blocks that separated her house from the bus stop at the corner of La Avenida de los Héroes (The Heroes Avenue) and Roosevelt Street where her home was located.

"Good evening, ma'am," said the bus driver after Sebastiana deposited a fifty-cent coin in the metal container next to the driver. "Where are you going this evening?"

"To the end of the avenue," Sebastiana said. "But I'm going to get off at the stop next to the El Camino bar."

"Be careful, ma'am," the driver added. "At this time of the morning, most of the customers are already somewhat drunk."

"I have no intention of entering that den of vice and perdition; that cantina that as its name well says: 'El Camino' is the 'way' towards hell. I don't know why the mayor hasn't closed it. Like everything in this city, the owner must be his friend, and it's rumored that he frequents it late at night in the company of women of dubious reputation."

After walking two blocks, Sebastiana approached the bronze statue dedicated to the hero of independence located at the corner of the street; she looked at him with respect and devotion, as if she was venerating a saint and loudly said:

"If you were alive, I'm sure you'd have finished all the rot and vice of this city, including the dump of the cantina El Camino."

From the right pocket of her pretty white linen dress, Sebastiana pulled out a brown paper bag and carefully drew three dates from it. One she put it in the left hand of the hero, another threw it to the ground and the third again put it in the paper bag. Staring at the statue's still eyes again, she said aloud:

"Simón, every Monday at this hour I bring you this date so that you never forget me, remember me in your dreams, as I remember you in mine, do not forget how much you loved me, if it had not been for the war we would have married; we would have had many children and be eternally happy. Tell me that I can eat my date, give me a sign of approval, or I'll have to give it to that black squirrel that already ate his."

Without taking her eyes off the statue's immobile eyes, Sebastiana gave thanks to Simón, took her date from her bag and with great satisfaction kissed hit before eating it. The course of the night had consumed the emotions and the notion of Sebastiana's time. As she waited for the bus to return to her house in the dim light of the lantern that lit the bus stop, she looked at her silver wristwatch; the hands of the small garment marked four o'clock in the morning.

"China, pity me, hug me, give me a kiss," said the beggar, leaning on the bench at the bus stop, covering his half-naked body with a torn and dirty newspaper.

"You're disgusting and senile Baltasar, how can you imagine me hugging you, let along kissing you," Sebastian said.

"*China*, you soon forgot when we were young, when under the shade and the soft breezes of the branches of the elm tree next to the San Ignacio church you swore to love me, when in the moist grass you gave yourself to me without any prejudice, how soon you forgot, *chinita* of my soul."

"Baltasar, you are a vile drunk, I am an honest and married woman, please do not bother me anymore!"

"*China*, forgive me for interrupting your exchange with Baltasar," said Severino, the undertaker, as he pushed a wagon with a coffin of dark mahogany. "Will you buy me this coffin?" Severino asked Sebastiana.

"That coffin is very small and I do not fit in it," Sebastiana said. "You are wrong I have no amorous relationship with Baltasar, this dirty drunk who hasn't tried the water of a bath in who knows how long."

"*China*, allow me to take measurements of your body and make a coffin so that you fit into it and won't wobble on the way to the cemetery," Severino added.

"Severino, you are worse than Baltasar, you are degenerate, you want to touch me, and I will not allow you to put a finger on my body even with your measuring tape; I am a married woman and a very respectable, you cannot touch me, not even if I was dead," Sebastiana replied.

"China, are you going out today to do your walk as you habitually do? Celestino asked his wife when he saw her in front of the mirror of the room, while she, with a tortoiseshell brush, stroked her straight black hair to her bareback.

"I doubt it," said Sebastiana to Celestino, as she wiped the faint sacks under her almond-colored, and narrowed Chinese looking eyes with a cotton ball slightly moistened with tap water from the sink. Approaching the oval mirror that hung on the wall, she watched her paleness and with her ivory white hands, she slapped her cheekbones trying to bring some of her blood to her cheeks to color them. With a light rose-colored Kleenex, she wiped the red from her thin lips.

"But today is Monday; you always like to go for a walk early in the morning, what has made you change your plans?" Celestino asked, surprised.

"I feel tired today, I have been walking most of the night, today I do not want to walk," said Sebastiana.

"Tired?" Celestino asked in amazement. "You've been sleeping through the night, and when I got up to drink a glass of tap water, you did not even move, I'm sure I heard a slight snore."

"Yes, I'm tired, do not make fun of me, I don't snore; besides I am thinking of the black dog of Doña Lubina, the other day it scared me to death, it showed me his large, razor-sharp fangs and wanted to bite me, it launched himself at me with fury and drool on his snout, it almost bit my right leg. If you see how large and white the tusks were, larger than a wolf's, like those of a hungry lion. You have to talk to Doña Lubina to lock that beast."

"*China*, I think you're delusional, seeing visions, you've been sleeping a long time, Doña Lubina has no animals but a black dog, she hates animals."

"You never believe me, you always think I'm seeing visions and goblins, you always think I'm crazy ...!"

"*China*, I never said you were crazy, I just told you that Doña Lubina does not have any dogs."

"Someone has a dog then, maybe it's the twins, every night I hear him barking, it will not let me sleep."

Celestino did not want to continue trying to convince his wife that no one in the neighborhood had a black dog; it would have been known; everything was known in the neighborhood, there were no secrets there and less if someone had bought a black dog, he did not pay much attention to the complaints and visions that supposedly his wife was seeing. However, not wanting to arouse her suspicions, he decided to observe her and pay more attention to her complaints, especially when she mentioned having met Baltasar, the city drunkard, who had been missing for three years ago and with Severino the undertaker who had wanted to sell her a coffin.

Celestino did not understand what was happening to his wife, she had never acted that way. In the course of the following year Celestino observed that Sebastiana showed no improvement; on the contrary, he noticed her behavior had worsened. She was colder toward him, distracted and taciturn; she no longer wanted to sit in the living room by the door facing the street and growl at the twins who often passed by greeting her. Now she would sit on a chair in her room where she stayed the most hours of the day and entertained herself by looking through a window; gazing out into emptiness with a sad, empty, vague look. As she sat at the dining room table with her fingers, she drummed strange and uncoordinated sounds as if she were hitting the edge of a drum; she ate little, and neither did the rice with chicken, her favorite dish she fancied. Even more so, Celestino paid close attention after watching her every Monday throwing three dates in the backyard of the house, pretending to talk to a stranger whom she called Simón.

One morning Celestino said to his wife. "I am going to the Jew's house, Dr. Levowitz, he called me yesterday because it looks like he has a leak from his roof, then I'm going to my job, we're finishing the installation of the roof on Don Petronio's house. Now that the economy has improved the construction of houses has increased; I have submitted budget proposals to the mayoralty to install roofs on three houses, I hope they award me the contracts that would bring us extra money and so we can take that trip that you have always longed for."

"I don't know what you mean," Sebastiana said. "I do not want to go anywhere, you go alone. Do not delay, remember that Francisca is coming today ... that woman torments me day and night, I do not want to be alone when she comes."

"Francisca?" Celestino asked aloud as he closed the door to exit his house.

Celestino took advantage of the visit to Dr. Samuel Levowitz and after repairing the problem that was causing the leak, very worried and with the luxury of details explained to the doctor what was happening with his wife and her most noticeably odd behavior. Pensive and scratching the beard with which he covered his aged face, he turned to Celestino.

"Son," the doctor began. "What you're saying to me does not sound good ...; I do not like it at all. Some years ago, I had a patient who suffered from similar symptoms and after having seen and examined by several doctors, psychologists and neurologists she was diagnosed with a very bad decease, schizophrenia."

"What is that?" Celestino asked. "Give me medicine, a remedy to cure her. I think she does not suffer but I do, I am extremely worried and in silence, I suffer intensely, I do not like to see her that way. She was a cheerful, pleasant woman; she liked to dance, to laugh, all that ..., now she does not want anything, she just passes her time gazing vaguely out of a window."

"Imagine doctor," Celestino said. "The other day she told me a very strange story, she told me that when she was a child, she had been raped under the elm tree of the San Ignacio church by the drunkard Baltasar. That is not true, she was never abused, in addition to the side the church there are no trees and less an elm."

"I understand Celestino what you are telling me," answered the doctor. "I am very sorry but little is known about this disease; is a disease that affects the brain and progresses over time to the point that the person becomes aggressive and uncontrollable. They do not suffer and believe that they are not sick, they believe that the one who is sick is their partner or their relatives and, in many occasions, they violently take their feelings out against them and insult and humiliate them. It is the relatives who suffer and usually they insult and humiliate the most beloved; in this case, it's you. I'm so sorry," the doctor added again.

"What can I do, Doctor? Give me something to help her improve her condition, I'm desperate, before I came, she told me she was waiting for a so-called Francisca. I do not know who she is but she constantly mentions her. She says that Francisca torments her, that she pursues her throughout the house, that she tells her secrets. She's gone as far as telling me that I am being unfaithful to her, that I cheating behind her back with the mulatto Eulalia. Doctor, Eulalia does not exist and Francisca does not exist either, it's all in her imagination."

"I can prescribe some pills that help control the disease, but they are very expensive and not as effective. Another option is to apply electric shocks but these are dangerous since in some cases do not solve anything and can negatively affect the brain and aggravate the disease. I know my dear Celestino that the last option is to put her in a place where she is observed twenty-four hours a day, and soon you will not be able to leave her alone at home. All of these alternatives are extremely costly and you will have to deal with them. You will have to install many roofs."

"Will she die suddenly, or will her suffering be prolonged for a long time?" Celestino asked the doctor.

"The patient I mentioned to you lasted about ten years, but it's unpredictable how long they can last."

"Thank you, Don Samuel," Celestino said as he said goodbye to the doctor. "Forgive me for taking all this time. It was not my intention, but I'm desperate," Celestino added. "Don't worry about paying me for fixing the roof."

"Celestino," said Samuel. "Don't worry about my time, if you have any other doubts and if you notice that Sebastiana is worse come see me, if I am attending a patient please wait for me."

"Why have you taken so long? That roof repair you made at the Jew's house must have taken an eternity," said Sebastiana to her husband upon seeing him enter the house.

"*China*, I told you that I was going to finish the installation of the roof of the house where I've been working all this month. I also told you that I would stop by the mayor's office to inquire about the budgets I had submitted for the other jobs."

"The mayor is a scoundrel," Sebastiana said. "He will not give you any contract unless you give him a *mordida,* a bribe."

"China, don't think with so much malice," Celestino said, adding. "I had forgotten to tell you that I received a telegram from my brother informing me that on the way to Vista Alegre they would be visiting us for a couple of days. I am very happy because I have not seen him in almost three years."

"You can start answering your brother not to come to our house; I do not want to know anything about him or that wife of his. The last time they were here, all he did was go around and around the house, that made me very nervous and his wife is a degenerate alcoholic, she just spent her time drinking that disgusting vodka, that dirty and sinful drink. The two are going to go straight to hell."

"But *china*, my brother spent most of his visit watching TV with me and his wife is very religious, she has never tasted a drop of liquor."

"That's what you think; she would go into the bathroom with the bottle in her hand and come out with her eyes glassy ... You never believe me, who knows what that quack told you because, since the last time you saw him you have not stopped watching me, follow me everywhere, I cannot stand you. Go on to that trip with the mulatto Eulalia, yes her, you got crazy with the wag of her buttocks, go to your brother and his alcoholic wife, but don't bring them here. Leave me alone, let me live in peace."

Celestino had no choice but to tell his brother not to come to his house because he did not want to make Sebastiana worse. He had to join his brother in a nearby restaurant and lie saying that Sebastiana was ill with a high fever that could be contagious.

The next time Celestino visited the doctor, he was desperate and needed to tell him what had happened.

"Doctor, the situation with my wife continues to get worse. The other day she tried to leave home half-naked; when she dresses she puts on that white linen dress and her red shoes; the white dress is no longer a dress it's almost torn to shreds, every day is dirtier, and refuses to wash it." Celestino said to the doctor. His visits were more frequent, and the medications and prescriptions he had recommended were not improving his wife Sebastiana.

"You're going to have to make a drastic decision," the doctor told Celestino. "Seriously you will have to consider interning her because her attempts to escape will become more frequent and you will not be able to control her or stop her."

"Doctor," Celestino said. "The cost of the most economical center of this city is above my few means, I will have to sell my house. I do not want to send her to the center located in the city of Soledad. I have heard that patients are mistreated there; they are often beaten, shouted at, they are kept ungroomed and barely fed. I want to have my *china* nearby so I can visit her and avoid being mistreated."

"Do not despair, Celestino," said the doctor. "I'll see if I can use my influence with the mayor, he owes me a couple of 'favors' and it's time for him to pay me back."

"Oh! Thank you, Doctor, although you may not go to Heaven; well, you're not Catholic or religious, but I'm going to pray to the Virgen de Guadalupe — she's very miraculous — for her to keep in mind your good deeds when it's your time."

"Thank you, Celestino, for your good intentions." Smiling, the doctor said.

Returning to his home, Celestino sought out Sebastiana to give her the good news about having been awarded the three contracts to replace the roofs in three of the mayoralty's buildings.

"*China*, where are you, I bring you good news," Celestino said aloud as he searched the rooms and the rest of the house. He was so surprised when he exited onto the patio; he observed Sebastiana in her underwear throwing the dates at the squirrels and very solemnly crossed herself before the invisible statue of Simón.

'How strange,' Celestino thought to himself. 'Today is not Monday. What caused her to come out on a Saturday?'

"*China*, what are you doing half-naked in the courtyard?" Celestino asked, looking at the coat rack on which Sebastiana had hung the white linen dress, which she had cut into several strands.

"I cannot stand the twins, look at them on the roof, they haven't stopped throwing pebbles at me. You have to do something, call their parents so that they do something and stop bothering me; if you don't do anything I'll cut them just like I did with that dirty dress."

"Do not worry *chinita*, I'll talk to their parents so the twins stop bothering you, please give me the knife. Why did you shred the dress, is it your favorite dress?"

"Because I won't need it anymore, I am not going to wear it ever again."

"All right," Celestino told her. "I'll buy you another, a blue dress, that's one of your favorite colors too."

"I do not want you to buy me another dress, do not buy me anything, I do not need any more clothes," Sebastiana answered in disgust.

"Well, I will not buy you any more clothes, but please come into the house and put on your robe for dinner, I brought you your favorite dish."

"I'm not hungry, I do not want to eat anything, I'm very tired, the twins won't leave me alone, they have tormented me all day. I'll take a shower and go to bed, don't bother me anymore."

Sebastiana went through the dining room and looked at the rice and chicken dish that Celestino had brought her but did not pay attention to, she went up the ten steps of the stairs to the second floor. After showering, she lay down on her bed and covered up to her neck with a green blanket. Aloud she called Celestino, who immediately went to Sebastiana's call.

"*China*, why are you covered with a blanket, don't you realize it's very hot?"

"I'm cold; I did not call you to criticize me. I called you to tell you that when Severino comes with the coffin that I ordered, make sure that he has done it to my size, that the handles are made of bronze and that it is well varnished. Don't pay him more than a hundred pesos, and then put it in the center of the living room, and tomorrow I'll see what I do with it. Thank you, Celestino," Sebastiana added, looking at her husband with tenderness as she had always seen in the past, she turned to the wall and fell sound asleep.

The next day Celestino with the help of a friend took Sebastiana's body to the coffin which had been placed in the center of the living room as she had requested. There Celestino would have the wake; watch over his wife, his companion, whom he had called *china* for more than twenty years. With his hands, he tenderly stroked Sebastiana's black hair away from her face that had turned pale, ivory white. Gently he took her hands and crossed a rosary between them, placing them gently on her still breast. His beloved *china* had finally been freed from all her visions, her anguish, her fears, and all the goblins and characters who had tormented her mind for so many years.

Today, fifteen years ago the Canuto twins, the children of Clemente and Consuelo Canuto, were born. They were no longer brats — as Sebastiana once thought of them — they were already a pair of fine young gentlemen. Dressed in their finest suits, they were both standing in front of the Montenegro house, silently watching with great sorrow at Celestino and five of his friends, who, taking the varnished coffin from the bronze handles went down the three steps to the concrete sidewalk to carry the coffin with the corpse of Sebastiana towards the cathedral; with the corpse of the *china*, as she had always wanted to be called. This would be her final walk. It was at this point when Antonio, one of the twins, asked his brother Luciano:

"Are you going to go to the cathedral for the mass for Doña Sebastiana?"

"No!" Luciano said. "You go. I'm going to go to the church of San Ignacio."

"What are you going to do there, why not the cathedral?" Antonio asked his brother.

With a wicked smile on his face, Luciano replied:

"I'm going to meet with a most beautiful girl who has just come from abroad and on Sundays, wearing a nice bone white linen dress and bright red shoes, she waits for the last bell to ring for the five o'clock mass under the shade of the elm tree."

"You are crazy Luciano...!" Answered his brother.

Was Luciano taken by the dreaded decease?

Twenty Years Later

To my cousin Gloria María

All stories are true. But some of them never occurred ...
James A. Owen

Torquato Berindoague was a skeptical person. He doubted that someday he would find out why his parents had baptized him with such a horrible name. A name which had been the reason for mocking, jokes and concealed laughs during his school years and early adulthood. Friends laughed at him behind his back. His first girlfriend ended their short-lived relationship after realizing that her friends were making fun of her for dating a guy with such a terrible name.

When he was fifteen years old, he daringly asked his father why he had chosen to give him such a weird name. His father's response was even worse. He told him not to be disrespectful of his ancestors, especially of his great-grandfather Torquato after whom he was named. He told him that his parents had risked their lives to go on an arduous trip through the Iberian Peninsula and later across the Atlantic Ocean to come to America, leaving all their family and friends in Sitges, a small coastal town in the Mediterranean south of Catalonia.

May they Rest in Peace...! Torquato used to say when referring to his parents who had passed away not long ago. They had made an enormous sacrifice to have him educated at one of the best universities in Barcelona, hoping that he would become a lawyer someday. However, he didn't want to be a lawyer. Despite his aversion to the legal profession and in order to please his parents, he graduated with a degree of Doctor of Jurisprudence. They also helped him financially to set up his own law firm. However, he was unable to get a single client. Following his failure in the field of law, and without his parent's approval, he decided to start a career as a writer. That too failed, he was not successful as a writer. He couldn't even pay the fees to his editor or publicist for the two novels he ended up writing. Nor did he have any intentions of being a politician. He thought politicians had the reputation of being opportunistic liars and freeloaders that were not to be trusted. At one point, he considered a career in the medical field but realized he could never be a physician. He didn't have the stomach nor dedication to take care of sick patients and least of all to be a surgeon, he couldn't stand the sight of blood. He always liked numbers and finance.

Years after settling in New York, he tried to convince his parents to change his name, that ugly name with which he had been baptized. Their response was always the same: "... you have to honor the name of your ancestors, especially your great-grandfather...," and so on. For Torquato, such ridiculous reasoning seemed insufficient.

Years of ridicule and bitterness pushed him to eventually change his name to Benjamín Cohen, a name much more suited and in tune with businessmen, financiers and the like who worked in the Stock Exchange. He pursued in earnest his childhood dream, he would study finance; he wanted to be a stockbroker, a financial advisor and open an office in Wall Street, a few blocks from the New York Stock Exchange. After graduating from one of the best schools in that city he diligently became a financial advisor.

And so, with his newly adopted name, Benjamín Cohen opened his own office in one of the most prestigious streets in New York. He wanted to forget his past and start anew, but would he be able to erase from his memory the macabre crime he uncovered twenty years earlier, towards the end of 1940?

During the 1960s the stock market had already suffered many highs and lows. Benjamín Cohen had spent more than two hours explaining to his prospective client Saul Rabinowitz the different options available to invest his life savings. Saul asked Benjamín to create a not too aggressive investment portfolio, that is, a rather conservative one that would allow him to withdraw interest and dividends and in addition, receive a quarterly sum of four percent of the value of the principal.

Saul was already a man in his sixties, recently retired and did not want to take risks in the stock market investing all of his hard-earned life savings. In the conference room, Benjamín drew up the anticipated plan covering the entire blackboard, while explaining to Mr. Rabinowitz which securities would be the best in order to achieve his wishes. After his detailed presentation, he finally convinced Saul Rabinowitz to make a decision — and invest more than two million dollars. He then proceeded by signing the pertinent documents plus handing to Benjamín a certified check for the agreed amount. After exchanging a friendly hug, Saul left the office of Benjamín Cohen, his new and trusted financial advisor.

Minutes after Mr. Rabinowitz departure, Letty, Benjamín's secretary, walked into his office. She was carrying a cup of Colombian coffee — Benjamín's favorite —, biscuits and a copy of the *Excelsior,* the local newspaper. Although she was born in New York of Puerto Rican parents, Letty was fully bilingual. Ever since she was a child her parents emphasized the importance of learning both languages.

Letty showed Benjamín the front page of the newspaper wherein large bold letters, the front headline read:

AFTER TWENTY YEARS THE MYSTERY OF A VILE CRIME HAS BEEN SOLVED ...

Benjamín hurriedly tried to take the newspaper from Letty's hands to read on his own the details of how the crime had been solved, who had been the culprit or perpetrators, but she wouldn't let him, instead, she told him she would summarize it to him.

"It's about a crime that took place at the beginning of the 1940s. Yet, neither the federal authorities nor the local police had been able to identify the body of the woman discovered about twenty years ago by a young Hispanic man, a newcomer to this country. The young man's name was Torquato Berindoague."

She chuckled while trying to pronounce the name and said to Benjamín:

"What a strange name, the parents of this poor soul must have been drunk to baptize their child with such a name. According to the report," continued Letty, "the witness, Mr. Berindoague, vanished and was not heard from again, he disappeared as if by magic, after the intense interrogation he was subjected to. I don't blame him, with such a name and the shock of finding the woman's body he probably did not want to be involved. He was afraid and reluctant to answer more questions and decided to disappear."

"What else does the article say?" Benjamín asked his secretary who very conveniently had already sat down in one of the armchairs. He refrained from making any comments to Letty about the name of Torquato, his real name, and decided to listen to her.

Towards the end of August, the young man, Torquato, was enjoying a short holiday at a beach house in the plush seaside resort of Nantucket, Massachusetts with some friends and fellow university students. Early one morning, Torquato decided to go for a walk on the beach and after walking for about half a mile he took off his sandals and went into the water. He had not gone more than ten feet when he felt something brush against his leg. Without giving it much attention, he continued walking and again felt something brushing his leg. It was something sticky like a slippery mass. Thinking that it was seaweed or some other ocean plant, he curiously reached with his hand to pull it out. He grabbed the mysterious matter which felt softer and slimier than a piece of wood and as he looked down, he was horrified! What he thought was a piece of driftwood was the arm of a human being. Terrified, he pulled the arm and discovered that it was part of the mutilated body of a young woman possibly around thirty years old. With much difficulty, he dragged the body covered with sand and algae out of the water onto the sandy beach. Fearing to be blamed for her murder, he looked for someone to help him but there was no one around. At that time of the morning, residents of

Nantucket were just waking up late while trying to enjoy the last days of summer.

"Mr. Cohen, would you like me to continue?" Letty asked his boss.

"Yes, continue please," Benjamín said.

Although terrified by such gruesome discovery, Torquato started to analyze in detail the decomposing corpse. He noticed that the hands had been sawed off, maybe with a hacksaw. The toes had also been severed perhaps with the same instrument. He noticed her lips had turned bluish and her deep and hollow eye sockets were empty and full of sand. They were stained with a brownish substance such as the color of iodine, perhaps by sea salt. The neck showed signs of having been tied with a nylon rope or a woman's stocking.

As the waves gently moved the back of the head of the dead woman, he noticed a small orifice below the right ear, perhaps from a bullet of a low caliber revolver, as if someone had executed her. After performing an autopsy, the coroner confirmed that the small hole was caused by the projectile that had taken her life. Subsequently, the body had been mutilated to cover her identity. The killers had taken all precautions disposing of the corpse into the ocean, however, they failed to anticipate that the waves and possibly the currents were going to wash it back to the coast. Apparently, the perpetrators had to get rid of the evidence of their crime hastily and did not have time to tie the body to something heavy such as a cinder block, thus preventing it to rise to the surface. Someone had disturbed the act of disposing of it.

Torquato hastily headed for a sentry box on the beach to phone the authorities. Soon after the police arrived, a group of curious neighbors started to gather to look at the woman's body, speculating and making all kinds of wild guesses. Each one had an opinion while adding to the scene an air of mystery and intrigue. They could not understand that someone would have been capable of committing such a ghoulish and heinous crime in such a beautiful and peaceful beach resort. Some went as far as to suggest that it was a crime of passion or an execution-style murder with overtones of international intrigue.

Among the many details that the coroner discovered, was a tiny tattoo on the sole of the girl's partly mutilated right foot with the name of *Boris;* however, they had not been able to decipher its meaning or who *Boris* was. The name was not only strange but of foreign origin. It had been tattooed on the sole of the foot as if trying to conceal its identity. It could also have been the name of a family member, boyfriend, or her lover.

After noticing that Benjamín had grown somewhat distracted Letty asked:

"Are you alright Mr. Benjamín? Can I continue?"

"I'm sorry, I was just wondering, please go on."

Letty continued telling with horror to Benjamín the macabre story of the murdered girl:

The mystery turned out to be more intriguing when the coroner discovered in the stomach of the victim a small titanium plate with the inscription: *Uma Klika.*

After a detailed analysis, it was concluded that perhaps Uma Klika was the name of the girl. Apparently, *Uma* had swallowed the plate before her assassination to hide her identity and to make it more difficult to be identified ... On the back of the plate was a combination of letters and numbers: OL641WDC405YUG.

After thoroughly checking records of missing persons, birth and marriage records, schools and universities in Boston and other surrounding cities the local authorities weren't able to identify the origin of the dead girl. Unable to decode the mystery of her death and the plate, they decided to call the office of the Federal Bureau of Investigation.

Upon their arrival, the FBI determined that they needed to examine the body more thoroughly and to look for other evidence. They needed to transport the body and all the evidence to the specialized laboratories in the State of Virginia where they had more resources to help them solve the murder and the mystery of her death. In addition, they would widen the investigation and focus their efforts on the international field. Federal agents were deployed to Miami, New York, New Orleans, San Francisco, Los Angeles, and other cities to search the records of foreigners who might have entered the United States by land, sea or air.

The work was arduous and intense and given the high volume of documents to be analyzed, the investigation was carried out with unanticipated slowness. The initial result of all these inquiries by federal, and local agents failed to establish the identity of the young woman. Even after posting the story in local newspapers, it was not possible for the authorities to find relatives or anyone to claim her body. Therefore, the authorities, hoping for someone to come forward, waited for an additional six months. Without being able to get results, all documentation pertaining to the case was archived in the files of unsolved cold cases and a year later the remains of the girl, Uma Klika, were cremated.

"Was that the end? Did the FBI ever find out what happened?" Asked Benjamín.

"Wait, Mr. Benjamín, there is more. I have not finished," replied Letty.

"I am sorry! Please go on." said, Benjamín.

At the beginning of the war in Viet Nam, at the end of 1959, a marine colonel named Jack Legrand was assigned the difficult task of coordinating all intelligence activities with the Government of Hanoi. It was then feared that Chinese and Russian spies and operatives from other Eastern European countries had infiltrated the Communist forces of North Vietnam to advise and provide them with intelligence on the movements and advance of the South Vietnamese army and their American military advisors. Among the agents of the various espionage agencies, Legrand met a Jacques Pipán, a Frenchman who voluntarily had stayed in Viet Nam after the lost battle of Diem Bien Phu in 1954, when the French began their withdrawal from Viet Nam.

Legrand established a professional friendship with Pipán and during one of their talks, Pipán asked Legrand that upon his return to the United States he conduct an investigation to determine the identity of an agent who had disappeared and then been murdered, some fifteen years earlier, at a beach resort in the state of Massachusetts. At the same time, Pipán told Legrand that he and a Yugoslav official named Boris had met in the war-zone and who, before his death, had confided to him details about this case. However, Pipán had failed to find out from Boris, before dying, the name of the victim. He could only find out that the alleged agent had discovered the names of two communist spies who operated in Washington, DC, and was about to disclose their names to the relevant authorities at the State Department of that country.

"I suspected it," Letty said to Benjamín. "Just like one of the persons on the beach in Nantucket said, this had to turn out to be an international intrigue of espionage and mystery. Nevertheless, that doesn't mean that the crime was less horrific and I can't stop wondering what kind of torture the unfortunate Uma was subjected to at the end."

"Please continue Letty." Benjamín urged Letty. "Stop speculating, remember that Mr. McCormick is about to come in, he is very worried by the recent decline of the Stock Market. How did Legrand discover the identity of the victim?"

"Very simple!" continued Letty. "Remember the combination of letters and numbers etched into the metal plate that the coroner found in the stomach of the dead girl?"

"Yes, I remember, it was OL641WDC405YUG as indicated at the beginning of the article," Benjamín answered.

"Very well! Let me continue," said Letty.

When Legrand returned to Washington, he visited the offices of the FBI in Virginia and told the authorities the details of the conversation he had with his friend Pipán in Hanoi and the confession of Pipán's friend Boris before dying. Legrand was given the authority to review all the documentation on the victim believed to be Uma Klika and with the help of the combination of numbers and letters engraved on the plate, he concluded that Uma wasn't her real name any more than Klika, that was her *nom de guerre*. Legrand figured out, he deciphered what the combinations of letters and numbers meant: Her real name was Olga Latislova or OL, 641W meant her agent number assigned to Washington, and YUG meant

Yugoslavia, her country of origin. Boris — Latislova — the name tattooed on the right foot was the name of her spouse.

"What about the 405, what's the meaning of these three numbers?"

"I don't know, it was not mentioned, perhaps it was just a number to mislead people in case she was captured," answered Letty.

"What an amazing story!" Letty said as she got up to go back to her desk. "The mysterious case went unsolved for more than twenty years and finally was resolved during a foreign war. What a coincidence, Legrand to become acquainted with Pipán in the most inhospitable of places in this world, war-time Viet Nam. What do you think Mr. Benjamín? Do you think this story could be considered as the script for a movie of international crime and intrigue?"

"Miss Letty," Benjamín told his secretary. "You have a great and wondering imagination. To think that this story could be used for the script of a film! I am sorry, but I very much doubt that this would be possible. Thank you for summing it up to me."

"It is too bad, Mr. Benjamín, that Torquato Berindoague never found out the end of the story, who the perpetrators were or how the combination of letters and numbers helped Legrand solve the mysterious murder of the girl on the beach."

"Don't be so pessimistic Miss Letty," answered Benjamín. "Who knows if Torquato someday might not find a person as curious and dedicated as you are, who takes the time to bring him the newspaper, a dish of beveled glass with biscuits and a cup of aromatic Colombian coffee."

When Letty left Benjamín's office to greet Mr. McCormick who was already seated on one of the armchairs in the waiting room, Benjamín took the newspaper and reading his real name and surname — Torquato Berindoague — recalled his father's perennial response about why he had given him such a horrible and disgusting name. He could just imagine him saying: "You have to honor the name of our ancestors ..."

Storytime at the Park by Cecilia Ford

"... Abuelo, can you tell me a story?" Nicolás
asked his grandfather Eduardo ...

Abuelo, Can You Tell Me a Story?

To my grandchildren Cecilia, Dominic and Victor...

As they usually did every Sunday, Eduardo Balvarena and his five-year-old grandson Nicolás approached the bench and sat on one of the pathways at Las Mariposas Park.

"Let's sit on this bench," said Eduardo to his grandson, "it's a bit shadier here and we can see who goes by."

"This is good grandfather," said Nicolás, sitting on the corner of the bench.

Nicolás knew that every time his grandfather invited him for a stroll in the park, wearing his favorite faded denim overalls, he would get to savor an ice cream. His page boy style blond hair fell freely on his forehead and his bright green eyes watched everyone and everything.

The eucalyptus grove that adorned the park already showed signs of the beginning of spring and despite the cruel and icy winter, it was warmer than normal. Butterflies of various species and sizes, looking for nectar were perched on the flower buds that were about to bloom. The birds of different species and colors, with their loud chirps, bathed in the small water-fountain on one of the corners of the park. The yellow daffodils — one of the first flowers of spring — had already risen from the cold earth after a sleepy winter and carefully adorned the edges of the park's gardens.

On this day, the park was strangely quiet. One could not hear the bustle of boys and girls scampering behind squirrels and rabbits or scaring the Castile pigeons that abounded in the park. There were only three or four couples watching over their children who were carefully sliding on the aluminum slides and swaying on the colorful swings.

"Wait for me here on the bench while I go buy some ice cream from the street vendor," Eduardo said to his grandson as he placed the book next to Nicolás.

"What kind of ice cream do you want?" Eduardo asked his grandson.

"The usual, raspberry," Nicolás replied. "Thank you, grandpa, but don't take too long, don't start talking to your friends like you did last Sunday," Nicolás added.

"Grandfather," Nicolás asked. "What is the name of this book you are reading? Can I see the drawings?"

"Of course," Eduardo said to his grandson. "The book is called *Treasure Island* but be careful don't lose the page that is marked."

Eduardo Balvarena was an older man of about seventy-five. His thick white hair was covered with an "Indiana Jones" dark gray felt hat that covered half of his forehead. His sky-blue eyes were hidden by bushy eyebrows, also the color of his hair. On his bronzed, sharp nose rested a pair of round-rimmed eyeglasses. His slightly hunched body was covered with a white shirt and a dark gray pullover that matched the color of his hat.

"Good afternoon, Don Eduardo," the ice cream vendor said to Eduardo. "Does your grandson want his favorite raspberry ice cream?"

"Yes," answered Eduardo. "Give me a strawberry."

While Nicolás waited for his grandfather, he would entertain himself by looking at the drawings in the book that his grandfather had asked him to take care of. Suddenly he listened as if someone were calling him.

"Psssst!" ... "Psssst!"

Nicolás heard the sound of a small whistle. Surprised and curious, he looked around but could not see anyone.

"Grandfather hurry." Somewhat nervous he called his grandfather aloud. "The ice cream is going to melt."

"Psssst!" ... "Psssst!"

Again, Nicolás heard the soft, faint call coming from the back of the bench, but just as before he did not see anyone who could be making that peculiar noise.

"Grandfather," Nicolás said when Eduardo came over and handed him his raspberry ice cream. "Someone behind me has been making a very strange noise as if someone were calling me." Nicolás tried to imitate the faint noise he had heard. "It sounds like this: Psssst!"

"Yes, it sounds like someone called you," Eduardo said to his grandson. "But there's no one around who could have made that noise or that faint whistling. I don't think you should continue to look through this book because you are imagining too many things. I'd better read it to you," Eduardo concluded.

When he had finished the ice cream, as promised, Eduardo began to read the first paragraphs of the book to his grandson who listened very attentively. However, his reading was interrupted when he saw that Ernestina Domínguez had opened her kiosk at the main entrance of the park and decided to go over to buy the day's newspaper.

"I will be right back," Eduardo said to his grandson. "Don't move from here and be very careful not to talk to strangers, I'm just going to go buy the newspaper."

"It's okay, grandfather," Nicolás answered his grandfather with a resigned look on his young face. "What do you want me to do if I hear the same noise again?"

"Don't pay attention to it," Eduardo answered. "There's no one around here who might be doing that, maybe you are imagining it."

"My grandfather always thinks I'm imagining things," Nicolás said to himself.

Eduardo walked to the kiosk at the entrance of the park and, on the way over, he met his friend Venancio who returned from the newsstand with a newspaper under his left arm.

"Hello Venancio," Eduardo greeted his friend with a hug. "Ernestina came late today, what happened to her?"

"I don't know," said Venancio to his friend. "It seems that the brown cat she keeps inside the kiosk made a mess. He climbed on the shelves and broke the glass jars where she keeps the candy and other treats."

"What a pity," Eduardo answered. "I don't know why she still has that cat; it's more clever and older than Methuselah. See you soon Venancio, have a good day," said his friend Eduardo.

"Psssst!" ... "Psssst!" ... "Psssst!" Again, Nicolás heard the same tenuous and insistent hiss and again looked around but could not see anyone, but this time it occurred to him to look under the bench.

On the ground, hidden by the legs of the bench, Nicolás noticed that there was a hole where a small grey mouse peeking out and then back in again.

"Psssst! Nicolás" called the mouse.

Surprised and a bit fearful Nicolás watched as the little mouse looked out and hid his head in the hole near the leg of the bench.

"I have to be crazy; I cannot be hearing a mouse talking," Nicolás said aloud.

"No, you're not crazy, Nicolás," the mouse replied. "Listen to me, you can hear what you want, and with your imagination you can hear, fly, travel wherever you want; you can become a king, a president, a famous ballplayer, a professional swimmer; you can do anything," the mouse continued, wiggling his long whiskers. "I want to ask you a favor," said the mouse to Nicolás, who could not believe what he was hearing.

"Who are you and what do you want?" Nicolás asked the mouse, making sure that no one was watching him much less listening to him, but he could not hide from Libardo, another friend of his grandfather, who at that moment passed by where Nicolás sat and smilingly said:

"Hi Nicolás, are you talking to yourself?"

"No, Don Libardo, I'm trying to read this book aloud," Nicolás replied.

As Libardo walked towards the outside of the park Nicolás resumed his conversation with his new friend asking him:

"What is your name?"

"My name is Popo," answered the mouse.

"How do you know my name?" Asked Nicolás.

"Because I've heard your grandfather calling and I've watched you sit on the same bench on Sundays," Popo said.

Suddenly another mouse had popped out.

"And I, Nicolás, am Pipa, I am Popo's mate," she said very effusively, pulling her head out of the hole and putting it next to Popo's.

"We need a great favor of you because we no longer can put up with Rasputín," Pipa added.

"I don't know who Rasputín is," Nicolás said, shrugging his shoulders and looking with a surprised face as he peered around to make sure no one was listening.

"Rasputín is Doña Ernestina's brown cat," said Popo. "He is a scoundrel and a trickster; he won't leave us alone and we cannot go out at night in search of food."

"When Doña Ernestina does not leave him locked up in the kiosk, he lurks around all night," Pipa added. "The other night he took our Mirringa, and for lack of food Pitongo died on us."

"Who is Mirringa, and Pitongo?" Asked Nicolás.

"Mirringa was the youngest of our daughters. We could not rescue her when Rasputín took her," Pipa told Nicolás. "Pitongo was one of the newborns but he died for lack of food. All because of Rasputín, he's driving us crazy."

"That's why we need you to help us," Popo added. "You are the only one who can hear us; we needed someone with your imagination to communicate with us."

"What do you want me to do?" Asked Nicolás.

"I want you to get us a *cascabel*," said Pipa.

"A rattlesnake?" Nicolás asked somewhat alarmed. "I think that's a poisonous snake. Do you want to kill Rasputín?"

"We'd like to kill him after what he did to our Mirringa," Popo replied. "However, we don't want to hurt him, what we want is a *cascabel*, a metal ball with something inside to make noise to hang on his neck to hear when Rasputín walks around."

"Well, now I understand," said Nicolás. "I'll see where I can get one."

When Eduardo returned from the kiosk he said to his grandson:

"Well, Nicolás. I'm going to continue reading the story. Where did we stop?"

"On the second paragraph," replied Nicolás to his grandfather, looking slyly at the hole next to the bench's leg.

After reading the story for a while, it began to drizzle, so Eduardo and Nicolás decided to go back home. Nicolás turned his head and looked back at the bench where he had been sitting, enjoying the ice cream, the story, and the conversation with his new friends Popo and Pipa. As they walked back to his house Nicolás took his grandfather's hand and asked:

"Grandfather, is it possible to think of things that do not exist? Is it possible to imagine that one can be anything in this life?"

"Of course, it's possible." Eduardo looked surprised at his grandson. "We can imagine many things even if they are unlikely, we always have to be careful of not thinking or wanting something that we cannot reach or achieve. If you want something you have to be persistent and work hard to get it but your goals have to be realistic. Do you understand what I mean?" Eduardo asked his grandson.

"I think so," replied Nicolás, scratching his head with his hand.

"Are you thinking of the famous pirates of the story I was reading?" Eduardo asked.

"No grandfather, I was thinking of something else," said Nicolás.

Back at the house, Mariana Balvarena was embroidering a monogram on one of the linen handkerchiefs that she would soon give to her husband for his birthday while swaying in her favorite rocking chair next to the edge of her garden. Mariana liked to sit in that particular spot because it was where she could take advantage of the sunlight and see more clearly since at seventy years her eyesight had begun to fail. It was from this place that she could also enjoy the aroma of her rose bushes, listen and revel in the chirping of her colorful canaries that she very carefully housed in a nearby cage in the courtyard of her house.

At her age, Mariana still retained some traits of her youth. Her face had not yet wrinkled, although her black hair showed some silvery strands that accentuated her ivory complexion.

"Good morning grandmother," Nicolás said, kissing her on her cheek. "Can I ask you a question?"

"Yes, Nicolás," Mariana said to her grandson. "Each time you approach me so lovingly it is a sign that you want something. What trouble have you gotten yourself into? What is it that your imagination has cleverly invented? What do you want, dear?" Mariana asked Nicolás.

"No grandmother, I have not gotten into any trouble or made something up," said Nicolás. "Do you remember Sofía?" Asked Nicolás.

"Of course, I remember Sofía," Mariana said. "Our Angora cat who died last year. How beautiful she was; white as snow with her precious green eyes. I remember her perfectly because she liked to cuddle in my lap while I knitted," Mariana added, looking longingly at the cage where the canaries were chirping. "And what has made you remember Sofía after all this time?" Mariana asked Nicolás.

"Good grandmother," said Nicolás. "It's not Sofía that I remembered; it's the bell you used to put on her neck, I wanted to know where it was. Did you save it after she died?"

"I suspected it, my dear, I never thought you liked cats," Mariana said. "What do you want the bell for? Mariana asked Nicolás.

"I want to give it to friends I met in the park on Sunday, they need it to put it on Rasputín, the brown cat of Doña Ernestina, the owner of the kiosk."

"Yes, Rasputín," said Mariana. "That shameless and daring cat that often came from the park to our house in search of Sofía. Luckily, I always kept her in a safe place, and he never managed to put a claw on her."

"Yes, that one," said Nicolás. "Rasputín is bothering Popo and Pipa and the other night he took their Mirringa."

"Popo and Pipa, Mirringa, who are they? Are they other cats that Rasputín is bothering?" Asked Mariana.

"No! No! grandmother, they are not cats, they are just new friends of mine I met at the park," Nicolás replied.

"Okay, Nicolás ..." Mariana said resignedly since Nicolás was not giving her more information about his new friends. "You and your mysterious projects, look for the bell on top of the cupboard in the kitchen, that's where I put it when Sofía died."

"Thank you, grandmother," Nicolás said, embracing and kissing his grandmother on the cheek.

"Grandfather, at what time are we going to the park?" Asked Nicolás to his grandfather, while making sure the bell was in the right pocket of his overalls.

"We'll go after lunch," Eduardo said. "Your grandmother has gone an extra mile to fix lunch; she has prepared a delicious stew."

At about two-thirty in the afternoon, Eduardo and his grandson, Nicolás, headed back to Las Mariposas Park.

"Nicolás, are you going to want your raspberry ice cream?" Eduardo asked his grandson.

"Thank you, grandfather, I don't think I'm going to have ice cream today," Nicolás replied. "With the apple pie that grandma served for lunch, I'm pretty full. But you can go visit Doña Ernestina, buy your newspaper and talk for a while with Don Venancio, I think I just saw him entering the park," Nicolás added. "Find out what mischief Rasputín did and ask her if she wants to put a *cascabel* on him so she knows where he's going. When you return, you can continue reading me the story of the pirates. I promise I will not talk to anyone."

With a puzzled look of on his face, Eduardo looked at his grandson and wondered what he was up to when he hurriedly wanted to get rid of him and he had not even wanted to have his favorite raspberry ice cream.

"Very well, Nicolás," said Eduardo. "You're up to something, you must have something planned, that little mind of yours is amazing. Do not worry, I'll be back soon. I'll tell you what happened to Rasputín." He glanced at his grandson as he headed to the kiosk.

Nicolás watched his grandfather go to the kiosk and once he figured that he could no longer hear him, he took the *cascabel* of his pocket and shook it at the edge of the hole where Popo and Pipa lived. Nicolás did not have to shake it more than twice. At the sound of the bell, in unison, Popo and Pipa poked their heads out making sure no one saw them. They looked very happy with the bell Nicolás had in his hands.

"Hello Popo," Nicolás said to the mouse. "I have the bell you asked me for. It was given to me by my grandmother; she had it saved after her cat Sofía died."

"Thank you, Nicolás," said Pipa. "We don't know how to thank you, you have saved our lives, now we can go out at night to find food and we will know where Rasputín roams."

"I thank you too," Popo said. "But something is still missing."

"What else do you need?" Nicolás asked, surprised. "We already have the bell."

"But ... who's going to put the bell on the cat?" Asked Pipa.

"My grandfather," Nicolás replied, with great wisdom. "He is very friendly with Doña Ernestina."

Just as Nicolás had assured his rodent friends, Ernestina had agreed to the suggestion of her friend Eduardo to put the *cascabel* on Rasputín to know where he was hanging around and that way, she would not have to lock him in the kiosk.

After reading more than eleven pages from the book *Treasure Island* to Nicolás, Eduardo told his grandson:

"Nicolás, this afternoon has been very fruitful, we have advanced with the reading of the book and we convinced Doña Ernestina to put the *cascabel* on Rasputín. Don't you think we should go home now? It's getting late." Eduardo asked.

"True," replied Nicolás to his grandfather, while looking toward the hole in the ground at the edge of the bench's leg. "Thank you, grandfather, for bringing me to the park every Sunday, I like looking at butterflies and squirrels ..."

"I read you some stories, too," Eduardo added. "I trust you like everyone I've read to you."

"Yes, I like all the stories you read to me, grandfather," said Nicolás. "But ..."

"Abuelo," Nicolás replied to his grandfather Eduardo. I want you to tell me a story, one of those you know how to tell, not one from a book, one of yours. Why don't you tell me a story?"

"All right," Eduardo said to his grandson. "I'll tell you one, this story is one of my favorites," Eduardo added.

Nicolás sat down on the bench to attentively listen to the story his grandfather was about to tell him.

"Once upon a time." Eduardo began "there were two little mice that lived in a park called Popo and Pipa ..."

"Grandfather!" interrupted Nicolás. "Did you know that story too?"

Eduardo did not answer, he just looked at his grandson and they both exchanged smiles.

The Anonymous Manuscript

U sually, the mailman brings the mail to our door around two o'clock in the afternoon. He never fails; rain or shine, whether it is snowing, thundering or lightening... he is always punctual.

I do not know why the postman was late today. When he delivered the mail, it was past five-thirty in the afternoon. It had begun to drizzle. Excusing himself for his delay, he handed me the regular mail plus the usual advertisements announcing all kinds of sales, including those of nearby grocery stores offering bargains on different cuts of meat and sausages to be grilled the following Sunday, Labor Day.

With the falling drizzle, the ink from the ads had begun to stain the postman's fingers as well as the rest of the correspondence. All the other envelopes with bills of the utility companies, plus a letter from the Department of Motor Vehicles reminding me to renew my car's registration, had been carefully tied with a blue rubber band.

Included with the mail, he delivered a stained manila envelope. The envelope had been carefully and neatly addressed. The upper and lower parts of the envelope were secured with transparent adhesive tape. The postage stamps had also been carefully aligned on the top right as if a ruler had been used according to their value. The total value of the postage stamps was five dollars and forty-five cents.

After placing all the correspondence on the dining room table, my first intention was obviously to open the unexpected envelope. However, before opening it I stopped momentarily to admire the variety of stamps of different birds and flowers and to find out who was sending it. The envelope weighed more than usual. I did not recognize the name of the sender nor did I know anyone who lived in the city of Weed in California.

How strange? I thought to myself, as I took out the contents of the envelope. I do not know this person. Perhaps the sender made a mistake, perhaps his intention was to mail it to someone with a similar name as mine.

Although the sender had been extremely careful aligning the stamps, he was less careful about fastening together the two hundred and seventy-five pages, including a letter addressed to me. Glancing at the document, I noticed that it had been written with a font very similar to the one I normally use.

"Too much of a coincidence," I murmured, but I did not think it was of much importance.

Some of the loose sheets slipped out of my hands and fell on the carpet in the dining room. I picked them up and put them back in the respective order.

Without paying too much attention to the letter that came with the document, I realized that the other two hundred plus pages were the manuscript of a novel titled *La Ira de Guadalupe,* the Ire of Guadalupe. The title was well centered in the middle of the page and to my astonishment, the author's name was, Guillermo Aragón, me.

The way in which the document was written; the index, the margins allocated to each page, the introduction, the quotation of a famous writer, references … was a sign that the writer had taken extreme care to ensure that nothing was missing, that it wouldn't be necessary to make editorial changes, it was fully ready to be sent to a publishing company.

A novel? Again, I asked myself. I am not a writer; I entertain myself writing short stories which I send to some of my friends. How weird! I thought. It has to be a mistake.

A novel? I wondered again. I do not know where to begin or where to end. It has to be a joke. Yes! Someone is making fun of me.

After asking myself all these questions and making all the customary conjectures, I decided to read the letter enclosed with the manuscript. The letter was properly addressed to me and to my amazement, in addition to the letter, the sender had included another envelope containing five one-thousand dollar bills.

"These bills are brand new," I said aloud. "They have not even been circulated." With much curiosity, I proceeded to read the letter. Below are excerpts of the text:

Dear Mr. Aragón:

My name is not Rodrigo Villagrande, neither is the address in the remittance correct, I chose them at random. I do not live in California; I live in another state in this country. Do not attempt to find me, do not try to find out my nationality; I can tell you in advance that I'm not from Latin America …

You may be rightfully wondering why I am writing to you and why I am enclosing the manuscript of a novel and the money. While I was researching information for the novel, I learned that many years ago one of your great-great-grandfathers was swindled out of a plot of land in the Salinas Valley by one of my ancestors. I realize that this sum is just a fraction of the value of the land stolen; however, it is my way of paying a debt left unpaid…

I decided to send you the manuscript of my novel so you can publish it under your name. I know that you are not a professional writer but I understand that you like to write short stories, some of which I have had the opportunity to read…

To save you from incurring any expenses, I have included five one-thousand dollar bills. I am confident that this sum will be enough to publish the novel ... If the cost is lower you can keep the rest of the money ... You also can keep any honoraria from the sale of the novel, and I am truly sorry for what happened in the past...

Kind regards,
Rodrigo

I could not hide from my spouse the anxiety caused by the dilemma I found myself in. I didn't know what to do. I could not accept the money any more than publishing a novel that I had not written. That would be plagiarism.

"What I am going to do with the money? I don't know the person to return it to. Oh my God! What kind of mess have they gotten me into?" I mumbled.

My wife, who was listening to me mumbling also shared my concerns and said: "Before you continue thinking about what you're going to do, why you don't you start reading the manuscript and see what it is all about, perhaps you'd find out what's behind all this mystery? The title sounds intriguing to me," she added.

Reading the manuscript took me until the early morning hours of the next day. And as I was reading it, I couldn't stop thinking about what to do next or how I could get out of the mess I was in.

"What is *your* novel about?" my wife asked, ironically smiling while taking a sip of a cup of tea.

"It's about a tragedy, about a migrant worker named Guadalupe, a Mexican immigrant," was my response. "It's interesting," I added.

"You always find everything you read interesting," my wife replied, "What's the story about, where does it take place, who are the characters? It has to have a shocking ending; I am curious about Guadalupe and why was he so irate?

"It's about the abuse encountered by migrant workers in California. It takes place, in the Salinas Valley, there are only three or four characters, but I don't know if you are going to like the outcome since it does not have a 'punchline' or a dramatic ending or any of those classical phrases of the famous novelists. I will summarize the novel for you."

"Fine, please start." My wife answered while sitting back on one of the kitchen chairs.

Calixto Madrigal de Villareinosa, was a landowner, proprietor of hundreds of acres of fertile land in the Valley of Salinas in California who like many others, inherited lands from his ancestors, the first Spanish colonizers who had settled in California.

From the large porch of his enormous ranch located on the slopes of the Gavilán Mountains, Calixto delighted himself each morning, admiring through his binoculars his vast fields of artichokes, asparagus, lettuce, celery and strawberries, planted along the Salinas River. The crops reached as far as north of the valley. The bright black earth on his property was one of the most fertile in the region.

Calixto had spent a fortune installing water extraction pumps to be able to irrigate the fields of his extensive property. He took advantage of the labor provided by migrant workers who came from poor disadvantaged towns in Mexico. Calixto paid them as little as possible for their hard labor. He housed his workers and their families in small shacks without heat and sanitary facilities, then deducted rent from their meager wages.

The crops were sold to the fruit and vegetable packing companies in the cities of Castroville, Gonzales and Salinas, who in turn sold and transported them to the myriad of markets and supermarkets across the country.

"Very interesting" interrupted my wife. "What is the problem then if everything is going so well for Calixto? He continues to benefit and fatten his coffers at the expense of the migrant workers."

"The problem he is experiencing is with the cultivation of citrus fruits, mainly with lemons, the Meyer species. Something is going wrong; he does not know whether it is the harvesting of the lemons; the way they are being transported, or maybe the way they are stored in the packing houses," I said to my wife and continued narrating ...

The lemon trees were laden with lemons but he was not making the same profit as he was from the artichokes and other crops. Calixto suspected that perhaps the workers were being lazy, stealing from him or smuggling out the lemons to sell them at local markets. He suspected that the foreman was in cahoots with others, he also suspected Guadalupe and Gabriel who were the last hands to be hired.

Both Guadalupe and Gabriel met during their journey to El Norte. Guadalupe was one of many thousands of migrants who came to this country illegally by way of Arizona, and like Gabriel, swum across the Río Grande. Migrants who come this way are referred to as *mojados,* wetbacks. They suffer hunger, humiliation, abuse and other vexations at the hands of the *coyotes* whom they hire to help them cross the border.

"I find nothing unusual so far," interrupted my spouse "these poor people are robbed, raped, imprisoned, and sometimes deported on a daily basis. You haven't told me anything new."

After firing the foreman, Calixto hired Clementina Brown, a woman who worked at the Martinez Detention Facility as a correctional officer. Clementina was a tough woman in her forties of Mexican and British descent. As a child, she had been abused by her father, an immigrant from England, and also witnessed how he abused and mistreated her mother, a native of Guadalajara, Mexico. She resented how her mother always looked the other way and paid little attention to her complaints. Clementina carried these awful memories which left her scarred for the rest of her life. She had been the subject of ridicule and bullying during her school years. Clementina had developed a personality complex and a hidden hatred for men, and for unknown reasons, her hatred had been directed against men of Mexican origin.

Clementina was a despot! Because of the abuse that she inflicted on the prisoners, mainly Mexicans, she had been fired from the Detention Facility. Now she directed her hatred against the migrant workers, mainly against Guadalupe and his friend Gabriel. Daily she vented her frustrations and hate on Guadalupe whom she humiliated by insulting him and calling him all kinds of names, constantly mocking him whenever he could not tell correctly the number of baskets of lemons collected that day. She called him ignorant, illiterate, and unable to count or write. Gabriel and the rest of the migrants resented the fact that a woman was their supervisor; however, they all endured the abuse and insults. But Guadalupe hid the hatred and anger he had accumulated against her.

On a Monday afternoon, after completing his daily work, Guadalupe entered Clementina's office carrying a basket full of lemons. As usual, Clementina started insulting him for coming into her office while she was on the phone. Guadalupe could not bear her insults anymore. He lifted the basket full of lemons above his head and threw it violently in Clementina's face. He pulled out a knife and stabbed her in the chest several times killing her on the spot.

He had to flee. Guadalupe had to flee. His friend Gabriel, who witnessed the tragedy felt it was his duty to notify the police. But to give his friend time to get away, Gabriel waited until the middle of the night to inform Calixto of the crime, who in turn immediately notified the police.

Guadalupe escaped by boarding and hiding in one of the trucks loaded with lemons heading towards the city of Monterey. Upon arriving in Monterey, Guadalupe hid among the rocky shores, where the homeless roamed under the pier. To them, he was another vagrant who was looking for shelter, for a place where to spend the night. They gave him a blanket to weather the cold breezes blowing from the Pacific. But his welcome was short-lived when he tried to take some food from one of their plastic bags. One of the homeless chased him out while brandishing a knife. Guadalupe ran as fast and as far as he could until he reached Lovers' Point in the town of Pacific Grove, where he drank some water from a public fountain.

He tried to hide behind a local motel, but his ragged and filthy clothes gave him away. One of the motel workers ran him off the motel grounds. It was too late, he was a marked man, he wouldn't be able to stop any place without being noticed. The police had given notice to all of the surrounding cities. He could not escape. His name was being broadcast on the radio and his photograph shown on television. In an effort to escape he decided to walk along the coast to avoid as much as possible being detected, but it was too late. The homeless near the pier had already betrayed him and notified the local authorities.

Guadalupe decided to continue southward along the coast and spent the night hiding in a cave-like formation near the water. Early the next morning he heard footsteps nearby, he hid further inside the cave, it was just a lone fisherman looking for a place to cast his line. As he left the cave, he figured out that the rocky cliffs at Point Lobos and Big Sur were too steep and it would be more difficult to move forward. He had not had any water or a morsel of food in a day. Guadalupe was a desperate man. He didn't know what to do. He started to feel regretful of downloading his wrath against Clementina.

On the evening of the second day, he noticed a church. It was the Carmelite Monastery, about a quarter of a mile from the trail he was traveling. It had started to get dark. He hoped to seek refuge there and that perhaps the nuns would give him some most needed food and water. Like a haunted animal, under the cover of the evening shadows, he stealthfully approached the main door on the atrium, knocked several times to no avail. No one answered. Under the cover of darkness, he walked toward a nearby peach orchard where he desperately devoured some of the unripened fruits and spent the night under one of the trees. Just as he had made it to the orchard, the night before, he carefully walked away from the Monastery grounds and decided to change his path and head south toward the Santa Lucia Mountains where he thought he would go unnoticed. But that would not work. The sheriffs with their well-trained tracking bloodhounds had smelled his scent and picked up his trail. Exhausted and thirsty he decided to hide near Palo Colorado, a small community of unconventional people who had built their homes under the cover of eucalyptus, cypress and redwoods. Without asking questions, a young couple offered him water and some freshly baked bread and gave him directions to reach the mountains through a least traveled road. They also warned him about wild animals in those woods.

Following the directions given to him by the friendly couple, after many hours of walking he reached a small plateau covered with tall grasses and saguaro cactus. He had seen those cactuses in Arizona and thought he was getting closer to the border. He noticed a willow-covered patch and headed toward it hoping to find some much-needed water. Nearby he discovered a small stream. Upon reaching it, Guadalupe without thinking and to quench his thirst threw himself into the stream's crystal-clear waters. He drank his fill but tiredness overcame him. On the sandy bank, Guadalupe found comfort and fell asleep without noticing that among the willows and tall weeds bordering the stream, the yellow and curious eyes of a mountain lion hidden behind a piece of driftwood silently stalked him; the mountain lion attentively had watched his movements waiting for the right moment to attack.

The sheriffs and the dogs reached the plateau and the stream where Guadalupe had quenched his thirst the night before. But Guadalupe offered no resistance. His lifeless body lay in the same place where he had fallen asleep. His throat and flesh around his neck had been torn. About fifteen meters from the lifeless body, the yellow eyes of the puma curiously watched the group while licking its dirty and bloody skin.

"What a sad end!" my wife remarked. "Poor Guadalupe, he left his country looking for a better life and ended up in the clutches of a wild beast. I find the story very sad, however, I doubt anyone would be interested in reading this novel and least of all purchasing a book about it; it's just one of many migrants' stories. Why not ask your friends with whom you are going to have lunch next week their opinion of what to do with the novel, *your novel,* and more importantly with the money?"

Two days later, during the anticipated lunch with my friends, I told them of my dilemma. As I suspected, each had his own opinion:

"I'd keep the money and forget about the novel," one of them said.

Another suggested ironically: "You have to be honest, publish the damned novel, maybe you become famous and you win a literary prize."

"Take your wife on a cruise, I doubt that novel is worth the paper it's written on ..." said another.

"Ask a Lawyer," added the lawyer friend.

"Be charitable," said the religious one of the group, "make a donation to the church and don't worry about publishing the novel."

"Publish the novel under another name, don't use yours," was the comment of another.

"Forget about the novel and all the comments we've made," one of them said, "why don't you throw a big party at your house and invite us all, but to begin with, why don't you start by treating us all today to this lunch?"

When I returned home in the afternoon, my wife eagerly wanted to know the result of my inquiries. As soon as I opened the door, she greeted me in the hallway, holding the small package I had hidden to give her on her birthday.

"How was your lunch?" she asked somewhat sarcastically.

"Lunch was fine, but I could not get an opinion that was worth it. My friends took it as a joke."

"I figured they would take it as a joke. No one was going to take this seriously."

"What are you doing with that package? Where did you find it?" I asked her.

"I found it while cleaning the cabinet where you keep your books. What is it?" she asked curiously.

"It's something I found at Mi Pueblo, our local Spanish market. I wanted to surprise you on your birthday. Open the package," I suggested.

As she opened the package, with a wide smile on her face she said:

"Wow, it's a bottle of Florida Water Cologne! Thank you very much, I suspected it. What does this have to do with *your* novel?"

"Nothing," I replied, "I just wanted to surprise you and show you that this cologne is still around."

"But Guillermo, what are you going to do with the novel and the money?" she insisted. "I don't think the novel is publishing material, nobody is going to buy it. Don't waste your time!"

"I don't know what to do. What would you do?" asked Guillermo.

"Forget about publishing anything, let's keep the money. I don't know how much you paid for the Florida Water Cologne; with the money, you can buy me a bottle Channel No.5 perfume! Let's pay some bills, and if there is any money left, let's go to Europe and take a cruise on the Rhine River..."

The Blue Jay

O ne Friday afternoon in May of 1965, a blue jay named Pepé was perched on a faded board of a fence. This fence circled the property of Esperanza Ríos, located on the outskirts of the city of El Carmelo, on the central coast of California. Unlike Pepé — a perennial show off — Flora, his mate preferred to hide behind the shiny green leaves of the oak tree next to the fence. With her shiny black eyes, Flora exchanged glances with Pepé as they curiously observed the two women nearby.

A few yards away, Esperanza and her neighbor, her very dear friend Carlota, relaxed in comfortable armchairs on the porch of the whitewashed bungalow to enjoy the amazing views of the Pacific Ocean. The sun would soon be approaching the horizon. It was at that time of the day when both Esperanza and Carlota would sit down to rest from their daily chores and share a glass of Portuguese Port. They watched the majestic waves violently crash against the rocky precipices of Big Sur.

They both enjoyed that particular hour of the afternoon when the day vigorously fights the encroaching night, which in the end triumphantly wins the struggle and slowly steals the day's precious light. The colors of the firmament gradually change from a pearly white to light tones of pink and faint hues of red, just like the pale petals of the rose bushes surrounding the fountain in Esperanza's garden.

The years had started to take a toll on Esperanza, however, she refused to be humbled by the unforgiving passing of time. Her hands were strong and rough, a sign of the many years she had labored at her small ranch. It was because of this hard work that she had managed to keep her youthful figure. Under the bright and punishing California sun, the white complexion of her face had turned honey brown, like the nectar of the blue agave. It complemented her sky-blue eyes and silver hair.

Esperanza lived alone, so she looked forward to afternoon visits from Carlota. The blue jays would approach when the women would sit on the porch to share their stories.

"The blue jays aren't good birds," Esperanza said, shaking her head, as the jay made a loud screech.

"Why do you think so, Esperanza?" Carlota asked, taking a handful of peanuts from the pocket of her apron. "I believe that they are good birds. They are smart and friendly! Did you know that they are native of North America, they live in the wild and are most noticeable in the eastern and central parts of the United States but they also are found in the west, like in California?"

"Yes! I read about their origin in a magazine, I thought they just lived in residential areas, their blue color is very beautiful, and the black collar stands out and makes them very different from other birds ..."

"Not only they are smart and friendly, but they also have learned to mimic human sounds and those of other birds, namely hawks, but their most common call is the one which in some cases could be alarming like a scream; like if they were alerting you of something." Said Carlota. "There are different varieties in another part of the Americas, like in Mexico and Central America, which are very distinctive, over there they are called "urracas" or "magpies.""

"You seem to know a lot about the jays." Added Esperanza.

"I remember my grandmother, mi Abuela, telling a biblical legend related to the urracas," said Carlota. "According to this tale, when Jesus Christ prayed at the Mount of Olives, a group of ill-intentioned women pointed out where Jesus was to the soldiers and Pharisees, and so he was taken prisoner. To punish this evil betrayal, God turned the women into urracas. This is one of many tales she told us when we were children and we believed everything." She tossed a peanut off the porch and the jay swooped over to retrieve it.

"Look at him!" Esperanza answered. "Coming here every day at the same time, and with his deafening shrieks, begging for some peanuts. I call him Pepé. I am sure that his mate, Flora, is nearby, hiding in the leaves of the oak tree."

"Let's see!" laughed Carlota. She tossed another peanut and sure enough, Flora darted out of the oak tree to get a peanut of her own.

"Did you know, Carlota, that my husband was also called Pepé? It's for that reason that I named the blue jay after him. He brings me many memories of him." She poured two small glasses of the ruby-colored wine and handed one to Carlota.

"Esperanza," Carlota answered inquisitively, "you have never spoken to me about your husband!"

"Pepé was not his real name. His father used to call him by that name, but his real name was José. Pepé was just his nickname."

"What caused you to think of him?"

"Do you see that ship out there?" She pointed out toward a ship which at that moment was cruising along the Pacific coast. "My husband was a very restless person. He loved the sea. He talked about it all the time, how he wanted to go to from one port to the next, looking for adventure."

"Why have you never mentioned him until today?"

"It is painful to talk about him. I have always wanted to know what happened to my husband after he left me," Esperanza added.

"I only knew of him here and there. I don't know if he is still alive or if he is dead."

"How many years has he been away?" Carlota asked, very intrigued.

"Many, many years, my dear friend!" Esperanza replied while gazing at the ocean. "The sea was his downfall. He was not too attached to the land. Pepé was one of the descendants of the Esselen tribe, the native Americans who populated these beautiful lands of California," Esperanza continued. "He was unlike his ancestors who loved their land. He was so different!" she sighed. "Perhaps it was the sea which took him. I don't really know! I was never able to change his mind or stop him from leaving. One day he left and never returned."

"We had only been married a few years when Pepé inherited this ranch from his grandfather," added Esperanza. "It was a large ranch with very fertile land. At that time, we had about two hundred heads of cattle. Pepé managed the ranch and cared for it for years. To be honest, he was never happy with the management of the ranch; he despised it, he was just not interested. Suddenly the Great Depression came, and everything fell apart."

"How could I forget!" said Carlota. "Those were terrible days, with hunger and poverty everywhere. Jobs were scarce; people didn't have enough money, not even to buy the bare necessities."

"Like many other ranchers in the region," Esperanza remembered, "we had to provide housing to a large number of people coming from Oklahoma, from Arizona, who were escaping dust storms and droughts. To add to our misery, they took advantage of our hospitality and started to slaughter our cattle, not just to feed themselves but to sell the meat as well. Those were extremely heartbreaking and desperate times."

"All of this economic and social turbulence," added Esperanza, "drastically affected Pepé. He did not know how to get those people off of our property. He would go around the ranch's boundaries trying to prevent squatters from stealing, but all his efforts were in vain, useless. One day he was almost lynched, and that was the end of ranching for him. He was worn out, afraid. He became very quiet and withdrawn. A few weeks after that, I woke up one morning and he was gone. I believe the ocean was his lover who took him away from me."

Esperanza added a bit more port to their glasses. After a few quiet moments, Carlota said, "I didn't realize you have been here by yourself for thirty years."

"Not entirely by myself!" Esperanza chuckled. "I still have ten cows, a donkey, two goats, three pigs, half a dozen chickens and a horse. The donkey didn't last long, but it wasn't a surprise. That tricky donkey was old. I had to sell the goats and the pigs. The feed was so expensive it was not worth keeping them. I sold five of the cows, and with the rest, I was lucky to double the herd with some help from my neighbor Laureano's bull. I sold some, keeping the best for myself. Now I have a total of twenty cows and five calves. When the horse died of old age, I purchased another from Laureano. Fortunately, I didn't have the need to sell the chickens and they have multiplied. Their eggs are quite popular at the farmers' market. That's how I made it through the Depression and then the war."

"You are fortunate to have a reliable ranch hand," observed Carlota. "I can't remember a time when I haven't seen him."

"Yes! Dionisio. He started working for me at a very young age. He is from Mexico. He helps me take care of the ranch, including milking the cows, cultivating the vegetable garden, and collecting the eggs and ripened peaches to take to the market. Sometimes he helps me with churning butter and making cheese. Dionisio is a capable man, a good man, and most importantly a very honest man. Even so, with every passing day, it's becoming more difficult to care for the ranch. I don't know how much longer I will be able to survive."

After pausing for a while, the blue jays started squawking, as if to fill in where the women's conversation had stopped. Carlota threw a few peanuts out for the jays.

"What about Pepé?" asked Carlota.

"His absence devastated me. Nevertheless, I am amazed by my ability to maintain this parcel of land. I take pride in my name Esperanza, which means "hope." I am an eternal optimist. I am always hoping that he will come back someday," Esperanza admitted.

"Do you know what happened to your husband?" Carlota asked.

"At the beginning, Pepé wrote to me to say he went north, toward the city of Monterey. It was there where he was able to secure a job on one of the cargo ships belonging to the Pacific Maritime Company. I believe that the ship had been commissioned under the Los Lobos name which sailed from San Diego to Alaska. At first, they transported sea otter pelts, and later sardines. I cannot imagine what my husband did aboard the ship when the only thing he knew how to do was raise cattle. I suspect they were in dire need of able hands and hired men even if they had no experience."

"All was well at the start," Esperanza added. "He would write to me every month with numerous tales of his sea-bound experiences. He wrote about finally having realized his lifelong dream. Often, he would send some money, but it was not even enough to pay Dionisio's meager salary. Fortunately, Dionisio was content with just having a roof over his head and some food to eat.

Some of his letters arrived from Santa Cruz; others came from San Francisco and Los Angeles. The later ones I received were mailed from a port in Alaska. I recall his enthusiasm so vividly. He was so happy. He told me that he would be boarding a large vessel headed to Japan with a large shipment of abalones."

"Esperanza," interrupted Carlota. "I had no idea how much you have suffered. I suppose these experiences have made you strong enough to endure all of these sorrows."

"No, my dear friend!" answered Esperanza. "On the contrary. With all this adversity and the passing of the years, I have turned very fragile. It's very similar to what happens with the day; we have our vibrant awakening but as the day wanes, the dark shadows of the night eventually take over. No matter how much we try to avoid them, to delay them, they always triumph. I am reaching that point. Would you please pour me another Porto?" Esperanza asked her friend. Carlota refilled the glass and threw another peanut. Pepé darted after it before Flora had a chance to emerge from the oak tree.

"You see?" Esperanza said. "He is so selfish; he is going to swallow the whole thing. He will not share it with Flora, his mate. He is just like my husband, only concerned with himself!"

While Esperanza observed her friend feeding the blue jays, namely Pepé, she said, "Carlota, you shouldn't feed the blue jays. They are going to get used to you feeding them and become lazy. They'll be negatively affected, especially in the winter months when food becomes scarce."

"I am conscious of that, but I pity them. I don't like to see them so desperately hungry."

As the two friends enjoyed their drinks, they turned their attention to the small fountain in the garden, where a group of pigeons shared some water with a quail family.

As respectfully as always, Dionisio approached the ladies on the porch. One of the cows had given birth and he needed to pick up the vet since the calf was having some difficulties. He added that soon they needed to start picking the peaches from the orchard before they ripened so they could take them to El Carmelo's central market. Esperanza thanked and informed him that the following week she herself would start the picking.

Soon a thick mantle of fog approached the two friends, obstructing the ocean view they had been enjoying all afternoon. Both of their faces became damp from the mist being carried in. While Carlota refilled their glasses, Esperanza brought out some small wool blankets to cover their bare shoulders and protect them from the cool breeze. After so many afternoons together, they were both accustomed to the fog and the cool mist. Carlota wanted to continue listening to the story her friend was narrating to her.

"Five years after Pepé left in search of adventure in the seductive ocean," Esperanza continued, "I found out that a disastrous accident occurred. During one of those fierce winter storms with hurricane winds of more than one hundred miles an hour, a ship called Los Lobos was violently tossed against the rocky shore. It was the ship where Pepé was supposed to be working. The captain was not able to steer far enough from the shore and the ship split in half. Most of the crew perished. All the cargo — valued in thousands of dollars

— was lost. Those who survived the catastrophic accident were transferred to the city of Monterey, and the badly wounded to the nearby hospital."

"What a tragic and horrible end for Pepé!" Carlota exclaimed in dismay.

"Well, that is what I feared. I traveled to Monterey with Dionisio. We went to the offices of the Pacific Maritime on Alvarado Street. After reading the ship's manifest, the superintendent informed me that Pepé was not among the dead or wounded. Luckily for him, he had been transferred to another ship earlier that year. The superintendent did not have the name of the ship nor its route, though he suspected that the ship's name was El Dorado which cruised between Japan and Seattle, Washington."

Carlota breathed a sigh of relief, and Esperanza continued. "In the years which followed the horrific accident, he never wrote to me again. I sporadically received news of him from sailors and other people who had seen him. One day a fellow sailor stopped by my ranch to tell me he had seen him at a bordello in San Francisco. I never was aware that Pepé frequented those houses of sin, but I suppose he changed after being away for so many years. It was to be expected. On another occasion, a friend of his wrote saying he had met him in Oregon, at the port city of Astoria near the Columbia River delta. That was the last news I heard. It is as if he had been swallowed by the ocean."

"Don't be so pessimistic," Carlota encouraged her friend. "One of these days Pepé will show up. He will knock on the door and overwhelm you with gifts and objects he collected on his travels in foreign lands."

"I am not pessimistic," Esperanza replied. "I am being realistic, Carlota. Pepé is a man carrying many years on his shoulders. His night will catch up to him if it hasn't already. Life without a predetermined route can make a person more fragile. I only wish that if he, in fact, is dead that he did not suffer at the end. I pray to the Lord to look after him. But despite all his selfishness and absence, I have never stopped loving him. I have always longed for his return. Perhaps, just like you say my dear Carlota, someday he will return to be by my side so we can end our nights in our little ranch, together."

The sky was turning a deeper blue. Carlota finished her third glass of Porto and decided to say goodbye to her friend. She tossed the last of the peanuts to the blue jays who swooped down to retrieve them. Smiling, Esperanza shook her head and handed her friend a dozen brown eggs from her chickens.

Two weeks after her last visit to Esperanza's ranch, Carlota, without announcing herself, went back to see her friend once again to enjoy the stunning views of the Pacific. She came earlier in the day than usual; she heard a family of dolphins had recently been spotted frolicking near the beach facing the ranch house, so she came during high tide to be able to see them. Carlota went by the garden and as usual, she sat on one of the armchairs on the porch to wait for her friend. She watched the quail family by the fountain. From behind the wide leaves of the agapanthus, she noticed a brown cat spying on a mother quail and her tiny chicks. He would have to wait for another day for his meal, as the loud and annoying shrieks of the blue jays, Flora and Pepé, alerted the mother quail who quickly ushered her little ones to safety.

Patiently, Carlota waited for her friend. She figured Esperanza was attending her chores inside the house. Soon she realized she did not hear any sounds from inside. At that moment, Carlota decided to look for her in the house.

"Esperanza?" Carlota called before opening the door and walking in. She went to the kitchen and the bedrooms but could not find Esperanza. She returned to the porch and started to call out to her friend again. Suddenly her calls were answered with the shrieks of a jay. Pepé like a maniac darted from the fence at the edge of the peach grove and landed on the porch step. Carlota had never seen him this close. His bright blue feathers were puffing up and his shrieks were louder than usual. He flew back to the fence and then back to Carlota. It was as if he was guiding her toward the place where her friend could be found.

Intrigued by the shrieks and odd behavior of Pepé, Carlota followed him to the peach grove. As she approached the entrance of the grove, she saw Esperanza. She was sitting against the trunk of one of the peach trees and her face was as yellow as the faded grass on the grove. Next to her was a white wicker basket full of the peaches which she had finished picking. In her hands was a copy of the Monterey newspaper. With teary eyes, Esperanza showed Carlota the headline of the newspaper. It described the sinking of El Dorado in the violent waters of the Pacific; it was the ship where Pepé, her husband, had sailed to Japan. It had been totally destroyed by one of the typhoons commonly encountered near the coast of Japan.

"Please read the list of the ones who perished," Esperanza asked her friend.

After a few moments, Carlota quietly said, "Pepé is on this list. There were no survivors. I'm so sorry."

Flora, the female blue jay flew over to join her mate on the fence. With their shiny black eyes, they curiously stared at the two women. Esperanza grabbed her chest with her right hand and reached out to Carlota with her left.

"Carlota, I can feel my heartbreaking. Perhaps it is Pepé, my husband, who guided you this way. The blue jay saved my life. You were right. The blue jays are good birds."

While Esperanza expressed her emotionally filled words, Carlota noticed that Esperanza was not well. Her face had turned greenish-gray and beads of perspiration appeared on her forehead. Without thinking about twice, Carlota called out to Dionisio, who she had seen nearby on her way to the orchard. The blue jays started making agitated calls as if trying to call him over too. He hurried over when he heard all the commotion and gasped when he saw Esperanza.

"We need to take her to Monterey immediately," urged Carlota. Dionisio ran to get the truck.

"Carlota," Esperanza murmured. "If I don't survive, I want you to have my small ranch. Please take care of it. The day after your last visit I made all the legal arrangements with Horacio, my lawyer. I signed all the transfer documents to your name. In other words, this ranch already belongs to you." Before Carlota could reply, Dionisio appeared with the truck.

Carlota held her friend's hands on their way to the city. Esperanza made an effort and raised her head from the pillow Dionisio had positioned to ease the trip. "It was Pepé," whispered Esperanza. "He came back to be with me like you said he would. He is here with me! My dear and good friend Carlota, whenever you see a blue jay, throw him a peanut, and always remember: it could be your Pepé."

Esperanza did not survive the massive heart attack she suffered when she learned the news of the shipwreck of El Dorado, where her beloved Pepé had perished. Carlota and Dionisio buried Esperanza's ashes next to the dilapidated fence facing the Pacific Ocean, where the blue jays sat daily.

The Tile Setter

It was seven-thirty in the morning. That Sunday morning, Ramón Mercado was hoping to catch up on some much-needed sleep. Having worked until past midnight all day Saturday, he thought he deserved to stay longer in bed and perhaps his wife would surprise him by serving him his favorite breakfast: sunny-side-up fried eggs with two strips of crispy bacon, a side of hot buttered grits and a slice of toasted French bread. Ramón must have been dreaming, there wouldn't be any special treatment or staying in bed later than usual. He was abruptly awakened by the noise of the bathroom shower going full blast and his wife Lorena complaining about the tiles in their bathroom. He didn't know why his wife was taking a shower so early, she normally showers in the evening. Perhaps, Ramón wondered, she was going to early Sunday mass. When she came out of the steam-filled bathroom with a towel wrapped around her body and another on her head, she told him:

"Ramón, once and for all, you need to take care of the problem in our bathroom, some of the tiles in the shower are so loose that one of them fell off and broke as it hit the floor. Besides, I have told you many times that I don't like the pale-yellow color, it's antiquated, I want to replace the entire bathroom with more modern looking tiles. In the meantime, the least you can do is get out of bed and go to the hardware store to see if you find a new tile to replace the one that just broke. Also, while you are there, bring me some samples of new tiles to start selecting for a new bathroom."

After preparing his own breakfast, Ramón drove to the local hardware store. He was determined to find a match for the broken tile and select some samples to bring to his wife for her to look at. He was tired of listening to her complaining every time she took a shower.

As he entered the hardware store, he did not waste any time looking for grass seed or fertilizer for his lawn, he headed straight to the tile section to search for a mosaic tile to replace the broken one. He was trying to match the color of the piece of the broken one he had brought with him when a man approached him from behind. Ramón noticed that the cart the man was pushing contained seven tile boxes, glue and mortar necessary to tile an entire bathroom.

"Excuse me, sir," he said. "I noticed you were looking in the tile section trying to match a broken tile with another of similar color; if you need help selecting any material for your job, I can be of help to you. My name is Abelardo Romero and I am a tile setter by profession."

"My name is Ramón; I am trying to replace a broken tile in my bathroom which fell off while my wife was taken a shower."

"Nice to meet you, sir, it's a shame the tile broke; however, it is going to be difficult to find an exact match, especially if the bathroom was built sometime in the past. The best thing you can do, Mr. Ramón," suggested Abelardo, "is to remove all the tiles and install new ones. I could do the job for you and give you a reasonable price; and as I said before, that is what I do for a living, I am a professional tile setter."

"That's exactly what I intend to do, I am selecting some samples to bring to my wife. How can I get in touch with you? Could I have your telephone number?"

"No need to phone me, sir, you can find me here on Sundays, it's my day off, and I come here to get supplies for my next job. If you decide to retile your bathroom, you can find me in the tile section next Sunday at around ten."

The following Sunday, as Abelardo suggested, punctually at ten Ramón met Abelardo in the tile section. His wife had selected the tiles she wanted for their bathroom and chosen a new shower head as well. He wanted his wife to be happy. Happy wife, happy life! He thought to himself.

After discussing some details of the job: cost, materials and such, Ramón decided to hire Abelardo's services since the price he quoted was more reasonable than the other estimates he obtained from two other tile setters. A week later, just as he had promised, Abelardo arrived at his house to start the job.

As he was accustomed to doing with other hired workers, Ramón started a friendly conversation with Abelardo while he worked. It was during one of their initial talks that they exchanged details about their countries of origin, work experience and how they both came into this country. While working hard and well, Abelardo told him that he was originally from Honduras, and modestly admitted that although he was a professional tile setter, having learned the trade in his homeland, his brother Bruno was a much better glazed-tile setter than he.

"Is your brother in this country? If he is so good as you say, why doesn't he work with you?

"It's a long and sad story Mr. Ramón, I don't want to bother you with it. Besides, it's all in the past, my brother is dead."

"I am sorry to hear that, please tell me about your brother and how you came to the United States and especially to Maryland? I want to hear..."

"Okay! If you insist, it is not my intention to bore you with his story. My brother was an artist when it came to the installation of glazed tiles," said Abelardo. "He was the best tile setter at the company where he worked. He would install tiles on cement, bricks, wallboard and other materials. The designs he improvised were famous throughout the neighboring cities. Wealthy people would seek him out to do their patios, kitchens, swimming pools ... He was a master installer and I am sure he would have made lots of money in this country; unfortunately, he was not as lucky as me," added Abelardo "a bullet crossed his way and stopped him from living in this country; I feel responsible for his death; it was me who encouraged him to come to live in the United States."

At first, Ramón thought Abelardo was going to open up and tell him his brother's story, but suddenly he raised his head and looked him square in the eyes, then hesitated for a moment and stopped talking, as if all of the sudden, he had been hit by lightning.

Perhaps, Ramón thought, I reminded him of a person who could denounce him to the immigration authorities or "la migra" as this agency is often referred to. Ramón understood his apprehension and concern and decided not to ask Abelardo any more questions about his brother. However, after talking about other less important matters, considering perhaps that he did not pose a threat to him after all, Abelardo continued confiding again in Ramón. Again, without being asked, he told Ramón that he would tell him in detail what happened to his brother but only on one condition. Abelardo paused, looked at Ramón and said:

"Mr. Ramón, I think I can trust you; I will tell you what happened only if you keep it a secret and refrain from mentioning my brother's real name or his daughter's, or their place of birth, towns and cities they crossed. Especially, if you ever decide to tell this story to someone, please do not mention the fact that my brother committed a crime."

"Please do not worry Abelardo, I accept your conditions and I promise I won't discuss or tell this to anyone, and if I ever decide to write about it, I will not disclose their names. Rest assured, trust me, you can start anytime you wish."

"We came from a very poor family; my father abandoned us when we were very small. We were four brothers; I was the oldest and Bruno the youngest. Overcoming many difficulties and hardships, my mother gave us the best education available, the best she could with her meager means. Luis and Roger, my other two brothers were killed in a bloody firefight during a revolution in my country ..."

While Abelardo was talking, Ramón was surprised to hear how well he communicated; the way he articulated his thoughts, pausing and emphasizing the appropriate words; he seemed to be listening to a man with a higher level of education than the one he told him he had received.

"We lived with our mother," Abelardo continued "in a small wooden house on the slopes of a mountain located to the north of the country; it is known as Mitombillo. The morning fog which enveloped the nearby mountains was late to dissipate, but it wouldn't stop

Bruno or me to wait only until dawn to do our chores and rush to work.

Carrying our backpacks on our shoulders, we descended the steep slopes, sometimes overtaking others trotting down, to be the first ones to arrive at Azulejos S.A., a tile factory in the town of Hornillos. It was at this factory that my brother Bruno learned how to install glazed tiles to perfection. He trained under the supervision of a master Italian tile setter, who taught him the art of cutting and installing mosaics in the most amazing shapes and most beautiful designs I have ever seen. As I previously mentioned to you, Mr. Ramón, my brother was a master setter, an artist, if you had met him you would have hired him in an instant. You would have been delighted by the designs he created. It was also at that factory that he met María, a girl of humble origins, and after a brief courtship, they married. A year later, Ignacio, a son, was born but unfortunately, he died from an undiagnosed infant disease. Soon after, they were blessed with the birth of a girl, Mariíta, who brought back happiness to the young couple."

Abelardo continued narrating, in great detail, the information about his brother Bruno. He told Ramón how, after the death of their mother, in September 1993, they decided to sell her house and split the little money they obtained from the sale.

"Unlike my brother, who decided to stay in Honduras," said Abelardo, "I decided to venture traveling to this country or to El Norte, as it's often referred to. Notwithstanding all the obstacles which I encountered on my way, I overcame them and after trying my luck in several cities, I settled in the city of Rockville, in the state of Maryland."

"In the evenings," he continued "I went to school to learn English to be able to communicate with the large majority of my clients. And with the help of a U.S. citizen, who sponsored me, I was able to obtain legal status in this country. Nowadays, I have my own business, specializing in the installation of flagstones, tiles as well as glazed tiles. When I have several jobs at the same time, I hire a couple of *muchachos* on an hourly basis. I saved enough money to put a down payment on a small house and buy a used Ford pickup.

I decided to come to this country, but my brother did not want to accompany me; he did not want to leave his wife and his daughter. With the proceeds from the sale of our mother's house, plus what he had saved he moved to the capital city where he could get more clients and thus provide a better living to his family. Although the economic condition of the country favored him monetarily, his luck did not last long. As the economy collapsed, work became scarce and fears about the political and economic conditions worsened among the population. In view of such insecurity, wealthy people abstained from investing in unnecessary projects."

"Workers competed against each other," added Abelardo. "They would fight for the few existing jobs; companies would take advantage of this situation by offering only the lowest wages. Bruno was not able to find a job; his scarce resources were rapidly dwindling. On one occasion, he applied for a job advertised in the local newspaper and when he arrived at the job site, he found fifteen other workers competing for the same job.

Neither my brother's experience nor his acquired fame mattered; what mattered was who was willing to work for the wages paid. When I learned what was happening in the country and of the precarious situation my brother was facing, I contacted him and offered my help to bring him to this country. More than once, I tried to convince him to change his mind, but he wouldn't budge, he hoped the economic conditions would improve. However, that never materialized, on the contrary, things were getting worse; stores, markets, private homes were being robbed and vandalized, crime was rampant and, on the rise, food was scarce, people were going hungry."

While Abelardo was narrating all these events, Ramón did not dare interrupt him. But it wasn't possible anyway, he couldn't stop.

"Later the drug dealers and the gangs started terrorizing the population. Crimes among themselves and against the rest of the citizenry increased throughout the entire country. The kidnapping of young boys and girls became more frequent, and to obtain their freedom, criminals were requesting large sums of money for ramson. When I learned about all these awful conditions, once again, I contacted my brother, who by then, had finally realized what the country was going through and was concerned about the country's precarious situation. His daughter, who had just turned fifteen, plus the fact that she could be in danger of such crimes extremely worried him. But again, he would not accept my offer to help him, nor my suggestion to leave the country.

The situation in the entire country continued to grow worse, robberies, kidnappings were on the increase. Three months later, after my last conversation with him; he received a call from a friend telling him he had overheard a plan to have his daughter kidnapped; his precious fifteen-year-old daughter who, at her age, had developed into a very attractive girl. The fear of losing his beautiful daughter convinced him to finally accept my offer to come to this country. He decided to leave but he would just bring his daughter with him. His wife needed to stay in order to look after her ill and aging mother of more than eighty years."

While Abelardo was telling Ramón about the country's precarious conditions, thefts, assaults, plus the danger Bruno's daughter faced, he could not help thinking that he had heard many similar stories and Abelardo's was just another one of the many reported in the newspapers. However, to avoid appearing insensitive to him and to his family's sad story, he continued listening.

"Since I was not able to find the same 'coyote' — who helped me during my crossing — in order to smuggle him into this country, I needed to hire another one who had a good record of guiding a large number of migrants across the border. After selling some jewelry, plus other personal effects, my brother was able to put together the sum of three thousand dollars. With the three thousand that I gave him, he got together the six thousand dollars required to pay for the operation."

"Tell me how would the trip take place?" Ramón interrupted Abelardo who was carefully cutting the corner of one of the tiles to perfectly fit it in one of the corners of the bathroom wall.

"They traveled by bus," said Abelardo "for six thousand dollars the 'coyote' covered transportation expenses, housing, bribes or *mordidas* to pay the authorities at the border crossings. To keep his daughter safe from the attention of undesirable people and risking abuse, he cut her hair short like a boy's and dressed her in blue jeans and a very loose shirt to hide her young breasts. He asked her to avoid speaking with anyone and pretend she was mute.

At the beginning of July 1977, they said goodbye to his wife and her ailing mother, and at a pre-arranged place in the outskirts of the city, they boarded the much-anticipated bus that was going to take them to El Norte."

"How smart of your brother, to disguise the looks of his pretty daughter!" Ramón said to Abelardo.

"Yes, it was smart of him to do it, but he could not hide it for very long, I will explain. Although their trip towards the border was somewhat different, the route was very similar to the one I traveled.

Occasionally, the 'coyotes' traveled through many different side roads to avoid the police but eventually, they returned to the main highway. The local authorities were well aware of their routine and of the shady deals related to the traffic and transportation of such a large number of people. My experience was very similar to my brother's. Before reaching the border, five buses joined the caravan; men, women, small boys and girls of different ages, some with families, others traveled alone. The prettiest women were separated by force from the group as well as girls older than eleven or twelve years of age. If they were not abused by the men on the buses they were abused by the 'coyotes.' Some were taken to local whore houses to be prostituted; some would be returned; others disappeared and were never seen again. The most endangered ones were the good-looking ones, who often were sold to other traffickers. While all these outrageous abuses were taking place, no one dared say anything. Terror consumed everyone, no one dared to speak up or to complain. In one instance, a man complained when another man tried to sexually abuse him and he confronted his aggressor. The next day he was found dead, stabbed to death with a knife in his neck. It was heartbreaking, no one reacted, they feared for their own lives.

On other occasions, if someone complained, they would throw

them off the bus, steal their savings and abandon them in an isolated road to be eaten by the predators. You could only guess what would be the end of those poor people!

For reasons unknown to me, the 'coyote' in charge of the group in which my brother was traveling treated him better than the rest of the group. Earlier, he must have realized that Bruno's *son* was not a boy, as he appeared to be, but a girl who could be abused or trafficked as they did with some of the other girls and women.

I learned later, that he also had another plan. He had found out that my brother was an expert glazed-tile setter and he wanted to take advantage of his expertise, going as far as to offer him a deal. He would return one thousand dollars to my brother provided he would install a special tile design in the bathroom in one of his houses in the city of Arriaga, in the southern state of Chiapas, Mexico.

As far as my brother was concerned, the installation of glazed tiles was not an issue or an arduous job, and although the job would delay his travel plans for at least four or five days, and so he accepted the offer. He needed the money as it would be helpful to have extra cash once he crossed the border. Upon reaching the next country and without any justification, an army patrol stopped the caravan. One of the 'coyotes' in charge of another group complained to the soldier arguing that all pertinent documents were in order. An irate sergeant grabbed him by his shoulders, shook him abruptly and laughing aloud, he pulled a gun from his holster and coldly shot him in the head. Although they had witnessed a cold-blooded crime, no one said anything.

The soldiers ordered everyone off the buses, separating the women from the men, then they grabbed the women and dragged them to a nearby wooded area where they raped them indiscriminately. One could hear their terrifying moaning and screams. When they finally came back from the woods, it was easy to see how the thorny bushes had scratched and torn apart their clothes. Their bruised legs and arms were a testimony of how they had been beaten and abused. Thank heaven, they did not realize that Bruno's *son* was a girl, and so she was spared that ordeal. The indiscriminate orgy lasted three days until the soldiers had fully satisfied their sexual urges. Not until then was the caravan allowed to continue, leaving the body of the 'coyote' in the open, barely covered with a few dry branches."

As Ramón was listening to Abelardo's horrifying story about the brutality and mistreatment these poor souls were subjected to on their way to El Norte, the only words he could utter were:

"How terrible! What a horrible experience!"

"Once they arrived in Arriaga, all the unfortunate migrants were informed that they had reached their final destination, the rest of the trip toward Reynosa, a city close to the Río Bravo del Norte in the northern state of Tamaulipas, would be made on their own. They were also advised that they could — illegally — board a freight train which traveled frequently from Arriaga to the city of Reynosa. The so-called train was called 'La Bestia,' (The Beast). Don't ask me, Mr. Ramón, why they called the train by that name, but perhaps due to the beastly abuses and brutal acts committed on board.

To comply with his part of the bargain, regarding the installation of the tiles, the 'coyote' separated my brother and his *son* from the rest of the group and took them to his house located in a neighborhood of dubious reputation. At that house, the 'coyote' put them into an obscure room in the rear of the house, which appeared to be a storage room filled with debris, old furniture, broken items covered with dust and soot; dirty rags and old newspapers.

In one corner, my brother noticed two coffins stacked one on top of the other but he did not dare ask about or open them fearing a mean reply from the 'coyote' or to find something inside he did not want to see. The only window in the room was sealed with four rough boards screwed to the frame and the meager light coming from a light bulb hanging from the ceiling was not even enough to light up the room. It felt like a cold, dirty prison cell. To make matters worse, the 'coyote' threw them an old and stained mattress, instructing them that this would be their bed while they stayed at his house. My brother anticipated the worst, he should have turned down the offer of the one thousand dollars, but it was too late, he was trapped. Not having a choice, he decided to do the best under the circumstances and do the tile setting job as fast as possible and protect his daughter from the claws of the filthy 'coyote' who, for unknown reasons, had realized that his *son* was not a boy. How did he find out? I do not know," concluded Abelardo.

Up to this point, Ramón did not interrupt Abelardo's story, it was not necessary. Abelardo raised his head, and with a glazed tile in his hand, looked him in the eyes and said:

"Mr. Ramón, I don't even know why I am telling you this horrible and disturbing story? The only thing I'm asking of you is to understand why my brother acted the way he did."

"I am listening." Ramón said, "and rest assured that I would understand and accept your brother's anticipated and justifiable behavior."

"No!" Abelardo explained. "You cannot even imagine what came next. You will find out that my brother was in a position where he had no choice but to do what he did.

The next day my brother started to do what the 'coyote' asked him to do; removing the old tiles from his bathroom. He removed the wall holding the tiles, leaving the construction bricks to which the piping system was attached in the open. According to my brother, the framing trusses measured more than six inches thick, spaced between twenty to twenty-two inches apart instead of the sixteen inches which is what is normally used in accordance with the U.S. construction code.

The 'coyote' had all the materials ready, anticipating my brother's acceptance to do the job. He had bought the best supplies; luxurious glazed tiles — typical of his country — plus a large number of beautiful mosaics of different sizes and colors. His plan was for my brother to install a mosaic and tile design of his face conjoined with the face of a famous revolutionary hero of his country, I believe it was Emiliano Zapata.

By then, the 'coyote' had started to spy on Bruno's daughter and make obscene comments, which my brother was unable to stop. He did not want to antagonize the damned 'coyote' who could, in an irate attack, obstruct his final destination by killing them both, burying them in the coffins at the corner of the dark bedroom.

Pretending to be asleep, the 'coyote' took advantage of my brother's absence — he had gone out to search for some food at a nearby market — and entered the room where the girl was alone. My brother's absence was short but long enough for the dirty and inebriated 'coyote' to start raping his daughter. When Bruno saw what was happening, he grabbed a two-foot-long iron pipe and violently hit him on the neck.

His intention was to separate him from the partially naked body of his daughter. He succeeded, but not as he had intended. The coyote fell on the floor, his dark brown, almost black face turned pale-yellowish like death itself, he did not articulate a single word or move a muscle. My brother had no idea whether he was dead or alive. Horrified, he took one of the glazed tiles and held it close to his mouth to see if he was still breathing, but there was no sign of it. Next, he tried to check his pulse but he was too nervous to detect any. Lastly, he tried feeling his carotid artery and failed again, there was no sign of life. He concluded the coyote was dead."

"How horrible!" Ramón said. He couldn't think of any appropriate comments to Abelardo's tragic story. He then sat down on the floor of the bathroom to be able to continue hearing such a terrorizing story.

"Trembling and disconcerted for the act he had committed, my brother didn't know what to do. He thought that if he called the police, they wouldn't believe him and they would apprehend him and charge him on the spot or kill him and his daughter without asking any questions. He was an illegal migrant in a country where these types of crimes are committed against transients all the time. Desperately, he thought about hiding the corpse in one of the coffins in the room; but this was not the best solution, the decomposing body would betray him. He looked around and entered the bedroom of the supposedly dead 'coyote.' He didn't know what to do; he couldn't think of a place where to dispose of the body. He went to the bathroom where he had been working. His daughter was crying in one of the corners of their bedroom.

The only thing exposed was the construction bricks supporting the bathroom walls; and again, he noticed the unusual separation and depth of the wall trusses. Without giving it much thought, he dragged the body — which wasn't showing any signs of life — towards the unfinished bathroom. With a superhuman effort, he raised the body and placed it in between two of the trusses. To prevent it from collapsing, he tied his wrists and feet to the exposed pipes with electric cables. He grabbed a piece of his oily hair, tied it into a knot and nailed it to the brick wall to keep his head from falling. He then filled the empty spaces with newspapers and old rags that he found in the bedroom where they had spent the night. He hurried to cover the improvised grave with the wallboard the 'coyote' had imported from abroad making sure it was securely nailed down."

"What a macabre experience your brother had to endure. By the way, you are telling me the story with so much detail, it seems you were either there or perhaps you were a witness ..." Ramón commented to Abelardo.

"It appears to be so, Mr. Ramón, but it was my brother who told me the story, and every detail of what happened has permanently remained in my mind."

"Suddenly, as he was getting the walls ready to install the tiles and the mosaics" — continued Abelardo — "someone knocked on the door. Not knowing what to do and in horror, he pretended to be calm, and to avoid suspicion he opened the door. The persons were acquaintances of the 'coyote,' and my brother, without hesitating, told them that he had gone out with other migrants and he was not sure when he was coming back. Fortunately, they believed him and left. No sooner were they gone that my brother, with heroic effort went on with the installation of the glazed tiles with the design requested by the 'coyote' but instead of the swine's figure and his country's hero he laid out a tile design with the 'coyote's face and that of the devil, both coming out of a flaming inferno.

Two days later, after finalizing the macabre task, my brother and his daughter waited until nightfall to leave the cursed house when suddenly, coming from the bathroom, they heard a muffled scream and the faint knocking against the tiled wall. It sounded as if someone was drumming his fingers against a table. From the tub's faucet, they saw purplish drops, like blood mixed with rust, as if the bathroom was possessed by an infernal being, it felt as if the house had been possessed by the devil. My brother did not stop to go back and find out where the sounds where coming from. He knew! They left hurriedly and walked across dark isolated streets, and with the help of two other migrants they headed to the place where 'La Bestia' was waiting; it was the freight train they needed to board to escape to the city of Reynosa.

The freight train cars were fully loaded with migrants of different countries pursuing the same destination, cross the Río Bravo del

Norte and reach El Norte. To avoid being drenched by a torrential rain they had to seek refuge underneath one of the cars. They stayed there for four days eating whatever they could buy from street vendors nearby. What they witnessed during that period was indescribable: thefts, assaults, rapes ..., and to endure the lack of space inside the cars, they eventually traveled on top of the roof of one of the cars where they tied themselves down to avoid falling over.

The trip to Reynosa lasted three days and upon their arrival, they needed to contact and pay a different 'coyote' an additional sum to take them to the river bank where they would hide in the bushes for another six days. The other 'coyote' would take them to the edge of the river and give them the green light to go across. It was necessary to wait for the border guards to absent themselves temporarily. Once they signaled it was safe to cross, in the evening of the sixth day, along with nine other people they grabbed a larger than normal pneumatic tube and jumped into the water. They evaded pieces of wood, branches, trash and much other junk the river was dragging. Of the eleven who ventured into the crossing, only eight made it to the other side. They couldn't find out what happened to the other three, perhaps they let go of the tube and were dragged away by the strong current."

"Amazing!" Ramón said to Abelardo. "What happened next, who killed your brother and why?"

"I was waiting for them in a pre-arranged place on the United States side of the river, I can't divulge the specific site. I had borrowed a car from a friend to be able to drive my brother back to Maryland. After driving for more than a day, we made it to Houston where we rented a room at a modest motel outside the city. At about ten-thirty that night, my brother went out to purchase some sodas at a nearby convenience store. That night luck ran out on him.

When he was paying at the counter, two teenage boys came into the store brandishing pistols and demanding money from the cashier. The cashier objected and refused to give in to their demand and a shootout ensued, my brother and the cashier were shot and killed. It all happened so unexpectedly, so fast! After waiting for him for a while, I decided to go look for him at the convenience store but it was too late, the place was surrounded by cops. They asked me if I knew the dead person but — damn it! — fearing to be apprehended, I disguised my feelings and told them that I didn't know him.

His body was taken to the morgue and later buried at a public cemetery. After making sure that his body had been duly buried, I headed north, together with his daughter, who in the end turned out to be my best companion, his beautiful daughter who endured this arduous journey with him. She, fortunately, finished her education in this country and is currently a Spanish teacher at a public school in one of the southern states of this country."

"Yes, she was a lucky girl and what a sad ending to your brother's life," Ramón commented. He then thanked him for sharing his story.

Two days later, Abelardo finished the installation of the glazed tiles in Ramón's bathroom, and when he offered to pay him with a check, Abelardo asked him to pay him in cash. Once again, he begged him to abstain from making any comments about the story and about his brother's ordeal, but if he decided to tell someone about it, to avoid mentioning names.

Somewhat over six months had passed since Abelardo finished the job of installing the glazed tiles and narrating the horrific odyssey his brother and daughter had experienced while traveling towards El Norte. Ramón forgot about the entire story and only told it to his wife, who was more than pleased with the color of the tiles and Abelardo's workmanship.

News about the horrible abuses and perils that so many people endure every day are published in the local newspapers and on television. Ramón had not paid too much attention to such reports until one afternoon, the bell rang twice at the front door of his house. He was leisurely reading the newspaper and since he was not expecting any visitors at that hour, he ignored it, thinking it could be someone trying to sell something, but twice again the bell rang. When he finally opened the door, he was confronted by two men who politely showed him their police identifications from the state of Sonora. Ramón asked them what brought them to his house. They answered that for approximately ten years, they had been on the trail of a man who was a tile setter believed to have been involved in the disappearance of a 'coyote' in the city of Arriaga in the state of Chiapas, Mexico. They showed him a picture of a young man whose features were very similar to those of Abelardo and asked him if he had ever contracted the services of someone like him.

Ramón replied to them that yes, not long ago he had hired a man called Abelardo, adding that he wanted to contact him recently to recommend him to a friend but could not; he did not have his telephone number.

"Thank you very much, sir," one of the agents said, "his name is not Abelardo, that's one of the many names he occasionally uses."

And as pleasantly as they had introduced themselves, they said goodbye without offering him their business cards. After they left, Ramón shut the door, went back to reading the newspaper but he couldn't help wondering:

Could it be possible that Abelardo and Bruno were the same person? Could the story Abelardo told me about his dead brother Bruno be a fabricated story, perhaps to hide his true identity? And as he sat down in his armchair, he shrugged his shoulders and said to himself:

"I very much doubt that I will ever find out the truth."

Discord Among the Insects

Guadalupe Guandique's heels clicked on the tiles as she entered the foyer. She was glad to be off the hot, dusty streets of town and back inside her cool airconditioned house. After admiring her lovely new hairdo in the mirror, she turned her attention to the view outside the large sitting room window. She loved looking at the creamy white roses and scarlet poppies in her luxurious garden. A trio of white iron chairs sat empty on the patio under the majestic maple tree which dutifully hid the sun's rays on this humid July afternoon.

Guadalupe stepped away from the window, unaware that a plot was being hatched among the pachysandra, gladiolus and fragrant carnations. A collection of delinquents had gathered to plan an assault on the mansion. The villains raised their eyes to, of all things, Guadalupe's house, which provided a bit of shade in which they could hold their meeting.

Gathered this day were Toña the fly from Veracruz, Pepe the cricket, Tina the red ant, Chucho the wide-eyed bumblebee, Luisa and Pepa the shy lice sisters, Pascual the mosquito, and Gina the mysterious spider. Also present were Celia the energetic cicada, Rogelio the sly grasshopper, Anabel the colorful, delicate monarch butterfly, and the Chinese ladybug brothers named Hunan, Yo-Ke-Se and Ke-Se-Yo. Finally, off to the side but not forgotten was Bonifacio the lazy, stinky bedbug.

The miniature army began by discussing the point of entry. They agreed the front door was the best option and hoped for an opportunity such as Guadalupe opening the door to welcome a visitor or to accept a package from the mailman. Next, they established who would give orders, who would be in charge of fair distribution of rations, who would write the laws and who would approve them.

Beneath the dining room window, they could hear the crystal and silverware being set out and smell the assorted cakes, honey, and fruits on their way from the kitchen. As the aromas wafted down on cool drafts escaping from inside, they groaned over how they were famished and about to suffocate from the heat and humidity. They daydreamed of the cornucopia awaiting them inside the air-conditioned walls of Guadalupe's house.

When it came time to determine how to take action, however, they were at an impasse. No one in this distinguished cast of characters had been able to discern the best way to synchronize their advance toward Guadalupe's house. Before long, the meeting became a hullabaloo with everyone speaking at once. It was the baritone voice of Rogelio the grasshopper that rose over the others and brought the mayhem to a halt.

"Silencio! A decision will never be reached in this pandemonium. We should consult the field marshal. He will know what to do," said Rogelio, referring to Plutarco the toad, whom they called the "General."

The toad with sparkling eyes and olive-colored wrinkled skin wore a smug smile from ear to ear. From his usual spot among the matted, wet maple leaves he had been observing the agitated discord among the insects. He emerged when he overheard they were seeking his counsel. They approached Plutarco and formed a semicircle in order of rank before him, each wanting to hear what the General had to say. In the middle, Tina the ant dug up a tiny mound of dirt, forming an insect-sized podium.

Toña the fly, the most aggressive of the diverse cast, stepped forward. She had assumed — having asked none of her comrades — the role of speaker. "Gracias," she humbly thanked the General for graciously receiving them on such short notice. She told him all about their army and the elaborate plan to infiltrate the house in search of cool air and a free lunch.

When Toña was done, Plutarco was silent. He stretched his left haunch and yawned twice. "Absurd!" he said at last in a deep, resonant voice. "What an ill-conceived plan. You all are fools." He shook his head and closed his eyes.

Astonished at Plutarco's negative reaction, the revolutionaries looked at one another. They could not believe their ears. Toña, the most ambitious, was furious. "Bah! I should have known better than to come to you. You have no idea what delights are in that kitchen! Never mind, how would you know? You spend your days down here with the worms under these disgusting, rotting leaves. You wouldn't know a good deal if it hit you on the ..."

"Eeeeek!" Toña's tirade was interrupted by the shrieks of Miguelito the mouse, who came shooting past them like a bullet from the nearby rocks with a face full of terror. And with good reason, as immediately the insects' antennae fluttered under the silent flapping of the wings of Aron the hawk, who was pursuing Miguelito for his next meal. Luckily, the clever mouse disappeared into a hole in the trunk of the tall maple just in time. Toña turned to face the band of invaders.

"We will continue with our plan!"

Anabel, the monarch butterfly, raised her hand. "Toña, I must excuse myself from this mission. I am better off with the nectar from the lilacs, and I need the sunlight to gather strength for when I fly south next month. Besides, I do not wish to wind up on the end of a pin among the other winged creatures decorating the walls of Guadalupe's office." Before Toña could speak, Anabel flew away.

Pepe the cricket hopped to the podium. "I am sorry, I must

leave also. I just remembered that two weeks ago my first cousin Pepín made his way into the house through a crack in the back door. Hungry as he was, he lunged at what he thought was nectar in a small plastic tray on the floor, however, it was a sticky trap strategically placed by Guadalupe in the basement, and ..." Pepe shuddered at the thought of his dead cousin, which made his hind legs rub together and create a loud, out-of-tune trill. He startled himself with his own dissonant symphony and leaped away. Rogelio the grasshopper, Pepe's second cousin, also shuddered, shouting his apology as he fluttered away.

Toña cast a scornful glance over the group which gradually was disintegrating, abandoning her and the illicit project.

With an unmistakable high-pitched buzzing Pascual, the mosquito flew forward to the mound of dirt.

"Toña, count me out. I prefer to seek out my meals outside at dusk, 6:30 to be exact when Guadalupe and her husband relax in their chairs. I always make my move when they least expect it, just before they spray on some foul-smelling oil, which has the same revolting odor as the citronella plants Guadalupe placed in pots around the patio last week."

While everyone pleaded their case, Plutarco the toad enjoyed the drama unfolding before his droopy-lidded eyes.

Celia the cicada spoke next, presenting a compelling argument. "Ummm, the time has come for me to go underground for several years. The recent rains have softened the soil enough to begin my descent into the deep earth. I must rush off or my family will leave me behind. See you in 17 years!" She took off with a deafening roar.

Chucho the bumblebee declared that he, like Anabel, preferred nectar and zoomed off toward a collection of bright orange poppies.

The podium was vacant momentarily while Luisa and Pepa, the lice sisters, heatedly argued over which of their arguments was better. The ladybug brothers squabbled over whether they should seek the advice of the Japanese beetles, their distant relatives, residing in the neighbor's climbing roses. Tina the ant had fallen asleep, tired from all her digging.

"Por favor, I hope you understand," said Gina the spider, who had been patiently listening to everyone. "I have to go back to work." She opted to leave the group to continue to weave her delicate silken web.

"I will go with you, Toña." Bonifacio the stinky bedbug was the only one who dared join Toña on the dangerous mission.

Toña rolled her eyes. "Compadre, you are slower than a turtle with his back legs tied together. How can you possibly believe you will ever make it to the entrance of the mansion?"

At that moment the stragglers heard the sound of a car pull up and park in the driveway. In unison they turned with curiosity to see Sacha, Guadalupe's niece, step out of her bright blue car. She swept her long dark hair over her shoulder and brought out a basket from the back seat. Toña's eyes widened, her front and back legs rubbing together. The basket was full of candies of all sizes and colors, juicy pears, shiny red apples, a small gold box of the most delicious chocolates and a bag of caramel popcorn. Balancing the basket carefully, Sacha tucked a brightly wrapped package the size of a shoebox into her tote bag and walked up the steps. Guadalupe opened the front door to greet her niece, who had just arrived to spend the weekend with her and her husband.

The door was ajar. This was the moment everyone had been waiting for.

"Meet me inside," Toña said quickly to Bonifacio.

"How will I find you?" he asked.

"Don't worry. I'll know when you arrive!" she called out to him as she flew fast like lightning toward the door that was left open. A cool draft engulfed her as she zoomed through the foyer toward the dining room.

"Ay caramba! Tia Lupe, when you opened the door for me I saw a fly come in the house," said Sacha.

"Don't worry. I will get the swatter and take care of it. It's probably in the dining room. That's where the flies come in looking for food. We will find it soon," said Guadalupe.

Sacha and her aunt and uncle looked for the fly in and around the dining room but soon gave up in favor of opening a bottle of red wine and listening to Sacha to play the guitar. They did not give the fly a second thought as if it had never existed.

Toña had strategically placed herself in a corner where she suspected Guadalupe would set down the basket. Toña the greediest, the most revolutionary of the discordant group of insects, intended to stuff herself with the leftovers of the delicious dinner being prepared for Sacha's arrival. She would have the banquet all to herself!

From her hiding spot in the pleats of the dining room curtains, Toña observed as the family enjoyed their meal, her mouth-watering. Guadalupe had prepared her niece's favorite dishes: roast pork leg with vegetables and potatoes, and sliced baguettes with garlic butter. The meal concluded with Sacha's chocolates. Guadalupe started serving coffee when Sacha handed her uncle the gift box from her tote. He unwrapped it and pulled out a handheld vacuum. To Guadalupe's delight and Toña's horror, he began picking up all the crumbs, leaving not one single morsel behind.

Three days after the delicious dinner, it was time for Sacha to go. Her sandals went flip-flop on the stairs on her way to the basement to retrieve some jars of Guadalupe's famous canned peaches to take home. She looked out the window and admired the hydrangeas bordering the garden when she noticed a piece of lint on the windowsill. After a closer look, she chuckled to herself and called out,

"Tía! Come see what I found. It's that fly we were looking for the day I arrived. It's dead with all its legs in the air."

Sacha turned away, not noticing a tiny bedbug slowly climbing up the other side of the glass.

"Dang," said Bonifacio.

Analysis of a Story

*... Making bad decisions is a part of life. Blaming others
for your decisions is a bad choice ...*
Anonymous

It's all about a word, namely the word "but." Also about how many times a particular word is used in a not-so-long short story.

My wife is one of my best critics. Without her methodical analysis, my writings would probably be just a set of ideas. She warns me that if she does not understand what she is reading, no one else would. She tells me: "I do not understand this!" "What do you mean by that?" or "Don't repeat the same word." "Instead of 'but' use 'notwithstanding or however." Additionally, she corrects and tells me to avoid using "nicaraguismos" which are idioms used in my country mostly understood just by Nicaraguans. I am including her in this group since she is so used to listening to me that she also uses "nicaraguismos."

I like the word "but." In life, there is always a "but." For example, someone may say: "I went to the theater and I really enjoyed the performance, but ..." or "I read your story and I liked it so much, but ..." The word "but" is very important. Can you imagine life without '*no ifs, ands, or buts*?' What would become of us if there were no "buts?" What would we replace them with?

But, what has all this to do with this story?

Bear with me!

On the subject of literary critics, I would like to make the following distinction. There are literary critics who make a living critiquing the works of others and there are professional editors who read the content and correct grammatical errors, spelling and punctuation. They may suggest changes to the text to enhance it, to make sure it flows naturally for the reader to easily understand what has been written. There are other literary critics who "think" they know how to evaluate the content of a story without having any professional training or experience; these are the ones who usually say: 'I liked what you wrote ... but you need to explain what happens at the end ...' I don't take their comments seriously. I categorize them as "inexperienced critics."

I consider myself among the inexperienced ones. I am not a literary critic, nor do I pretend to know how to critique a novel, a short story, a poem, particularly when it is written by a famous writer. However, — I use "however" trying to avoid using the word "but" — after reading a good number of novels, plays and short stories written in English and in Spanish, by famous writers and Latin American storytellers, I consider myself capable of distinguishing between the good, the bad and the mediocre.

It is rather interesting to analyze how a famous writer describes a situation such as the act of donning a simple garment like a pullover and makes it a complex and suspenseful event. I would like to clarify that the word "pullover" is also used in several Spanish speaking countries. It may be an Anglicism or an adaptation of the word which in English is spelled "pullover" and is a piece of clothing usually made of a warm material such as wool, has long sleeves, and to put it on, it has to be drawn over the head. It is also known as a "sweater."

Often, I have been tempted to start some of my writings in the same way as a few of the tales are started in the famed and amazing book *The Thousand and One Nights.* I remember reading some of those stories when I was growing up. I remember how some of them would begin with the familiar phrase: *Once upon a time there was a beautiful princess who lived in a distant and magic land* ... and so on. I'm going to start this brief analysis emulating these same lines.

Here it goes.

Once upon a time, there was a famous writer and storyteller, known worldwide, who during his lifetime wrote a large number of books — novels, essays as well as short stories. This writer — born in Belgium — for many years lived in a distant land in the southern cone of the Americas, Argentina. His name was Julio Cortázar. He was extremely prolific, with an amazing imagination and an astonishing ability to describe his characters and situations.

One morning in February 2013, I woke up early and after having a light breakfast I sat down in the living room in a comfortable armchair to start reading one of Cortázar's books of short stories. After randomly and arbitrarily browsing through the titles, I paused at the title of one of them that caught my attention. It was a tale in which someone is blamed for being late for a family meeting. It is always easier to blame someone or something else for your own mistakes.

In Spanish, the story is titled *No se culpe a nadie* or No One is to Blame. Later that day, while having lunch with a friend, I briefly narrated the highlights of the story to him. He listened attentively to my narration and after I finished, with a puzzled look on his face, he said: "What a boring and stupid/pointless story. What a waste of paper ...!"

I was surprised by my friend's remark; however, I thought that perhaps he was not impressed by the story itself due to the manner in which I narrated it to him. It is not my intention to blame him for such a lack of appreciation for the writing of such a famed storyteller. Maybe the fault was mine.

In short, this is what happened in the story. The author or the protagonist of the story was going to meet his spouse in front of a store to select a wedding gift. That is the beginning of the story. I say the author or the protagonist since I do not know who Cortázar is actually referring to. As usual, very skillfully he hides and disguises the identity of the protagonist without mentioning his name or that of his spouse. It's as if he is subtly hiding behind a door with opaque glass.

The author begins the story blaming the cold weather, the cold weather of autumn. He says: *The cold always complicates matters; in summer we are all so close to the world, skin to skin. But now at half-past six, his wife is waiting for him at a store to pick out a wedding gift. It's already late and he notices that the air is cool ...* He tries not to blame *anyone* but, I repeat, he already begins his story by blaming the *cold*. With this sentence, he opens the door to justify that he considers it necessary to wear something warm, in this case, a blue wool pullover to mitigate the cold caused by the wind blowing at that hour of the sunset: *I have to put on that blue pullover ...* and in front of a mirror he starts whistling a tango to amuse himself.

Starting with those introductory phrases, the author then brilliantly describes how the protagonist becomes entangled with the pullover, which in turn — the pullover — tries to avoid being worn and fights him, as if this piece of clothing was aware of the hurriedness and impatience of the man who does not want to keep his spouse waiting.

Cortázar continues: ... *autumn is all about putting on and taking off pullovers...* Here he blames the season and later his shirt that prevents the wool of the pullover to slide over his arm: *It is not easy, perhaps owing to the shirt's sticking to the wool of the pullover ...* Impatiently and despairingly he pulls the pullover sleeve until he sees that his fingers have managed to overcome the resistance of the pullover's sleeve, as they — the fingers — are already starting to feel the mild cold after having been stuck in it, feeling the friction of the pullover's wool: ... *And yet, in the twilight, the finger has the appearance of having been shriveled up and placed towards the inside, with one black nail ending in a point ...*

In the last two paragraphs, I use the word pullover nine times, including here. At this point, I would like to ask the reader the following question: Don't you think that it would have been more appropriate to title this tale: *The Pullover?* Perhaps!

Let us continue.

Somewhat desperate, the man begins to imagine that the pullover is resisting because he made the mistake of putting one of his arms through the pullover's neck and his head through one of the sleeves. It is then, when he starts to suffocate in the stale breath coming from his mouth: *It seems absurd to carry on whistling in the sudden blue darkness enveloping him, and it begins to feel hot. His face, still part of his head, ought to stick out; but his forehead and his whole face remain covered and his arms are barely halfway through the sleeves ...*

He starts to feel that his face is about to emerge: *... his head is about to make its way out but the blue wool is pressing against his nose and mouth ... suffocating him ... obliging him to breathe deeply while the wool gets moist against his mouth ...* which causes the blue color of the pullover to come off, and he thinks his face is staining blue: *Moreover, there is the taste of the pullover, this blue taste of the wool that must be staining his face, now that the humidity of his breath is mixing more and more with the wool, even if he cannot see it, because if he opens his eyes, his eyelashes bump painfully against the wool ... He is certain that his wet mouth is being enveloped with blue, then his nostrils, then his cheeks ...*

He continues, saying that perhaps it would be better to start all over again and take off the pullover.

Up to this moment, he has focused all his energies on trying to slip his hands gently through the sleeves of the pullover in order to keep his face from getting stained blue. He hasn't even remembered that his spouse is waiting for him in front of the store to buy the wedding gift. In an effort to remove the damned blue pullover, he has made several turns around his room trying to get rid of the pullover that has him completely trapped. The cold room is a silent witness to the royal battle that is taking place between a man and a garment.

In short, I guess the man is finally freed from his executioner. I say guess since the author at no time indicates that that it is the case. The very astute Cortázar lets the reader conclude that that was what happened. Cortázar, behind the opaque glass, like a master puppeteer, is manipulating the man and giving life to a piece of clothing which, in its inertia, imprisons the man in its blue wool, driving him crazy for not being able to rid himself of his oppressor.

The culmination of the battle is not the end the reader imagines: a victorious man emerges. Quite the contrary, the author concludes the story with a sentence which in my view is implausible and not related at all to the theme of the story. It reads: *... So as to arrive at last somewhere else without a hand and without pullover, somewhere where there may be a fragrant air that wraps and accompanies him and caresses him and twelve stories.* Perhaps my judgment and conclusion are incorrect, or I just didn't understand the significance of the story.

As previously suggested, I was interested in this story not only because of its title but also because of the many times the author mentions the word pullover. To make sure of what I had read, I reread it more than once. I even took the time to count the number of times he mentions the word "pullover" and also estimated the total number of words. I estimated that approximately two thousand five hundred words made up this amazing tale, in which the word pullover was used twenty-six times.

I ended up concluding that one does not err by repeating the same word several times, as I have done here, and as does the famous author Cortázar in his story. Sometimes, it is necessary to use and repeat a particular word, as long as that word is properly used and woven well into the theme of the narrative.

However, I am not going to disregard the observations of my best critic and editor. Nor am I going to stop using the word "but," provided it is properly used, in accordance with the subject of the written narrative.

While I was writing this brief analysis, I was driven by my curiosity to wonder what Cortázar would have said if he read this comment about his story, which I have titled *Analysis of a Story*. Perhaps he would have said:

"*Che pibe not echés macana ...*" (Hey kid, don't be so annoying), "*who authorized you to fiddle with my story?*"

Or,

"*Che ñato que macanudo está tu cuento, pero ...*" (Hey kid, your story is excellent, but ...)

A Despicable Betrayal

To a good friend

A dark blue 1956 Pontiac GTO sped along the Malecón. The ocean waves, agitated by the recent tropical storm, ruthlessly struck the seawalls and soaked the broad promenade, just as they had thousands of times in countless hurricanes before. It was the fall of 1959, and Miguel Ortega was driving towards the clinic of Miramar in the city of Havana. The torrential rain that had drenched the island for the past three days overpowered the windshield wipers, obstructing Miguel's view. After each stop sign, he pressed the accelerator hard. He needed to get to the clinic soon.

Adriana, his wife, who was nine months pregnant, sat uneasily in the adjoining seat. The child they had been eagerly waiting for, was a few days overdue and until now, seemed to be taking his time before making his appearance. He suddenly decided his arrival into this world, needed to be as dramatic and fast as the winds buffeting the island. Adriana feared she would not make it in time to the clinic where her physician was waiting for her and would have to give birth in the car in the middle of a hurricane. An hour after entering the maternity ward she gave birth to a healthy and beautiful nine-pound baby boy with crimson cheeks and gray-green eyes. They named him Javier.

Adriana came from a distinguished family from Havana. Like most girls her age at that social level, Adriana had lived a quiet and happy youth, enjoying the good fortune and the best education that her parents offered their only child. She earned her Ph.D. in Philosophy and Literature at the University of Havana. Like Adriana, her husband Miguel was also from a well-known family. He had a degree in Civil Engineering from the University of Havana. It was at the university where Miguel met his wife.

Miguel worked as an inspector in a government agency which required him to travel periodically throughout most of the country. Sometimes his frequent travels and prolonged absences justifiably worried Adriana who, in those times of political uncertainty and abrupt changes in the country, feared for his safety.

Like the waves that struck the island during the birth of little Javier, the violent waves of a power-hungry revolution voraciously sought to erode the foundations of the island and its inhabitants. The majority of the population discussed their concerns in secret, for fear of reprisal should they be overheard in public.

Gradually, Fidel Castro was pronouncing himself as a staunch communist. He was radically inclined toward a socio-communism by his hatred of social classes and what he called "bourgeoisie." He was nothing more than a social misfit, resentful for being born a bastard of an illicit relationship of his father and his maid. The revolutionary dictator, emulating the Russian dictator Joseph Stalin, had initiated the purge of those collaborators whom he felt could overshadow him and interfere with the implementation of his communist and leftist ideas, even though most of them had fought with him shoulder to shoulder in the Escambray Mountains. In 1961, two years after the triumph of the Revolution, Castro made it official; he declared himself a Marxist-Leninist.

The changes that Castro implemented just a couple of years subsequent to his taking over were staggering. Suddenly private enterprises and businesses were being confiscated. The agrarian reform was introduced and children were being sent to the fields to help with the sugar harvest.

Wealthy people who were opposed to Castro's communist ideas began leaving the island. The exodus was by sea and by air. The flights, known as "freedom flights," were taking off daily from the Rancho Boyeros Airport in Havana to Miami, Florida. The exit of small vessels full of terrified citizens increased. Relations between Cuba and the United States were discordant, yet they were not strained enough to break diplomatic relations. Although Castro had not fully closed the doors, little by little it became more difficult to leave Cuba.

Adriana, like thousands of Cubans, feared the communist indoctrination, the suppression of human rights, loss of their freedom and even for their own lives. She was scared of losing the *patria potestad,* as the government was threatening to start taking legal guardianship of children from their parents. The failed invasion of the Bay of Pigs in April 1961 contributed to worsening diplomatic relations between the United States and the revolutionary government of Havana.

Miguel feared being imprisoned for having worked with the "bourgeois" entities. He initiated the necessary formalities to leave the island without telling his wife. While Adriana may have been unaware of her husband's plans to escape, she often felt that Miguel was unfaithful to her. His prolonged absences from home plus his indifference toward her led her to believe he had a mistress in another city. Adriana's love for her son Javier, who was approaching his second birthday, kept her from confronting her husband and she opted to turn a blind eye.

The freedom flights gradually diminished. The strangling noose that Castro wrapped around the neck of his people slowly tightened. Miguel surprised Adriana by informing her that he had obtained a way to leave Cuba. Even more surprising was the fact that he would go alone, not having been able to secure passes for her and their son. He promised her that once established in exile he would do everything possible to send for them and start a new life, free of the fear in which they lived. Stunned and without any choice in the matter, Adriana agreed to her husband leaving the island and accepted his promise to send for her and their son in the near future.

Shortly thereafter, in October of 1962, the communist government of Moscow installed missiles on the island aiming them toward the United States. An insulted President Kennedy declared a state of emergency and threatened to destroy the missiles unraveling a confrontation with the Soviet Union widely known as the Cuban Missile Crisis. An enraged Castro cut off diplomatic relations with the United States and in retaliation, unleashed his anger toward his own people by canceling all flights and sea travels.

It is not known if Miguel anticipated what was to happen in Cuba or if his departure before the crisis was a pure coincidence. Adriana tried to talk herself out of thinking that Miguel knowingly managed his own escape and purposefully left her behind with their two-year-old son.

Adriana suffered from the absence of her husband and the anguish of not knowing his whereabouts, which was further worsened by the closure of the free exits out of the country. It was very difficult to communicate with Miguel, but Adriana was a determined and strong woman, and with that determination, she was finally able to reach him by telephone. He told her that he was employed by an agricultural company in San Francisco, that he was being substantially remunerated, and that he would soon send for her and Javier, telling her how much he loved and missed them. While Adriana was relieved to have heard his voice, her thoughts were filled with doubts, and it was difficult for her to shake them off.

Given the restrictions that the Castro government had implemented, it was almost impossible to escape the island. Desperately, people began doing the unimaginable to leave Cuba, attempting to leave in small unsafe boats, in makeshift rafts made of car tires among other things to reach freedom. The ninety miles of sea between Cuba and the tip of Florida became a watery grave for many innocent and brave Cubans who ventured to cross them. Thousands perished due to undercurrents, sharks, heatstroke and starvation on their voyage across the Straits of Florida. Those warm waters witnessed the most tragic misfortunes that Castro had forced upon his own subjugated people.

On a hot and humid afternoon, Adriana approached the U.S. Embassy to find out the necessary requirements for her and her son to reunite with her husband. After being sent from one person to the next and receiving nothing but vague answers, Adriana finally found out that in order for her to leave the island she needed the approval of her spouse. Using her scarce resources, Adriana contacted her husband informing him that the government of Cuba required his approval in order for her to leave the country. After a long pause, Miguel denied her the necessary permission, telling her that it was not the right time, as he was still trying to find a home worthy of her and her son.

Adriana realized at that moment that she would have to resolve the situation of her and her son herself. She immediately started taking serious actions to leave Cuba, despite the uncertainty of what awaited her in the United States.

She could not go to her parents for help who, due to their age and hopes that the situation in the country would improve, had chosen to stay in Cuba. They could only give Adriana moral support and encourage her to go ahead with her plans to leave the country. Fortunately, Leticia, Miguel's mother, for whom Adriana felt great respect and affection, was willing to accompany her. Leticia and her husband were well connected with the government in Havana. These contacts proved to be very valuable as she began making the necessary arrangements to leave the island. In addition to helping her daughter-in-law, it was Leticia's intention to stay close to her beloved grandson. She also longed to see Miguel, her only son, even if it meant leaving her husband behind in Cuba.

In the meantime, the suspensions of departures remained in force. Although Castro remained intransigent, he periodically accepted the humanitarian shipment of food and medicine from the United States government and from private and religious entities. These were transported, depending on the quantity, onboard medium size vessels or on larger scale ships.

Suddenly a window of hope opened for Adriana and her family to escape. It was a combination of factors, the first fueled by the need for food and medicines that were scarce in Cuba. Castro negotiated with President Kennedy to send more than $53 million in food and medicine in exchange for freeing more than a thousand political prisoners who had been captured during the failed Bay of Pigs invasion and were being kept in Havana jails. A large number of these prisoners would be transported to the United States by air and the remaining group by sea. The exchange would take place once the agreed medical supplies were delivered in Havana.

Days before the Christmas holidays, the African Pilot ship arrived at the port of Havana with its precious cargo of food and medicines. In an inconceivable gesture of humanitarianism, albeit temporary, the dictator announced that he would allow a limited number of Cubans to leave the country on that ship. Castro emphatically warned that he would only allow those who could prove that they had not been involved in subversive acts against the Revolution, and would have to be cleared by the Committee for the Defense of the Revolution of their respective neighborhoods. He would also allow Cubans who could prove to have parents, children, spouses or very close relatives in the United States. The primary function of the so-called "Committee" was to monitor residents and to report to the higher authorities any act violating the Revolution, among imposing other civil restrictions.

The second factor was when Adriana, already accustomed to the usual negative outcome experienced on previous occasions yet full of determination, approached the Committee for the Defense of the Revolution for her neighborhood where she was interviewed by the main comrade. Right away he informed her that there was no possibility to approve her petition. Desperate, she humbled herself before the interviewer, begging him in the name of the *Virgen de la Caridad del Cobre*, to find in the remotest corner of his heart a trace of pity for her, her son and her mother-in-law and grant her permission to leave the country. The comrade did not give in to Adriana's pleadings and maintained his position, saying that he was a revolutionary without any religion and did not waste time praying to any virgin. From then on, agents of the Committee began to watch Adriana's house, day and night.

Adriana anxiously informed her mother-in-law Leticia about the unsuccessful meeting with the comrade. She feared that the quota of Cubans to be approved to leave on the humanitarian ship African Pilot would soon be filled. Leticia offered to ask her husband, who also had contacts with the authorities, to speak with the head of the Defense Committee in his neighborhood, a religious and trustworthy man with greater authority than the atheist comrade in Adriana's neighborhood. After receiving verification of their information and personal background both in the capital and in exile, Leticia finally obtained a safe passage for the family. The next step would be to board the ship that would promptly leave the island after unloading its cargo of medicines and staples.

At dawn on December 26, 1962, Adriana, Javier and Leticia were driven by Leticia's husband to the port of Havana, where they would board the African Pilot, the ship that would take her into exile, to Miami, and to face her husband. Adriana felt dizzy from a whirlwind of emotions. Jubilation from obtaining safe passage clashed against the fear of it being taken away at the last moment. Her heart pounded with anticipation of finding out Miguel's true intentions and whereabouts. She felt a lump in her throat because she knew that this was not just any trip. As they neared the ship, deep in her heart she knew that she could not turn back, and even worse, that she could never return. In the few steps she would take to board the ship, she would be forever walking away from her beloved Cuba, her parents, her friends, her home, and the beautiful sunsets of that Caribbean. Adriana gazed misty-eyed at the sea that she would soon cross, at the royal palms that adorned the avenues of her beloved Havana, the city that had seen her born, grow, educate herself; the one who had witnessed her happy adolescence and more.

She hoped her mind would preserve those memories forever. She choked back her tears so as not to distress her little Javier.

As they approached the dock, the car driven by her father-in-law was suddenly stopped by revolutionary agents. In a humiliating gesture, they were ordered to get out of the car and to walk the rest of the way to the pier to board the ship. The elastic band around Adriana's waist where she had hidden a few hundred dollars was starting to irritate her, and her arms trembled from carrying Javier. The Prussian-blue wool dress, which she wore because it was a cool December, was beginning to suffocate her. The anxiety combined with the grief of leaving behind all she loved and knew tortured her. All those tumultuous feelings were suddenly put on hold when a militiaman with a Kalashnikov rifle across his chest abruptly stopped the group of walkers. Adriana feared the worst, her heart pounding. Suddenly the bearded dictator, followed by a group of militiamen, approached the checkpoint in the middle of the pier, and asked for the list of passengers, caressing the beard that distinguished him. He turned his gaze to Adriana and approached her, then took Javier in his arms, telling her:

"Hola Adriana. What a cute boy! Why do you want to take him away from Cuba?" Adriana did not respond. Sweat started trickling down her neck, not only because of the intense heat but for fear that the tyrant would take away her son.

"Adriana, do you remember the days when we attended the university together?" Castro continued.

She did not answer him initially. But, suddenly, swelling with courage she calmly replied to the dictator.

"I remember you without a beard, dressed in a pressed, white long sleeve guayabera. I hardly recognize you now."

With a sarcastic smile, he returned the child to the arms of Adriana and said plainly:

"Have a good trip, señora."

He turned around, keeping the list of passengers in his pocket, took a final look at the travelers and left without saying a word.

At around six o'clock in the afternoon, after enduring all day under the blazing sun, the African Pilot raised anchors, taking off from the port of Havana, with the loudspeakers playing *La Internacional*, the internationally known communist hymn. At the same time, the crew began to sing the National Anthem of Cuba, emboldened and imbued with emotion. Promptly the ship's captain urged them to wait to be in the open sea to sing and celebrate.

At sunrise on December 27, 1962, the African Pilot dropped its anchors in the warm waters of the port of Miami. The travelers crowded on the deck of the ship, embraced effusively, some applauding, some shouting. Some sang the National Anthem of Cuba, others hummed the National Anthem of the United States, some tried to imitate the famous Beni Moré and the *guarachera*

Celia Cruz; others prayed as they turned their gaze to the horizon, perhaps seeking a final glimpse of the beautiful country they were leaving behind. While some cried, others remained silent looking at each other and enjoying the feeling of being free, finally a few steps from the land of freedom. The land where they can freely express themselves without fear, where their rights as human beings will be respected and not humiliated; the land where they will be able to start a new life, the land where they can meet with their loved ones. Adriana, holding her sleeping son, kissed her mother-in-law's cheek, tears rolling down both their faces.

Upon landing in Miami, freed members of the Bay of Pigs group were separated and moved to a predetermined site and then sent to a temporary camp on the outskirts of Miami. The remaining civilian crew members on four buses were taken to the Tower of Liberty located on Biscayne Boulevard in Miami Beach. It is in this Tower where Adriana and her mother-in-law Leticia were interrogated by Herbert Matthews, the famous editor and reporter of the New York Times who at the beginning of the Revolution announced to the world that Castro was alive in the Sierra Maestra when he was presumed dead worldwide. It was here that they also verified that all of their documentation was in order, where they were provided with a voucher to purchase three items of clothing, a basic stipend to survive in the coming days, plus plane tickets to their next destination. Adriana had chosen to go to the city of Stockton, California since she suspected that her husband had lied about living in San Francisco. The interrogation and verification of documents would take two days. At dawn on December 29, Adriana's family boarded a plane bound for Stockton.

At midnight, a group of citizens who volunteered to care for Cuban exiles welcomed the travelers at Stockton airport and transferred them to a modest hotel in the center of the city where they would stay for a few days.

The next morning, after breakfast in the hotel's cafe, Adriana rented a car and drove by herself to an address her husband Miguel had given her once upon a time, an address she had saved as carefully as when one store a precious stone, a diamond. She climbed the three concrete steps leading to the front door. She pressed the buzzer, waited for an answer. Nobody answered. She pressed again and began to wonder if the house was vacant. She walked around the property, which was neatly kept and not overgrown or unattended. She knocked on the back door which appeared to lead to the kitchen. Again, no answer. She felt frustrated, having spent part of her little money on a rental car just to hit a dead end. Whose address was this? Confused, she returned to the hotel to inform her mother-in-law of her failed effort. Leticia suggested to Adriana to dial the telephone number where she had communicated with Miguel from Cuba. The response obtained was discouraging as the phone number had been disconnected. Disconsolate, she tried to find out the name under whom that number was registered, but the telephone company gave her a vague answer.

The doorman of the hotel, an older man of Mexican origin, had been listening to the conversation of the young woman and her mother-in-law in Spanish. After noticing her anguish, he apologizes for eavesdropping and suggests calling the police who could perhaps help her locate her husband. Adriana does not hesitate. When two agents greet her in the lobby of the hotel, she provides them with Miguel's personal information and a photo she had brought from Cuba. She informs them that her husband was allegedly working in the city of San Francisco. Adriana also gives the authorities the address of the house she had visited the previous day and asks them to find out if it is actually vacant and if possible, inquire who owns it. The authorities do not commit themselves but offer to help.

Three days passed without hearing back from the police. The stipend they had received in Miami plus the cash she had smuggled out of Cuba was rapidly depleting. On the morning of the fifth day, the policemen reappeared at the hotel with the news. They had found her husband who, like Adriana suspected, was not in San Francisco but currently resided in Stockton. Additionally, they told her that the house located at the address she provided was inhabited by a Cuban man and his wife, a native of the city of Matanzas named Joaquín Gutiérrez who had just returned from being away on vacation.

Without wasting any time, Adriana headed back to Mr. Gutiérrez's house, hopeful that he would provide her information on Miguel's whereabouts. When Mr. Gutiérrez opened the door, Adriana identified herself as Miguel Ortega's wife, adding that her mother-in-law and her two-year-old son, after much effort had been able to leave Cuba, that they were in a downtown hotel and that she was trying to find the whereabouts of her husband Miguel. Mr. Gutiérrez, as if anticipating Adriana's visit, courteously invites her into his home, asks her politely to sit down and introduces her to his wife who, after hearing the knock on the door, had come out to greet her.

It is easy to hope that everything would be cleared up for Adriana during this visit, that Joaquín Gutiérrez would divulge where Miguel was, where he worked, his telephone number, his address in the city of Stockton, and much more. But not everything is so easily solved or so quickly. Joaquín Gutiérrez simply said that he knew Miguel, that he lived in that city but he did not have Miguel's address or phone number. Frustrated, she returned to the hotel feeling empty-handed. As she entered the lobby, Adriana was approached by a well-dressed, middle-aged woman who identified herself as a social worker affiliated with the Stockton police department. She invites

Adriana to sit on one of the yellow vinyl chairs — the ones imitating fine leather — located in a semi-private corner of the lobby.

Adriana is confused yet hopeful for some good news. Very matter-of-factly, the woman tells Adriana that Miguel Ortega, her husband, was living in Stockton with his new wife.

During his trip to Miami, Miguel had met a Spanish woman named Gloria who was returning to the United States after a short tourist visit to Havana. This brief encounter in the air turned into a passionate love affair on land. After spending a few romantic days enjoying the sun on the beaches of Miami, Gloria invited Miguel to visit her in the city of Stockton where she worked as a professor at the state university. Miguel accepted the invitation, later relocating to that city. He eventually moved into her home and soon after, sealed their love relationship by marrying her. Never did Miguel reveal to his new bride that he had a wife and son waiting for him in Cuba.

Adriana freezes as the blood drains from her face. There is a deafening buzz in her ears. She feels as if the world is disappearing under her feet. She wants to vomit, to expel all the jumbled feelings that had taken possession of her since her last days in Cuba. Gathering her last bit of strength, she restrains her feelings and quietly thanks the agent. She returns to the hotel room where she locks herself in the bathroom. She looks in the mirror yet does not recognize the woman staring back at her. She crumples to the floor and turns on the shower in the hopes that her son and mother-in-law won't hear her sobbing.

Alerted perhaps by his friend or by the social worker, Miguel rushes to the hotel and asks the porter for the number of the room where his family is staying. He hurries to room number 221 on the second floor. Sitting on the edge of one of the beds, while his son played on the floor with a miniature car, Miguel arrogantly tried to justify his inexcusable, devastating and blatant treachery without any guilt or remorse. He does not succeed in convincing his mother and much less his wife. Just as she had filled herself with courage when Castro approached her on the pier of Havana, Adriana calmly exposes her lying husband of the theatrical farce in which he is living. Immediately demanding a divorce and clenching her teeth she tells him:

"You have committed a despicable betrayal, the worst crime that a man can commit, miserably deceiving your wife, and your son! You do not deserve God's forgiveness and will never get mine!"

Soon after, in the neighboring state of Nevada, a divorce officially ends their marriage. Leticia has decided to stay with Adriana. With few financial resources, the young mother does not know what to do, or who to turn for help. She does not know anyone in Stockton, or anyone to guide her on what to do.

When one fears that the sky is shattered, or when one feels that all the doors have closed, always and I underline always, a silver ray of light reflects in the calm waters of an immense sea, there is someone with an open hand who says, "Come, I will help you!"

Two days after the dramatic and devastating meeting with her former husband, in the lobby of the hotel which she would soon have to leave, Adriana met with Miguel's friend Joaquín Gutiérrez, who had come to visit her accompanied by his wife Alina. After exchanging hugs and the customary greetings, Joaquín confessed to Adriana that he was aware of what had happened and apologized for having denied knowing her husband's whereabouts. In turn, he tells her that the doors to his house are fully open for her and her small family.

Not accustomed to accepting gifts out of pity, Adriana declines the offer. Joaquín insists and convinces her by saying that it will be temporary to allow her to organize her thoughts and plan her next steps. Adriana accepts the invitation to move in with her new friends, where she would stay a little more than two months.

During the months at the home of the Gutiérrez, Adriana does not rest. Like the Phoenix, she awakens and springs out from the desert sands and decides to make the best of her new city, that city that had given her shelter. After a short period, she was able to revalidate her university degrees and later accepted a position as a Spanish professor at a school in the city. Once settled into her new job, earning a modest salary enough to support her son and mother-in-law she is able to rent a small home. The lights of the lanterns that shined on her new home not only illuminate the streets of the neighborhood, but also begin to shine around Adriana's life.

By mid-April 1963, the sporadic rains falling in the coastal and central part of California had dissipated; the Pacific sea breezes had faded and the severe winter snows in the nearby mountains melted away, giving rise to the scorching heat in this part of the state. When the meadows and hills covered with green mantles caused by the fleeting downpours turn into yellow gold, the Gutiérrez adorned the small garden at the back of their house in preparation to celebrate their wedding anniversary.

Adriana, one of the many guests, wore a beautiful summer outfit very appropriate for that time of the year. Joaquín, the host, put the finishing touches on some savory steaks on his newly acquired grill. Since she did not know most of the guests, Adriana, sporting a white brimmed hat, with a glass of soda in her hand, retreated into one of the corners of the patio close to the table where some of the guests enjoyed the drinks that the Gutiérrez were serving. The aromas of the delicious food and the laughter of the guests made the atmosphere familiar and friendly.

One of the guests, Bryan Wilson, a US Army brigade colonel who had learned of Adriana's educational background, approached her politely. After introducing himself, he engaged in a casual conversation, in which nothing concrete is discussed. However, the colonel, knowing Adriana's academic background, had a purpose in mind. During the course of the conversation, he informed her of an open position as a Spanish professor at the Monterey Language School in the city of Monterey, on the central coast of California. He tells Adriana that she would be an ideal candidate and encourages her to apply.

Since Adriana lacked knowledge of the history of Monterey, the first capital of California, she excused herself. The colonel smiled after hearing Adriana's answer and tells her that many foreign languages were taught at that school to members of the US Government. Relieved and encouraged, Adriana thanks the colonel and this time accept his card where he had written the address of the school.

After a battery of interviews with army officers in charge of the administration of the Monterey Language School and obtaining the required clearance of the United States Government, Adriana accepts the position of Spanish professor. Later, accompanied by her mother-in-law Leticia, who keeps her promise to stay with her, and her son Javier, they move to the city of Monterey, staying in a rental apartment near her new job.

During this difficult and dramatic period, Javier has only noticed very superficially all the vicissitudes and sacrifices that his mother has made in order to escape from the communist island, including all the hardships to which she has been exposed upon her arrival in this country and the unmasking of the farces and lies which his father had made them go through. Javier only remembers seeing his father briefly in the lobby and in the hotel room in Stockton. Years later, Adriana's parents leaving everything behind, left Cuba via Spain where Don Ignacio, her beloved father soon passes away. Adriana's mother-in-law, after a few years in the United States, leaves Adriana and her grandson and joins her son and later returns to Cuba.

During all those years Adriana had stood out as one of the best Spanish professors at the Language School. She had been distinguished with numerous recognitions and prizes. All of Adriana's achievements had resulted in well-deserved promotions and in salary increases which allowed her to move from the apartment to a modest home that she purchased with her savings. It is then that Adriana brings her mother from Spain and lives with her for many years enjoying her much loved grandson Javier.

Adriana eventually meets Alex in the corridors of the School. They had participated in social gatherings held annually with the professors of the various linguistic departments of the School. Alex Adriano, a young unmarried man from a city south of Moscow, was a Russian professor at the School. About mid-1972, Adriana and Alex occasionally sat together in the cafeteria to share their lunch. As could be anticipated, they start a friendly conversation exchanging details about their lives among many other things. During those brief encounters, Alex was not only overwhelmed by Adriana's beauty, but he was also impressed by her culture and her vast knowledge of art and music. Alex fell madly in love with Adriana and showered her with gifts, theater invitations, and in the end, asked her to marry him.

Adriana wanted to leave her son something more valuable than a house or a handful of dollars. After all, money vanishes like the smoke of a cigarette in the air, material things come and go. Adriana wanted to leave her son something more valuable, and there is only one thing that Adriana had not been able to achieve, and that is the legacy of her love for Cuba. She wanted to give her son her memories of all those tropical sights, the Caribbean sun, the white sands of the island she was forced to leave many years back. She wished to make a copy of all that history, the one she copied in her mind, a book of her memories printed with indelible ink of when she left her beloved Cuba that hot day of December 1962 more than half a century ago.

Adriana is unsure at first that she can achieve it; she doubts that she can imprint her memories into her son's mind through books, magazines, maps, and stories. No! She will not be satisfied and will fight to the end to pass those live postcards to her son.

"Live, yes, what better than a visit to Cuba!" she said and at the same time she asks herself:

"How can I do it? I am not allowed to travel to Cuba."

Adriana is more than accustomed to overcoming obstacles and will not give up until achieving her dream.

More than half a century after leaving Cuba, Adriana and her son Javier climb the steps of flight number 2075, an American Airlines flight bound for Havana. This time Javier is no longer a child. He is a man and just as his mother helped him up the stairs of the African Pilot, the ship that brought them to the land of freedom, he now takes his mother's arm to help her climb the stairs to the airplane. At last Adriana triumphs. The dream that she held onto for so many years has become a reality. In a few hours, she will be standing on the soil of her beloved Cuba. She has returned to her beloved island. She has fulfilled her dream!

Yes! Adriana and Javier returned from Cuba. What happened during that visit? What were her son's impressions, hers? It is not known.

Dreams or Nightmares?

The interpretation of dreams is the royal road to a knowledge of the unconscious activities of the mind.
Sigmund Freud

According to Isabel Allende ...*when we dream we enter into a mysterious dimension where we live another life. In certain cultures, the dreams are an essential part of existence, they guide, inform, connect, prophesize, alert, and are the connection with the spirits and divinity ...*

Much has been written about how to interpret our dreams. I also have read some books about this mysterious and fascinating topic. I learned that they last only seconds and take place when we are deeply asleep or at a very early hour of the morning when we are to be awakened. Most often we wake up after each of our dreams.

To me, dreams are a question mark, a mystery that my uncomplicated mind has been unable to decipher. Most of my dreams, which I could easily call nightmares, occur at any time during my sleep. During my dreams, I am capable of visualizing beautiful landscapes, amazing situations, unbelievable acts and things, absurd events, premonitions ... which I am unable to see or visualize in real life.

The following is a narrative of three of my dreams which I was able to capture, remember and record with a great deal of difficulty; even more difficult was to organize them in a written form.

The first one could be titled "the scaffold" or "the execution," the second could be called "the train" and the third "the calling."

I disagree with Allende's theory that through dreams I live in *another life* or if *they are the connection with the spirits or the divine.* I would like to leave it to the reader to interpret their meaning.

I. The Scaffold

The carpenter in charge of building the scaffold took a large maul with his right hand and with his left a nail about twelve inches long and one inch in diameter. With some difficulty and using all his strength, he took the heavy maul and stroke the nail on the head. The thickness of the nail broke the board into several pieces. It was then that someone in the multitude of people who had gathered in the plaza to witness the execution shouted: "Imbecile! Find a smaller nail so you don't break the board. Why don't you use a regular hammer?"

The carpenter turned and searched for the person who had yelled at him but he could not find anyone. There was nobody present; the plaza was empty.

The executioner tested the trap door where the prisoner who had been sentenced to die by hanging was to stand. He let go of the heavy sandbag and the trap door violently swung open hanging just from two steel hinges.

It was around five-thirty in the morning. The execution was going to take place at six in the morning, before sunrise. I knew that I had only a very short time left to live. I was thirsty ... I asked for some water but they denied it to me.

The sheriff tied my hands with a rope behind my back and helped me go up the ten steps toward the platform of the scaffold. The black hood that covered the executioner's head had only holes for his eyes and nose. Gently he took me by my shoulders and slowly walked me toward the trap door at the center of the scaffold. With both hands the executioner placed a black hood similar to his over my head, except mine did not have any openings for the eyes or nose. With the right hand, he took the heavy rope and put it around my neck making sure that the noose was set on the left side of the neck. He tested the rope to make sure that it was strung out tightly. I hesitated some while stepping onto the door with my right foot, then my left. I could clearly hear the murmur of the audience. I clenched both hands into fists as if to gather as much strength as possible to prepare for the violent jolt that would break my neck. The thought of a slow death terrified me. I wanted a quick death ... I did not want my body to be left dangling in a void.

Someone in the audience shouted again: "Why don't you hang him once and for all and get it over with?"

Through a tiny rip in my black hood, I tried to identify who had raised his voice calling for my death. But there was no crowd. The plaza was empty. The sheriff, the executioner, and the judge were the only ones' present.

The judge ordered the executioner to proceed with the execution and the executioner pulled the rope, releasing the door beneath my feet. The sandbag fell down and violently struck the earth below leaving the four by four opening where my body had been left hanging with my feet touching the empty space; I felt the noose pressing on the left side of my neck, asphyxiating me. My body had not fallen, my neck was not broken. I was still alive ... and I woke up.

II. The Train

The train rolled along over the steel rails without making a single sound. It appeared as if the wheels had been made of black rubber. The trip from Montenegro to Las Palmas was taking longer than usual; two and one-half hours. The heat inside the car where I was sitting was suffocating. Holding on to one of the golden-colored metal bars and to the back of the benches along the aisle, I tried to open each one of the windows but it was not possible. It appeared as if they had been nailed shut, not ever to be opened. The Indian, who was seated in the back of the car and pretending to be snoozing, noticed that my effort was in vain. He then broke the glass of one of the windows with the top of a bottle and from it, he drank a greenish liquid. Looking at me, he shrugged his shoulders and motioned as if saying: "Go ahead; I just took care of your problem."

I approached the window with the broken glass and took a long deep breath, stuck my head out and looked toward the front and back. I was unable to understand how the cars of the train were being pulled forward; there was no locomotive pulling the endless number of yellow cars.

Suddenly, all dressed in green, the conductor crossed over one of the cars and approached the Indian and rudely asked him to show him his ticket. The Indian did not have it, raising the conductor's doubts as to how he had boarded the train.

Infuriated, the conductor took the Indian by his blue pullover and threw him out of the broken window. As he hit the ground he was suddenly devoured by a swarm of silvery giant ants, similar to a school of hungry piranhas. Without thinking and fearing to end up like the Indian I told the conductor I was getting off at the El Sauce station.

Two girls dressed in school uniforms sitting in the middle of the car were staring at me, giggling as if I had clowns all over my face. They also informed the conductor they would be exiting at the El Sauce station. Meanwhile, a middle-aged slightly balding man carrying a bunch of gladiolas was looking sneakily at the conductor, at the two girls with school uniforms, and at me. I was trying to avoid his sneaky look.

When the train approached the next station, the station of Las Flores, two women who were waiting for the train on the platform hurriedly approached the door of the car and showed the conductor their filthy tickets. The conductor would not allow them to board the train because of the stench of rotten meat coming from the baskets that they were carrying on their heads; it smelled as if they were carrying a dead animal.

From the broken glass window, the one broken by the Indian, I could hear the obscenities the two women were yelling at the conductor, and with rage, they threw their filthy tickets at him.

It was at this station where the slightly balding middle-aged man stepped down from the car bumping against one of the women. The other woman pushed him to the ground causing him to drop his gladiolas in the mud. Unable to clean the mud off his gladiolas he started to weep to the point the tears fell off his cheeks, staining his white shirt.

The train was noticeably picking up speed. It was as if the train's black wheels were rolling over white buttered rails. The conductor tried to stop it but was not successful. Suddenly the train stopped abruptly and the conductor pointed toward me telling me that this was my station. When the door opened, I looked outside; I attempted to exit the car but I couldn't … the steps were missing. The only thing that I was able to see was a gelatinous mass covered with millions of buzzing greenish flies and in the distance, I saw a brilliant light. It must have been the sunlight filtering through my window that woke me up.

III. The Calling

It had been raining most of the night. At first, I heard a light drizzle falling but the rain got stronger as the night wore on. I could clearly hear the rain gurgling through the aluminum gutters and downspouts at the corner of the house. I was able to see the green hands of the clock on the wall of my bedroom. It was four-thirty in the morning. The rain was falling torrentially.

I was not able to contain my curiosity. The noise from the people outside sounded like the noise of water pouring outside the glass window of my room. As I normally do when I get up, I combed my slightly graying thick hair. Taking the hand lantern from the night table I approached the edge of the window. I moved the embroidered drapes toward the left side and looked outside to see what was happening.

I could not be more surprised. I could not believe what I was seeing. Someone had enclosed the entire perimeter of our house with a ten feet high brick wall. I could still hear the noise being made by the people on the other side of the wall. However, the darkness of the night prevented me from seeing what was happening on the other side. I could not make out who was making such a loud noise. The light from my lantern was not strong enough to illuminate the houses on the other side.

I did not remember having seen anyone build such a wall. Suddenly the rain stopped. I walked outside the house and with much difficulty, I climbed the ten-foot wall. What I saw was shocking to me. There was a blinding light originating from the faraway hills. 'It could not be the sun,' I thought, rubbing my eyelids trying to get used to the light. "It is only four-thirty in the morning," I said to myself.

My neighbors' houses had all disappeared. There was a big crowd of people. Someone in the multitude yelled at me, "Get down from the wall and come join our group," but I could not identify the one who was calling me.

Fearing the worst, I launched myself over the wall believing that my fall would be cushioned by the thick gray grass below, but the ten-foot fall seemed more like an eternity. I felt my body floating in an endless vacuum until I finally landed in a spongy substance similar to the marine sponges that are extracted from the depths of the ocean.

A white-haired older woman with a very friendly face took me by the hand, showing me the way toward an enormous wooden stage where there was a large group of men and women of different nationalities. They were all dressed in brilliant red tunics, their heads were adorned with golden tiaras, and everyone wore belts made out of golden painted laurel leaves. Each had a small harp and as I approached them, they started playing a beautiful melody which I had never heard.

On the left-hand side of the stage, a chorus accompanied the harpists and on the right side, a group of children danced to the sound of the melody being played. All were dressed in bright yellow tunics.

I was so absorbed admiring such a beautiful spectacle and listening to the beautiful but unrecognizable tune, I did not notice a child approaching me. He was of medium stature, not older than ten years old; his eyes were blue and his blond hair was lighter than gold. His head was adorned with a tiara covered with diamonds, rubies, and emeralds. With his right hand he took my left hand and looking at me in the eyes he asked me,

"Did you come to pray?"

How deceiving are our dreams??!

A Rogue Wave

A love story

To my granddaughter Cecilia

G ood afternoon, my name is Jorge Esparza, today is July 31, 1999. I find myself sitting on a wooden bench in Lovers' Point Park in the small town of Pacific Grove, California. I am delightedly admiring the beautiful views which the Pacific Ocean offers me at dusk and waiting for the celebration of the Feast of Lanterns to begin.

I take advantage of this opportunity when my wife and my two children have gone to buy some sodas and hamburgers at the nearby restaurant, to share with you a beautiful but tragic love story. I am an older man, close to fifty, my hair has begun to whiten, and after years of being exposed to the sun while working in the vineyards, the color of my skin has tanned dark brown. I do not consider myself a handsome man, nor slender, I am of medium stature scarcely six feet tall, nevertheless, in my youthful days, I must have made a good impression on Marta for her to notice me and later share with me the rest of our lives.

When I met Bernardino, we were both barely five years old. Bernardino was eleven months older than I was, and perhaps this was the reason why instead of calling me Jorge, he affectionately called me Jorgito. At that age, he felt more important than me. He tried to teach me how to do this or that, maybe he thought he was my older brother. Although we differed in age, this inconsequential difference did not diminish the friendship and affection we had between us. I did not like being called Jorgito, but I chose to ignore him; we were very good friends and I was not going to allow a nonsense like that to cause discord between us. After all, that was my name. To annoy him or to avenge myself, instead of Bernardo, I called him Bernardito, but later I ended up calling him Bernardino. He didn't care.

Lorena, my younger sister, was only ten years old and did not have many friends in the neighborhood, the girls were all quinceañeras and did not pay much attention to her; she had no choice but to play with us the street games that we often played on the dusty streets of the neighborhood where our two families had their humble houses.

My parents and Bernardino's parents had emigrated from Guadalajara in the late fifties looking for a better life or in search of "the American dream" as it is if often called. They both decided to settle in the city of Gonzales where they coincidentally ended up buying their houses on the same dusty street. It was the proximity to the fertile fields of the Valley of Salinas that made them chose that particular California city. My father worked in the fields growing asparagus and artichokes and Bernardino's father labored in the orange and olive groves.

As boys of no more than thirteen or fourteen years old, we ventured on hunting expeditions beyond our dry, arid valley and into the cool waters of the Salinas River. Lorena did not accompany us on these expeditions. Armed with a .22 caliber Winchester we hunted for rabbits or pigeons on the slopes of the Gavilan mountains, those beautiful mountains where the cliffs scrape the skies, where the eagles nest and the condors soar; those granite peaks to the east of Gonzales, or Pinnacles, as they are called. My father was never supportive of our escapades, but we were adventurous boys with energies to burn and in the end, he turned a blind eye and enjoyed grilling the rabbits which we managed to hunt.

My sister was not fond of our escapades either, she felt left alone but she entertained herself by reading fairy tales and romantic novels by Corín Tellado. At night Lorena daydreamed, she would think of the afterlife, and often gazed out her bedroom window at the moon. She would light yellow and red candles, passionately dreamed of the Pacific Ocean and although she had never seen its waters, she longed for one day to be able to see that ocean, to be able to touch its waters with her own hands.

My father was always protective of Lorena, she was his little queen, the light of his eyes, his only daughter. Among the many stories that my sister read, one of her favorites was the story of the Feast of Lanterns. This amazing tale is about a fleeing Chinese couple — Queen Topaz and her low-born lover, Chang —. The representation of this story is annually celebrated in the small town of Pacific Grove. At the end of every month of July, Lorena begged my father to take her to that town next to the city of Monterey on the central coast of California.

I have learned that for more than one hundred years the citizens of Pacific Grove have commemorated the Feast of Lanterns with a festival and a pageant along Lighthouse Avenue ending at Lovers' Point Beach. The celebration coincides with the end of the Chautauqua Assembly, a cultural and educational gathering that originated in the state of New York at the end of the 1800s near the lake of the same name. The festivities in Pacific Grove are a family event attended by students from neighboring schools and a large majority of its citizens. People also arrive from Monterey as well as from other nearby towns. Most of the local homes, as well as the stores along Lighthouse Avenue, are decorated with colorful silk or paper lanterns with Chinese motifs. These multicolored lanterns are hung from the porches of homes as well as from branches of the beautiful cypresses that adorn the broad boulevard.

To be able to narrate this love story accurately, I had to search the contents of a blue trunk that my sister, very carefully kept at the foot of her bed. The trunk later was stored together with the rest of her books in the attic of our house. That's where I found an old book with notations in the margins, underlined phrases, and paragraphs highlighted in bright yellow or red, the same colors as the candles she lighted. The small book was quite worn perhaps by the number of times she had read it. The book described in detail the origin of the Feast of Lanterns.

No one knows exactly who was the first person to tell the story of the lanterns, which is based on another tale, the Legend of the Blue Willow, a fiction story for children. It is believed that the first one who narrated it was a Chinese storyteller who began by describing the love of a young man, Chang, for a pretty maiden named Koong-se and how both flew into the heavens and eternity in the form of two white doves. The story unfolds in a faraway land called Cathay, now known as China. During the reign of the emperors there existed a high official of the Chinese empire, a powerful and wealthy Mandarin named T'so Ling who possessed vast properties of very fertile land ... His daughters, six in all, whom he had procreated with his beloved princess, were his most precious possessions. They all had been named for precious stones. Koong-se, his eldest daughter, the one he named Topaz was the light that brightened his eyes. Topaz spent her leisure time in her little summer house amusing herself by weaving beautiful tapestries of white silk and listening to the tales and adventures of old Cathay that were told by her faithful former wet-nurse Chun Soy.

So proud was her father of Topaz's beauty that he dreamed of crowning her as the queen of his vast domains, and without thinking, he decided to execute his plan. He summoned the nobility, all the princes and potentates, the lords and rulers of his immense dominion and other high officials to witness the coronation of his beautiful and beloved daughter Topaz. Among the guests came an old Mandarin who, as a gift for the coronation, brought with him an immense wooden chest filled with gold and precious stones. His gift extremely impressed T'so Ling, Topaz's father, who decided that the old Mandarin would be an excellent and formidable husband for his daughter, and without consulting her, resolved to combine the coronation and the wedding of Topaz with the rich Mandarin.

Upon learning of her father plans Topaz, who had fallen madly in love with Chang, she felt revolting disgust and her disenchantment with her father was such, that in order to take revenge on him, she decided to throw herself into the dark waters of the sea with the purpose of drowning and freeing herself forever from his domination. After discovering what his daughter had done, T'so Ling alerted all the neighbors who jumped into the sea in their canoes and small boats lighting up the night with their bright lanterns in search of

Topaz who had already met her beloved Chang. Even though T'so Ling had offered a large sum of money as a reward, no one had been able to find her since she and her lover Chang had escaped into eternity in the form of two beautiful white doves.

In the version that is commemorated in Pacific Grove the lovers, like the chrysalis of two butterflies become two beautiful monarchs painted orange and black, fleeing and flying towards the beyond, towards the blue and purple firmament of nightfall.

That's how the story of the Legend of the Blue Willow went.

My parents, good observers as they were, and with many years of experience, had noticed what was happening between Lorena and Bernardino. They watched as they both looked at each other, they held hands while they walked to school. That innocent friendship had grown into a mature love relationship. They both had secretly sworn to each other once at a mass they attended in the church of San Marcos. My sister and Bernardino were madly in love with each other. Neither my father nor Bernardino's were like Topaz's father who objected to his daughter's marriage to the humble young Chang. Although Bernardino was not wealthy like the old Mandarin, nor did our parents own large swaths of land, they both approved of their relationship. Bernardino, my childhood friend, could only offer my sister his fervent love and so had told my parents when he asked for Lorena's hand. However, both my parents and Bernardino's agreed that the wedding would have to be celebrated after they had completed their studies.

Lorena's beauty was enviable, she had turned into a lovely young woman. She was of medium stature with pale white skin. She had brilliant black eyes and her straight jet-black hair fell down to the middle of her back. Bernardino was a handsome young man who, by his way of consciously upright walking looked like a very important person.

Bernardino was able to get an education and finished his studies in accounting thanks to the help of his parents. To be close to his beloved Lorena he decided to return to Gonzales and obtained a job at a fruit processing plant in that city. I, on the other hand, chose not to attend college; I decided to work at one of the vineyards in Napa Valley where after working for two years, I obtained a master sommelier's certificate which allowed me to secure a job in a vineyard nearby the town of Calistoga, north of Napa Valley. It was there where I met my wife and we currently reside.

Not surprisingly, one of my sister's wedding requests was to have Bernardino take her to the town of Pacific Grove to witness the celebration of the Feast of Lanterns. Her dream of so many years was finally becoming a reality. Not only would they spend their honeymoon in that picturesque town by the Monterey Bay, but they would also be present during that celebration, the one she had dreamed of for so long. What more could she ask, to be with her beloved Bernardino on that memorable occasion? The date for the festive event was set for July 30, 1971. Lorena had just turned twenty-one.

As I mentioned, my father was not a wealthy man, nor did he have vast properties of fertile land like Topaz's father T'so Ling, the Chinese Mandarin in the Legend of the Blue Willow. However, to mark the occasion of Lorena's wedding, they invited their neighbors and friends, hired a band of mariachis to enliven the party in the Mexican style. To celebrate the happy occasion my mother cooked traditional and delicious Mexican dishes of different varieties. Happiness reigned in our house; Padre Alberto, who officiated the wedding ceremony, was also present to bless both families which now bonded as one.

At the end of the happy wedding celebration, the couple drove over an hour to the town of Pacific Grove where they were to spend their honeymoon night at the Seven Gables Inn across from Lovers' Point Park. To Lorena, it seemed unbelievable that after so many years her dreams were so close to becoming a reality, she was about to witness the longed-for celebration of the lanterns with the man she loved. At dusk, all the preparations for the start of the Feast of Lanterns had been completed and to be closer to the performance Lorena and Bernardino selected the best spot where they could witness the entire show. But Lorena wanted to be even closer to the ocean, to be able to take pictures, to be able to touch and feel the ocean for the first time. Bernardino objected but she insisted.

My father often warned us not to get close to uncharted waters, 'there are treacherous waters' he would say. He could never understand why some people insisted on being as close to the water as possible. They would climb slippery and rugged rocks, sometimes falling and hurting themselves, others not so lucky would fall in the ocean. Among some of my father's warnings was the one about never turning our back on the sea. That so attractive and mysterious ocean can change in a split of a second and become violent.

Already the sun was hiding on the other side of the Pacific. The waters were calmer than on other occasions on that last day of July. The sky had a bluish-gray color as the sun was starting to set. Confident of how peaceful the ocean looked, Lorena insisted on descending the rocky cliff to stand by the rocky shore, to touch the cold waters of the Pacific with her bare feet.

Lorena and Bernardino were so absorbed enjoying the beautiful spectacle and the colorful sights of the sky, that they turned their backs to the ocean. Suddenly, and without warning, a shocking and enormous wave rushed violently toward where the newlyweds stood wrapping them in a gray sheet of foam and dark water. Bernardino desperately struggled and was able to cling to one of the slippery rocks lacerating his arms and legs, but Lorena was not as fortunate and unable to do so, she disappeared under the waves. Hysterically, Bernardino shouted her name and after hearing his desperate calls, all the participants of the event of the Feast of Lanterns, in their small canoes threw themselves into the sea in search of Lorena. Everyone wanted to help, it all happened so fast. But their search was useless, in vain, the dark and cold Pacific Ocean had taken Lorena; its hungry and violent waters had swallowed another victim, claimed another life. Without wasting time or giving it a second thought, Bernardino hurried to alert the Coast Guard, who unsuccessfully searching all night, did not find Lorena.

Bernardino did not know what to do, who to turn to; he was devastated, he wanted to take his own life. He felt guilty and responsible for the death of his lovely wife. He thought he should have stopped her from going down the rocky promontory. It was a tragic accident and he did not know how and what he was going to tell their parents. In his folly, he lost consciousness and later woke up at a nearby hospital. He cried disconsolately, he felt life was pointless and empty. A violent depression seized him.

My childhood friend came to me in his dark hours, and together we explained to our parents the unfortunate and tragic accident. They were devastated as well but never for one moment blamed Bernardino for the death of their daughter, my sister Lorena.

A year after the tragic accident, Bernardino invited me to accompany him to Pacific Grove to commemorate the disappearance of his beloved wife. He wanted to be present during the celebration of the Feast of Lanterns to throw a bouquet of Lorena's favorite flowers — the beautiful reddish and orange poppies, the flower of California — into the sea. I accepted to go along with my friend. We stayed at the same place where a year earlier, he and Lorena would have spent their honeymoon, the Seven Gables Inn. The following day at dusk the sea was unusually calm, the sky was displaying its favorite colors, gray, pink, ruby, and purple. As we both approached the rocky promontory at Lovers Point Beach, Bernardino acted nervous, as if he was in a hurry. He took a few steps ahead of me and seemed not to be paying attention to the celebrations and fireworks exploding in the sky all over the Bay. He stared at me with that look that had always characterized him. I was afraid and didn't know what he was about to do. He took the bouquet of poppies in his left hand and with his right gripping mine, said:

"Goodbye my brother and dear friend, forgive me for all the pain I have caused our respective families. Today I have decided to take these beautiful poppies to my beloved Lorena." He turned around and jumped into the ocean. He swam far until I could no longer see him.

I chose not to rescue him, nor alert anyone.

This is how I remember my sister's story!

Witchcraft

O n Friday, July 16, 1961, José María Gutiérrez carefully parked his dark gray 1959 Toyota on R Street, one of the streets that cross 16th Street in Washington, D.C., a block and a half from the Grand Temple of the Rosicrucians. The scorching July heat and humidity would have encouraged anyone to dress down, not to wear a coat and tie, but nothing could prevent José María from wearing the new dark brown polyester suit he had bought the day before at the Sears Roebuck department store. He was going pay a surprise visit to his friend Cornelia Ruiz hoping to renew those feelings he once felt for her many years ago. José María had not seen Cornelia in the past six years, it was during this period when she had changed her address after the death of her husband Pedro.

José María got out of his car, put on his coat and deposited four twenty-five cent coins in the parking meter. After making sure all the windows and doors were closed and locked, he started walking toward the house of his dear friend Cornelia.

"Could she be as beautiful as the last time I saw her?" José María anxiously asked himself.

Pulling a white handkerchief from his right trouser pocket, José María wiped the sweat from his forehead and then straightened the knot of his black tie while making sure that the light brown handkerchief that peeked out of his coat pocket was well fitted and still perfumed with the scent of Agua Florida cologne. From the pocket of his white shirt, he pulled out a tiny yellow paper where he had written her address in Washington, D.C. He unfolded the paper to make sure the address was correct. It was, he was just half a block from where he had parked his car.

Before he rang the bell, and in anticipation of seeing Cornelia after so many years, José María nervously looked at himself again in a small mirror he kept in one of his pockets, he wanted to make sure he looked his best. José María was a man of medium stature, with a light brown complexion; his eyes were the same color as the suit he wore, brown. The small cut on his upper lip was well hidden under a slight mustache very close to his aquiline nose; the little hair he had left was combed toward his wide forehead to cover the baldness that overwhelmed him. Although José María was a man in his fifties, his friends called him El Nene, the Baby.

"You look good José María!" He murmured to himself, making sure his brown shoes were also clean and shiny. He walked down the three steps in front of the door and rang the doorbell.

As he waited, he heard a crackling voice coming from inside the house: *"Open the door Pedrito, someone is ringing the doorbell."* A few seconds later Cornelia opened the door, not Pedrito.

"Oh, Don José María, what an unexpected and pleasant surprise to see you after all these years, I am so glad to see you!" In a half-weeping voice, Cornelia welcomed him. "Thank you very much for coming. Please come in." Cornelia invited José María, who hugged her and kissed her on the cheek.

Cornelia was touched by the unannounced visit of her old friend. Like José María had feelings for her, she also had amorous feelings towards him; however, despite being so happy to see him, it was difficult for her to hide her sadness.

Cornelia could not have been more than fifty years old; she was a woman of medium height and looked younger than her age. Her straight hair, with a flaming reddish tinge, was cut short, graciously framing and accentuating her white complexion; her lips were painted the same color as her hair. Her shining black eyes, although sad, showed features of a cheerful and vivacious past. Cornelia was still an attractive woman.

After the death of her husband Pedro, for a modest price, Cornelia had rented a small basement apartment in a two-story row house on R Street, Northwest. She occupied the largest of the rooms and her son Pedrito occupied the smaller bedroom. Cornelia still owned the French Provincial style furniture that her husband gave her as a wedding gift. The atmosphere in the apartment was stale and the humidity was very palpable. To mitigate the odor and humidity she had opened the kitchen and living room windows which led to an adjacent alley. The dining room was rather small and the furniture fitted snugly against the dark green walls where three pictures of royal palms and other beach motifs hung close to each other. Very attentively Cornelia took off José María's coat and hung it on a coat rack near the front door and courteously offered him to sit down on a red upholstered brocade chair.

"Can I offer you anything to drink? Like a cold lemonade?" asked Cornelia.

"No, thank you very much, perhaps later," said José María.

"Open the door Pedrito, someone is ringing the doorbell." Again, the husky and brittle voice was heard coming from the kitchen area.

"Don't worry Don José María," said Cornelia. "It's Napoleón, my foul-mouthed parrot who repeats whatever I say, even when no one knocks on the door. Please ignore him."

Answering Napoleón's call, Pedrito, Cornelia's son, dressed in shorts and a white T-shirt with a small hole under his right arm rushed to the living room.

"Unnnudo!" "Unnudo!" "Noooo!" "Unuuudo!" said Pedrito, who had trouble expressing himself due to his muteness. "What do you want, Pedrito?" Cornelia asked her son. "Say hello to Don José María and go back to your room and watch television."

Pedrito was no longer the same Pedrito that José María had seen six years earlier, now he was a twenty-six-year-old man still living with his mother due to his muteness and a mild mental disability.

"Noooo!" "Noooo!" "Noooo!" "Unuuudo!" Pedrito answered, and as he was exiting the living room, with his right hand he waved goodbye to José María who responded by also waving with his right hand.

"Pedrito is a grown man, what a shame about his impairment." José María commented.

"I know, but he is my son, and I cannot afford to place him in an institution. It's a cross that I have to carry ..."

"Tell me, Doña Cornelia, how's your daughter Vivian, what is she doing lately?" José María asked.

"Oh! Don José María!" Cornelia said, wiping the tears from her eyes, "If you only knew what happened to my daughter after her marriage with Rodolfo, Don José María," Cornelia added, "I don't know how much you remember about Vivian. She turned out to be a very pretty girl, not much taller than me. She had beautiful black hair and blue eyes. Her skin was white and fair, I don't know how she was born so light-skinned, probably she inherited it from her Spanish grandparents who came from Barcelona. For her age, she acted very mature and a bit precocious. My husband was always afraid that she would end up hanging out with the wrong crowd, it was for that reason my husband and I allowed her to marry Rodolfo at a such a young age, she had just turned eighteen."

"Was Rodolfo, Spanish or Latino?" José María inquired.

"Rodolfo was Brazilian, he was a young man from a very prominent family in Río de Janeiro. He was tall, handsome and hardworking and very much in love with Vivian. They were a very young happily married couple about to start a new life. But it was Rodolfo who drove her into evil ways."

"I remember your daughter well, Doña Cornelia, but I hadn't seen her lately, it's been a few years. From what you are telling me she grew up to be a very beautiful woman," said José María.

"Yes, she was very pretty, it was the scoundrel of Rodolfo; he was the culprit of what happened to Vivian."

"What happened to her? Why do you blame your son-in-law?" asked José María, curious and concerned.

"Would you like something to drink, a soda maybe, Don José María?" Cornelia asked.

"No, thanks again," replied José María.

"As you know, Don José María," said Cornelia, "my husband Pedro was from the Dominican Republic, from a town called Palo Hondo where the practice of witchcraft is very common. He was a close friend of a Haitian black couple of Nigerian descent who were well known for practicing that religion. He lost track of them when we went to live in Santo Domingo, the capital, where my parents also lived. My parents thought of Pedro so highly that they invited him to come and manage the leather business they owned. We were doing so well, but it was those Negros who started my husband in that religion, in witchcraft, which has nothing religious about it. I never liked their relationship; it wasn't a healthy friendship, so I convinced him to move to this country."

"But why do you also blame your husband for your daughter's troubles?" asked José María.

"Because when we arrived in this country sixteen years ago," said Cornelia, "Pedro met the witches again. Luckily, after Pedro died, we did not see them again until six months ago when Rodolfo, my son-in-law, met a black Haitian named Lázaro Rubiblanco at a bar on Kalorama Street in this city. It was then when this Lázaro learned that Rodolfo was my husband Pedro's son-in-law. It was Rodolfo who brought them to our house and that's how they met my daughter Vivian," Cornelia added. "I never trusted them, they always looked suspicious to me.

Let me tell you, Don José María, about that Lázaro Rubiblanco, whose only whiteness was in his surname. He was as black as a night without stars and he came with his wife Paula to visit us at our house. That was when they both met my daughter Vivian. At that time, I did not pay too much attention to the way they looked at my Vivian, but later I started noticing the way they were staring at her, they would not take their eyes off her; he and his wife watched her with obsession."

"It was good of you to notice how they were looking at her."

"It didn't help, that was the beginning of the tragedy," Cornelia said. "After that visit, Lázaro and his wife invited Rodolfo and Vivian to spend a weekend at a farm near Richmond, Virginia. I did not suspect in the least the intentions of those scoundrels, and that's why I did not object to their invitation. On the contrary, I found it very nice of them since they had been longtime friends of my husband, you know!"

"I understand, but what made you suspect something was happening?" asked José María.

"The following Monday," said Cornelia, "when I saw my daughter at the grocery store I noticed her somewhat pale and unusually quiet, but I assumed it was because they had been partying the night before and went to bed late; however, I had that motherly instinct, I had a feeling that something was not right. That evening, when I saw Rodolfo, I asked him why Vivian looked so pale and withdrawn, he gave me a very vague explanation. He was not specific. On the contrary, he was rather evasive and did not want to look at me face to face, like when someone avoids looking you straight in the eye. I thought he was not being honest, that he was hiding something."

"But that happened only once," said José María.

"I wish it had been only once. The invitations to the farm

continued every weekend. Whenever I talked to my daughter, she would tell me she was not feeling well; that she felt very weak and although she was eating substantially and well, she was worried that she was losing weight. Besides, she was avoiding me, she did not want to share what was happening; she stopped coming to visit me."

"And what happened?" asked José María, quite concerned.

"After not seeing her for almost five weeks, Don José María, Vivian came to see me one day and I cried up to the sky; my daughter was thinner than a sack of bones and paler than ivory, I do not know how to explain what I felt."

"Did you call the police?" asked José María.

"Yes, I called the police!" Cornelia said. "I told them about her husband, her friends and about their visits to the farm in Virginia. But they told me that they could not open an investigation without proof or evidence; that it was very difficult to blame someone on suspicion alone; in short, they could not help me. I was desperate, not knowing what to do. I could not sleep nor stop thinking about it. It took a lot of courage on my part, and I made up my mind to do my own investigation. I found out where the farm was located and decided to go pay a visit. The following weekend I asked my friend Eduviges to take me to the farm."

"But that was a little risky, you could have gotten into lots of trouble and they could have hurt you," said José María.

"I didn't care about that at the time, Don José María," Cornelia said. "I had to find out what was happening to my daughter. What those witches were up to, what they were doing to my daughter."

"But why do you say they are witches, Doña Cornelia?" José María asked.

"You cannot imagine. What I witnessed was horrible!"

"What did you witness, Doña Cornelia?" asked José María, now extremely worried.

"Although I knew where the place was, it was not easy to find the farm, but after driving for almost two hours on the main highway, we drove another twenty minutes to a place on the banks of a river," Cornelia said. "I do not remember the name of the river but I do remember that the farmhouse was not visible from the gravel and cobblestone road. It was hidden among tall trees surrounded by bushes and brambles. Eduviges parked the car making sure they could not see it and we waited until past eight o'clock at night. The heat was suffocating, the wait was endless and unbearable, the mosquitoes and other insects were relentless, but we waited, we had to witness what was happening."

"How scary and dangerous!" exclaimed José María. "What did you see?"

"A little after eight-thirty," said Cornelia, "I saw six black men and four black women come out of the house, and as I suspected they were wizards and witches. They were all dressed in white robes with white bands tied upon their heads; they walked slowly, then they stopped abruptly, then they started walking faster and again stopped suddenly. One of them separated from the group and started lighting a fire about twenty yards away from the house, also lighting candles around a carefully chosen space they had meticulously swept with brooms.

Later, three other witches came out with several drums and began to play music with a rhythm that I had never heard before. It could have been an African beat, it was weird, loud. The flames of the campfire accentuated the silhouettes of the participants who were drinking from gourds some strange liquor or God knows what kind of concoction; they smoked, danced, jumped, their bodies contorting, raising their arms toward the sky shouting some gibberish, the most strange words, like: 'Ochúm,' 'Ochúm,' 'Ochúm,' 'Babalú ayé,' 'Babará,' 'Babaré,' 'Ararú,' 'Varará,' 'Achanqüé,' 'Achingüé' ...'"

"That sounds like invocations, a ceremony or a ritual," said José María, very much astonished.

"At about ten or ten-thirty the Negroes seemed to be in a trance," Cornelia went on, "Lázaro came out of the house, dressed in a white robe with a white cloth wrapped around his head, snail shells around his neck and carrying an image of the saint known as Santa Barbara. But that was not all," Cornelia continued. "Behind Lázaro came the wretch of my son-in-law Rodolfo leading my daughter Vivian by the hand. He laid her on the ground near the fire and to my surprise and horror, the witches took the candles; placed them around my daughter and covered her from head to toe with a blood-stained sheet, it looked like chicken blood. Who knows what they had given to my poor daughter, who also gave the impression of being in a trance. My friend Eduviges was horrified, she was trembling with fear; neither the heat nor the bites of the insects could stop her from shaking."

"How awful!" said José María, who had already started feeling a cold sweat dripping on his back, and wouldn't stop wiping his forehead with his white handkerchief, which he held with a trembling hand.

"Lázaro," said Cornelia, "began to dance around Vivian's body to the beat of the drums and the shouting of the other Negroes; with palm fronds, full of some kind of incense smell, they started to hit Vivian's still body. Lázaro drank a potion from a large gourd he held in his left hand; he would rinse his mouth with it and spit a greenish liquid onto my daughter's body. At the same time, he would throw puffs of smoke from the tobacco he was smoking. Suddenly he stood in front of her and in a hoarse voice, that was not his own, with a tongue that was not his own, sounding the snail shells that hung around his neck, began to recite aloud more of that gibberish: 'Aró' – 'Aró' – 'Makanqüé' – 'Efimeré' – 'Mokinqüó' – 'Papá' – 'Basi – o – Batalá' – 'Machimeré - o - Qüé.'

Then suddenly, Lázaro, wielded a knife, pointing it at Vivian as the matadors do at bullfights; and that's when I could not control myself anymore. And, overpowered by my emotions as if I too were possessed, I sprang out of my hiding place and shouted: 'STOP, STOP, VIVIAN LISTEN TO YOUR MOTHER PLEASE!'"

"What happened then?" asked José María, wiping the sweat that was running down his neck.

"Vivian took a surprising leap, tossed the bloody sheet from her body and ran toward us," said Cornelia. "My friend Eduviges had turned on the engine of the car; Vivian and I jumped inside and Eduviges started off at full speed, leaving behind the witches who wouldn't stop shouting and jumping with satanic and erotic movements. In our eagerness to escape alive, we did not want to look back at the spectacle we were leaving behind. And we could still hear the sorcerers trotting and shouting after our car."

"Extraordinarily amazing how you rescued and saved your daughter out of that horrible and evil inferno!" said José María.

"Yes, Don José María!" Cornelia cried sadly. "But unfortunately, that was not all. When Vivian got into the car, she told me she was extremely tired; that she needed to sleep. She did, but never woke up. She died in my arms during that tragic ride."

"How horrible, Doña Cornelia!" said José María. "What a tragedy to see your daughter die in your arms."

"Yes, Don José María!" Cornelia said, wiping the tears from her eyes. "The witches killed her! They killed my daughter!"

"What happened to her husband and his friends?" asked José María. "Did you call the police?"

"Not only did I call the police," said Cornelia, "but I also accompanied them to the house in Virginia. You would not believe what we found, or didn't find, all of the witches were gone; there was no sign of the ritual or ceremony that we had witnessed; there was no trace of a fire, nothing at all, it seemed as if they had been swallowed by the earth. The owners of the estate, an elderly couple who was back from a trip to North Carolina were surprised to see the police. They could not offer any information because they did not know the existence of the individuals I was talking about. Everything was a mystery."

"And Rodolfo, what explanation did he give you?" asked José María.

"Rodolfo is a sonofabitch, a bastard, and a coward ... pardon my language" said Cornelia, gritting her teeth in her mouth. "He has also disappeared and I have not been able to find him; his apartment in Maryland is empty and the building manager told me he had paid the rent. He suspected that Rodolfo had left the country without giving him any information. Would you like to have a glass of lemonade or a little sip of Bacardi rum?" Cornelia asked José María.

"No, thank you, Doña Cornelia," José María said, wiping the sweat from his forehead. "Maybe some other time."

"They're ringing the doorbell ..." came the rumbling thunder of Napoleón the parrot, but this time it did not finish the phrase as he used to with ... *"open the door Pedrito,"* as if someone had abruptly interrupted him.

Suddenly from the kitchen, like a desperate madman, Pedrito jumped in the middle of the living room. His sweaty body covered with a white robe and a white band clinging to his head adorned with green and yellow feathers. He looked as if he was possessed by the devil. In his right hand, grabbed by the neck he brought Napoleón the parrot, its eyes popping out of their sockets, and as he violently twisted its neck, Pedrito, overcoming his muteness shouted out:

"ARÓ - ARÓ – MOKINQÜO - NAPOLEÓN ..."

"What's the matter, Pedrito, are you going crazy, and why did you kill Napoleón?" Astonished and with her eyes wide open, Cornelia asked her son as she stood up from the chair. But Pedrito wouldn't stop contorting. As he walked back to his room, he raised his hand holding the dead Napoleón, the parrot, he shouted again:

"ARÓ - ARÓ – MOKINQÜO – NAPOLEÓN DEAD ..."

Drying the copious sweat that covered his face, José María quietly rose from the red brocade chair; took his brown polyester coat and headed for the front door.

"I'm sorry, Doña Cornelia," he said, hurriedly going up the steps. "But I have to leave. Again, I am very sorry for the tragic death of your daughter."

"Please forgive me Don José María," said Cornelia. "I do not know what has gotten into my son's head. I hope you come back another day to visit me and I hope this is not your last visit. Next time I would like to invite you to have a bowl of chicken soup; I prepare some very tasty soups."

"Thank you, Doña Cornelia," said José María, replying to Cornelia's invitation as he exited to the sidewalk.

Hurriedly, he walked to where he had parked his Toyota, and wiping the sweat that still covered his face, José María said to himself:

"The hell with the chicken soup; that house is haunted ... Who knows what those wizards and witches gave her daughter and son ...?"

When the Bells Stop Ringing

Founded in 1524 by the Spanish conqueror Francisco Hernández de Córdoba, Granada is the oldest and one of the largest cities in Nicaragua. The majority of the population of Granada is Catholic and fervently attends Sunday mass at the church in their neighborhood or of their predilection. The names of the churches in Granada were given according to the neighborhood where they were founded. For example La Iglesia de La Merced, La Iglesia de la Virgen de Guadalupe, La Iglesia de San Francisco, El Templo de Xalteva and La Capilla de María Auxiliadora. The Catedral of Granada is one among these historical Houses of God which are found along La Calle Real, as it was called at that time. These churches start at the northern part of the city with El Templo de Xalteva and end near the shores of Lake Nicaragua, also known by its indigenous name, Lake Cocibolca, with La Iglesia de la Virgen de Guadalupe.

These churches are beautiful historical and architectural temples that were built by the Spanish conquistadors during the time of the colonization. The ornaments adorning them were brought from Spain by Spanish friars, who were masters of goldsmithery, cabinetmaking and artists of many crafts.

They are virtuous places where devotees offer their prayers to God, Jesús Christ, the Virgin Mary, or to the saints of their devotion. In difficult times of the country — as it was during the Civil War of 1855 to 1857 — some of them, like El Templo de Xalteva was used as a military fort. However, in this story, one of them, the Catedral of Granada, was used for a less virtuous or religious act.

There is an old tradition, observed by many, which suggests that upon arriving for the first time in a city, one must visit its churches in order to learn about their historical value as well as some of the town or city's customs and beliefs, among other things. In other words, these religious temples, although many have architectural similarities, they have their own legends and spiritual and historical meaning as well.

In many of the small towns of Nicaragua as well as in the larger cities, gossip, stories and tales about colorful characters have always been abundant. These stories are passed along from our grandparents, parents and relatives as well as by the gossipmongers of the respective towns. Granada is no exception. There are true and invented stories, but usually, most have nuances of truthfulness as well as fiction, depending on who is the storyteller. The narrator will usually add to the story whatever comes to his mind, making up colorful characters and events in order to embellish it and make it more appealing and interesting to the listeners or readers. With this in mind, I will narrate the tale of what transpired in one of these religious temples, the Catedral of Granada.

The main characters portrayed in this tale are four teenagers who had not yet passed their fourteenth or fifteenth year. Like most kids their age, they lived in that confusing stage when they are not adults and yet they are no longer children. It's a hesitant, not well-defined age that so often makes them stop to think which path to follow. They knew about things their parents tried to hide from them. They also listened attentively when their parents spoke behind closed doors thinking that their children weren't listening. They had an idea or maybe suspected how babies were born. They thought they knew how to do "that," (to have sexual intercourse) although they had never tried it.

They also listened to stories about people being unfaithful in their marriage. They were told by their parents and by their religious educators that doing "that" outside of marriage was a mortal sin and it had to be confessed to a priest while inside a booth called "confessionary." They also knew that there would be consequences for this sinful act and that a punishment would be imposed. That punishment would be in the way of penance; such as praying an Our Father and three Hail Mary's plus the promise of not to do "that" again.

The Central Park of Granada is adorned with a beautiful fountain in the center surrounded by ample walkways, bordered with almond trees, mangoes, palms as well as many other tropical trees and plants. A colorful kiosk is located at each of the corner entrances to the park. These kiosks serve as social gathering places for the young and the not so young adults of the city. They are also places where tourists, shoe-shiners, vagrants and, sporadically, drunks stop by, just to hang around and watch people go by. Visitors often sit down at tables to savor the popular *vigorón* (yucca with pork rinds), local refreshments, colorful milkshakes and sodas, or purchase local artisans' trinkets, while admiring the girls walking by as they provocatively move their hips to catch the admiration of the male population. The girls respond to the loud whistles and flirtatious remarks by accentuating the movement of their hips. That Friday afternoon of May 1956, after the early morning downpour, the sun shone brilliantly above the trees' canopies in the park and a warm mist of damp earth evaporated off the ground.

Alfredo, El Chiriso (Spiked Hair), René, El Chele (The Blond one) and Roberto, El Garfio (The Hook), were seated at one of the kiosks' tables and impatiently waited for Jacobo, El Chino (The Chinese-looking one). They did not know why he was late; they did not want to order another round of refreshments. They all had to hurry to their respective homes as dinner time was approaching.

No one knew why Roberto had been nicknamed El Garfio, but it was rumored that as a child he had fallen from a swing and landed on his index finger, and the 'quack of the doctor' who, dishonestly pretending to have medical skills, had tried to straighten it and left it in the form of a hook.

As they were getting ready to go home, they saw that Jacobo turned the corner of the Calle la Calzada. He hurriedly crossed the busy central plaza and panting, out of breath, he gave his three buddies all kinds of excuses for being late.

Alfredo impatiently asked: "What took you so long? Have you noticed how the barber cut your hair? It's so short that makes you look more Chinese than you already do. Your ears stick out on both sides of your head like the wings of a plane, and your nose looks more hooked than a hawk's beak."

With a disgusted look on his face, Jacobo told Alfredo: "You are such an asshole! You are always criticizing how people look. Have you looked at yourself in a mirror lately? Your nose is so flat that it looks like a smashed tortilla, and your hair is more spiked than ever, it seems that on your way here you passed under a magnet."

"Let's stop this name-calling nonsense, it's getting us nowhere. I was late," continued Jacobo, "because I was hiding under the table in the dining room listening to my parents and I couldn't come out until they got up. You cannot imagine what I just heard!"

"You know it's getting late?" René asked him. "Soon we'll have to go home, what you heard better be good!"

René was called El Chele because his golden blond hair was always brushed against his forehead covering one of his light blue eyes. René's muscular body was like that of a boxer's, even though he'd never lifted a single weight; he looked like Joe Palooka.

"Don't spin the subject and tell us what you heard, it must have been very important for you to have come this late," said Roberto to Jacobo. "It has to be one of those big bombs, a juicy gossip."

"Do you know Doña Prudencia?" asked Jacobo.

Prudencia Flores was the neighborhood gossip. However, she did not live up to her name, she wasn't "prudent" in the least. Her round, white marble face looked like the marble color of a gravestone, and her jet-black hair was pinned up with a bow attached to the back of her head with a hawksbill comb like the ones used by Spanish señoritas. Prudencia was a worse gossip than even the so-called Tula Cuecho, a woman infamous all over the country for her biting and venomous tongue.

René, a little impatient, said:

"Yes! We know of Prudencia, she is better known as the town virgin and of the flaccid flesh."

"Why do they say that? Why is she called the town virgin?" Alfredo asked René.

"Because she's past forty, and at her age, it's rumored that she has not yet seen a naked man, and her wrinkled flesh looks like the flesh of an old virgin," replied René.

I don't know why people referred to Prudencia in such a contemptuous way. True, she had not married, and that at her age — early forties — she probably had not seen a naked man. But she was not an ugly woman; she was relatively attractive.

"You're a worse gossip than Doña Prudencia," said Roberto.

"That's what the venomous tongues say, and you know there are plenty of them in this city," René said.

"Jacobo, why don't you finish telling us what you heard while you were hiding under the table?" impatiently asked Alfredo.

"I will, but you promise me that whatever I tell you, it's not going to go beyond the four of us, that it's going to be a secret."

"Yes!" Alfredo, René, and Roberto answered in unison as if they were singing in the Catedral's choir.

"They say that a 'good girl' is meeting with Roque 'the mulatto,' you know, the 'sacristan,' in one of the bell towers of the Catedral and is having an affair with him."

"In the bell tower of the Catedral? With the sacristan? With Roque, the mulatto?" asked Alfredo, René, and Roberto almost in unison.

"And who is the 'good girl'?" René asked.

"I don't know," Jacobo said. "But Doña Prudencia seems to know. They say that no one has seen her enter the bell tower."

Roque, the sacristan, was a well built and muscular mulatto. From pulling the bell-string up and down, his arms had developed like the arms of a boxer.

"Yes, with Roque, the mulatto," Jacobo added. "They say he is a Canary."

"What's a Canary, besides playing the bells, he also sings like a canary?" Asked Alfredo.

"No hombre! Don't be so stupid," Jacobo answered. "He is Canary, he was brought by the bishop from the Canary Islands, those near Spain, on the west coast of Africa, that's how they call the natives of those islands; you have to polish up your geography."

Alfredo was not stupid, he was always asking silly questions and his classmates believed that he was really a fool, but he was neither. He liked to ask questions to confirm and make certain that his knowledge of the subject was correct.

"Doña Prudencia says that Roque, the mulatto, in addition to ringing the bells also plays the harmonium, that old instrument in the Catedral which needed to be repaired. Roque was able to do it plus giving it a good tune-up, now it sounds better than when it was new," said Jacobo, adding that Roque had studied music when he lived in the Canary Islands.

"Jacobo, why do you keep repeating the same stupid thing after every name? 'Roque, the mulatto, Doña Prudencia, the old virgin of fluffy flesh,' stop it, we know their nicknames," said Roberto somewhat disgusted.

"I'm sorry, I will not repeat them again," Jacobo said. "I don't know if you've noticed how the bells ring so much better ever since Roque's playing them, he gives them a livelier rhythm very different from the one given by the other bell ringer. He combines the sharp notes very well with the sound of the big Bell, the one called the Tenembaum."

"What are you saying?" René asked. "Why do you call the biggest Bell the Tenembaum?"

"Because that Bell was donated by the wealthy Don Filadelfo Tenembaum. He imported it from Spain. You know, Don Fila, the rich Mac-Duck, who lives in the big mansion across from the park and who for any good reason throws the most luxurious parties."

"Don't bother us with the nicknames anymore; tell us once and for all, what does Don Fila's Bell have to do with the gossip of Doña Prudencia about the 'good girl,' Roque, and what is happening in the bell tower?" asked Roberto.

"Doña Prudencia says, as the venomous tongues of this town, and you know who they are ..."

"Yes! Yes! We know that there are a lot of them in this city," René interrupted, more impatiently. "When are you going to let the cat out of the bag? When are you going to finish telling us the damned story?"

"Well, the ringing of the Tenembaum Bell has to do with the gossip," continued Jacobo. "When Roque begins to ring it, it is when he is having sex with the 'good girl' and when they finish doing it, is when the bells stop ringing, not only the Tenembaum but the rest of the bells. And Doña Prudencia says," Jacobo added, "when 'that' happens, Quique, the altar boy, accelerates the ringing of the little bells."

"It cannot be, it's not possible," said Alfredo, shaking his head from side to side. "I do not know much about love or sex, but it is not possible to make love and ring the bells at the same time. And what the hell does Quique, the altar boy, have to do with ringing the small altar bells?" asked Alfredo.

"You know nothing ..., you don't know a damned thing," René said. "And least of all, you know anything about love."

"Doña Prudencia says," continued Jacobo. "That three Sundays ago, when she was attending the six-o'clock mass, the bells stopped ringing, and Quique, the altar boy, started ringing the altar bells faster than ever. That made Padre José so nervous that he almost dropped the chalice with all the hosts. Luckily he had not consecrated them."

"I don't think anyone has seen the 'good girl' enter the church, let alone go in the bell tower, nor seen her face," Roberto added dubiously. "I don't believe any of this crap."

"Don't go so fast, Roberto," Jacobo answered. "Two weeks ago, after the six-o'clock mass, someone claims to have seen a girl hurrying out of the church, she's suspected to have come from the bell tower and she may be the 'good girl.'"

"Who was it? Could they identify her?" asked Alfredo.

"No!" No one has seen her face. She wears a dark dress like the ones worn by women when in mourning, and she covers her face with a black embroidered mantilla."

"I think this is another of Doña Prudencia gossips," René said. "I think there is no such thing as a 'good girl' going up to the bell tower to do 'that.'"

"And why in hell you keep saying 'that'? We all know what 'that' is already." asked Alfredo.

"Now I am more convinced than ever that you are totally stupid," said Jacobo. "If you think you know what is to do 'that,' why don't you take a walk around the San Francis Chiquito brothel, which is three blocks away behind the Iglesia de San Francisco and ask one of the "muchachas" to make up with you, but oh yes! you will have to pay her at least five pesos for her services."

"Men, you mess around so much, you boast that you know what 'that' is and you have not done it either, I bet neither of you has ever been close to a girl," Alfredo replied.

The four boys were so involved discussing the rigging of the bells and the meaning of "that," that they didn't notice when, as silent as always, the drunkard Baltasar showed up and approached them begging for a few coins.

"Look Baltasar," Jacobo said as he came close to their table. "Leave us alone, this time we do not have any money, nothing to give you. We are discussing a very important matter."

"Baltasar, don't come near us, you smell like a garbage can, you must have been drinking since very early, we're almost dizzy from the stench coming out of your mouth," Alfredo barked.

"Leave us alone, we told you that we don't have a single penny, go on and sleep it off under a mango tree, in the mango grove by the lake," René said.

"All right, kids," Baltasar said in his coarse, deep voice and scratching his unshaven chin said: "It looks more like you are telling a gossip, one of the good ones; it must be the one about what happened in the bell tower." And as he was leaving, he burst out laughing.

No sooner had Baltasar left, the bells of the Catedral started ringing and the four of them gazed curiously toward the bell tower.

"Quiet! Shut up," Jacobo warned. "Germán is coming, he's looking for a fight."

"Don't tell him anything" Alfredo said, "or invite him to sit with us, remember that what we're talking about is a secret and should be kept between us four only. He is such a bully."

Almost all the boys in town were afraid of Germán, since, for just a single glance, a comment, or anything, he could get pissed off and start a fight. None of the boys his age or older dared to confront or contradict him. Germán luckily passed them without stopping.

"Look, Jacobo, this story is already getting to be too long. We were interrupted by Baltasar and now Germán. Why don't you finish telling us what the hell happened in the bell tower? My parents will soon be calling me to dinner," said Roberto.

"Remember the burial last week?" According to Doña Prudencia that was Roque's burial."

"Rooooque?" they all asked surprised in unison.

"Yes!" Jacobo replied. "It seems that the bishop kept it all quiet, under his cassock and did not want anyone to know what had happened."

"Don't fool around anymore!" René said, getting up and shaking the dust off his pants. "If this is another one of your stories, I'm leaving, you're worse than Doña Prudencia."

"Wait, don't be so impatient! According to what I heard; the bishop learned of the rumors about what was happening in the bell tower. He asked Padre José to keep an eye on Roque and the bell tower-door, to see who was going up and who was coming down. That Sunday, at the six-o'clock mass, when the Tenembaum Bell stopped ringing, and when Quique nervously began ringing his bells, all the parishioners looked at each other and — of course Doña Prudencia was also there — Padre José dashed to the bell tower, all sweaty and panting he managed to climb all the steps, about sixty-two of them," mysteriously said Jacobo.

"Well, what did he find?" René asked.

"Did he find the 'good girl' having sex with Roque?" Asked Roberto.

"Worse yet," Jacobo said. "What Padre José saw was impossible to believe, terrible and macabre, you cannot imagine it."

"You are so full of shit Jacobo, your eyes have started to brown up, don't hold us in suspense," Alfredo added. "Finish the story, what did Padre José find?"

"In addition to being ignorant, you are so vulgar, Alfredo! Where did you learn that kind of language? Let me continue. Roque's eyes were bright and half-sallow, his face half swollen and bluish, and his tongue tilted out of his mouth, it was the lifeless body of the mulatto, hanging from the rope of the Tenembaum Bell. The stool on which he climbed to reach the rope was lying on the floor. But that's not all. Very close to the stool Padre José found a folded in half and wrinkled note."

"And the 'good girl,' was she there?" Asked Roberto. "What did the note say?"

"No! the 'good girl' was not there. I don't know how Doña Prudencia knows so many details," continued Jacobo. "They must have been confided to her by Padre José. She says that the note was somewhat tear-stained and some of the letters were blurry but you could still read:

Dear Roque: I am very sorry and with my heartbroken, I must tell you that our relationship has to end. I cannot continue seeing you, do not ask me why, it is not for lack of love, someday you will understand.

I love you,
D."

"D.?" Rene asked. "How many girls have names that begin with a D?"

"There's Dorita, Damaris and Desiré," Alfredo said.

"There's Dianita, Dulcecita and Dalia," added Roberto.

"Which could it have been?" René asked.

"According to Doña Prudencia, at the wake of Roque, the mulatto, they saw two of them who discretely wiped their tears with a white embroidered linen handkerchief."

"Who? Who?" asked Roberto.

"I don't know," Jacobo said. "She did not want to reveal their names."

"Why do you think that Doña Prudencia, who is such a gossip, did not want to say their names?" asked Alfredo. "Ha! Ha! Ha! Because she is a witch, the town virgin with her flaccid flesh," he answered himself.

"Alfredo, you are not only dumb and vulgar, but you are also crazy," called Roberto.

"I don't know why she didn't, who can guess what people think?" said Jacobo, the most philosophical of the group.

"Who knows what women think," said Alfredo.

"And what do you know about what women think or what they don't think, when you don't even know what a Canary is," René said.

There was a pause, and again the ringing of the bells was heard. It was the second call for the five-thirty afternoon mass. The four friends, after silently gazing at the bell towers of the Catedral, exchanged inquisitive glances.

In the distance, one could hear the sound of a Victrola coming from one of the other kiosks playing a popular song:

... Señora, te llaman señora, y eres más perdida que las que se venden por necesidad ... (... Lady, they call you a lady, but you're more perverted than those who sell themselves for money...)

Lucila's Secret

E milia María and her sister Lucila María lived with their mother on a small ranch they inherited from their father upon his death. Even though both sisters were the pride and joy of the Oyantes marriage, Venancio, and Celia María, for some obtuse whim of nature Emilia's skin color was lighter than Lucila's. Both were of medium height and although very similar in their physique, Emilia's light green eyes and almost blond brownish hair differed from Lucila's bright black eyes and jet-black hair. Because of her dark skin, her friends and family affectionally referred to her as La Negra. Besides their difference in skin color, Emilia was more industrious and more demure than Lucila, who was a flirt who liked parties and men's attention. The Oyantes were very religious, and in honor of the Virgin Mary, they baptized their ranch with the name: Las Tres Marías, or the Three Mary's.

Although their means were not abundant, the Oyantes couple enjoyed a comfortable life, which allowed them to send their daughters to Santa Margarita, a private school for girls located in Montejo, the largest city in the region of Aguajal. After graduating, Emilia chose to stay in Montejo to continue her education, and during that time she fell in love with a handsome young local lawyer. Eventually, they got married and decided to live permanently in Montejo. Lucila, on the other hand, decided to return to the ranch and help her mother with the cultivation of tobacco and the making and sale of cigars.

During her childhood years, Lucila spent most of her free time taking care of her parents and helping them with their daily chores. She attentively observed her father's maintenance and cultivation of tobacco in their *vega*, a fertile plot of land near the Aguajes river. At the same time, she would help her mother and two female employees with the delicate task of cutting and wrapping pre-selected tobacco leaves and packing the cigars in small boxes of fine wood, to be exported internationally. To differentiate their cigars from others of lower quality, these boxes were stamped with the trademark of the family, golden ringed *vitolas* where the name Tabacos Las Tres Marías was decorated with three images of the "Virgen de la Altagracia," in honor of the revered Virgin of the Dominican Republic.

Lucila not only learned, with delicate precision, the wrapping of the cigars, or *puros* — as she called them — but also learned to smoke the cigars, which she carefully wrapped with the best leaves. The income of the Oyantes depended on the local and foreign sale of the cigars and plant seeds, which were well coveted for being some of the best in the region.

The friendly relations with the family of Manuel and Concepción Recio, their neighbors, had deteriorated gradually. The Recios owned a sugar mill adjacent to the Oyantes' *vega*. It was said that they had emigrated from Cuba many years back. The Recios accused the Oyantes farmers and workers of trespassing into their well-tended sugar cane fields and surrounding hills and there illegally hunt, steal pigs, hens and other poultry, even cattle, and one or two goats. It is not known exactly whether the claims and accusations of the Recios against the Oyantes were valid or unfounded since they had no evidence or proof of these allegations.

Lucila paid no attention to such quarrels. Unlike other girls her age, she would escape every afternoon to a hiding place she had discovered under a tall, leafy and shady chilamate[3] tree located in the adjoining line between her *vega* and the sugar plantation of the Recio ranch. Lucila took advantage of the shade the beautiful tree of dark green leaves provided her during those days of calcinating heat; hiding among its robust roots where she would smoke the cigars wrapped by herself with the finest tobacco leaves of her *vega*. That was her secret place to enjoy the stillness, the solitude, the silence, — broken only by the chilamate's arms, swaying in the refreshing breeze — to disappear from everyday life, to yearn, and dream of the day she would find her Prince Charming. She dreamed of marrying him and as she had read in the fairy tales, to live happily ever after. These escapes to her hiding place were so frequent, that Lucila had already threshed a path between her tobacco plantation and the sugar cane fields of her neighbors.

For Lucila, the years went by without haste. She lived happily doing her daily routine; the cultivation of her *vega*, occasionally visiting her sister and her lawyer husband in Montejo, but what really pleased her most, was being able to hide in her private secret place under the leafy chilamate, where alone she could enjoy her cigar, exhaling puffs of smoke towards infinity, watching her dreams disappear — just like the smoke of her cigars vanished among the branches of the tree. Lucila had turned twenty-nine and had not yet met her knight in shining armor.

When the Recios couple died in a tragic automobile accident, Manolito, their only son and sole heir of the sugar plantation, whom his parents had not trained in the day-to-day operations of the

---

[3] The chilamate is a soft wood tropical tree of the fig family which can be found throughout Latin America. Although it is a free-standing tree with buttress roots snaking to the ground, it eventually anchors them to the floor. It is a tree that attaches itself to a host tree eventually strangling it. Its fruit is favored by howler monkeys. The chilamate grows up to 26-135 ft tall.

plantation, found himself alone without even knowing how the sugar cane was sown, and much less the process involved to produce a single grain of sugar. The productivity of the sugar mill deteriorated, the sugar was no longer of the same quality, the molasses went from being of the first quality to second best or even third; distillers of the region avoided buying what had once been high-quality molasses, now they chose molasses from other mills. The decay was also noticeable in the sugar cane fields ... there was a year when the sugar cane was not harvested. It rotted, and when they tried to recover what was left, it was too late, it was a total loss.

In addition to the economic debacle of the sugar mill caused by Manolito's disdain or ignorance, he found himself alone in a foreign country, outside of his native country. He became so affected by his misfortune that he decided to sell everything he had inherited from his parents and return to Cuba, his beloved and longed-for island. Manolito not only sold all materials and equipment of the sugar mill but the *bateyes* or dilapidated barracks where the tenant farmers and other workers of the mill lived, as well as livestock, poultry and many personal family heirlooms.

Among the potential buyers of the abandoned sugar mill, and the sugar cane fields were the owners of other nearby mills who wanted to take cheap advantage of the state of deterioration of the property and thus increase their own holdings. American speculators also arrived with their respective lawyers wielding bright, newly printed dollars. It was as if the sea was suddenly filled with voracious hungry sharks that had smelled blood in the water. All wanted not just a piece of the property, but the property as a whole.

In making the decision to sell the sugar mill plantation, Manolito did not realize that by selling to foreign entities, he was fomenting foreignism, the absenteeism of ghost proprietors interested only in their financial well-being or that of their corporation. The owners of such entities did not take care of their property and even less ventured to visit their acquired properties, limiting themselves to hiring administrators who, at times, lacked the necessary knowledge to manage a successful sugar mill enterprise.

While all this personal and financial drama unfolded in her neighborhood, Lucila continued to improve her tobacco crops, selling her cigars, her seeds and seedlings, and at the same time improving cultivation of her *vega*. Manolito, on the other hand, did not care about the property, his only desire was to liquidate everything and leave the country. Without consulting an attorney or anyone else, he decided to sell everything to the highest bidder, to Razpon & Melenkamp, Inc., a conglomerate of Russian and German investors, who at once decided to change the name of the plantation from The Recio Plantation to El Habra.

During the farewell banquet for Manolito, the local authorities offered speeches and emotional words praising the Recio family for having fomented and increased the sugar industry of the region. The Recios had played a very important role in the economic and educational development of Montejo. They had participated very actively in donating large sums of money for the construction of a new hospital and also a new school for underprivileged children, along with many other charitable activities. This family was so cherished by all the community that the mayor of the city publicly asked Manolito to change his mind, to stay and live permanently in Montejo. But all efforts to convince him were in vain, they vanished like the smoke Lucila saw disappear through the branches of her favorite tree.

Days later Manolito left for Cuba, stopping in Spain where he still had relatives that he had not visited for some time. While in Spain, the news spread everywhere, in the newspapers, radio, television; Fidel Castro had taken over his long-cherished island. That unexpected news was to change all off Manolito's plans. He would have to stay in Spain. That was his exile, Manolito would never return to Cuba.

The train coming from Arenal, one of the Pacific main ports of the country, arrived in Montejo on a sunny and humid Monday afternoon, in the middle of June 1960. A large number of neighbors and observers, including the mayor of Montejo, came to the railway station to witness the arrival of the new representatives of the Razpon Company, the new administrators of the El Habra mill. Together with her sister and husband — who as a result of his political maneuvers had already been appointed district attorney or prosecutor of Montejo — was Lucila, wearing a fashionable summer outfit and a wide-brimmed hat to protect herself from the scorching midday sun.

Furnishings, modern appliances, trunks, personal luggage, a brand-new model Mercedes Benz, that was brought by the engineer Andrés Sokolov and his young wife Irina, were lowered from one of the train cars. Andrés was the representative of the company Razpon & Melenkamp Inc. Two other cars were loaded with state-of-the-art machinery and equipment to revitalize or rather reconstruct the abandoned, dilapidated and newly christened sugar mill El Habra. In addition to all the luggage and machinery two German Shepherd dogs and three elegant and spirited horses came down, one of them a beautiful sorrel. Among all the equipment, from the passenger car emerged Viktor Mosktrenco Atarré, a chemist by profession, son of a Russian father and Spanish mother. Both Sokolov and Mosktrenco presented their unofficial credentials to the mayor, who in turn, very politely welcomed them, wishing them the best of luck in their new venture and inviting them to a reception in their honor at the mayor's office. The mayor, a bald, squat man, supplemented his income with bribes and graft received from the city's businessmen. Sokolov was introduced to the Montejo authorities as the Chief Executive Officer or CEO of the sugar mill, having among his functions, administrative and social liaison with the authorities of Montejo. From then on, some of the citizens of Montejo would refer to him just as "el CEO." In that city, no one wasted time or opportunity to baptize its citizens or visitors with the best and most accurate nicknames.

Viktor Mosktrenco Atarré, the chemical engineer, would oversee the technical operations and supervision of the sugar production. Viktor was a tall handsome man, his athletic build distinguished him from the rest of the new arrivals, who were mostly of Asian descent or *chinos,* as the majority of the citizenry called people with Chinese looking eyes. Viktor couldn't have been older than thirty-five years. His white complexion contrasted well with his blond hair, almost brown and disheveled, which, with a careless gesture, he constantly cast back. Viktor's steely blue-eyes scanned curiously and carefully the crowd of onlookers, political and military officers who had come to greet them at the train station. At one point, his roving eyes met the bright black of Lucila's, who in turn discretely looked into the steely eyes of the newcomer. Although her dark color complexion made her stand out from the rest of the crowd, to attract even more attention, with well-studied disdain, she removed the wide-brimmed hat that adorned her head, blowing her jet-black hair from one shoulder to the other. Viktor and La Negra Lucila, exchanged curious smiles and, along with the rest of the guests, entered the spacious room where the mayor offered the new arrivals a splendid and well-intentioned reception. The ambitious mayor, as a minor government official, never wasted the opportunity to ingratiate himself with visitors to the city. These attentions were overemphasized in the case of wealthy foreigners.

Lucila and Viktor, having been introduced by her brother-in-law — the district attorney — politely chatted briefly about the city, the climate and social activities. But that brief and insignificant encounter was enough for them to captivate each other. He was overwhelmed by the natural beauty of Lucila, and she was impressed by the masculinity of Viktor and his foreign accent in which he expressed himself in Spanish.

In spite of the initial chemistry they felt for each other, both pretended not to notice that mutual attraction; instead, they continued with their lives, Lucila, with the cultivation of her *vega,* Viktor engaged in the necessary task to reconstruct and revitalize the abandoned sugar plantation.

The progress that the foreigners achieved to improve the production of sugar, its export and the sale of the molasses to the liquor manufacturers and distilleries of the region started to show. And gradually as well, the sugar mill recovered its vitality, the improvements were obvious, and the new machinery helped much with its recovery.

As a young bachelor in town, the amorous tentacles of Viktor Mosktrenco not only spread to the city of Montejo but other nearby towns. Viktor, being a good-looking man, had a strong Don Juan complex. He believed himself to be a veritable Adonis, fully deserving of the attention, praise and flattery offered by everyone around him. For a little more than a year after his arrival to the city, he was busy courting and wooing the single girls and even one or two married ladies of the Montejo society. Those who fell into his amorous web, victims of his attention, collapsed in his arms as ants fall into thick and sweet honey. They were lured by his masculine endowments or his ostentatious and luxurious gifts, which sometimes included large sums of money. It was even rumored that Viktor frequented the brothels of the city, mainly the one called El Emporio. In social circles, it was rumored that the mayor, the sole beneficiary of that den, and in payment for his protection, enjoyed the exclusive amorous services of Lucrecia, the brothel's madam. It was also said that one of Viktor's favorite whores there was Brigitte, well known in male circles as "the Frenchy," not only for her name and her French accent but for her bodily endowments and exotic sensuality with which she satisfied her clients.

Some of Montejo's girls boasted that Viktor — Montejo's Don Juan, as some had already nicknamed him — had proposed to them marriage, for it was his intention to settle down in the city. It truly was his primordial desire was to get married and to have a son. However, none of the so-called marriage proposals had been verified; otherwise more than one of the girls would have accepted Viktor's alleged marriage proposals. But someone else in the city had stolen Viktor's heart. That, someone, was Lucila Oyantes, la Negra *veguera*. Their business interests widely diverged; however, since that brief encounter over a year earlier at the railway station and the mayor's welcoming reception, the amorous feelings between the two had not changed.

Her mother flatly opposed Lucila budding relationship with the "foreigner," as she referred to him. Vehemently, she did not tire of alerting her daughter to the customs not only of an unknown man of Russian origin, men in whom she had not a trace of confidence. She found them false, conceited and roguish; abusers of their partners, drinkers ... and so she would let her daughter know. She also did not waste any opportunity to make Lucila aware of the risk she faced if she formalized relations with Viktor. In addition to his womanizing, Viktor was a sugar master, and Lucila and her whole family were tobacconists; she would dishonor the memory of her father and his trade for which she had fought and labored all her life, for the tobacco cultivators against the sugar barons, the landowners, foreigners, absentee owners ...

But Lucila did not heed her mother's warnings. Like a small night-life butterfly attracted by the glitter and the flickering of a candle's flame, she knew, just like the insect that approached it, if she came too close to the flame she would burn, and by then, it would be too late to reconsider and escape from danger. She feared being abandoned if Viktor was transferred to another country, she could not accompany him, her life was in Montejo, not abroad. She would never leave Montejo; she would die there.

Despite all of her mother's warnings and of her own fears, Lucila decided to marry Viktor. She would inform her beloved mother of her decision after it had happened, knowing she would suffer unspeakably, but her decision was made, she would marry the brown-haired man, with steely blue eyes, those same eyes that had crossed hers at the train station.

On a fine spring day, while the fragrant jasmines and fragrant cestrum nocturnum adorned the local gardens, Lucila informed Celia María, her mother, that during a simple and private ceremony she had been married to Viktor before the judge of Montejo. She would move to a house on the grounds of the El Habra adjacent to the old house of the Recios — the former owners of the mill — where the "CEO," Andrés Sokolov, the new administrator of the mill, lived with his wife Irina. Viktor had refurbished the small house in anticipation of his marriage to Lucila. She also informed her mother that despite having married Viktor Mosktrenco, she would not adopt his surname, she would retain her own, Oyantes. Although very sad, her mother accepted her daughter's decision to have married the "foreigner."

Even though the newlyweds had tried to minimize the publicity of their marriage, it was not possible for them to prevent the press, radio and other means of communication from publicizing the event that had just taken place in the court of Montejo. Gifts, congratulations, and good wishes rained from the most remote corners of the region, for both were well known, especially Lucila, whom they had known since her childhood.

On their return from the honeymoon, they both took care of their businesses. After six or more months after their marriage, happiness reigned in both El Habra and the Las Tres Marías estates, except for Lucila's mother who barely, forcibly, accepted her son-in-law.

There are some who say that when a child grows mischievous, it is difficult to break his old habits, his tricks, and mischievousness, and as a grownup, he will continue being unruly and cunning. The same applied to Viktor Mosktrenco. It was very difficult for Viktor to break with his old habits especially his misdeeds, love affairs and escapades. Since Montejo was a quaint small city, it was very difficult not to know of the activities of its residents, plus there were always the gossipers who took it upon themselves to make sure Lucila became aware of her husband's infidelity.

Despite Lucila's entreaties, Viktor ignored his wife. He had gradually neglected her woman's needs until the day the straw broke the camel's back; she no longer endured his misdeeds or the gossiping that ran throughout the city. She informed her husband that she would return to live on her estate with her mother. She packed what little she had, and after less than eleven months of marriage, she left El Habra and returned home. Viktor wouldn't even try to stop her. Upon returning to live at Las Tres Marias, Lucila did not tell her mother the true reasons why she left her husband.

Two months after Lucila returned home, the press, radio, and television announced the disappearance of Viktor Mosktrenco Atarré. The chemical engineer of the El Habra sugar mill, the Don Juan of Montejo, the handsome "foreigner" who had stolen the hearts of many of the girls of the city had disappeared without leaving a trace, a note. In the social club, in the private homes, in the court offices, in the office of the crooked mayor, in the barrooms, cantinas, even in El Emporio — the well-known brothel —, in the most secluded corner of the city, everyone was talking about it. It was — as some would say — the talk of the town.

No one could explain what the motive of Viktor's disappearance had been. At the railway station, he had not been seen boarding a train, he had not bought a ticket at the bus station, local authorities did not know his whereabouts, his automobile — a sports Jaguar — was still parked at one of the mill's garages. Everything was a mystery, speculation, gossip, spreading all over.

Upon hearing the news, Celia María, Lucila's mother, knocked on the door of her daughter's room to inform her about her husband's disappearance, however, she refrained from telling her that she had been foretold, before Lucila married the "foreigner," that one day he would disappear as if by magic, leaving no trace; that he would evaporate and puff away like the smoke of the cigars she smoked. Lucila's reply to her mother was brief, somber and devoid of emotion:

"Mom, thank you, I heard." Then she closed the door of her room almost on her mother's face.

For the next nine months, Lucila barely got out of her room. Sometimes her mother brought her food, and sometimes she would come out grumbling. She stopped doing her usual walks to escape under the branches of the leafy chilamate, her favorite tree; and she even quit smoking her favorite cigars. No one could explain what was happening to her, what she was suffering from, or the sorrow which afflicted her and led to her confinement. What was the mystery, the secret that had caused her to isolate herself from her family and friends? When asked about her husband, she avoided the questions; she would not respond, lock herself in her room with the windows closed and curtains drawn so no one could see her and let no one witness her grief.

Soon after her self-confinement, books which she ordered from the local bookstore began to arrive, plus those she ordered by mail from the capital city. Lucila started reading Latin-American writers of the time such as Quirós, García Márquez, Donoso, Cortázar, Rulfo, as well as Spanish translations of Poe, but her favorites were the writings of Alejo Carpentier. Her mother did not know what happened to her daughter, she once contemplated taking her to a psychiatrist thinking she was suffering from depression, but she gave up the idea. Lucila wouldn't cooperate. While Lucila avidly read, Montejo's authorities could not find Viktor's whereabouts, they had no evidence or information to guide them, nothing ... the mystery of his disappearance traveled to Germany and the Soviet Union.

Bartolillo, Lucila's nephew, was not mentally retarded; he was just a fool, a blockhead, a boy who, at the age of eleven laughed at everything and everyone. He laughed at the flight of a bird, a fly perched on a breadcrumb, the creaking of crickets at dusk, everything provoked an uncontrollable giggle ... His surreptitious laughter irritated the people around him. His parents feared taking him to visit their friends, at school they could not stand him, his friends had dropped him. Only his grandmother could tolerate him and his pointless laughter.

On one of his visits to his grandmother at the Las Tres Marías, one rainy morning, while Bartolillo was looking out from one of the windows in the living room, laughing aloud after seeing two pigs wallowing in a puddle of muddy water. He continued to laugh stridently at seeing three police cars approaching his grandmother's house. His laughter did not cease when four officers came out of the cars with their revolvers drawn out while the others surrounded the Oyantes home. Hearing the quick, nervous tone of his grandson's laughter, Celia went down to the living room to make sure nothing unusual was happening to Bartolillo.

Suddenly she heard someone insistently tapping the iron knocker of the front door of the house. Celia opened the door and was aghast when four policemen, pointing their weapons at her, barged into her house, strategically positioning themselves inside the large, cool and somber living room to make sure that no one was going to escape. Bartolillo was so scared that he stopped laughing and quietly tiptoed up the stairs to the second floor. Celia was a bundle of nerves; she had never imagined herself in such a situation, surrounded by armed police, aiming their weapons at her. After regaining her calm and with a gesture of disgust she addressed the policeman who appeared to be the leader of the group:

"Excuse me, officer, what is all this trampling about? You are raiding my house, you have entered it, like savages, as if this honorable home was a lair of criminals; you haven't had the decency to tell me what is that you are looking for. You owe me an explanation.

You very well know that my son-in-law is the district attorney of Montejo, that we are a very honest family. You better have a very good reason that justifies your presence, otherwise, I will take up this inexcusable intrusion with the Governor."

"My apologies, Mrs. Oyantes, I am Captain Fernando Aquilino," replied the captain, "these are my agents. They only obeyed my orders." And addressing the other three, he ordered them to put down their weapons.

"Now, could you tell me, what is the reason for your deplorable visit, Captain Aquilino?"

"Yes ma'am, excuse our discourteous intrusion into your house, but our visit is justified."

"Sir, Captain, please tell me once and for all, without subterfuges or without beating around the bush, what is the purpose of your visit?"

"Yes, ma'am. We have an arrest warrant for Mrs. Lucila, your daughter, for the murder of Mr. Viktor Mosktrenco Atarré," said the captain, showing her a document signed by the judge of Montejo.

"I didn't know he was dead, that's all I needed," Celia said in disgust. "Blaming my daughter for the death of such a scoundrel, that 'foreigner' who has done nothing since his arrival to this town but to mock all of us, to seduce our girls and other so-called 'ladies' whose names I prefer not to mention."

Standing at the edge of the second-floor staircase, upright and haughty, prideful, dressed in the finest of her outfits, a long white dress with a red band tightly fitted around her waist, Lucila, with her characteristic calm and with the disdain of a queen said to her mother:

"Calm down mom, I've been listening to your conversation with the captain, do not worry."

Slowly, as if she had rehearsed it, wearing a pair of red patent leather shoes, the same color as the belt around her waist, Lucila descended the seven steps that separated the ground floor of the house with the upper floor.

"If the captain has an arrest warrant against me in which I am charged with committing a crime, he must execute that order. In spite of being innocent, I voluntarily surrender to the authorities to be tried, and I repeat, I am innocent of the crime. I will defend myself before a judge and I will be set free."

"Proceed, sir," Lucila said extending her arms to make it easier for the officer to handcuff her. And addressing her mother who already wiped tears from her eyes with a crimson handkerchief, she said:

"Calm down mom, do not cry, everything will be fine."

In the presence of the judge, Luciano Estefano, — an older gentleman, affable of face and big-hearted, and very familiar with the Montejo families and their business — Lucila petitioned not to be heard by a jury, instead, she asked to be tried directly by the judge; petition which was granted. However, the judge warned Lucila that if found guilty of her husband's murder, she would be sentenced to no less than twenty-five years in prison.

The district attorney, Lucila's brother-in-law, had refrained from being the one to substantiate the accusations against her sister-in-law fearing that during the trial, Lucila publicly denounce him for having made amorous advances behind her sister's back. In his place, the judge appointed Genaro Alació, the deputy district attorney, a tall, thin and austere man, with a sharp, hard and piercing look. It was rumored that Alació, at the age of fifteen, was either abused or had a consensual relationship with a mulatto worker at the Recios' sugar mill. No one could attest to this as being true or pure speculation.

The news of the murder, and how Lucila Oyantes had been apprehended as the culprit of her husband's murder, spread like wildfire through the countryside, the capital, and surrounding towns. The people who knew Lucila and her parents, in astonishment, asked themselves how such a religious, decent and hardworking person could have murdered her husband. A great majority conjectured, and in advance declared her innocent. But also, there were those ultra-religious ones, who criticized her, for they considered the cultivation of tobacco to be a diabolical trade. Tobacco had been used first by the Indians, later by the black slaves in their occult ceremonies. They considered that it was not a business fit for a woman and as a result that occupation had led her to commit illicit and even criminal actions.

That morning, on the day of the trial, the room where the fate of Lucila Oyantes would be decided was filled with curiosity seekers, friends, admirers, the nuns, Sisters Victoria and Lucrecia; other teachers of the Santa Margarita school where Lucila had attended high school were also present. The CEO of the El Habra mill who represented his company occupied one of the reserved seats in the courtroom. The CEO had abstained from bearing witness against Lucila considering that Viktor's personal activities were not incumbent on the Razpon enterprise ... Also present were some sugar cane cutters and tobacco hands, as well as some of the whores who chose to absent themselves from the brothels, including Brigitte, the supposed lover of Viktor, the "foreigner." Also, in the audience, was Baltasar, a small-town drunk who, from his country of origin, had traveled to witness such a famed event.

The trial room hummed with a speculative murmur, the secret talks were abundant, and so was the nervous giggling ... None those present could control themselves from chit-chatting until the judge interrupted the lively crowd with three strong strikes of his gavel — made of imported Bubinga wood — against the reddish base or *peana,* made from the same hardwood, of the top of his lathe-dark mahogany desk. Lucila, dressed in light green — the prisoner's uniform — was led in by a court's guard, followed by the deputy prosecutor, the supposedly gay lawyer. The judge instructed her to sit on the chair next to a small bench, the so-called bench of the accused, near the deputy prosecutor's table. The sudden silence in the room was only interrupted by the clicking of the journalists' cameras who did not cease to take photographs of the defendant. The judge ordered the deputy prosecutor to begin his exposition of the facts. He said:

"Mr. Genaro Alació, Deputy Public Prosecutor of this Honorable Court of the city of Montejo, please initiate this trial by succinctly stating the motives or reasons why Mrs. Lucila Oyantes is accused of murdering her husband Viktor Mosktrenco Atarré. I repeat Mr. Alació, be brief with your exposition."

"Yes, Your Honor, I will be brief." The deputy prosecutor replied.

"It turns out, Your Honor, that after having reported to the authorities of the incursions of certain persons in the property of the El Habra sugar mill, including in the sugar cane fields ..."

"Mr. Deputy Prosecutor," interrupted the judge, "please be more specific, to whom are you referring when you say 'certain persons'?"

"Exactly I don't know for sure what kind of people the representatives of the El Habra mill referred to when they notified the authorities about the theft of a cow and two goats, property of the mill."

"Silence!" the judge admonished the audience, who had interrupted the deputy prosecutor with shrill comments when they heard about the theft of a cow and two goats.

"Proceed please," added the judge.

"Thank you, Your Honor. It turns out that in response to the alleged thefts, Mr. CEO hired the services of two police officers to investigate who the thieves were and from what ranch they made their incursions, and in turn to guard the grounds of the mill and to patrol its surroundings. With the help of two German Shepherd dogs, for several weeks the investigations carried out by the agents had not yielded any positive results. It was during the sixth week when patrolling the grounds around the borders of the Las Tres Marías estate and the El Habra mill the detectives saw a beautiful, leafy tree of robust external roots, and in order to mitigate the heat, decided to come closer and enjoy the shade and the soft breezes provided by the tree."

"Listen to me well, Mr. Deputy Prosecutor, I must remind you that I am not willing to listen to whether or not a tree exists, whether it is leafy or not... limit yourself to the relevant facts, nothing more ... Please proceed ..." the judge instructed the deputy prosecutor.

"Understood, Your Honor," said the deputy prosecutor. "As they sat on the edge of the tree, the dogs began to bark at a small earthen promontory and instinctively began to scratch and dig the earth. It was then, that in less than two or three feet deep, they uncovered the remains of Mr. Viktor Mosktrenco, I say remains because the body was already in an advanced state of decomposition having been devoured by worms."

"And how, Mr. Deputy Prosecutor, do you intend to prove that it was Mrs. Lucila who committed the murder?"

"Immediately a medical forensic specialist was summoned to the site, and by the teeth, Mr. Viktor's brownish hair — which was still intact —, plus other personal items such as a wallet, a ring bearing the emblem of two Soviet eagles, which he was wearing at the time of his death, made it easier to identify his remains. Likewise, the coroner discovered that the deceased had fractured two or three vertebrae in the nape of the neck, concluding that that had been the cause of his death. In his official report, the coroner also described that someone had struck him very hard in the lower back of his head, perhaps with a rough object. In addition, it called their attention that in his left hand the deceased was holding a golden medal on a chain belonging to Mrs. Lucila, with her name and date of birth on it. A small dagger was also discovered, lying next to the corpse. Very close to the grave, a small space was noticed, kind of a hiding place, where a number of cigar butts were found. Moreover, after further investigations, it was possible to verify that Mrs. Lucila Oyantes was the only person who frequented this 'hiding place.' It was there where she enjoyed smoking cigars from her tobacco shop. Apparently, the victim had approached the place by horse, because despite the time that had passed since his death, it was still possible to distinguish some blurred traces of shoed horse hooves, which was confirmed by the equestrian outfit worn by the deceased plus the boots of fine leather he was wearing, purchased at the leather store of Montejo, a fact that was verified by the owner of the leather store, Mr. ..."

"Very well Mr. Deputy Prosecutor," interrupted the judge, "do you believe that everything has been elucidated by you to this Honorable Court of the city of Montejo is sufficient to convict Mrs. Lucila and condemn her for the murder of her husband?'

"Yes, Your Honor, I think it is sufficient."

"Do you have any witnesses to corroborate your accusations?'

"No, Your Honor, I have no witness."

"Then, if you have nothing more to add and no witnesses, I suppose you have concluded with the presentation of all the facts. Therefore, no data or any other evidence that you may obtain in the future will be accepted by this Honorable Court."

"Yes, Your Honor, I have concluded with the exposition of all the facts in my possession."

"Mr. Domínguez, please take note of what has been discussed." the judge instructed the young man serving as the court stenographer.

"Very well," the judge addressed the court, "we'll take an hour recess, and upon our return, we will listen to the accused. I hereby declare closed this session of the Honorable Court of the city of Montejo. This meeting is adjourned and we will reconvene at 2:00 pm."

After two in the afternoon the judge, the Honorable Luciano Estefano, opened the session and with three strong strikes of the gavel again silenced the crowd, including the curious who, knowing that it was the turn of the accused to take the stand, had gathered in the corridor adjacent to the courtroom.

"Mrs. Lucila Oyantes, please stand up and approach the table next to the Deputy Prosecutor. During your testimony or presentation of the facts you will have to stand unless you are told otherwise, you will address this rostrum when instructed and, moreover, you must limit yourself, succinctly, to the exposition of the facts, obviating parables or similar devices to enhance or embellish your narrative. Understood?"

"Yes, Your Honor, understood."

"Go on, Mrs. Oyantes, please."

"Thank you, Your Honor. I met Mr. Viktor Mosktrenco, my late husband, at the railroad station upon his arrival to Montejo a little over two years ago. During the reception offered by the Mayor, we exchanged glances, made small talk ... and soon after, we fell in love. During the next year after that initial encounter, Viktor started besieging me with his amorous advances and although I was in love with him, I avoided him." Lucila paused.

"Understood Mrs. Oyantes, please continue."

"As it is now known to all here present, and this entire city, in the afternoons, I escaped from my ranch to relax, to daydream, alone in solitude under the tree mentioned by the deputy prosecutor. It is there that I would daydream about those fairy tales, while I smoked one of the cigars I personally rolled with the best leaves of our *vega*. I presume that Viktor learned, I don't know how, of my usual get-aways, since on several occasions I saw him prowling very close to my hiding place under the chilamate. It was during one of those afternoons when I amused myself watching two doves making love on one of the branches of the tree, I heard the approach of a horse. I tried to put out the cigar that I was smoking, but it was too late, the smoke gave me away. Viktor was riding a beautiful sorrel-colored horse; it was like seeing the prince of the fairy tales I had been dreaming about and had been eagerly waiting for. Like when I first saw him at the railway station, I was convinced that I was in love with him. Viktor got off the horse, very cordially extended his hand to me, and straight out told me that he wanted to have a son with me."

"And what was your response?" the judge asked.

"For me, Your Honor it was a great surprise; I did not expect such a proposal. My response was obviously negative. I told him that I would not be another of his concubines, that I was not that kind of a woman. If he wanted to have a child with me, he would have to do it properly, by law, by marrying me. In addition, I told him that I was aware of all of his love affairs, including his relationship with the prostitute Brigitte, who I understand is present in this room."

"Mrs. Lucila," interrupted the judge, "limit yourself to the exposition of the facts; avoid making comments about persons who are present in this room. Mr. Stenographer, erase the last comments made by the accused. Please continue, Mrs. Oyantes."

"Forgive me, Your Honor! Openly, I told him that if he was to marry me, he would have to give up all his conquests and activities of dubious nature. Very gentlemanlike, Viktor immediately accepted my demands and conditions, repeating to me that he was madly in love with me and that he wanted to marry me and start a family and stay permanently in Montejo. Again, he stressed that he wanted to have a child with me. After all his declarations and commitments, he mounted his sorrel horse and disappeared in the sugar cane fields at a gallop. As it is known to this Honorable Court, it was here, in this same court, that I subsequently married Mr. Viktor Mosktrenco. Most of all, I would like to tell the Honorable Judge, that I have not committed the crime of which I am accused, I am innocent."

"Your innocence or guilt, Mrs. Oyantes will be determined by this court, please continue with the narration of the facts."

"After marrying him, I went to live at the El Habra mill, in a house that Viktor had refurbished. Everything was going well for the first few months after returning from our honeymoon in Spain, where he took me to meet his mother, who truthfully was a beautiful person. However, my ordeal began three or four months later. In public, Viktor gave the impression of being a kind, polite, socially correct man, but behind that façade, he was a very violent man. He started showing his claws when after many attempts, I could not get pregnant. His amorous advances turned into violent advances, sometimes forcing me, against my will, to have sex with him. I went to be examined by the best gynecologist of Montejo, who in his medical report specified that I had no impediment for procreating; however, Viktor refused to undergo a similar examination by a urologist. He boasted of being very macho ... I would have said the opposite; he was rather a sterile narcissist. Upon learning the results of my medical examination, he became more violent and for days in a row, he locked me in a dark room where he continued to rape me against my will. He would undress and hit me with the same whip he used on his horses. On two occasions he punched me, almost broke my nose, and on another, he kicked me in the stomach. He was physically and verbally abusive. I did not know what to do, I was afraid to tell my mother or denounce him to the authorities since he was well respected in town and no one would believe me. Until one day, after nine months of enduring his violent advances and abuses, I told him that I was going to move back to live at Las Tres Marías, my ranch. He did not even object to my decision, when he saw me leaving the house he just stood under the threshold of the door — with his legs spread out and his hands akimbo — laughing out loud, threatening me that one day he would run into me and would take revenge for abandoning him."

"Silence please!" said the judge to the audience, for it had burst into loud murmuring. "Continue, Mrs. Oyantes, pardon the interruption."

"I continued my normal life, as I had before I married; taking care of our *vega*, supervising the cutting, wrapping, and packing of our cigars and most recently, following up on a special order from a French customer who had requested a shipment of *rapé*. Also, I continued my usual visits to my hiding place under the branches of my favorite tree. Fortunately, Viktor's threats had not come true, I had not seen him, nor had he looked for me. It seemed as if the earth had devoured him. I thought to myself, that in the face of my past ordeal, that was the best thing that could happen to me, while, before the pertinent authorities, I filed the necessary papers to divorce him."

"Very good Mrs. Oyantes!" someone shouted from the hallway.

"Silence!" said the judge.

"Maybe," Lucila went on, "what provoked my husband's ire was that my lawyer presented him with the divorce papers. Maybe he had not anticipated it, hopefully assuming that I would return to him, submissive and regretful. But he was wrong; I couldn't stand him anymore. On one of my returns to my hiding place under the chilamate tree, while I sat, smoking one of my cigars, he suddenly reappeared, mounted on his sorrel horse. At once, I could see he had not come with peaceful intentions, I had lived with him long enough to know his attitude and violent gestures. Like a wild man, he dismounted from the horse and began to yell at me while at the same time he threw a punch at me, which I managed to dodge. That infuriated him. He grabbed me by the waist and began to tear off my clothes while threatening to rape me. We struggled for a few seconds, which seemed like an eternity, but I finally got free of his forceful embrace. He stepped back a few steps and withdrew the knife he always carried on his belt, lost his balance and slipped backward on leaves wet from a recent drizzle. He then tried to recover his balance by taking hold of me and ripping a chain from my neck. But he could not regain his balance. He fell backward hitting himself in the neck against one of the roots of the tree. As he lay motionless, I thought to myself that this was another of his ruses to get me close to him and grab me again. Seeing that there was not a single muscle moving in his body, that his eyes would not open, very cautiously I approached him. I told him not to play dead, and when he did not respond, it was then that I noticed the blood coming from a cut in the back of his head. When he fell back, his neck had crashed against one of the roots of the tree. He had broken the back of his neck."

"You bastard 'foreigner!'" someone shouted.

"You son-of-a-bitch!" another voice yelled.

"Silence!" the judge interrupted. "Sheriff, please take these vulgar and rude people out of this room."

"Go on, Mrs. Oyantes," the judge instructed Lucila.

"I'm thirsty!" Lucila said.

The judge, addressing the courtroom clerk, said:

"Haven't you heard that the lady is thirsty? Please bring her a glass of water."

"I didn't know what to do." Lucila continued. "Horrified, I noticed his face emaciating, it had turned from pinkish white to ashy gray. I presume that's the color of a dead person since I had never seen a dead man before. My hands were shaking, my heart was beating so fast, I felt it coming out of my chest; I felt that my temples were going to burst. I looked around for someone who could help me, but I did not see anyone. Then I rushed to my house, to find someone, to tell my mother. When I arrived home there was no one around, my mother wasn't there. A couple of hours passed, and during that period of time, I thought the only thing I could do was to bury his body. I thought if I informed the authorities, they wouldn't believe me and would accuse me of having killed him."

"What did you do then?" asked the judge.

"I took a small shovel from the garden and ran back to where his body was. I think it took me between an hour or two, maybe three, before I got back there. I'm sorry, I do not remember exactly."

"Did you bury the body of the deceased?"

"No! Your Honor."

"If you didn't, who buried him?"

"I do not know, Your Honor. The body had disappeared. Someone had taken it or buried it. I do not know who it might have been. I searched my surroundings but found no one, not a track, not a trace. The sorrel horse had also disappeared, I suppose it was frightened and returned to the mill. I was so afraid, I felt nauseated, I sweated copiously, I feared that someone was watching me, that someone had witnessed what happened and was waiting to kill me. I felt the earth sinking under my feet as if I was falling into a deep and black abyss. Although the tree was my favorite place for many years, I did not dare to stand alone under its shade, I grabbed the shovel and ran, frightened that someone was following me, spying on me ... When I arrived at my house, my mother had already returned from the city. When she saw me coming in, looking disheveled, in a bad state of nerves and sweaty from head to toe, she asked what had happened to me. I said nothing, I went up to my room; I took a bath and went to bed without a word to anyone. And so, Your Honor, I have remained for the last nine months, after that horrible violent encounter with my former husband. I have voluntarily secluded myself; reading relentlessly until the day the police came to arrest me. That's the end of my story, Your Honor."

"Thank you, Mrs. Oyantes. Have you concluded your testimony?"

"Yes, Your Honor, I have nothing more to add."

"Mrs. Oyantes, please understand that according to the law, I have to ask you the following question: Do you have a witness?"

"No, Your Honor, I don't have any witnesses."

The judge looked at the clock that hung from one of the walls of the courtroom, which showed four-thirty in the afternoon, and was about to end the session when suddenly, amidst the murmur of the audience, through the cramped corridor, pushing and elbowing, a small thin man, with sallow complexion and slanted Chinese looking eyes, dressed in blue jeans and long-sleeved plaid shirt — out of respect for the court — a worn dusty straw hat in his hand, forcefully was fighting his way toward the judge. Addressing the judge, he said:

"Your Honor, my name is Ángel Chong, but my friends call me Angelito, I am Mrs. Oyantes' witness. I can testify and corroborate that everything the lady has narrated is true."

The murmurs of the audience in the courtroom increased. People said to each other: "That's the *chino* Chong!" "It's Angelito!" "Yes, it is the Chinaman, the cane cutter, the hired hand ...!"

"Silence!" interrupted the judge with a strike of the gavel. "This court is a place of honor, not a public market." And he then addressed the alleged witness:

"Mr. Chong, this is not a joke, here, the fate of a person is at stake, we are judging the guilt or innocence of Mrs. Lucila Oyantes. Are you willing to swear before this Honorable Court that what you are about to say is the truth and nothing but the truth?"

"Yes, Your Honor, I hereby swear that what I am going to say is the truth and nothing but the truth."

"Before you proceed with your testimony, answer if you know the defendant, Mrs. Oyantes?"

"Personally, Your Honor, I don't know her, I have seen her on the grounds of the sugar mill and later at the place where Mr. Viktor lost his life."

"Well, go on," said the judge

"On the day of the fatal accident, I was on my way to the railroad station skirting the tobacco and the cane fields, when suddenly I heard the voices of a man and a woman heatedly arguing under the shade of a tree on the edge of the canefield. Curiously, I approached the scene and to prevent from being seen, I hid behind the bushes nearby. I witnessed how the lady tried to defend herself from the blows the gentleman threw at her. He shouted insults at her, threatening to kill her. It was then that he stepped backward, pulled a knife, but couldn't hit her, he slipped and fell on his back. She tried to approach him cautiously, but I could see that the man did not react, he was motionless. Then I could see her anxiety and nervousness as she saw blood flowing from the man's neck. She looked around as if seeking help. I did not dare to leave the bushes, for I did not know what was happening and I do not like to interfere with other people's problems. Then she ran off and, as she passed by where I was hiding, I could see she was trembling with fear."

"And what did you do after she left?" asked the judge.

"I decided to come out from hiding and approach the gentleman. It was then that I could tell that he was dead; his face was already beginning to turn yellow, ash color. I peeked at the back of his neck and noticed a wound, I thought he had cut himself by falling against one of the roots of the tree. I was afraid that someone would see me and think that I had been the culprit of what had happened, and then I decided to wait and see if the lady would come back. So, an hour or two passed ... I did not want to wait for nightfall, I had to get to the train station to catch the last train to the capital. When I saw that the lady did not return, and not wanting to leave the body in the open, exposed to be eaten by a wild animal ... I decided to bury it. This task was not easy for me since he was a big man and weighed a good two hundred pounds. I dragged the body to a small earth mound where, with my machete, I dug a pit, not very deep, about two to three feet deep, I threw the knife and the body into the hole to avoid the attention of wild animals. I prayed for him a Holy Father, asking God to forgive him for the bad deeds he might have done, and hurriedly left for Montejo."

"Why didn't you notify the authorities, Mr. Chong?"

"Well, in fact, Your Honor, I did inform the authorities. When I arrived at the city, before going to the train station, I stopped at the police station, which is three blocks away from the station. As I entered the reception room, I realized that they were celebrating perhaps a birthday or other festivity and did not want to interrupt the party. The officer I spoke with to notify what had happened, barely thanked me. He only asked for my address, informing me that in case they needed more information, they would contact me. Feeling that with that, I had done my duty as a good citizen, I walked to the train station and caught the last train leaving for the capital. Days went by and the police never contacted me. I assumed that they had solved the case and I did not give it another thought, until recently when I heard the news that a lady had been apprehended and that she has been accused of the murder of her husband. Again, I found myself at a crossroads: testify or be silent. I decided on the first. That, Your Honor, is all I have to say."

"Thank you, Mr. Chong," said the judge. "You may sit down on one of those chairs."

"You are welcome, Your Honor, thank you for listening to me."

"Well!" the judge said. "It's almost five o'clock. If the accused or Angelito don't have anything more to add, I hereby declare this session closed, till tomorrow at 10:00 am."

At ten o'clock the next morning, like the day before, the courtroom was filled to capacity. There was not even room to stand. Ceremoniously but with the economy of movement that characterized him, the judge approached the rostrum and sat down, taking up the gavel; but this time he did not have to use it. The silence was sepulchral; the sound of a fly could be heard. The silence was suddenly broken when from her chair, one of the nuns, Sister Victoria, called on the judge:

"Your Honor, please excuse my irreverent interruption, but for the love of God, Your Honor, you have to exonerate our dear and former student, Lucila Oyantes, from all culpability."

"Long live Sister Victoria!" "Long live Lucila Oyantes!" spontaneously clamored the courtroom.

"Silence! Silence! exclaimed the judge. "Ladies and gentlemen, after hearing the arguments of the Deputy Prosecutor, the statement of the facts by Mrs. Lucila Oyantes, and the testimony voluntarily offered by Mr. Ángel Chong, pardon, I mean by Angelito, I consider that the rules stipulated in the penal codes and jurisprudence tomes of city have been met; therefore, in view of the authority conferred upon me as appointed Judge of this Honorable Court of the city of Montejo, I hereby declare Mrs. Lucila Oyantes exonerated of all charges against her brought before this Honorable Court and so it will be duly recorded in its records. Mrs. Oyantes, you are free to go." And with one strike of his gavel, the judge said: "Case closed! This court's session is over." The clock showed ten-thirty in the morning.

Applause, hurrays and cheers spontaneously burst throughout the room, the cameras continued to click, the journalists were hurrying out of the courtroom to inform their respective newspapers about the outcome of the trial, to be the first ones to report it. Lucila, however, did not utter a single word; she looked at her mother, looked down at the marble floor of the courtroom and cried.

On her return to Las Tres Marias, her *vega*, Lucila walked to the living room ... She turned on the record player and played one of her favorite long-play records, that of the famed Spanish singer Sarita Montiel, *El último cuplé,* The Last Torch Song, and selected the Argentine tango: *Fumando Espero,* Smoking I Wait:

Fumar es un placer genial sensual
Fumando espero al hombre a quien yo quiero
tras los cristales de alegres ventanales

Y mientras fumo, mi vida no consumo
porque flotando el humo me suelo adormecer...

To smoke is a wonderful, sensuous pleasure...
Smoking I wait for the man I love
behind the glasses of gaily-colored windows
And as I smoke, my life I don't waste away
because floating the smoke I usually fall asleep

Many years later, Lucila, by then an older woman, was rocking in an armchair on the porch of her home. She was enjoying the deep greenness of the tobacco plants in her *vega* when the tranquility of the afternoon was interrupted by the noise of the motor of an approaching car. Lucila was pleasantly surprised when she saw Ángel Chong getting out of the Chevrolet with a bouquet of red roses in his hand.

"Angelito, what a surprise! So many years since the last time I saw you! What brings you here? What a beautiful car!"

"I came to say goodbye, Mrs. Lucila, we sold our small home on the other side of the valley and we are moving to Guatemala. My wife has family in that country. Yes! With some of our savings, I was able to buy this car." And smiling he said: "Now I don't have to walk through cane fields anymore."

"Sit down Angelito." Lucila pulled up a chair for him to sit on. "If it had not been for you, I would have spent the last twenty years in jail."

"Thank you, madam, I did what my conscience dictated to me at that moment. I'm a little hurried, I brought you these roses to adorn your living room. I have to leave."

"Thank you so much! Wait one moment please, Angelito." Lucila got up from her chair, went inside the house, and then came out with a wooden box of cigars in her hands.

"This box contains the twenty best cigars of this entire region, they are my favorite, I want you to have this to remember me and the tree where as a young woman I entertained myself smoking, dreaming ... watching my thoughts disappear like the smoke of my cigars. I wish you good luck Angelito, I will never forget you."

"Goodbye, Mrs. Lucila, I will never forget you either."

He left without turning back, got into his car, started the engine and in a cloud of dust disappeared in the distance. Lucila smiled.

"... I guess I am on my own now ...!"

To my son

... life is a story, what we remember today is not
the same as what we lived yesterday ...
The author

I. Crossings

For reasons unknown to me, most of us humans enjoy crossing things or objects. We like to do crossword puzzles, we do cross-marks when filling applications, and we often say expressions such as "I will cross that bridge when I get there" and many more. Additionally, we also like jumping over puddles; we cross rivers and sometimes lakes; we even cross an ocean but most commonly or routinely we cross a road or a street just to get to the other side.

In the years I have been living on this beautiful earth, I have also crossed many things. In several of my trips to Europe, I have crossed the "pond," as the Atlantic Ocean is commonly referred to.

Crossing the "pond" for the first time, going to that part of the world was exciting to me and to my wife. But we did not see anything during that crossing; it was very difficult to see anything when you are up flying at thirty-four thousand feet in the middle of the night. However, we saw a dark-blue sky painted with millions of stars and with a crescent moon curiously following us across the majestic ocean.

We have navigated the Danube and the Rhine rivers as well as Lake Onega in Russia; crossed in a hydrofoil the Gulf of Finland to reach Peterhof Palace, the summer palace of Peter the Great in Saint Petersburg, Russia.

With regards to puddles, I would be lying to you if I said I have jumped in a puddle of water — when I was a small boy back in my home country, — because I never did. I always watched other kids jumping and splashing in the middle of it and getting their shoes and clothes dirty. It must have been fun; perhaps I should try it sometime. Back home I crossed a few rivers like the Tipitapa and the Ochomogo just to mention a couple. Once I swam a short distance across from one island to another in Lake Nicaragua, only to be chastised by my father and mother after proudly telling them of my adventure and hearing both of them say to me: "... you are lucky you are telling us the story, you could have been bitten by a shark ..." There are freshwater sharks in Lake Nicaragua which lurk mostly beneath calm waters and in rivers. However, crossing Lake Nicaragua later with my father was the most memorable crossing that I had experienced in my life.

In this country, I have also done a few crossings of my own. I have crossed, by car and by barge the Potomac and the mighty Mississippi as well as the awesome Columbia River, the river traveled by the famous explorers Lewis and Clark, which took me from Oregon to Washington State. I have crossed by ferry from the mainland to Orcas Island, one of the San Juan Islands in Washington State as well as others. By plane, I have crossed the country several times but again it is very difficult to see and appreciate anything from thirty-plus thousand feet; I was just able to see a beautiful aquarellic painted landscape below and cotton-like clouds in between.

Several years ago, I told my wife that I wanted to take a trip across the United States and I wanted to do it either by train or by car but I never pursued it. Perhaps she thought that I wasn't serious or that the trip would prove to be too long. So, I gave up on that idea. The opportunity to fulfill that itching desire came up again when our son informed us that he was going to visit a school friend who had moved to Portland, Oregon, but the real opportunity materialized one year later after he visited his friend and decided to move west.

II. In search of a bike trail

He always liked bicycles. Ever since he was a small boy of two or three years old, he liked to ride his big-wheel tricycle and speed down sidewalks and in the absence of brakes, he used his small feet and whatever tree he could find to help him stop. We always feared he would break a leg or an arm, fortunately, he never did. While he was growing up, he rode dirt bikes with his friends along the neighborhood and in a few trails. The Washington DC area was not very friendly to cyclists at that time.

He rode bicycles in several area trails while he was going to school at Virginia Tech, as the Virginia Polytechnic Institute and State University are most popularly known. He was always looking for the perfect trail. He purchased and sold some of his bikes just to purchase a new one or one more modern and better which would allow him to achieve a more thrilling ride. Of course, in the process, he became an expert bicycle mechanic.

He tested other trails on the eastern shore of Maryland and in West Virginia, alongside the Potomac River and other small trails by nearby lakes and small rivers in Maryland. After his graduation from Virginia Tech he purchased an apartment in Glover Park, an upscale area near Georgetown and American Universities, and instead of driving or riding public transportation, he opted to ride his bike to his new job in Bethesda via the Crescent Trail. However, he always longed to ride better and more challenging trails like the ones available in Moab, Utah and in Oregon; both of these are like magnets to cyclists, professional as well as amateurs.

III. His mind was made up

It took him approximately one year and two glasses of wine since his visit to a friend in Oregon for him to get enough courage to tell us that he had decided to move away from the Washington, DC area. Most Sunday's afternoons we would sit down to watch the Washington Redskins football games and share a homemade dinner with the rest of the family.

It was around the middle of May of 2007 when he broke the news to us.

"Well," he said, "this is the deal." Whenever he wanted to tell us something important, he would always start with that statement.

"I have decided to move out; I have quit my job and advertised my condo up for rent. In the meantime, I am moving back with you guys so I can get my place ready for rent."

Both my wife and I knew that this was coming, sooner rather than later; it was a matter of time for him to make his move, but we nonetheless decided to ask him the reasons for making such a drastic decision.

"I want to try to make it on my own," he said. "I am tired of this area. I know I have a good job and also the possibility to move up in the company, but I want to move out to the west coast, Portland, Oregon to be exact."

"Aren't you happy here?" my wife asked him. "You have everything here, you have your own place and a car, a job that you just quit but you could get it back, and you have your family here." My wife continued.

"What, who do you have in Oregon?" I asked. "You don't even have a job, a place to live."

"I am not unhappy," he replied. "But I am too comfortable here, it is the same routine; come here on Sundays, watch the ball game, grill some, drink some wine ..." he continued. "... I have been under the parental umbrella for quite some time and as I said before, I want to try to make it on my own, away from here ..."

And so, the conversation continued with our son both of us trying to convince him to reconsider his decision by looking at the advantages of living in the Washington, DC area. We pointed out the different job opportunities that were available here, it's the nation's capital and the seat of the Federal Government. We were not successful. He was going to go away.

However, since we had a trip to Russia planned for the middle of May of 2007, I asked him to wait until our return in early June. In the back of our minds, we always hoped that he may change his mind. He would not.

It was at this time that I also told him:

"If you don't mind, I would like to make the trip with you, I always wanted to drive across the United States," I said. "What do you think?"

"I don't think so," he promptly replied. "There is no room in the car, I am taking all my stuff and you know that my car is not that big," he said. "And besides," he continued, "this is my trip and I want to make it alone."

"I know is your trip," I said. "But I would like to make you an offer that I doubt very much you will refuse, and perhaps you could reconsider."

"I'm listening," he said. "What's your offer?" he asked me.

"If you allow me to accompany you," I added, "I promise you that you will be the one calling the shots about what route to take, where to stay, and so on, and in addition," I said, "I will finance your trip."

"What do you mean?" he asked me.

"I will pay for all the food and lodging as well as for gasoline."

He hesitated for a moment but finally said;

"OK, you are in."

IV. Preparations for the trip

Fortunately, I was wise enough not to tell my son that in addition to wanting to drive across the United States, another reason was to be able to keep him company along the way. At the slightest suspicion of my intentions he probably would have rejected my offer no matter how attractive it was. After all, he was my son and I wanted to be with him just in case anything happened to the car or to himself or any other unexpected emergency. I never thought about anything happening to me, being a heart patient who had undergone by-pass surgery a few years before, but that did not matter; it was the least of my worries.

"You are joking," my wife said when she learned that he had agreed to let me make the trip with him.

"Why?" I asked her.

"Two non-talkative individuals," she replied, "going alone on a six or seven-day trip, across this huge country, from the east to the west coast."

My wife knew that I was not too much of a talker and she feared, knowing that our son was not a great communicator himself that the trip would end up in a communication disaster. She was wrong.

Upon our return from our Russian river cruise, my son and I set out to make the preparations for the trip. A trip that will become

215

the second most memorable for me. I had crossed Lake Nicaragua with my father, now it was time for me to go across this vast and beautiful nation with my son. Not many people are as fortunate to be able to share a trip with their father, and now I was going to share a long trip with my son. I never knew how my father felt about sharing his trip with me, but now I was going to have this once in a lifetime opportunity to experience a trip with my son.

Of course, the first thing we did was to visit the offices of AAA. We needed a map of the United States and several individual maps of special places to visit as well as the mandatory roadmap or "Trip Tic."

"Where are you guys going?" the clerk at AAA asked.

I started to say to California but my son interrupted me.

"We are going to Moab, Utah, then to Yosemite National Park and then to Monterey, California."

"That's a beautiful country," he said. "I wish I could go with you guys."

Normally when somebody asks you about a trip that you are taking or about to take, he or she is ready to do anything to join you in your expedition, whether or not an invitation was extended.

"But you have a job," I said. "Would you quit your job?"

"In no time," the clerk replied.

Then I felt a kick on my left foot. It was my son telling me to shut up.

Next stop was Best Buy. In addition to the maps, we needed a Global Positioning System, a.k.a. GPS to guide us on our trip. Among the several brands available we chose a medium-priced Garmin.

"This is a good brand," the clerk at Best Buy said. "One of its good features is that it calls the name of the streets and roads and it stays charged for two hours at a time."

"Where are you fellows going, are you planning a trip?" he asked curiously.

Since I did not want another passenger or another companion on our trip, I just told him that I wanted the GPS to help me navigate the streets of Washington.

"Don't you know your way around?" he asked. "How long have you been living in the area?" was his next question. "I agree, you need more than a GPS to help you with the Washington streets," he said. "They are a mess and they are constantly being re-routed."

"Yep! you are right," I said. "They are a mess." End of conversation and questioning.

From Best Buy, armed with a brand-new GPS, we headed to REI, Recreational Equipment Inc., one of my son's favorite sports stores. We needed some supplies for the trip, such as a pair of hiking shoes, although I was not planning on doing any hiking, also needed was underwear made of a special material which dried very fast. It would come in very handy since I was packing just the bare essentials.

Most of us guys are terrible when it comes to packing, especially personal items for a long trip. My son was the opposite. He was as neat as they come as well as a terrific organizer. He packed some of his clothing in boxes instead of suitcases; his kitchen utensils and china in another box; shoes in another; a large four battery flashlight was placed under the seat and a small one in the glove compartment. A medium toolbox was included with auto tools, including a set of spark plugs and cables; small and larger wrenches to fit the majority of the nuts and bolts of his black Honda CR-V and, of course, tools for the two bicycles which he had disassembled and strategically mounted on the inside of the truck and to allow more space the two back seats had been tilted forward. The reason I say that he had the bikes strategically mounted is that he anticipated removing them in the evenings when we went to sleep in a hotel or motel, as he did not want to call attention to the bikes and have somebody break one of the windows to steal them.

I suggested that for protection we should take a gun, but he wisely objected to the idea; we probably would not have used it even if we were threatened. Instead, he suggested that we take several bottles of water and beer ... We were not planning to have a party but one never knows when they could become handy. In a medium-sized cooler, we stored the beverages; a six-pack of Sierra Nevada beer, sodas and a bottle of Chardonnay, just in case thirst became an issue. My wife suggested that we take a roll of paper towels, to clean anything that could get soiled during the trip.

The gas tank was filled up to the brim; brakes checked, tire inflation including spare checked, coolant checked, engine oil and filter recently changed, windshield wiper fluid checked; blades brand new; timing belt and water pump fine as well. The mechanic that did the inspection told us that everything else was OK. We were ready to go!

I was only allowed to take a small L.L. Bean backpack with a pair of jeans, the fast-drying underwear, socks, several t-shirts, four polo shirts; shaving and grooming equipment as well as my assortment of pills, a toothbrush, toothpaste, my Canon Power Shot S3, cap, small binoculars and my Ray Bans. Later I would regret not listening to my wife who suggested that I take a jacket or a sweater just in case it got cold during the trip. Why would I need one? It was June, the beginning of summer. I was wrong; I should have listened to her.

V. Ready to go!!

The night before, after the sumptuous dinner that my wife prepared as a farewell dinner, we spent some time sipping *Sambuca di Amore* and reminiscing about the family trips we had taken together to

Bonita Springs, Florida in our Volkswagen bus for fifteen straight summers; talking about where we were going to spend our first night, reviewing some of the maps and other minor details. It was agreed that I would drive mornings and that he would drive afternoons as well as when going uphill when we reached some inclined roads, namely the Colorado Rockies since I did not want to risk not being able to shift soon enough and mess up the gears. His CR-V was a stick-shift. I knew how to drive stick-shifts since I learned to drive in a stick-shift car, but it had been a while since I had driven one. Honestly, the main reason was that I had the tendency of snoozing during most afternoons.

Being as thoughtful as she was, my wonderful wife had prepared our first lunch the night before. Breast of turkey sandwich on rye with mustard and mayo for me, and ham and Swiss cheese on wheat with just mustard for our son accompanied with plantain chips, chocolate chip cookies and a couple of napkins; the sandwiches were lightly toasted.

Strangers have often told me that I don't look Hispanic; in general, I don't know how Hispanics look or who could be shelved in that category. Perhaps the comment about my looks is prompted due to the fact that I am not a short person or perhaps for the lightness of my skin. I am not a very tall individual, I measure about 5'11" but with my new hiking boots, I could be scratching the 6' mark. I am relatively slender, with an average looking face, brown eyes and medium-sized nose and with a full set of graying hair.

My son, unlike me, is a tad shorter, but he is also light skinned and slender with short cut brown hair and bright greenish eyes. I am humbled to say it because he is my son, but overall, he is a very good-looking guy.

If it wasn't for my accent, we would both blend easily among the different groups of people who make up the population of this country. This was our intention, to blend.

At 6:30 am on June 7, 2007, after a light breakfast I kissed my wife and headed for the driver's seat of the CR-V while my son was taking care of last-minute details in the back of the car. Through the rear-view mirror, I could see my wife in her robe hugging her son before closing the garage door. Being as strong as she is, I knew that she was holding back some tears, but she would not let us know. Instead, she wished us both a safe trip and to make sure that we had a great time and to call her every day to let her know where we were or where we would spend the night and most of all to make sure we took lots of pictures.

She realized at that moment that the most precious men in her life, after her father, were leaving. She knew that one, the oldest, was coming back, but not the younger one.

VI. We hit the road

The first few hours of our trip were uneventful. We jumped on I-270 northwest toward Frederick, Maryland, a few minutes after driving on I-495. At that time of the day the temperature was comfortably cool; however, I knew it would soon rise and I felt that the khaki shorts and the blue polo I was wearing would be the right thing for the trip. My son programmed the new Garmin.

Before reaching Frederick, we faced our first confusion. The posted signs indicating the road to follow were not as explicitly defined as we would have liked but soon enough, "the bitch in the box," as my son referred to the female voice calling out the directions in the GPS, made the decision for us. This was not to be our last encounter with confusing road signs. This country is plagued by such anomalies. I often wonder how people don't get lost more often.

At around nine in the morning, we veered onto Route 70 and we skirted Pennsylvania towards Wheeling and on to Columbus, Ohio, driving almost parallel to the Mason-Dixon Line. The country was awakening as we made a slight detour to reach Route 70 again. People had started to hit the roads in trucks; trucks transporting produce, lumber, furniture, gasoline, home building materials as well as gardening and household appliances; trucks moving stuff from families going someplace else; vans, sport utility vehicles, campers, house trailers, regular cars, and many more.

North America is a country on the move. People move from one place to another; north, south, east and west. They move seeking an adventure, to visit relatives and places; others move in search of better jobs or just because they were unhappy with the place they lived. A large majority of these people don't have a place to call home; they, as it is said, "lack roots." I left the roots of my birthplace in search of an education but after a few years, I established a new set of roots; I had a family, a house and other unmovable property which is what defines the meaning of roots. Although my son had an unmovable property, a fully furnished apartment, to him it was not a condition to set up roots yet, in addition, he was unhappy where he was living thus making it the main reason for him to uproot himself. He had joined the multitude of Americans who were looking for a different place to live, a job or just an adventure. Unlike me, he was a true American in the full sense of the word. I was just a transplanted American tagging along, going along for the ride, just to keep him company.

After stopping at one of the six hundred plus Cracker Barrel Restaurants in the country to supplement the sandwiches that my wife had deliciously prepared and to perform some physical functions, we decided to entertain ourselves by counting how many Cracker Barrel signs we would encounter along the way. The signs stopped showing up after we crossed the Mississippi River near Omaha, Nebraska. We counted about sixty-three signs.

Since we were going to cross the Appalachian Mountains in anticipation of encountering steep hills, as part of our early arrangement, he suggested that perhaps it would be better if he took the wheel for a while.

While he was driving, the Garmin was disconnected to allow him to plug in his earphones. I distracted myself by studying the map to try to decipher the maze of blue and red lines and the miniature shields marking the numbers of the highways and roads. I was mainly interested in comparing the data in the maps with the information being provided to us by the "voice" in the GPS. Also, I was curious to verify what a friend told me a few years back about how even numbered highways crossed from east to west and vice versa and the odd numbered ones crossed the country from north to south and vice versa. Information confirmed.

At around noon, after going through Zanesville and driving by Columbus, Ohio, we stopped for lunch at a rest stop. The sandwiches that my wife had made for us had had no time to gather any dust; they were devoured in no time. My son decided that it was all right for me to drive again. As we exited the rest stop a sign along the road suggested: "next rest stop, thirty miles."

I like to call rest stops road emporiums. They are facilities located on most of the major Interstates which crisscross the country providing travelers with a place to rest, to examine their routes or reconsider others, to eat, and to empty their bladders. Some of these emporiums are marketplaces full of vending machines which for a quarter, a dollar or two anybody can purchase crackers, chewing gum, sandwiches, peanuts, chips, coffee, soft drinks, bottled water and much more stuff. Even in the men's rooms, one would find personal items such as toothpaste and brushes, combs, deodorants and even condoms. I don't know what is available in the ladies' rooms since I have never entered one. Although some of these stops are manned to provide a hot meal, a hamburger or a hot dog or to provide directions like the welcoming centers, the majority are not. I often wondered who supplied these centers, in particular, the ones that are isolated with no signs of civilization for miles around.

"We are making good time," my son said, "let's try to make it to Peoria."

"But that is in Illinois," I said, "isn't that a little too far?"

"If we don't find any delays," he responded, "we can make it; remember that we will be crossing a time zone pretty soon."

From the start, we had avoided traveling on back roads; we had decided that we would travel the Interstates whenever possible.

"Besides," he said, "I want to go as far as we can today because I want to stop for a couple of days in Moab, Utah and we don't know if we are going to go across the Rockies without any problems."

"Ever since we stopped at AAA you have been saying that we were going to Moab," I said. "What's in Moab that is so important?" I asked him.

"Have you ever seen red rocks? Big red rocks?"

"No, I haven't," I said. "How big?"

"Biggggg, and beautiful!" he responded.

"I thought that your interest in this place had to do with your bicycling. I did not know about the rocks."

"That too," he said. "You are going to like it."

"Where did you learn about these places?" I asked. "You have been talking about the Glaciers that shaped this land, about the Ice Age, how the Grand Canyon was formed and all these things. Where did you learn all this?" I asked again.

"You have always told us that the only way to learn is by reading. So, I have been doing that ... reading," he said.

"That's pretty good," I said. "You have to tell me more as we go along."

By 3:30 in the afternoon we encountered heavy traffic as we bypassed Indianapolis and hopped onto I-74 toward Peoria. Welcome to Illinois, the Land of Lincoln, read the sign as we were crossing into the State of Illinois a few miles before the town of Danville.

Every state in the country is named after an important person, a plant, a bird, you name it. New York State is called the Empire State; Indiana the Hoosier State; Louisiana the Pelican State; South Carolina is known as the Palmetto State; and North Carolina as the Tar Heel State, and so on and so forth.

The Welcome to Illinois sign reminded me of many of my countrymen and relatives who had recently arrived in this country. It was customary to send a picture back home in front of the sign welcoming you to the state that you were entering, plus a picture of you standing next to a late model automobile even if that car did not belong to you. I would not even dare ask my son to stop as we entered each of the states we traveled through and have my picture taken pointing toward the welcome sign. He would have had a fit.

We made it to Peoria by 6:30 pm a little before seven, almost twelve hours after we had left Bethesda. We settled in a motel, located past the city and the Illinois River, which offered a good rate of about $75.00 with continental breakfast included. At the restaurant where we had dinner that evening, the locals were still recalling how Illinois State had beaten Penn State.

VII. The Corn Flakes States

The next states that we were going to cross; Iowa and Nebraska, are part of the mid-western states or most commonly recognized as the Corn Belt States. Why? The name says it. Corn is grown there.

Humorously, I decided to call them the Corn Flake States or Corn Flake Alley.

We did not waste any time during the so-called continental breakfast. I had orange juice, a muffin, and coffee. My son had the same and he refilled his thermos with coffee from the percolator in the lobby. He likes to drink several cups of the black liquid in the morning. We had refilled the gas tank the night before.

We did not have to travel too long before we hit the cornfields. Cornfields after cornfields as far as our eyes could see. We watched those cornfields swaying back and forth by the gentle breezes blowing from south to north and from east to west, just to be interrupted by the sight of trucks on the highway or a small house in the distance. A small house that could have been a large house, perhaps the owner of the fields lived there, but to us, it was a small speck of sand in a sea of corn stalks.

From Peoria, we drove northwest toward Davenport, jumped onto I-80 to Des Moines and continued on to Omaha, Nebraska where we crossed the Mississippi River.

The day could not have been clearer. There was not a single cloud in the sky. My son was speeding above seventy-five almost at eighty miles per hour, trying to make it to Colorado by nightfall. I was enjoying the view; the amazing sight on both sides of the road, corn and more corn. It was after passing Omaha, close to the town of York when I heard the loud boom. It was like the boom heard after a jet plane breaks the sound barrier, a sonic boom. The breeze had stopped and the cornfields were no longer swaying.

"It has to be a plane, possibly one of those fighter jets," I said while scanning the skies for an aircraft through the open window of the CR-V.

"I am sorry Pops," he said. "There are no major airports or Air Force bases around here."

'He knows,' I thought to myself. He had done the reading.

"Look ahead," he said, pointing ahead of us. "I just saw a lightning strike on the left of us. Listen to the thunder."

Lightning was ahead of us. It was as if the heavens suddenly needed to punish the earth for its present or past sins, and we were in the middle of it. How did it know that we were among them, sinners? Lightning was striking left and right in broad daylight. It reminded me of a brutal thunderstorm I had encountered while crossing the Florida Everglades with my older daughter when she was eleven years old. It rained buckets. I was afraid then, and again I was afraid now. But this time there was no rain, not even a trickle.

I had heard, I don't recall from whom or where, that lightning often strikes ahead of a major storm, be it a thunderstorm or a tornado.

"I believe we are going to be hit by a tornado," my son said. "Look toward your left, it seems that is coming from the south. Look at the black clouds. They are taking the shape of a funnel."

"Holy crap!" was my only reaction. "Can you increase the speed?"

"I am already going to eighty-five! We don't want to be stopped by a cop," my son replied.

"You're right, but I do not want my life to end in one of these cornfields, in the middle of nowhere," I said. "I have seen on TV how tornadoes can toss a car like a toy," I added.

We sped toward where the lightning was striking, fearing for our lives, but just as it had suddenly struck, it suddenly vanished leaving no trace of what could have been a horrendous experience.

As we traveled on I-80, we passed Kearney, Lexington, and Cozad. What a relief! We had survived Corn Flake Alley without even tasting a kernel of corn or a single cornflake. I had never seen such a spectacle; the vastness and the evenness of the cornfields.

VIII. The Colorado Rockies

We continued on I-80 along the North Platte River and a little after Big Springs we veered south onto I-76 toward Denver. We had made it to Colorado a little before 6:00 pm.

We had reached another time zone, but instead of the extended sunlight, it was getting dark and damp. A light drizzle was beginning to fall. The temperature started dropping and the drizzle turned into snow. I needed the jacket or the sweater that my thoughtful wife had suggested to take "just in case!" Like I said earlier, I should have listened to her.

My son noticed the shivering I was bravely trying to hide from him, and he kindly offered me a thoroughly worn and faded sweatshirt that at one time, perhaps when it was originally woven, was blackish in color. I never gave it back to him. I still have that faded garment and every time I wear it; it reminds me of that first time I wore it.

"I would rather not go through Denver," I said to him. "What do think?"

"I don't either," he said. "Why don't we find a place to stay before it gets darker? If we continue, we run the risk of finding all the places already booked," he added. "I don't think that snow will be a problem. It is not sticking to the road."

We hunkered down in a town called Brush a few miles before Fort Morgan. The vegetation was different than the cornfields we had left behind. It was shorter and darker green; perhaps it appeared that way due to the evening darkness. The motel was also dark and damp and so were the rooms. But 'What the hell,' I thought, 'we are not planning to buy the damned place.'

Fortunately, the room where the continental breakfast was being served was already open by five in the morning. We thought we would be the only ones at that hour but there was another couple in the room already making waffles. In addition to coffee and hard-boiled eggs, we loaded up on the apples which looked pretty red and juicy. We had decided to take Route 34 after going by Fort Morgan toward Greeley. We headed toward the zenith. We felt the altitude as we started up the Rockies. Daylight made its appearance a little after six-thirty. We were rewarded with a shower of trees of all shapes and sizes and different shades of green accentuated by the rays of the brilliant sun. Conifers of different species like pine, cedars, and firs tall and small guarded our uphill trek on both sides of the road. The view was awesome.

Route 34 proved to be long and a road of many twists and turns. As we went up, I distracted myself by admiring how the sights we had just passed were shrinking behind us. Deer and elk abounded. As we inched forward, we made a brief stop at Pony Tracks Trading Post. It was a small souvenir trading post along the winding road. He decided to taste one of the apple pockets that the wife of the owner had recently baked.

As he was purchasing the goodies, I took advantage to use the facilities. It was at this point that the friendly owner, an older gentleman in his late seventies, offered to take a picture of us. It was then that he noticed the tags in my son's CR-V. I wish he hadn't.

"You are from Washington, DC," he said. "I have never been to Washington; I wish I could go there sometime. Have you ever seen the President?"

To prevent a conversation that God knows where it was going to lead or how long it was going to last, I decided to tell the nice gentleman that we had not been to the White House and we had only caught glimpses at the President when he is being driven in his limousine, if we were lucky. When one speaks about Washington, DC, the President and other politicians, one always risks engaging in a political discussion. I was not prepared to entertain a discussion of such a nature.

"Although I would like to go and visit Washington," he said looking melancholically toward a sign that he had painted on a sheet of aluminum with the Rockies in the background which read *Slice of Heaven* he said, "I don't think I will ever leave this place. This is my slice of heaven."

We thanked the gentleman for his hospitality and headed up the mountain.

After traveling on Route 34 or Trail Ridge Road as it's also known, for another hour we finally reached a rest area near the summit where vehicles were starting to crowd around.

"I wonder what is going on," I said to my son while he was trying to find a place to park the car.

"I don't know, I am going to go and ask the Park Ranger up by the restrooms," he replied as he exited the car.

While he went up to speak with the Ranger, I amused myself taking pictures at the sights below. I admired the vastness of the valley and the winding road we had just traveled which looked as if someone had threaded a needle with a thick brownish thread.

I was also admiring a couple of youngsters who were jumping from rock to rock. I was fearful that they would tumble down into the valley below, into the abyss. They were following me wherever I moved, hopping from rock to rock. They also insisted, almost begged me to take a photograph of them. I couldn't resist. Finally, I obliged and snapped their picture. They told me their names but they sounded foreign. So, I decided to give them different names; I called then Red and Sunny. They also asked me that if I ever wrote a story about this trip to please include a picture of them. Unfortunately, I couldn't, include their picture, the only thing I can say is that they were the most beautiful little birds I had ever seen.

Fifteen minutes later after my son had managed to speak with the Ranger. He came down and told me the bad news.

"It snowed last night," he said. "Two feet. We are stuck here for at least a couple of hours until the plows clear the road; no one is being allowed to go up."

"What option do we have?"

"Go back down, and try crossing via Denver," he said.

"I don't think we want to do that," I replied. "I don't mind the wait."

"I agree," he said. "But while we wait," he added, "we can go and hike up the hill."

"What if they open the road while we are away," I said. "I think we better wait." He agreed and went back to where the Ranger was speaking with other travelers.

That was the excuse I gave my son. In reality, I was afraid that my 'blood pump' would have a fit when it realized how high we had come. The elevation was about 12,000 feet. I was afraid that it would throw one of its tantrums and retaliate against me by suddenly stop pumping. I did not want my son to have to deal with such a situation, not on this trip that was so significant to him.

The road was opened sooner than we had anticipated. We headed to the summit of the Sierra Madre, the Colorado Rockies. On one side a wall of bluish ice about fifteen feet high hugged the narrow road; on the other side, there was nothing, except for the ten-foot-high metal rods, placed every thirty feet or so, to guide the plows to prevent them from falling into the emptiness below.

I have never been up so high in my life, and I doubt that I would ever again go as high as that instant unless I climbed Mount Everest or the Kilimanjaro, but such a climb was not included on my "bucket list." In school, I had briefly read about the Sierra Madre and how it extended from North America to the outermost ridges of South America, but I never dreamed that someday I would be on one of its zeniths; to me, that moment was as if I was on top of the world.

As we reached the summit, we veered left and headed south. A few miles down we saw the sign "Continental Divide." We had just finished clearing the snow off the sign to be able to take a picture when we heard a roaring thunder. 'Not again,' I thought, 'we are far from Corn Flake Alley.' As I turned my head to see where the noise was coming from, I saw four men.

"Son," I told him, "we don't have a weapon to defend ourselves; we are being mugged by those four guys."

As they dismounted their Harleys, they headed towards us. All dressed in black leather jackets and pants decorated with what looked like silver spikes, each six feet plus tall. One was removing his shiny helmet, also black and putting it in his left arm, tugged against his body. One of them said;

"Morning!"

"Morning!" my son answered. "We're just finished clearing the sign to take a picture, and we will be on our way after that."

"We also stopped to do the same," said the tallest and the heaviest, the one who was removing his helmet as he spoke.

"Where are you guys heading?" I nervously asked.

"We are heading east," said the third, the one that appeared to be the oldest with a thick reddish beard who looked like the king of the Vikings.

"Where are you two fellows heading?" asked the one with his helmet in his arm.

"We are going west," I said.

"Do you mind if we take a picture of the two of you?" he asked.

"No, we don't mind," said my son. After a brief exchange, we headed west and they headed east.

Once in the car, my son asked me about the significance of the Continental Divide. I explained to him that it was an imaginary line or an invisible line which had to do with the direction that rivers flowed from east to west. Rivers east from the Divide would empty onto the Atlantic Ocean and west of the line would empty onto the Pacific.

"How did you know all this?" he asked me.

"I read about it," I replied. "Do you think you are the only one who's been reading stuff for this trip?" I asked him. "Besides," I said to him, "it was written in the sign."

"Huh!!" He mumbled.

From there we continued southwest bordering and, in some instances, crossing the Colorado River.

After catching up with I-70 again, we decided that the next stop would be Moab, Utah, taking breaks of course for gas and for restroom necessities. We still had some hard-boiled eggs and some apples. That would be enough until we reached Moab. We passed Riffle, De Beque, Fruita and after Thompson, we veered south onto Highway 50.

IX. Arches National Park

Bowen Motel was a small motel in the center of Moab. A very neat and clean motel surrounded by rocks the size of a small mountain; buttes as they are called. I realized at this point what my son had been telling me about rock formations; they were red, not a brilliant metallic red, but a volcanic burnt red. I had never seen such a palette of color in rocks.

We checked in at around five-thirty in the afternoon. We felt the heat; we regretted having left the cool breezes and the different shades of green of the Rockies. This was dry land, hot and desert terrain but awesome. There was plenty of daylight ahead of us. We decided to shower and rest for a while instead of immediately venturing outside to explore the small town.

We walked on what I would call Main Street, not more than ten or twelve medium-sized blocks. I don't think I would distance myself too far from the truth if I stated that there is a Main Street in every city in America. There must be a reason, but I don't know what it is.

On our way back, we entered a bar-restaurant hoping to get a beer or two as well as something to eat. As we sat at the bar the bartender asked us:

"What's your pleasure, gentlemen?" while with a white cloth and in a circular motion he wiped the crystal clear and spotless wooden top which appeared to have endured several coats of polyurethane.

My son said, "We would like to have a beer."

"I am sorry." the bartender apologized, "but this is a dry state. You are in Utah," he said. "We only serve alcoholic beverages to members."

In the past, I had the opportunity to work with a Mormon and I was familiar with the customs of their church including the fact that they did not drink alcoholic beverages. Still, I was a bit surprised at the suggestion of the bartender that we had to be "members" to be able to have a beer. Perhaps, I thought it was different if you lived in Utah.

"Do you mean I have to be a member of the Church of the Latter Days Saints to have a beer?" I asked.

"Oh no!" He laughed. "You have to be a member of the 'pool' club, the billiard club, or we could serve you a beer if you order something else," he said.

'Why didn't he say so from the start?' I thought to myself.

Great, we ordered some chips and salsa on the side and had a couple of beers. Later we had dinner.

"Remind me," I told my son, "not to come back to this place again."

Early the next morning after having a very hearty breakfast we drove a little more than a mile toward the entrance of Arches National Park where we purchased the entry tickets. We made up for the previous days when we were in a hurry and had only muffins and boiled eggs for breakfast. But since the boiled eggs were free to take, we packed a couple and some apples to help us mitigate the hunger during the day since there were no food stands or vending machines inside the Park.

It would be presumptuous of me if I thought that I would ever visit the planet Mars. I will never, in what remains of my time on this planet visit Mars, and I doubt very much that I would in my afterlife. As far as I am concerned Arches was the closest I would come to be on Mars, provided that all scientists and experts in astronomy are correct in saying that Mars is the "red planet." To me, this was my red planet.

As soon as we entered the Park my eyes were rewarded with the sights of skyscraping red rock formations that I had only seen in magazines and in the cowboy movies I watched during my younger years back home when the hero after rescuing the heroine from the villain rides onto the sunset. I don't really know where those movies were filmed but it seemed they were filmed here.

I was snapping pictures left and right. I couldn't decide which was the prettiest. I was afraid I was going to miss one. If I had attached all the pictures in this story; there would be no room for the text. In some instances it seemed as if some extra-terrestrial had carefully placed a rock on top of the other, one never knows, perhaps that was the way it happened, it was an awesome sight, one not to ever be forgotten.

As we toured the park we came across the rock formations for which the Park is named after, in the form of arches, amazing.

After driving and walking through the Park during most of the morning, admiring and photographing our Martian landscape, we decided to hit the hard-boiled eggs under the meager shadow being cast by the CR-V. It was after our brief lunch that my son told me that he wanted to hike up. He wanted to see an arched rock, that after years of exposure to the elements it was very thin and according to what he had read it was bound to crack and fall.

I was reluctant to go up with him but bravely I said yes. I did not want him to think that I was afraid of going up the five-thousand-foot-high place where the rock was situated. He suggested I take at least two bottles of water and something to munch. I complied and in each of my short pockets, I put a bottle of water and one apple. He did the same but no apple. It was a little after one in the afternoon, and to say the least, it was hot. It was a dry heat, not the humid type of heat that I was used to in the hot summer days in Washington.

I always have thought the world was full of crazy people who would do anything to prove a point, but I doubted very much I would find one here, in a desert-like atmosphere. I was wrong. I am not talking about a mentally ill individual; I am talking about the shirtless fellow, with just a brief set of shorts and running shoes that was jogging up the hill.

"That guy is going to drop dead," I told my son.

"He appears to be in good shape," was his reply.

The higher you go up the thinner the air gets. This is not a scientific theory and even if it was, I am not a scientist to make that affirmation. I felt it while at the summit in the Rockies, and I was starting to feel it again as we went up. My 'blood pump' was getting excited.

As we approached the top of a very large flatly shaped rock formation, we found the jogger. Not dead but sprawled on top of the rock with his arms and legs open wide. His companion was blowing air and pouring water on his face. I felt like telling him, "You should have known better, you crazy fool," but I abstained from making any comments.

"I think I am going to wait for you here," I told my son.

"Why are you out of breath?" he asked me. "You shouldn't have any problems. You run every day," he added.

"Yes, you are absolutely right, but I run on a flat surface and not up to a rocky hill five thousand feet high," I said. "Besides I don't want to end up like that guy."

"Okay," he said. "You can wait here, drink plenty of water even if you are not thirsty, that way you will not get dehydrated, and if you eat your apple make sure you don't throw away any leftovers, you will be polluting the park if you do."

My son is always concerned about the environment. I don't blame him; I wish there were more people like him. But I did not listen to him this time, about not disposing of the remains of the apple. After I had finished eating it, like a small child, I threw its core down on the rocks, wanting to see how far it would go. It went far. After my apple and after drinking my first bottle of water the sun was punishing me, perhaps because I had not listened to my son and thrown the apple down the rocks, so I went down and sat under the modest shade of the CR-V.

"What did you do with the apple?" he asked me when he joined me one hour later after coming down from his climb.

"I gave it to a rabbit," I said.

"There are no rabbits here."

"What about a deer?" I asked.

"Whatever..."

Back at the motel, we agreed that we had seen most of the Arches and he had gathered plenty of information about the numerous bike trails in the area, and perhaps we should hit the road the next day, one day earlier than we had anticipated. We checked the tire pressure and the cooling fluid made sure the AC was in working order, filled the gas tank and called it a day. We were headed towards the desert; we were going to go across Nevada.

As Utah passed us, and Nevada welcomed us I thought about my Mormon friend whom I had not seen or heard from. He was a high-level bishop in the Church. Perhaps he had moved up and was currently performing higher-level functions in the Church in Provo. For sure he had not become a member of the exclusive R.I.P. club. I would have known since I am an avid reader of the obit column.

I worked for many years for an organization which assigned titles such as "specialists" to those employees who performed specialized functions. On our trip, we met a class of people who unlike the "specialists" I had worked with, are true "specialists" in their profession. These are the truckers. They know every detail of their trade, they are those who roam the country east to west, north to south; they are a very special breed of people.

Truckers know every single detail about the vehicles they drive day in and day out in order to make a living. There are small trucks, medium sized ones and the so-called eighteen wheelers. Truckers know the type and size of the engine of their vehicles and they can tell if the truck is in good or in bad health just by listening to the purring of their engines. They don't need maps or GPS's, they know every road by name and by distance; the size and capacity of their gas tanks; how the wind is blowing and in what direction; if there is a storm on the horizon; how far it is from here to there, but most importantly they know where to stop to eat and get gas, they know which truck stop on the road has the best hot meal and or a hot bath, they know where other truckers congregate to exchange information about the conditions of the road ahead and the one they have just traveled. We needed to find one of those "truck stops" before crossing the desert.

After exiting Moab, we jumped onto I-70 towards Salina, and on I-15 to Beaver. After driving shortly on I-15 we took road 21 passing Milford and Garrison to 50 toward Ely. Ely was our destination before we headed to the desert toward Tonopah where we were planning to spend the night.

"At Ely," I told my son, "we should find a place to have something to eat, fill the gas tank and check that everything visible in the CR-V is in working order, and if we can let's stop at a truck stop."

The sign read "Ol a's Dinner." I figured that the name had to be "Olga's," and the number of trucks around it gave the impression that there was a trucker's convention inside the diner. This is what we were looking for, a truck stop.

I guessed it was Olga; but it could have been Betty or Sue, the waitress behind the counter who welcomed us with a loud "Howdy boys!" as we entered the joint. We scanned the place and sat at the two remaining vacant stools at the end of the counter. I ordered a hamburger with fries and a cup of coffee. My son instead had scrambled eggs with hash brown potatoes and coffee as well. The blueberry pie under the glass dome on top of the counter looked very inviting but I resisted the temptation.

We had to be very attentive to be able to understand the languages being spoken inside the diner. I thought I had an accent, but mine was a Spanish accent. What I was listening to was a mélange of languages and rhythms as the English language was being spoken. I thought that having lived in New Orleans for some time would qualify me to understand the different tones and accents of America. Words were being shortened, extended and accentuated in a form I had not heard before.

I had heard about how New Yorkers talked, how Bostonians had a very peculiar way of pronouncing some words; I knew how Louisiana and Mississippi natives spoke because I had listened to them, which brings me to a brief story about a cleaning lady from Mississippi reporting to my landlord that the vacuum cleaner had broken, she said, "Miss Dora, the cleaner ain't no good anymore no more." Four negations in just one sentence.

The "ain't" contraction so commonly used including by me, as well as how the language was articulated in the southern states with a beautiful swaying of words, was almost like singing. I had heard about the Texas "twang," and had read about the unbelievable shortening of words by the so-called Okies from Oklahoma, including the pronunciation by the Kentuckians which I had heard in the movie "Deliverance."

It was amazing how all this variety of idioms and accents were being spoken under the umbrella of a single language: English.

X. The Nevada desert

As we had agreed at the start of our trip, I would refrain from carrying on any prolonged conversation with people whom we would meet along the way to prevent them from detecting my accent and to prevent them from asking the very familiar question, "You have an accent! Where do you come from?" I told my son to approach the trucker inspecting the engine under the hood of one of the trucks parked outside the diner and ask him a couple of questions about crossing the desert.

After inspecting our CR-V and kicking its tires (I don't know why people kick the tires of cars they are looking at), he courteously told us that we would make it across the desert with a full tank of gas and still we would have some to spare.

"However," he advised us, "buy enough water, and check your cooling fluid because it can get really hot there."

My son thanked him for his advice to which he responded, "Much obliged, and happy trails."

"He is a Texan," I said to my son.

Instead of the title that I have given this story, I should have named it "I have never seen that before..." because I had never seen dust funneled twirls ten to fifteen feet high arising from the scorching earth and disappearing into thin air no sooner than they had formed. Sagebrush was abundant in the desert; I had not seen such plants before either.

Neither had I seen a mirage, an illusion that tricks your eyes into seeing small bodies of water in the flattest parts of the desert when in reality there are none. Something else that caught my attention was the neat and extensive wire fence installed on both sides of the road.

"I wonder why they have that fence; there is nothing here, no animals that would cross the road, nothing," I commented to my son.

"Tumbleweeds," he said.

"Do you see those dry bushes which look like balls piled against the fence?"

"Oh yes!" I replied, "I have seen them in the Western movies ... What is wrong with them?"

"They are called tumbleweeds. They are dry bushes that when blown by strong winds can travel at high speeds. Their dry branches are very hard and sharp like spikes and they could hit your car and damage its body and puncture the tires flat."

"Wow! I never heard about that," I said.

Up until now, my bladder had behaved; it had not shown any of its sudden outbursts requesting to be emptied. Now it was texting my brain asking it to tell my son to stop because it was carrying too much fluid and it needed to get rid of it.

"Hey," I said to my son. "Could you stop the car and pull over?"

"What for"? he asked me, "We don't have time to take pictures."

"I need to pee."

"But you just went an hour ago. I can't stop in the middle of the road; someone will see you."

I said, "There is no one around, we have not seen a car in more than one hour, and the car that we spotted one hour and a half ago went by twenty minutes ago."

After driving for a one-half mile he stopped.

"You are going to pollute the desert and somebody is bound to see you," he said as I opened the door and exited the car ready to answer my brain's call who in turn was responding to my bladder's text message.

"Perhaps the only somebody around here who could see me is the lizards and the scorpions and I doubt that they would risk leaving their shady burrows just to witness my polluting act," I said.

"Besides it is so hot here that maybe it will evaporate before it hits the ground." It didn't evaporate.

Since in every desert there is a carcass of some animal or another, I have to mention that the only carcass that we saw was that of a dog or a coyote that probably got lost and could not find water soon enough.

The McDonald's at Tonopah was crowded when we arrived a little after five. It was full of soldiers. I could not tell if they were from the army, marines or air force. What I recall is that they were loud and rowdy; they must have been from a nearby base. The town was almost deserted, perhaps due to the unbearable heat. The motel where we were planning to stay did not look very inviting. It was at this point when my son asked me:

"What is the name of this town"?

"Tonopah," I answered.

"This is a ton of shit," was his reply. "Let's get the hell out of here."

I looked at the map and the closest town in the vicinity was Bishop. Since we still had a couple of hours of daylight, we headed toward Bishop which was not far after crossing the California state line. What a relief to see the Sierra Nevada Mountains approach us in the distance as well as the air-conditioned air. So much for Nevada! ¡Adios!

Bishop was a nice little town, a town full of tourists the majority of which were going toward or coming back from Yosemite. At the Holiday Inn in addition to the bikes, we had to unload everything because my son had seen a couple of suspicious characters looking at the license plates and inside the car. We did not want to risk being robbed.

XI. Yosemite National Park

I should remember the name of the town; the one that we had driven through the next day after checking out of the motel while driving north toward Yosemite. I should remember it because of the stench of cow manure which stretched one mile before and one mile after, but I don't. I am almost sure that it was before heading up the Sierra Nevada mountain range. I feel sorry for the people who live there; however, they are probably used to by now.

The things to do at Yosemite are countless. Trails for hiking and camping places are readily available near mountain lakes and small creeks as well as rock climbing. There is no shortage of attractions in the park. However, the major tourist attractions are Glacier Point, one of its highest points from where one can admire the Half Dome, the monster granite formation that looks as if it has been sliced in half with a very sharp knife; El Capitan, a very popular magnificent granite rock, a magnet for rock climbers who risk their lives and spend two or three days climbing it. Many have fallen to their deaths in the process. There is also Bridal Veil Falls, a waterfall that vigorously precipitates toward a rocky floor in the form of a veil; and of course, the land of the giants as I call the beautiful redwoods or the Sequoia trees that majestically congregate at the Mariposa Grove.

The Forest Ranger informed us, "The Sequoias are the oldest living thing on earth, they survived the ice age and the receding glaciers. They have survived storms and fires and there is not a single termite that dares to penetrate their bark."

The only thing I can add to what the Ranger said to us is that they are the high ranking bishops of the forest and the witnesses to our journey. Being the oldest living things on earth they have been witnesses to many generations of humans and for sure they will be here for many more thousands of years, long after my journey ends.

Both of the descriptions are accurate but none tops the description of these giants like the one written by Steinbeck in his book *Travels with Charley*. He wrote:

...The redwoods, once seen, leave a mark or create a vision that stays with you always. No one has ever successfully painted or photographed a redwood tree. The feeling they produce is not transferable. From them comes silence and awe. It's not only their unbelievable stature, nor the color which seems to shift and vary under your eyes, no, they are not like any trees we know, they are ambassadors from another time...

Beautiful description!

We did not try to paint them but we tried to capture their beauty with our cameras and yes, we were awed by their stature, and indeed Steinbeck was correct, they are the ambassadors of the forest.

After hiking the redwood grove we headed toward Glacier Point forty-five minutes up the mountain range where we could admire and photograph the Half Dome. Words cannot describe the beauty of what we saw on our drive up.

Due to the altitude at Glacier Point, we failed to connect with the Days Inn Motel located in the town of Oakhurst near the southern entrance to the park. After admiring the beauty of this massive granite rock we decided to call it a day and continue with our exploration the following day.

I was familiar with the area since I had visited the Park before, and the clerk at the desk, in addition to the AAA discount, added another ten percent for senior citizen discount.

"Did you feel the earthquake?" she asked us as we were checking out the next morning.

"We had our beds rattled at around three in the morning, but we thought it was one of those eighteen wheelers going by making all the noise," my son said.

"Oh, no! It was an earthquake, there ain't no trucks going by here at that hour," she said.

After breakfast, we headed back to the Park. We did not have to pay again since I had my Senior Pass for life which my son had suggested that I purchase for $20.00 when we entered the Park for the first time.

We headed to El Capitan where with our binoculars tried to spot the crazies trying to climb up. We were able to spot only one about halfway. The Ranger told us that it was his second day. Imagine sleeping on the side of that granite monstrosity in a hammock, attached to God knows what. Again there are people who not only challenge nature but also themselves. More power to them.

Later we headed toward the Bridal Veil Falls, the waterfall which falls to earth in the form of a Veil. We were lucky to witness the beauty of nature which is more notable during early June when the snow is melting at higher elevations thus making the waterfall fuller and stronger. During late August the fall relies less on the melting snow and the fluidity of the water depends on the little rainfall which scarcely falls during this time of the year. Sadly enough our journey was coming to an end.

While we headed toward Monterey, our final destination, we entertained ourselves by trying to identify the different types of orchards along the way. The easiest to identify were the citrus fruit trees; the cherry and olive trees were more difficult.

We crossed the Salinas Valley, the Salad Bowl of the United States, located between El Gavilan and El Toro mountains. We could admire different crops; lettuce, strawberry, artichokes, and asparagus all among the few that I recall seeing.

We were not expecting my wife's aunt to be waiting for us with dinner since she didn't know our arrival time. We decided to stop at Doña Esther, a Mexican restaurant located at the center of the town of San Juan Bautista where the Mission of the same name was built years ago by Franciscan monks.

XII: Monterey

After a brief tour of San Juan Bautista, we headed toward Monterey. As I said before we had not anticipated that my wife's aunt would be waiting for us for dinner. I was wrong!! She was waiting for us with a sumptuous and delicious Cuban dinner of *Picadillo, Arroz Blanco, frijoles negros, and tostones,* to top it off. We had to eat it; we could not disappoint her.

During our three days stay in beautiful Monterey, we toured the familiar sights such as Cannery Row, Big Sur, Carmel, Point Lobos as well as others.

My Jet-Blue non-stop flight from Oakland to Washington, DC was to depart at 9:00 am. I warned my son that the morning traffic through San Jose and San Francisco was really bad and that we needed to get an early start. Additionally, we needed to start early since he had to continue on to Portland. So, we left Monterey a little before six in the morning after saying goodbye to my wife's aunt.

As we headed toward the airport, I could not help wondering about whether or not my son would return. I didn't know!! Why would he return? I never returned to my home country. What would he find?

Would he find what I would have found? Ghosts from the past? Would he find friends who no longer existed or the memories of his younger years? The distance to be traveled back home was short now, just a couple of thousand miles. However, as the Sequoias have passed my wife and me after witnessing the end of our journeys, the distance would widen and we would be just memories; ghosts quietly roaming the hallways of his mind.

We talked very little along the way. I thought about my wife's comment when she learned that our son had agreed to let me accompany him during his trip, "Two non-talkative persons traveling together." But it was too early in the morning to carry on a lively conversation. Perhaps we were both thinking that we soon would have to say goodbye to each other. We did not know when we would see one another again. Also, the trip to Oregon was not around the corner. He had a long way to go, and I could no longer tag along. Our journey had ended.

As he dropped me off at the airport, he asked me:

"Hey Pops, do you know where I could buy a cup of coffee?"

I replied: "I don't have any idea, especially here."

He then said: "I guess I am on my own now."

I replied to him: "I reckon so."

He thanked me for everything and drove away.

My Samovar

Inspired by a true story

I. The Soviet Union, 1931

During the 1930s, the years of World War II and after, the Soviet Union suffered heartbreaking blows from the iron hand of the bloodthirsty dictator Joseph Stalin, the Secretary-General of the Central Committee of the Communist Party. The population witnessed innumerable criminal purges ordered by the dictator; they suffered hunger, shortages of food, as well as many other injustices and vicissitudes. It was a time of great suffering for the whole country.

In the city of Penza, southwest of Moscow, as in the rest of the Soviet Union, the situation was no different. Food was scarce and work was hard to secure. Iván Nikiforovich, an engineer by profession, faced all these hardships while sustaining himself with his small wages and savings. Nevertheless, he never ceased worrying about the precarious situation his country was in. The imminent arrival of his eagerly anticipated son deepened his concerns about his family's financial condition. All those worries kept him awake at night.

At the beginning of August 1931, Irina Pyotor, Iván Nikiforovich's wife, nine months pregnant, busied herself in the small kitchen of their tiny apartment, making sure the coals she had lit in the samovar half an hour earlier were red and hot enough to place the water container on top of it. Iván Nikiforovich was a demanding man, he liked his tea hot, not warm, the water that Irina heated in the samovar had to be steaming, almost boiling. The tea and the slices of bread with fig jam had to be served to him at precisely the same time every afternoon, at half past three. Irina was a strong woman who faithfully heeded the demands of her husband.

The unbearable scorching heat, typical of the summers in Penza, prompted Irina to open the front door and the five windows of their humble apartment. On August 23 of the same year in the early hours of the morning, Irina started feeling birth contractions and hurriedly Iván Nikiforovich took her to the neighborhood state clinic. At around noon, Irina gave birth to a handsome nine-and-a-half-pound healthy boy. Iván, in advance, had selected the name he would give to his firstborn; that child would bear his name and would be baptized as Iván Ivanovich Nikiforovich. All was happiness and jubilation in the home of Irina and Iván Nikiforovich. Iván

Ivanovich, his first child, would immortalize his father, that child would continue the legacy of the family.

Upon arriving at the apartment with the new addition to the family, Iván Nikiforovich could not resist the temptation to celebrate the arrival of his son. He did not waste time inviting his friends and neighbors to share the joyful arrival. Glasses of vodka were poured in antique crystal glasses with silver ornaments he inherited from his ancestors. He served *kasha* or oatmeal porridge boiled with fruit, as well as pears, herring, smoked salmon, pickled gherkins, all these delicious delicacies accompanied with more vodka or a cup of tea, made with the piping hot water in the samovar.

Though the days and months passed and the economic situation of the country was not improving, Iván Nikiforovich considered himself fortunate, having a job in one of the state offices. Two years after Iván Ivanovich's birth, Irina surprised her husband with the news that she was pregnant again. A girl was born in December of 1933 whom they baptized Natalia. The Nikiforovich couple celebrated the birth of their daughter with the same enthusiasm with which they had celebrated the arrival of their son Iván. They did not skimp a penny on the celebration.

Stalin's pact with Hitler and the participation of the Soviet Union in World War II aggravated the country's economic condition. If food was scarce before, during the war the situation worsened, now everything was in short supply since all resources and efforts were devoted to the war industry. In spite of the bad economic conditions, the Nikiforovich were able to send their two children, Iván and Natalia, to primary and secondary schools in Penza.

The Nikiforovich family continued to enjoy a normal day-to-day life. While Irina took care of the house chores, Iván, in addition to his official duties, endeavored to help his children with their school and homework. But everything changed in late November 1948; the family had to face the loss of a family member.

As most Russian women, Irina was a healthy woman, she did not suffer from any illnesses; however, during that year the cruel Russian winter had begun earlier than normal. It is not known with certainty if it was the cold winter or the stress from raising a family under such dire economic conditions that affected her health but that year, Irina suffered a fatal heart attack while carrying out her house chores, and although the family doctor tried to save her, she could not be resuscitated. Irina died, leaving Iván — a relatively young man — alone with two children to care for.

Iván Nikiforovich did not have time for himself, his demanding job, plus raising his children and the house chores were overwhelming. Olga Mostrova, a humble woman of limited resources who had grown up in the countryside, in a settlement on the outskirts of

Penza, was a neighbor of the Nikiforovich. Olga lived on the same floor, separated by two other apartments. Olga was a calculating woman who did not wait long after Irina's death to seduce Iván by generously treating him to casseroles, pies, and other homemade food. She had him in her crosshairs. After a very short time the inevitable happened, Olga was invited to move permanently into Iván's apartment. She did not waste any time; she knew that other available spinsters in the apartment building were stalking Iván to court him and take advantage of his situation. They all knew that Iván was lonely and vulnerable and suspected that his pension as an engineer and a state employee was substantial. Iván Nikiforovich succumbed to the amorous and culinary advances of Olga Mostrova, joining her in marriage a few months later in the Orthodox church.

The marriage between Iván and Olga filled the void left by Irina in the home of the Nikiforovich. Olga had accomplished her objective, as eagles spy on and catch their prey, she had caught hers, she now shared the Nikiforovich apartment, his bedroom, Irina's clothes and hoped that once Iván died she would inherit his pension. In the corridors of the building, Olga mocked her neighbors, laughing, sometimes exclaiming loudly:

"He's going to kill me; he's going to kill me!"

All of her theatrical display was premeditated, she was laying the groundwork in case Iván tried to get rid of her and she would have sufficient witnesses to back her up in front of the authorities.

The union between Iván and Olga caused irreparable damage to his two children, Iván Ivanovich and his sister Natalia. Natalia could not bear the screams and laughter of her stepmother and feared for her father's health. She could not bear seeing her wearing her mother's clothes, Irina's pretty dresses, to see her sleeping in the same bed with her father; the same bed he had shared with her mother, the same bed where she and her brother had been conceived. It was a very hard blow for a seventeen-year-old girl.

Natalia Nikiforovich could not take it anymore. To escape Olga's lack of respect for her deceased mother, she decided to leave her father's house, without telling anyone where she would go, not even her brother. The union of his father with Olga Mostrova, also negatively affected her brother Iván Ivanovich, but Iván, being two years older than Natalia, endured in silence with a plan in mind. Soon after finishing his university studies and obtaining a degree in civil engineering in Penza, Ivan moved to Moscow. Among the things that he asked his father before leaving was permission to take with him the samovar in which his mother had always heated water for their tea. And so, it began, the separation of this Russian family, united at first by the love and care of a faithful mother, and destroyed, as many families were destroyed by the war, social anguish, the precarious economic situation endured by the Russian people, and by an unscrupulous woman who took advantage of the weakness of their father, a man who could not bear the loss of his beloved wife Irina.

II. Moscow

Iván Ivanovich Nikiforovich stepped off the train that had taken him from his hometown of Penza to Moscow. The man who got off the train was no longer a boy; he was a full-grown man six-foot-tall, with blond hair and steely-green eyes which accentuated his looks, he was a handsome Russian. In that tumultuous and strange city where he had never been before, Iván gazed anxiously at both sides of the train station platform. To get oriented in the big city; he began to look for a landmark or something that would guide his steps towards a building where he might rent a room. He found an apartment building where an elderly lady, renting rooms to students and travelers passing through, offered him an available corner of a room. He was to share with her a large room divided by a cardboard partition.

Iván considered himself very lucky. After having graduated as a civil engineer, he had managed to obtain several temporary, six-month contracts in Penza, his hometown, and now, more of those in the capital.

In those days of turbulence in the Soviet Union, only people who had secure jobs could rent a room. Even those who succeeded had to make do with a sofa, or a cot in a corner, sharing bathrooms and showers with other tenants or in the absence of these use public restrooms. Living conditions were precarious for the majority of the population, including Iván Ivanovich, whose meager resources were not enough to lead a comfortable life. Fortunately, Sveta, the owner of the boarding house, became fond of Iván Ivanovich, allowing him certain niceties, offering him better food and letting him boil water for tea in his prize possession, the samovar.

Iván Ivanovich remembers his first night away from home. He could not sleep; he was kept awake by the memory of his mother and her sudden death. He worried about the whereabouts of his only sister, the health of his father in the hands of the exploitative and manipulative Olga Mostrova; he longed for the warmth of his family. For a long time, Iván slept on a sofa at the corner of the room separated from Sveta's bed by a partition which did little or no help at all to avoid listening to her snoring as she slept on her back after drinking, every night, three or four glasses of vodka. But in spite of these inconveniences, he soon got used to them as he had no choice.

During the post-war years, economic conditions in the Soviet Union started to improve. Russian industry and reconstruction were gradually recovering; however, in spite of the economic improvements, political restraints did not diminish. The persecutions and abuses against the population and its human rights did not cease. Stalin did not loosen the iron grip with which he oppressed his people. Those who did not agree with his communist dictatorship were denounced, captured and tortured by his hired assassins. As punishment, dissenters were banished to the cold steppes of Siberia and sometimes summarily executed.

With the meager financial help that his father sent him and the good care is given to him by Sveta, who already considered him as her own son, Iván Ivanovich was able to fully apply all his energies to his work distinguishing himself over other fellow workers. Iván benefited every day from the welcoming appreciation of his supervisors and high government officials.

During his university years and while working in Penza and Moscow, Iván Ivanovich was slowly becoming disenchanted with the Soviet system of government. He was witnessing, living and suffering himself the abuses of Stalin's communist dictatorship. Iván was disillusioned with the government's policies, the misery, extortion and lack of respect for the basic rights of human beings. He did not know what to do, he did not know whom to trust. He was afraid to express his ideas, his anxieties to his father, his classmates, to Sveta; he feared to be exposed, imprisoned, sent to Siberia where without going to trial, he could be condemned to death solely for expressing his anti-communist ideas. He had to do something, he had to escape from the oppression, from the misery and hunger. He had to escape from such an oppressive system. He had to seek freedom, to leave the Soviet Union but he did not know where to go in order to free himself forever from the country that had witnessed his birth.

III. Services to the State

It was mandatory for each state university graduate to render services to the state. Prior to obtaining temporary contracts in both Penza and Moscow, Iván Ivanovich could not escape this obligation and after graduation, he was assigned to work in a company in charge of the construction of public housing. As he had been accustomed, Iván applied himself fully to his tasks, his knowledge and intelligence distinguished him from the rest of his peers. His work was valued by his superiors, and his dedication brought him promotions, salary increases plus other benefits such as tourist trips inside and outside Moscow to the beaches of Little Russia, as Gogol called Ukraine.

Iván Ivanovich recalls the waste of government resources, mainly of construction materials. Government employees did not care whether they were wasted or not, after all, it was not their property, it was state property, the state paid their salaries, whether or not they fulfilled their obligations. Why worry? The state provided everything.

While supervising a construction job, Iván Ivanovich recalls the time when he had to coordinate the delivery and distribution of iron, cement, sand and other concrete additives for a construction project. All these valuable provisions were brought from other nearby cities. He then witnessed a cement shipment which had arrived in a multi wagon train and left unattended, uncovered at the station. Due to lack of personnel to receive it, the workers in charge emptied the contents on the ground, next to the station, in the open and without taking the precaution to cover it to protect it. Witnessing such an act of irresponsibility, Iván protested vehemently to his supervisors but no one paid any attention to him, they laughed and mocked him instead. Two days later, it rained, and the cement turned into a solid mass. Waste such as the one witnessed gradually added to his disillusionment about the disdain with which the workers, supervisors, and state agents were conducting themselves. In short, the disenchantment with the communist-socialist system. It was a combination of events which led Iván Ivanovich to make the biggest decision of his life, to escape from the Soviet Union.

He was determined to leave the Soviet Union, though he could not tell anyone, his friends, his father, Sveta, nor much less his sister to whom, not knowing her whereabouts, he wouldn't even be able to say goodbye. He did not want to involve anyone because if the authorities discovered his escape plans, his friends and relatives would be imprisoned for not reporting them. To escape from the Soviet Union was considered a worse than capital crime, it was a betrayal of Mother Russia, and traitors were punished, authorities would seek them even in the remotest places of the earth to make them pay with their lives for their infamy. Iván Ivanovich was aware of what could happen to him, but he was tired, he was fed up. He could not take it anymore; he would escape as soon as the first opportunity presented itself. The opportunity came sooner than expected.

IV. Escape from the Soviet Union

While Iván was working in Moscow, conditions to escape were not favorable. Employment contracts were unstable and sometimes terminated without prior notice or justification. Additionally, all contractors' activities were supervised and scrutinized as if someone would read the small letters of a document with a magnifying lens.

By mid-1958, the authorities informed Iván that his contract in Moscow would be terminated. They also advised him of an opening for a longer-term contract in the town of Pern in the mountain range of the Urals. At that time, the Urals were considered as the dividing line between the Soviet Union and the West and because of the difficult working conditions in these inhospitable mountains, the salary would be higher and the benefits would also be better.

Iván did not hesitate, he knew that working in precarious conditions in such mountainous region would be beneficial and that outstanding officials were rewarded with trips abroad. After briefly training in "special" activities (Iván did not specify the nature of these activities), Iván Ivanovich moved to the Urals.

At the beginning of the winter of 1959, while working in those mountains, eleven officials who had diligently applied themselves to their work, but most importantly, because of their loyalty to Mother Russia, were awarded a six-day trip to East Berlin. At that time East Germany was a "satellite" state of the Soviet Union. Among the eleven engineers selected to make the trip was Iván Ivanovich, who had just turned twenty-eight.

The passport of each member of the group of the eleven engineers was retained by the Russian army officer in charge of coordinating the trip and of the close supervision of the visitors. This was a common practice of Russians to prevent those traveling outside the country from deserting. However, it was the opportunity that Iván had been waiting for a long time, he knew that he would not have another opportunity like this in the near future. Four days had passed since his arrival in East Berlin, the door that had opened was closing, he had to do something, but what? They would be taking the train back to Russia on the morning of the sixth day. Of the little money they were given, he still had a few Marks left; and that would be his excuse.

Iván Ivanovich Nikiforovich, at dusk on the fifth day, dressed in the only suit he was allowed to take out of the country, a dark brown suit and shoes of the same color, asked the officer for permission to go out and get some cigarettes at a nearby shop to take to his friends and to his landlady Sveta. That was his excuse, but Iván needed his passport. He asked the officer in charge of the group for the valuable document, who suspiciously looked him straight into his eyes as if anticipating what Iván was going to do, but Iván did not blink at the penetrating gaze of the officer. The request could not be denied him; the officer knew that as a foreigner he would need the passport to make any purchases.

Iván had no intention of buying cigarettes; the only thing in his mind was to escape, to leave, never to return. Once on the street in front of his hotel, to protect himself from the cold, he pulled up the collar of the dark gray overcoat and slipped on his leather gloves. He then lowered his gray hat to his eyebrows. Iván walked two blocks and making sure he was not being followed, boarded a taxi and asked the driver to take him to the border area between the two Berlins. It had started to snow, damp, cold snow, more like drizzle or hail.

STOP! shouted the soldier from the gate that guarded the border to West Berlin, an AK-47 in his hands. Iván Ivanovich froze. He felt as if an ice dagger had been embedded in his back, but without showing any fear he approached the soldier with a firm step. Iván coughed slightly to compose his quivering voice and showed the soldier his Russian passport plus other identification. Iván Ivanovich was calm, he could not back down, he had to overcome fear, and he no longer feared to be discovered, imprisoned or executed as a traitor.

He informed the soldier that he was traveling to West Berlín on a secret official mission to meet with another Russian agent who would give him secret documentation he could not divulge. To verify what Iván had told him, the soldier went to the phone in the checkpoint and dialed a number. Iván hid his fear, he did not feel the freezing temperature that had dropped below thirty degrees Fahrenheit. The frosted hail whitened his grey felt hat. The wait of fewer than five minutes seemed to Iván like an eternity; he felt his legs were beginning to falter. Then the soldier with the gun in his hand looked at him as if he was looking at a strange animal, aimed his submachine gun at Iván again, handed him his passport and the other identification, saying:

"These damned telephone lines never work, no one answers in the capital, sir."

Sighing deeply and controlling his nerves and emotions, Iván Ivanovich thanked the soldier and advanced to the checkpoint located in the longed-for sector of West Berlin, and freedom. Like a snake shedding its skin, Iván Ivanovich Nikiforovich had shed and left behind the poverty, abuse and corruption of the Stalinist communist system.

Iván paused for a moment, looked back and said in a low voice:

"*Rossiya do svidaniya,*" farewell Russia ...

V. West Berlin

The odyssey that Iván Ivanovich had just begun was not over. A soon as he approached the sentry box in the western sector, he was stopped by three US Army soldiers armed with automatic rifles, who began interrogating him, always pointing their weapons at him with their index fingers on the trigger, ready to shoot.

Iván Ivanovich provided the information they requested and asked to be taken to the United States Embassy, telling them in English, mixed with Russian and German, that he needed to see the ambassador.

At about 11:30 pm, a taxi dropped him off in front of the United States Embassy. At that time of night, the security guard in charge of the embassy, not having specific instructions or not knowing of anyone arriving at that hour, would not allow him to enter. He told Iván to return the next day, that there was no one who could interview him at that hour. Iván insisted, but the gate guard did not budge.

At the man's refusal, shivering in the cold, which had already begun to bite into his bones, his eyes watering, he sat on the cement sidewalk which was colder than the falling hail. Iván told the man that he would wait there until the next morning, even if he froze to death, and explained that he had nowhere to go, no money to rent a room in a hotel and that the only money he had left, he had spent on the taxi.

Fearing that the man, who claimed to be a Russian, would freeze and die before his own eyes, the guard made a phone call. Iván Ivanovich did not understand a word of what the man was saying; the only thing he saw was his gestures and his nervous hands pointing at him as he spoke. Obviously, someone at the embassy gave him the green light and allowed Iván to come in. The gate guard helped him get up from the cement sidewalk, handcuffed him, and led him into the lobby of the building. Iván had won the first skirmish of this first battle, but he still had not won the war, he had yet to cross many obstacles.

Once inside the embassy, another official removed his handcuffs and took him to a small room with one-way windows and furnished with just a chair and a portable cot. Iván asked for water and to be taken to a toilet, both requests were granted to him in the presence of the official who kept an automatic rifle trained at him. Once in the toilet, Iván bent down and vomited bile, he expelled from his body the anxieties, the fear and the anguish that had tormented him during these last days. All his movements were monitored and scrutinized through one-way windows. Back in his room, he slept the rest of the night.

The next morning, after a cup of tea and soda crackers, Iván Ivanovich was taken to a room lit with blindingly bright lights hung from the ceiling. The only furniture in the room were four folding chairs and a very large rectangular table where scissors of various sizes and other cutting tools had been put, such as those used by tailors and shoemakers. There were three men dressed, from head to toe, in white gowns with protective caps on their heads like the ones used by surgeons in an operating room, wearing masks covering their faces up to their eyes and surgical gloves. They looked as if they were going to perform open-heart surgery and Iván was the patient.

One of them, the tallest of the trio, in Russian, instructed Iván to remove his clothes, including his socks and shoes. Ivan obeyed the order without taking off his underwear. At this point, the smallest of the group, with a Russian accent and a Mongolian timbre, said to Iván:

"Take off your underwear too, sir."

Being naked made Iván feel like a plucked rooster. He had never taken off his clothes in front of strangers, and never before in front of unknown people dressed in white gowns. He was later offered a bathrobe.

Ivan could not believe what he was about to witness. First, they took his passport and now all of his clothes and shoes. Two of the men, the "tailors", as Iván later called them, with great care proceeded to fumigate his clothes. Then, without haste, they began to cut up every piece of clothing, and the third in the team, the "cobbler" started to cut his leather shoes into shreds.

As they cut, they analyzed the shredded clothes with magnifying glasses, then with a magnetic detector, searching, or trying to identify some sort of chemical or toxic material which Iván could have been trying to smuggle into the country. The "cobbler" dismembered the shoes and cautiously examined them. The entire operation took the examiners most of the day without finding anything suspicious or radioactive.

While Iván was quietly witnessing the destruction of his clothing, he thought to himself: 'Now I am really screwed! My clothes have been shredded, my shoes are gone, what am I going to wear? How will I get out of here?'

Soon his anxieties were calmed down. At the end of the session, Iván was taken to a different, windowless room with a bed and a private bathroom. On the bed, there were two brand-new suits, one dark blue and one gray, underwear, socks and a pair of brand-new black shoes, plus a wool overcoat similar to the one he was wearing before it was dismembered by the so-called "tailors."

An officer of the American Air Force dressed in a navy-blue uniform, knocked on the door and, in impeccable Russian, informed Iván that all the clothes on the bed were his to keep and that after he finished cleaning up and getting dressed, he would wait for him at the embassy dining room. Surprised, Iván smiled, thanked the officer, and thought: 'How generous are these Americans, they took away my old clothes and shoes and gave me everything new.'

And so, dressed in his new gray suit, Iván met the officer in the dining room and there began what amounted to a rigorous, extensive and lengthy interrogation which was to last for more than two months. Federal agents from several US government agencies, including the Pentagon, as well as agents from the United Kingdom and West Germany, took part in the questioning. He felt like a prisoner at the embassy, like a caged animal locked in a comfortable chamber.

Iván Ivanovich did not understand all the scrutiny he was being subjected to, after all, he was not a spy nor had he held any high official position in the Soviet Union, perhaps, he thought, all that attention was due to his most recent work at the Urals.

At this point, Iván Ivanovich thought that it would be better to change his Russian name to a Western name. Just as Iván had abandoned Mother Russia, Iván changed his first name and patronymic, the name his father had given him at birth, hoping to be immortalized by his son. Iván Ivanovich Nikiforovich from now on would be Alexander Adriano. He chose Alexander for his first name, because he was a great admirer of the famous and brave conqueror, Alexander the Great, and Adriano as his last name, because he wanted to honor his ancestors who came from the central part of Italy.

While Alexander was trying to get his bearings in West Berlin, and so in the West, the Russian officer in charge of the touring engineers had already informed the state authorities of the escape of Iván Ivanovich Nikiforovich. In Penza, State Security agents besieged the apartment of Iván Nikiforovich, informing him about the desertion of his son, asking him if he knew of his whereabouts. The interrogations were repeated monthly over a period of several years without obtaining any positive results, since Iván Nikiforovich and his daughter Natalia — who by then had returned to her father's house — were unaware of the whereabouts of Iván Ivanovich. They feared he was caught escaping and had been executed or that he had died in an accident.

Years later, Alexander, through American officials, learned that his name was part of a list of those who had escaped from Mother Russia, declaring them traitors to the Homeland. It was to be anticipated that the fate of these deserters, were they discovered or captured, would face execution or permanent exile in Siberia.

VI. Australia or America?

Over the next two years — perhaps less — Alexander Adriano, despite his limited knowledge of English survived by rendering translator and interpreter services to the United States Embassy in West Berlin. With the money he earned and with the help of embassy officials, he was able to rent an apartment in a four-story row house near the embassy, three or four blocks away.

Alex was not a genius, but he was very smart. He was aware of how the so-called "Enemy of the People," the "traitor" Liev Davidovich Trotsky, had been assassinated in Mexico; how the Russian State Security operated, of the methods used to execute traitors: poisoning or shooting them in the nape of the neck, using poisoned daggers, or by introducing radioactive poisons into the body while being treated at hospitals and clinics without leaving any traces. The tentacles of the Komintern extended to the remotest boundaries of the earth, very few escapees went unnoticed, and only a few survived escaped by evading them.

Living with such a constant threat, Alex developed a paranoiac fear not previously experienced, even during his years in the Soviet Union. Such fear and mistrust have haunted him his entire life like a dark shadow or like a leech permanently attached to his body.

Fortunately, Alex enjoyed good health throughout his life. However, one day, early in the morning, Alex felt a pain in his mouth as if someone was ripping off a piece of his head. He thought that the Russian hitmen had found his whereabouts and were torturing him.

But that was not the case, he had an abscess in one of the molars in the upper right jaw. As skeptical as he was, Alex would not run the risk of visiting a dentist's office. He preferred to ask his Ukrainian friend Boris, whom he had met at the embassy, and whom he blindly trusted, to do him the favor of extracting the molar with a rough utensil similar to a pincer without being anesthetized. He did not trust a dentist, he did not trust what a dentist could inject him with, maybe, instead of an anesthetic, he would inject him with a deadly poison.

People around him looked suspicious. He trusted no one, he would not take a drink of vodka or a cup of tea without pouring it himself. He longed for his precious samovar to prepare his own tea. Instead, he now used an old kettle given to him by an embassy official.

Alex tried to save most of his salary; he tried to dress as simple as possible to not attract the attention of others such as possible Russian operatives. His main objective was to leave Germany, to go to a place where he could be out of sight and minimize the possible pursuit of Russian officials.

On a cold night — *de duro cierzo invernal,* of a hard-cold northerly wind, as Agustín Lara sang in one of his famous tangos — Alex felt trapped within the four walls of his apartment; he felt stalked by the shadows of loneliness. That night, the howling winds penetrated through the cracks in the only window of his apartment. Without thinking about it twice, Alex made sure his wallet was in the right pocket of his trousers, got dressed warmly as if he was in Siberia, and ventured out, to the rundown cantina nearby. After sitting down at the bar, in a strategic location on the premises — always looking out the front door — he asked for a shot of vodka. Once his eyes became accustomed to the darkness, he turned his gaze to the other end of the counter and noticed a voluptuous young woman staring at him. Alex thought that the brown-haired woman, wearing a sailor's beret, dressed in jeans and a blue wool coat, could not be more than twenty-five years old.

The girl left her seat and sat next to Alex. She told him her name was Myriam, and insinuating herself sensually, asked for a glass of whiskey. However, that night Alex was not ready to take the bait and engage in an amorous relationship with a total stranger. After gulping his vodka, Alex left the tavern, and as he walked back to his place, he looked back every few minutes, making sure that he was not being followed, and rushed up to the second floor of his apartment building. The arctic winds hadn't stopped whistling through the cracks in the window.

Another time, while attending an official event at the embassy, Alex was approached again by an attractive woman — not as young as the one at the bar — but as he had done before, he avoided her amorous insinuations. Following these two unsolicited exchanges, Alex decided not to venture again into dangerous encounters but to submerge himself, like a submarine, to the bottom of a sea of celibacy.

In response to his desire to emigrate from Germany — which was a fact known to embassy officials — during one of his visits to the colonel in charge, Alex was informed that there were two countries he could be assigned to. One of those countries was Argentina and the other was Australia. In Argentina, he would work with a Polish Jew, owner of an electrical appliances store in Buenos Aires. In Australia, he would be employed as an assistant in a hatchery of venomous snakes in a farm outside the capital.

Alex refused both possibilities, claiming that in Argentina he ran the risk of being identified, as this country welcomed countless European immigrants who could be Russian agents. And as for the Australian post, Alex told the officer that he preferred to perish at the hands of the Russian hitmen to being bitten and poisoned by a viper in a remote place like Australia. Both possibilities were discarded. Alex told the colonel that he wanted to learn English and go to the United States, mainly to live in New York City. His dream was to become an American citizen.

Luck was at his side; he was about to achieve his goal.

VII. New York

Perhaps it was not what he had anticipated, but a new window was opening to him, much better than the possibility of going to Buenos Aires and superior to the alternative of getting into a venomous snake hatchery in Australia. The person in charge of coordinating his activities in Germany had learned that an architect's firm in New York was looking for a draftsman. Being a civil engineer by profession, Alex friends at the embassy thought that he would be the ideal candidate for that job. A few days later, Alex accepted the position.

Alex had never been outside Germany any more than out of Russia. Nor had he flown in an airplane before he would cross the Atlantic Ocean to the western world. Enthusiasm gripped him but anxiety prevented him from sleeping. Nevertheless, he trusted that his scant knowledge of English and what he had added during his stay in Germany was sufficient to communicate in the United States. And that it was not an obstacle, it was rather a challenge for Alex to learn a new language and settle in New York City.

Everything had been arranged, passport, housing in New York plus other documents for him to travel to his new country. Alex had committed to the US embassy or more specifically, to the United States government, that he could be called at any moment to appear before security authorities to assist them whenever they considered it necessary.

In compliance with such a commitment, before traveling to New York, Alex was asked to make a stop in Washington, D.C. where he would stay for a period of two weeks. Alex was very secretive and would not disclose to anyone the reason for his stopover in Washington, let alone what his mission was upon his arrival in the capital, where he would be interviewed by military personnel at the Pentagon.

Alex remembers that upon arriving in Washington, DC, state security officials were waiting for him at the airport. He was transported to his hotel in a black minivan and the following day to the Pentagon where he was informed of the reason for his visit. The unexpected telephone call at his hotel room was what he least expected; it was from his Ukrainian friend Boris, the person who extracted his tooth back in West Germany.

"Boris, what are you doing in the capital?" Alex asked his friend. "How did you know about my whereabouts?"

"I saw your name at the embassy in Germany, on a list of people who were traveling to the United States with a stopover in Washington," answered Boris. "They also informed me where you would stay. I came on an official mission. Tomorrow, army officers will interview a Russian agent at the Pentagon and they have requested my presence since the agent does not speak English."

Alex immediately fell silent, thinking that maybe Boris was a Russian spy who had infiltrated the embassy in Germany and now the Pentagon. Alex ended the conversation with his friend by addressing other issues without telling him that *he* was the one being interviewed the next day at the Pentagon.

The conference room where the interrogation would take place was located in one of the many underground basements of the Pentagon. The rough bricks and masonry walls in the room were painted faint gray. On a long dark wooden table, two projectors had been installed: one for films, another for photographs. Two screens hung from the ceiling of the room where the films and photos would be projected. The four US Army officers, all dressed in khaki, sat strategically in a semicircle.

When the door opened, an officer accompanied by Boris walked in. Alex did not know the rank of the officers, but he assumed by the number of yellow bars on the sleeve of one of the officers' uniform, that it was a colonel or a general. Boris was surprised to see that his friend Alex was the one being interrogated that morning, however, he simply greeted him very affectionately.

The colonel or general instructed the officer in charge to proceed first with the screening of one of three films. This exercise lasted approximately two hours. Alex immediately recognized the entire mountainous area as the Urals. He could not figure out how they had managed to film with such detail the area where he had previously worked. He suspected they had done it by means of a spy plane or another surveillance method.

Alex was able to observe a large number of rocket installations, missiles and other ballistic weapons aimed at Europe. During the afternoon and the next two days, the slideshows of photos and reels of film continued uninterrupted. Alex questioned himself about the importance of the pictures and films; he could not imagine what the cost of carrying out such an operation would have been. As he saw it, those pictures had no value, neither for espionage nor for war-related maneuvers. Up to this point, no one had bothered to ask him about what he had noticed in those films. The officers had not opened their mouths, and no one in the room had asked him absolutely anything.

At the beginning of the fourth day, fatigue and boredom had captured Alex's mind. One of the senior officers realized Alex physical and mental state and finally, in Russian, decided to ask him:

"Alex, could you tell us what is the meaning of everything you have observed so far? What are the intentions of the Soviet Union with so much weaponry?"

Alex remained silent for a few seconds, then promptly answered the officer:

"None," he said, "absolutely everything I have observed has no value. The Soviet Union has no plans to attack Europe and least of all has it warlike ambitions. All you have shown me is a farce, a deception; there are no rockets, let alone missiles ..."

The officer, surprised and with an upset look on his face thought that Alex was making fun of everyone present including his friend Boris who during all this presentation had remained silent, without uttering a single word.

"But what is the meaning of all we have seen?" asked the officer raising his voice in disgust.

"Everything your government has filmed and photographed," said Alex, "are pine tree trunks that have been shaped like rockets and missiles, painted in greenish-gray colors and strategically placed to fool the spy planes or whatever means you have used to photograph them."

"So that's all a Russian ruse?" the officer asked, surprised.

"That's what I told you, it's all a sham, there are no rockets," Alex concluded.

Both the officer and Boris looked at each other in a daze,

unable to comprehend what Alex had said to them in a few words. The interrogation continued for another day or two, less than the two weeks programmed by the embassy officers in Germany and the Pentagon. Alex's response was always the same. Alex's stay in Washington, DC was cut short and he finally headed for New York.

Alex did not remember the exact address of the firm of architects where he worked as a draftsman during his brief stay in New York. He vaguely remembered that it was close to a subway exit and close to the apartment house which the embassy officials in Germany had chosen for him to stay in New York.

After a few months without hearing from the embassy officers, Pentagon officials and his friend Boris, Alex presumed that they had cut the umbilical cord, that they would finally leave him alone, that he was on his own in the overwhelming metropolis, in a country where he did not know anyone and where his knowledge of English was severely limited.

To learn English, Alex attended a language school in the evenings after work, devoting most of his time to reading newspapers and books written in English. When his means allowed him, he would go to the movies and watch films to familiarize himself with the language. However, all his efforts were not enough to speak or write fluently in English. His supervisors at the firm of architects sometimes turned a blind eye and overlooked his errors, everyone liked him and appreciated his effort, but it was not enough to fulfill the job as a draftsman, he needed to learn English and look for other opportunities either in New York or in another city of the United States.

While Alex settled in and started to get used to the hustle and bustle of New York City, other events were taking place in the waters of the Caribbean Sea, specifically in Cuba.

The Castro revolution had triumphed in that tropical island. In 1961, Castro openly declared to the world his Marxist-Leninist tendencies; and in that same year, the world-known and botched invasion of the Bay of Pigs had taken place. The Soviet Union acceded to the insistent requests of the Cuban government to install missiles on the island, giving rise to the infamous Cuban Missile Crisis. Soviet "advisers" began arriving in Cuba. Among other things, the United States was confronted with a lack of security agents, of army officers who spoke Russian, and in the face of an imminent crisis, they decided to initiate a search for Russian native speakers who would be able to teach the language to army officers and security agents.

Alex was aware of what was happening in the world, and of the deployment of Russian agents in Cuba, however; his immediate concern was to learn English, and he concluded that if he kept postponing it, it would take even longer and it would be more difficult to get a better job. With a few savings he had left, he decided to enroll in a college near New York and take a six-month, intensive English course. A Frenchman, who had arrived at the architect's firm a year before, gave him all the information about the English course. The good handling of the English language by the Frenchman was what convinced Alex to make the drastic but necessary decision to go to school.

Days before finishing his classes, Alex underwent a thorough examination. His final requirement was to write a paper about the history of the War of Independence of the United States and present it to a panel of five professors. He passed all the exams and requirements with outstanding grades.

Upon returning to his work at the architects' firm in New York, Alex was greeted with a big celebration, toasting with his fellow workers in fluent English. Alex was so proud of himself that he dared to make a brief speech in his new language to thank his co-workers. However, before finishing his discourse, he was interrupted by a telephone call. One of his co-workers picked up the receiver and, turning to Alex said:

"A Mr. Boris is calling you; he claims to be your friend."

VIII. Monterey, California

Alex did not know what to think or what to do. 'Again, Boris is calling me,' he said to himself. 'Perhaps, I need to appear before another group of officers at the Pentagon or another government office.' He had to interrupt his speech, but nonetheless, everyone present applauded him and congratulated him on how well he spoke English. When he returned to his desk, he answered the telephone, and rather inquisitively, asked his friend:

"Boris, what do you want, is my presence needed in some other government office?"

"No!" his friend answered. "I need to talk to you urgently; I'll see you at Luigi's, the corner cafe in fifteen minutes."

Alex did not anticipate his friend's visit, nor did he know Boris was in New York, he only knew that he was already sitting at the corner cafe waiting for him. Alex apologized to his co-workers and hurriedly headed to the cafe where Boris was waiting for him, having ordered vodka for them.

"Boris!" Alex exclaimed, as he saw his friend with two glasses of vodka. "You are mad, it is too early to drink liquor, I prefer a cup of tea like my mother used to prepare in our samovar ... How I miss my mother, my family, how I miss my samovar!"

Boris was not anxious at this moment to listen to his friend yearning about his relatives, he would have to do it another time.

"Alex, I'm sorry, I do not have much time in New York, I have to take a plane back to Washington, I just wanted to inform you that at the Monterey Language School in Monterey, California, they need the services of a Russian native speaker, who speaks and writes Russian and can teach the language. I immediately thought of you and gave them your name, you're the right person, and it's the opportunity you've been waiting for. I have not been to Monterey, but I've heard it's a small town on the central coast of California, near the Pacific Ocean, with very nice weather."

"But I ..." Alex muttered.

"No ifs, ands or buts, you have to call the director in charge immediately," Boris said. "This is his telephone number, call him as soon as possible, tell him you are calling him on my behalf. Sorry, I cannot stay longer; we'll talk at another time. I think the government has finally left you alone. Who knows when they will forget about me?"

"Boris, please don't leave me wondering, who runs that school? Who pays the salaries?

Boris called back from the door of the cafe:

"Who do you think runs it? The Government of the United States, my friend! The United States! The salary is good and so are the benefits. Please don't hesitate and call! Goodbye!"

After completing a series of rigorous interviews with those in charge of the School, he proceeded to obtain the mandatory clearance of the United States government. Alex was starting a new chapter in his life, that of a professor of Russian, a position he held until he retired years later.

The plane in which Alex was traveling, early in 1962, landed a little after six o'clock at the small airport that serves the cities of Monterey and the Monterey Peninsula. Night had started to fall; the cold air blowing from the Pacific Ocean almost fluttered the gray hat Alex was wearing. After picking up his suitcase, he hurriedly left the airport in a taxi that took him to a nearby motel.

Upon arriving in Monterey, Alex rented — very close to the airport — a small townhouse, similar in size to the apartment in Penza where he had lived with his family. Not only did this small home revive many family memories, but it was located close to his new job. In addition, the house was furnished; therefore, he would not need to spend money on buying furniture. Saving was his most important objective, to save as much as possible in order to purchase a house.

Despite the security and comforts he now enjoyed, Alex had not lowered his guard, always alert for suspicious people. One day after returning from work, Alex poured himself a glass of vodka and proceeded to cook his favorite food, grilled salmon accompanied by boiled potatoes. After finishing his meal, sitting in a comfortable chair with a piece of apple pie and a cup of tea, Alex heard someone knocking on the door. He did not know who it could be, he was not expecting any visitors. Cautiously, not to be seen from the window overlooking a small garden, Alex went to the kitchen and wrapped a towel around a meat cleaver lying there; it was another instance when man forgets his fear and is willing to lose his life — because life is fear itself. When he crossed the dividing line between the two Berlins, he had also overcome his fear and he no longer thought about survival; when he was ready to face any foe. With the hand that wielded the weapon hidden in the towel behind his back, he went to the door and asked in a loud voice:

"Who is it? What do you want?"

It was then that he heard the voice of a child who said:

"Good afternoon, sir! Would you be interested in buying a subscription to the Monterey Herald?"

Suspiciously, Alex slowly opened the door and saw a boy with a newspaper in his hand, trying to sell him a subscription to the local newspaper. Alex smiled to himself.

Just as the political, economic and social oppression in the Soviet Union had affected the life of Iván Ivanovich Nikiforovich, now Alexander — Alex Adriano — causing him to leave his homeland, his family, and friends, in the city of Havana another person, Adriana Gutierrez, was facing the same vicissitudes caused by the political upheaval of the Castro Revolution.

Adriana, like thousands of Cubans, feared the suppression of human rights, freedom, and furthermore her own life. Already Castro had begun confiscating private properties and businesses, implemented the parallel suspension of free will and parental authority, and Adriana dared to make the most difficult decision in her life, to leave Cuba.

Both the fate of Adriana and that of Alex Adriano had been written; they met at the Monterey Language School, both professors, one of Spanish, the other of Russian. But it took ten years before they became serious about each other.

During the next eight or nine years, Alex diligently devoted his time to his teaching activities at the School, including writing a textbook in Russian which would be used — and is used to this day — to teach Russian there.

In his spare time and with the savings he accumulated during those years, he started investing in real estate. He would purchase small houses in desirable locations, renovate and resell them at a higher price and buy others. He was very successful in his real estate ventures and became moderately wealthy.

Alex did not hear again from his friend Boris, he was not called to appear before government officials or other security agencies, it was a quiet time of his life. He thought to himself they had finally let him live in peace. However, he kept thinking about his sister. He did not have any knowledge of her or his father's fate ... nor did he dare find out their whereabouts, fearing being discovered by the Russian authorities. He lived alone, with very few friends and without a female companion. Alex concluded that enough time had elapsed since his escape from the Soviet Union and his arrival in California and decided to re-start his personal life in this country, in this beautiful city located on the shores of Monterey Bay.

IX. Adriana

Adriana Gutierrez met Alex, the young single Russian professor, in the corridors of the School. For some reason or other, it was not the right time then to start a friendship and least of all a romantic relationship with him. They exchanged small talk at meetings, occasionally sharing coffee breaks but nothing meaningful that would develop into a serious relationship. Adriana's main objectives in life were her job and raising her son.

About mid-1972, Adriana and Alex coincidentally sat together at the cafeteria to share their lunch. As expected, they started a friendly conversation exchanging details about their lives among many other things.

That brief, casual encounter was what Alex Adriano needed to notice Adriana's beauty. That dark-brown eyed Caribbean brunette with a body that had nothing to envy the famous Italian actress Sofia Loren. It was as if a burning flame had been kindled in the depths of his being. He had been impressed by her vast culture, knowledge of art, music; in other words, Alex had fallen madly in love with Adriana and would not stop showering her with gifts, invitations to the theater and special events until he convinced her to accept his offer of marriage.

In 1987 the President of the United States, Ronald Reagan, with his famous words addressed to Mikhail Gorbachev, Secretary of the Communist Party "... *Mr. Gorbachev, tear down this wall ...*" challenged the Russian to tear down the Berlin Wall. The month of December of 1991 marks in the calendar of the history of the world the dissolution of the Soviet Union, consequently all the republics of the Union, including Russia, separated under the administration of Mikhail Gorbachev, thus marking the end of the Cold War.

After that historic event, and thirty-two years after escaping from the Soviet Union, Alex was given the opportunity not only to try to find his family but to consider traveling to Russia to visit them and perhaps recover his precious and longed for samovar.

X. Return to Russia, Natalia

Taking advantage of the chaos that followed the breaking apart of the Soviet Union, including most government entities as well as the security agencies, Alex decided to search for his relatives.

What better source of information than the local offices of the Red Cross. Without hesitating, Alex visited one of their offices and introduced himself as someone looking for his lost or exiled relatives. He gave the names of his father and sister plus telephone numbers where he could be contacted in case they were found. In turn, the local Red Cross sent an inquiry message to the central office in Washington, DC which was transmitted to its offices in Europe and subsequently sent to Moscow. After this entire operation that took about a month, his message reached his relatives in Penza.

Upon hearing on the phone, the sobbing voice of his sister Natalia, who after so many years, ignorant of the whereabouts of her brother, thinking he had died, Alex joined her with sobs and tears that were hard to contain. Both would have wanted to be together to hug and cry. Between tears and sighs filled with emotion, Natalia told Alex that their father had died and that his wife Olga Mostrova had left the city and returned to the countryside. She did not know if she was still alive. Natalia also told him that she was married and had three daughters and was still living in Penza. Alex told his sister that he had also married and that soon — accompanied by his wife — would be taking a river cruise from St. Petersburg to Moscow. Without hesitation, Natalia promised that she would be waiting for them in Moscow.

That spring morning — late May of 1992 — the cold Baltic air forced Alex and his wife Adriana to wear wool jackets. The M/S Rossia riverboat that would take them from St. Petersburg to Moscow was about to depart. They sat in two of the many seats on the deck of the ship's bow. Alex could not contain his emotion. Like a blotter absorbing spilled ink, he wanted to take in the beautiful landscape of the area through which they were about to sail, the cities and villages of which he had dreamed of for so long. After many years he had returned to his mother country, to Russia. Alex kept talking in Russian, with the captain, the waiters ... he was like a child opening his favorite birthday gift.

After visiting the Church of the Transfiguration on the island of Kishi located on Lake Onega, the cruise ship again sailed on the Volga River towards the city of Yaroslavl where they would stay for a couple of days. After a sumptuous Russian dinner of salmon and smoked herring, and after sailing up to the small village of Svirstroy, Alex excused himself to use the restroom. It was only half past eight and dessert and tea were being served, but Alex did not return to the dining room. Adriana didn't pay much attention to his prolonged absence and continued talking with the rest of the guests. But after an hour or so, she became anxious and started looking for him. Alex was nowhere to be found, it was as if the earth had swallowed him, or rather as if he had been dragged down by the river, by the majestic Volga.

Adriana kept asking the captain, the waiters, but no one knew where her husband might have disappeared to. Adriana started to fear that the worst had happened, that in the M/S Rossia there were agents of the KGB who had identified him, killed him and thrown him into the murky waters of the Volga. Then suddenly Alex reappeared, happily talking and laughing with one of the waiters. He had spent hours talking and reminiscing about Penza, his hometown, in one the cheaper class cabins of the ship. Adriana was so enraged by the absence of her husband, causing her such anxiety, that she could not utter a single recriminatory word to him for disappearing for so long. If looks could kill, he would have been in serious danger.

Finally, in the lobby of the Holiday Inn in Moscow, Adriana witnessed the anticipated and emotional meeting of her husband with his sister Natalia. They kissed and hugged each other; they laughed and spoke out lively; they looked at each other over and over. Alex asked her about the last years of his father and the cause of his death, mainly whether he had suffered. Natalia assured him that death had come quickly and that he had not suffered much, like their mother, he had suffered a heart attack. She also told her brother that soon after their father died, she had moved out of Penza to live on the outskirts of town, and with the little money her father left her she had bought a small farm where she now grew potatoes and vegetables which she preserved to be consumed during the harsh cold winter months.

Then Natalia handed her brother a box saying:

"This is for you, brother, remember Sveta, the owner of the boarding house where you stayed when you lived in Moscow? She brought it to our father only months before he died."

"Ah, Sveta!" Alex exclaimed. "The good Sveta, she and her snores ..."

Alex opened the box, took out its contents and with a smile on his face said to his sister: "It's my samovar! My samovar!" With tears in his eyes, he again hugged his sister: "Thanks, Natalia!"

Years later, after his return from Russia, when Alex least expected, he was contacted again. This time it was not Boris. It was a man who called himself Sergei. He requested a meeting at a local restaurant in downtown Monterey. Alex suggested instead to meet at a more open location near the intersection of Munras and Alvarado streets. Sergei asked Alex to travel to London and meet with a classmate from his school days in Penza who had been appointed to the Russian

Embassy in London. His mission would be to persuade his friend to desert his post and convince him to travel with him back to the United States.

Obviously, Alex did not accept that invitation, instead, he reported the incident to the security officer of the School and never heard from Sergei again.

This is the story of Iván Ivanovich Nikiforovich or Alex Adriano. He was pleased and relieved to have shared the details of the ordeal he survived during his exodus from the Soviet Union, he is forever grateful to his adopted country that welcomed him and he never regretted making that critical decision, nor did he ever looked back; he is a free man living the American dream.

To conclude this dramatic and emotional story, Alex added that he keeps in touch and occasionally visits with his friend Boris, who lives with his family in Santa Cruz, the coastal city north of Monterey. About his sister Natalia, Alex said he speaks with her once or twice every month and that she has come to visit him in Monterey several times.

During one of these visits, Alex invited my wife and me to meet Natalia to a luncheon in her honor. He also invited Boris and his family for that special occasion. I would be too pretentious to try to describe the different and exquisite Russian dishes that Alex and his wife Adriana prepared for that "Russian" lunch, which began at two-thirty in the afternoon with a special prayer and a toast to all the guests and lasted, between vodkas, wines and desserts, until close to midnight.

Before finishing the joyful and sumptuous meal, Alex, very proud of himself, approached the dining room table wherein the center was the splendid beautiful white and cobalt color samovar adorned with hand-painted inscriptions in Russian. As he had learned from his mother, he heated the water to serve a cup of an exotic tea from Ceylon for my wife and another one for me.

And to our delight, this is how my wife and I learned to savor a cup of tea served from a samovar.

Note from the author

My Samovar is a fictional mini novella and it must be interpreted as such. The story was written having as a backdrop a Russian samovar. There is a lot of rich history about this iconic symbol of the Russian tea culture. It is a symbol of hospitality and of wellbeing which dates back about three hundred years. Not only in the palaces of the Tsars was this iconic utensil treasured but also in the most humble households such as that of Iván Nikiforovich and his wife Irina Pyotor. The samovar became inseparably attached to Russian daily life, it explains why Alex was so attached to it, it bonded him not only to the Russian culture but most importantly to his family. Samovars were originally crafted in Tula, a city south of Moscow.

The story told here is a combination of reality and fiction. In some instances, historical events, places and people, although real, have been woven around the life of the protagonist, a Russian who grew disgusted beyond endurance with the communist-socialist system and the oppression and lack of respect for the human rights of its people. Such dire conditions prompted Alex to leave his father and sister in search of freedom and a better life in the United States.

Some places, persons and scenes were created to illustrate the experiences and vicissitudes endured by Alex during his life before and after leaving the Soviet Union, his Russia.

It took approximately ten years to gather all the facts to be able to write *My Samovar*. Some of the details were obtained from the protagonist during conversations while socially sharing drinks of vodka, glasses of wine, during dinners as well as other friendly gatherings. Often the information was offered fluidly, without hesitation; however, there were instances when Alex chose not to remember, stopping abruptly or claiming acute "lapses of memory."

I am forever indebted to my wife, who with her insight and discretion, would excuse herself to the kitchen at times to write down names, dates, and other information heard during our conversations; however, given the understandably suspicious and secretive nature of the protagonist, it is difficult to assert, with certainty, which facts of Alex's life are true or of his own creation.

The Quail Hunt

*For the wildest, yet most implausible narrative which
I am about to pen, I neither expect nor solicit belief.
Mad indeed would I be to expect it, in a case where
my very senses reject their own evidence....*
Edgar Allan Poe

The invitation was extremely alluring. Very difficult to pass up, especially when it was coming from the very rich Pánfilo Buenaventura, who invited his friends, Refugio Bolaños and Paco Ruiz, to spend the weekend at his summer home in the Monte Verde mountains, near the capital city of West Winston, about two hours away from the noise and traffic congestion of the capital. However, what made the invitation most attractive was the fact that Pánfilo had not invited their respective wives because he thought that they would be bored since he had planned a hunt for — according to him — the abundant and elusive quails in the nearby fields of his property.

Although Refugio and Paco were not attracted to the idea of traveling without their respective wives, neither of them made an effort to ask their friend to have them invited. Both were aware that Pánfilo's liquor and wine cellar was well stocked, and that Lee Chong, the Chinese cook, whom their friend had hired for the weekend had the reputation of being a fine cook, and without any objections, they decided to accept the invitation.

While both friends traveled to Pánfilo's summer home, in Paco's Jeep Cherokee, which he graciously offered to drive, Paco asked his friend:

"Listen, Refugio, have you visited Pánfilo's summer home in the past?"

"No, it is the first time he invited me, what about you?"

"Me neither, it is also the first time, we should consider ourselves lucky because I understand that Pánfilo is not the type to have too many friends, and although he has lots of money, he is very stingy and it's unusual for him to invite anyone to his house and least of all to his summer home. I am sure that his intention is to show off and show his new acquisition and, as an excuse, he has made up this quail hunt."

"Now that you mention it," said Paco, "have you ever gone on a quail hunt?"

"Never, I don't even know what they look like."

"I least of all," Paco answered. "The only thing I know is that

261

they are frightened very easy; if they get spooked, they fly away and while in flight one shoots them with a shotgun. I also understand that they are like small hens, very tasty and if Lee the Chinese cooks them, they will taste delicious."

"What do you mean that one shoots them with shotguns!" Said Refugio somewhat astonished. "We don't own any weapons, I have never shot a gun in my life and least of all a shotgun. We are going to be ridiculed."

"Don't you worry Refugio, I have never fired a shotgun either, but I am sure Pánfilo must have several, otherwise, he wouldn't have invited us. Besides, it doesn't matter, you very well know that his liquor cellar is well stocked and if we don't hunt anything, we will drink several of his wines, and Lee will prepare something to eat; he is not going to starve us to death."

Prior to arriving at their friend's summer home, Paco and Refugio, to avoid having to fill up the Jeep's gas tank on Sunday on their way back from the visit, they decided to fill it up at the next gas station. While they were paying for the ten gallons of gas, the man next to the counter engaged them in a brief conversation:

"I guess you fellows are traveling to visit Pánfilo Buenaventura at his summer home, and that he has invited you to a quail hunt."

"In fact, that's exactly where we are headed, how did you know about the quail hunt?"

"Because several of his friends have gone by this way, expressing their enthusiasm to hunt that small bird, but what they are not aware of is that there are no quails around here. The only thing which is plentiful in these lands is crows, rabbits, and once in a while, one spots some birds of prey. There is nothing around here, except for a small town about twenty miles further up and nothing else."

Somewhat surprised the two friends looked at each other, thanked the man in the gas station, and headed out to Pánfilo's without saying a word.

After taking a turn on the road, they spotted a sign which in bold black letters read:

LAS DELICIAS
Pánfilo Buenaventura
Owner

After about half mile ride on a dirt and gravel stone road, in the distance, they spotted Pánfilo's house. It was a small wooden house with an asphalt shingles roof. Bordering the house were a well-kept garden and grounds, which gave the impression that its owner paid for the maintenance since he was incapable of lifting a rake. On the porch, seated on an Adirondack style blue chair was Pánfilo smoking a Havana cigar.

Although Pánfilo was famous for being a show-off, he gave the impression of being a not so showy fellow. He was tall and skinny and with fine features. He was hiding his black hair which already showed some silver, under a multicolored baseball cap. Pánfilo couldn't be older than fifty.

On the other hand, Refugio was a man short in stature, of a muscular body, fine features and his brownish hair matched the attire he had purchased especially for the occasion. It was the much-anticipated weekend at his friend's house to participate in the quail hunt. Francisco, or Paco, as his friends called him, was slightly more obese than Refugio and Pánfilo but taller than they and his fine and stylized mustache hid a cut on his upper lip.

When Pánfilo saw the vehicle approaching, he got up from the chair and approached them to welcome them, thanking them for accepting his invitation and excusing himself for not inviting their respective wives. He instructed Lee to help with their luggage, serve some drinks and to start making preparations for dinner. Although it was summer, and there was still some daylight the clock on one of the porch walls marked six-thirty in the afternoon. Pánfilo liked to have an early supper, and without wasting much time he invited his friends into the living room. Although it was simple yet elegantly decorated with rural motifs, it gave the impression that it was Pánfilo's wife who had a hand in decorating it. Pánfilo continued to show his friends to the room located at the end of a narrow hallway where they would be spending the night during their visit.

After consuming two bottles of an expensive California Merlot, they devoured two pork loins accompanied with Asian greens exquisitely cooked by Lee. After dinner, while drinking cognacs together, Pánfilo detailed the plans for the hunting expedition early the next morning, naming the type of weapons they were going to carry. Knowing that neither of his friends had ever fired a shotgun before, he offered them to test their weapons and fire some shots in the firing range near the house before the hunt.

The second of July 2016, the day of the hunt, Paco and Refugio were awakened by the sound of dishes and casseroles. It was Lee making breakfast in the nearby kitchen.

Pánfilo, all dressed up with an African style attire — as if he was going to go hunting for rhinos — was already waiting for his friends outside the house with three of his best shotguns. He was ready to start showing Paco and Refugio how to fire the weapons and how to proceed when finding a quail. As a courtesy, his guests were to fire first.

Although neither Paco nor Refugio had much knowledge about this sport, they both inquired if there would be specially trained dogs to point toward a possible prey. Pánfilo explained that the two pointer dogs purchased from a trainer in England had not arrived on time for this hunt. Both friends exchanged curious looks, they would have to rely on their instinct when shooting. They hoped that the prediction of the man in the gas station was wrong and that they would find plenty of quails and not just rabbits and crows.

After making sure that everything necessary was ready for the hunt, such as water and backpacks with some provisions, Pánfilo started the expedition by heading toward some nearby hills, which they had to cross to reach a plain where they would start the hunt. Refugio, being a good observer, immediately noticed that Pánfilo was taking too many turnoffs, winding footpaths, and shortcuts; he could not understand why he did that. It was either because Pánfilo did not know the right trail or because he was lost. They had walked for more than two hours towards the foot of the hills and still there was no sign of the valley. However, neither Paco nor Refugio dared to inquire if the paths taken by Pánfilo were the right ones. Refugio had started to get skeptical; he no longer trusted his friend.

After crossing a small river, they finally made it to the top of one of the hills and saw a plain covered with grass which had turned golden yellow due to the absence of rain. The sun had already reached its zenith and had started to make itself felt among the hunting party.

"What a beautiful plain!" Exclaimed Pánfilo filled with emotion pointing toward the tall grass, which gently swayed by the gentle blowing of a light breeze.

"Beautiful spectacle!" Said Paco, echoing his friend.

"I agree with both of you, that it is a beautiful landscape, but I very much doubt that we are going to find any quails here," said Refugio. "I suspect that what we are going to find here is plenty or rattlesnakes, scorpions, lizards, and who knows what other type of reptiles, but quails, I doubt it. I am very sorry, but I am not going to go on, I will stop right here and go back to Las Delicias. Pánfilo could you give me some directions so I don't get lost. You guys go on, good luck and good hunt, bring lots of quails."

"You are nothing but a pessimist, I am sure we will find lots of quails; however, if you want to go back, I will tell you how. Are you sure you wish to go back?"

"Yes, I am sure!" Said Refugio.

"Very well, go down this hill, and after crossing the creek you will find a path in the form of a 'y' which splits into two trails; either path will take you to the house. Take the one on the left, that one although somewhat stonier is shorter and will take you faster to Las Delicias. Good luck and tell Lee to get the grill ready to roast the quails."

Refugio said goodbye to his friends, flung the shotgun on his shoulder and turned back.

When he reached the small creek, Refugio observed the path

in the 'y' form which Pánfilo had pointed out. He crossed the creek and he realized that the path on the left was indeed rockier and decided instead to take the one on the right, the one bordering the small river, hoping that at that time of the day it would be cooler and more pleasant.

After walking about twenty or more steps, Refugio realized that the path was taking him inside a wooded grove filled with thick leafy trees which he did not recall having crossed before. To make sure that he was on the right trail, he looked back, and to his surprise, the narrow path had disappeared. He also observed that very slowly it was starting to get covered with ivy and other strange and thick vegetation. Upon gazing at the river, he noticed that a thin thread of silvery water was the only thing running among the greenish rocks and the further he walked on the trail the water was disappearing. He felt trapped by fear, but he was not sufficiently afraid to turn back. He walked slowly inside the forest which was turning darker as he advanced; it was difficult for the bright sun rays to penetrate the thick tree canopies all the way to the path he was traveling, which was disappearing as he went on. The path was slowly covered with thorny brambles and small myrtles. It was at this point that Refugio realized that he was lost, that he had chosen the wrong trail; however, he decided to continue forward, he did not believe in turning back. He had not advanced more than ten steps when suddenly he heard the deafening sound of a shot and the echo vanishing in the distance. He thought that perhaps it was his friends who had managed to shoot a quail.

After walking about half an hour through the darkened forest, approximately half a mile, he observed the sun rays brightly shining over an open field, free of vegetation, trees, and of the thick brambles... He thought he was getting closer to the summer home and therefore accelerated his pace.

As he got to the open field, he noticed an enormous building. In its surroundings, there were all types of domestic fowl wandering around; peacocks, blue hens, yellow roosters, reddish hogs ... flying yellow and iridescent quetzals, black and albino crows, swallows, multicolored Castilian pigeons ... trotting minute horses and beautiful sorrels. In each of the four towers of the astonishing building, four white falcons with their wings open were perched in a protective stance as if guarding the building. He admired its granite decorations such as gargoyles of different sizes, figures of monks each with his unsheathed sword ... rock crowns decorations and crosses of different sizes ... everything was so beautiful ... it was something more spectacular than ever seen by Refugio during his forty-five years.

'It's a Cathedral!' Astonished Refugio said to himself. 'But it's not possible, I must be dreaming or it could be an illusion, a huge mirage. The man in the gas station told us that there was nothing here, absolutely nothing.'

The most amazing thing of all was that there was not a single human being around, just the flying birds and the animals, and in the huge atrium, a deer family wandered about. Notwithstanding the surrounding sepulchral silence, beyond the enormous black oak doors — which were widely opened — he could hear the murmur of voices, like the singing of canticles in foreign languages. Refugio thought he was hearing an old man's lament and the crying of a baby. He said to himself:

'If I am really lost, perhaps there is someone inside this building who could guide me and point out the way back to Las Delicias.'

Refugio was so perplexed admiring the beauty of the building that he lost track of time. He admired the distinctive colors of the glass on the large and tall windows adorning the structure. The enormous clock on one of the towers, loudly rumbled twice, marking two o'clock in the afternoon. Although he wished to continue admiring the beauty of his surroundings and the amazing medieval structure, he realized he could not waste any more time; he had to return to Las Delicias before dusk. He crossed the ample atrium, approached the huge doors and decided to go inside without realizing that the voices and canticles were mute and that there was no old man's lament or children's crying inside. However, in the middle of one of the naves — empty of furniture — there was a man who was slowly sweeping the black marble floor with a red wheat broom. The man was dressed in black, like a Carthusian monk, wearing a tall and pointed hat. He had ashy looking skin and his long white beard — pointed like the hat, reached his waist. Refugio asked him:

"Excuse me, sir, I believe I am lost, could you point out which is the best way to go to a house called Las Delicias?"

The man sweeping the floor raised his head and looked intensely at Refugio while speaking in a grave and hoarse voice:

"Follow this corridor, when you reach the middle, make a right turn, go down the fifty steps to the basement, open the first yellow door and you will find a narrow road which will take you to your destination."

Refugio shuddered, he almost fainted after seeing the face of the man who was giving him directions. It was the same man they had seen the day before at the gas station, now dressed as a sorcerer. It was the same man who had warned him and his friend, Paco, that they would not find any quails. As he pointed toward the end of the corridor, the man laughed ironically. Refugio was mute, astonished, he was not even able to thank him as he indifferently continued sweeping the marbled black floor.

Refugio's surprise, grew even larger when he started walking down the long and ample corridor. Refugio looked back, but the sorcerer had disappeared as if by magic. Refugio could not believe what he was witnessing, he was utterly confused, his eyes were about to come out of their sockets. His heart was beating so fast that he felt his temples pounding as if hundreds of drums were beating at the same time.

Both sides of the corridor were adorned with malakite columns which supported the enormous structure. In each of the columns, there were glass niches about fifteen feet high and six feet wide. Inside each of these niches, there was a man, a middle-aged man who looked like a Carthusian monk dressed in priest's attires of different colors: brown, red, yellow, blue, purple, black ... Refugio counted twenty-four columns, twelve on each side. All the men were standing up, each had a mitre in their right hand and a bishop's crozier in their left, like a cane to mitigate the fact of being standing. Most perplexing was their gaze, which was vague, empty ... As he approached one of the glass niches Refugio realized that the reason for the vagueness of their gaze was because they did not have eyes, they were all blind, their eyes had been pulled out.

Refugio could not believe what he was witnessing, it felt like a dream or a nightmare. He felt cold sweat running down his back like a freezing icicle. He felt as if a glacial cold had trapped his entire body, it felt as if hundreds of portable air conditioning units had been turned on at the same time. He made sure that the shotgun was still hung on his shoulder. He needed to make sure that he would be able to defend himself if something or someone attacked him inside this magnificent and magic temple. But his sense of security was illusory, he had never fired a weapon and very much doubted that fear would allow him to use it, he was a bundle of nerves, his hands trembled.

Refugio thought to himself:

'It is not possible to be so cold this time of the year inside this beautiful place, it is the beginning of July, the hottest time of the year.'

He was so distracted admiring the colorful attires of each of the wizards or priests inside the glass structures, that he did not notice that at the end of the marbled corridor, seated on a huge wooden chair adorned with silver, gold, and precious stones ... was a blue-skinned old man with eyes so red that resembled the flames of a bonfire. Next to him was a half-naked man whose color was as charcoal, who had a whip in the right hand and in the left, he was holding a gold dish with some of the eyes of the men encapsulated on the crystal niches.

Refugio was astonished. Once again, he felt the gun on his shoulder and very slowly approached the old man seated on the chair. Noticing the fear on Refugio's face the old man said to him:

"Don't you fear, my dear Refugio, my name is Nosór, I am the owner of this dwelling, I have lived here for hundreds of years. Those men you have observed and admired inside the niches are my subjects, I have trapped them and blinded them by plucking their eyes out to prevent them from escaping while faithfully serving me instead. Be careful with that weapon you are carrying, you will not have to use it at any time, there are no quails here and none of my subjects will do you any harm. For having entered this private and beautiful place for the first time, you will be allowed to exit, you will not be held prisoner. You will be able to go back to Las Delicias without any delays, it will not be difficult for you to find the way."

Refugio's heart was leaping from his chest, he was terrified, words could not come out of his mouth; however, as a gesture of gratitude to the old man or sorcerer, he knelt before him and said:

"Mr. Nosór, you have called me by my first name. How do you know my name? How do you know where I am headed, and that I carry this weapon to hunt quails?"

"Stand up Refugio, you do not have to pay homage to me. I am not a king, a pope, a potentate or anything of the sort. I am a humble and simple man who has self-exiled himself from the world, from the putrid world around us. From a world filled with envy, hate, violence, crime. Those men were non-believers, they could not see evil, I have blinded them and made them my slaves. They will live like that until the end of time. Serving me, yes, serving Nosór. You asked me how I know your name, very simple my dear, I listened to your friend Paco calling you by that name. When you entered this building, you told the man sweeping the floor where you were heading. I have been observing you ever since you crossed the creek and decided to choose this way. You are very lucky, you will be reunited with your friends. I will not hold you captive, you are an honest man, your name, Refugio, is very meaningful."

"Thank you, Nosór."

"Go on, go down the fifty steps, but before you exit through the yellow door, ask Ana, my maid, to give you a white bag. Take it, open it when you get to Las Delicias; don't do it before, open it when you get to your destination and enjoy its content with your friends. It's a gift from Nosór. Do not look back, you will not see anything. Be careful with Ana, she is seductive and a treacherous woman, she will try to confuse you and seduce you."

"Thank you, Nosór, I will do as you say."

Quivering and confused Refugio went down the steps toward the basement. In front of a table covered with dozens of lit candles was Ana, a beautiful woman of fine features and extremely white skin, of black hair falling to her waist, with emerald green eyes shining just like the precious stone. Ana could not be older than thirty. On a long and narrow table, there were ten bags of different colors. When she saw Refugio, Ana approached him seductively and took him by the left hand. Rubbing her Venus-like body against his she told him in a low and seductive voice:

"You must be the one sent by Nosór, you are coming for your

bag. Choose from these ten. The yellow contains gold, the green has emeralds they all have very valuable things, you can be very rich. Which one do you wish to take?"

"The white one, it was the one Nosór told me to choose, none other."

"Don't be such a fool, you don't have to obey the old man Nosór, take the yellow, it's filled with the finest gold to be found on this earth, you will be very rich!"

"No! I will take the white one."

"Very well Refugio, take the white bag and go out through the pink door, it will take you quickly to the home of your friends."

"I will exit through the yellow door, that's the door which Nosór said, I will obey his mandate."

"Go ahead you fool, go through the yellow door, it is at the end of the corridor."

Ana turned around, with a supernatural blow she extinguished all the candles and hurriedly climbed the stairs toward the atrium of the cathedral.

While following Nosór's advice to the letter, Refugio did not dare to look back, he was afraid of ending like the men inside the niches or like the woman who was described in the biblical story: like a salt statue. He opened the yellow door and exited into a narrow pathway, he did not stop, he followed the road while holding the white bag, which felt somewhat light; however, he did not dare open it to see what was inside until he reached Las Delicias.

He had not walked more than two miles when he saw Pánfilo's summer home. In the distance, he heard once again the booming of the clock on one of the towers. It was six in the afternoon. On the porch were Paco and Pánfilo, both sipping a glass of red wine. When they saw him, they both got up from their chairs to wish him a warm welcome.

"Where have you been all afternoon? We have been looking for you all over." Said Pánfilo, somewhat annoyed.

"We were so concerned, we thought that something awful had happened to you, we were ready to call the police so they would go looking for you," added Paco.

"I got somewhat lost, instead of coming by the rocky path, I decided to follow the one bordering the river, and I got distracted along the way."

"What do you have in that white bag, which you have not let go?" Asked Pánfilo.

"I don't know yet, along the way I bumped into an older man, who was also hunting and he gave me this bag. He asked me not to open it until I arrived at Las Delicias."

"What's the mystery! Exclaimed Paco. "You are already here, it's time for you to open the bag and see what's inside."

Refugio took the bag, carefully put the shotgun against one of the posts of the porch, carefully unknotted the knot and astonished he pulled out three quails. He also pulled out a note which read: *enjoy these birds with your friends.* Then, Refugio put the note in his pocket without sharing it with his friends.

"Refugio, you are such a liar, the story that some old man gave them to you is just a big tale. I am sure it was you who shot them and you just wanted to surprise us, and wow! what a surprise. Lucky for us because we hunted nothing. Lee — Pánfilo called the Chinese cook — please come over and start plucking these quails, season them well and get them ready for dinner."

Throughout the dinner, Paco did not say much. Instead, he kept looking at Refugio. During his forty-two years he had shared with his friend many stories and trips, he knew him well. He knew Refugio was hiding something from him but did not dare to share it with Pánfilo. Once in their room, at about midnight, with the moon gently illuminating their room, Paco, in a low voice, so Pánfilo and Lee would not hear, he told Refugio:

"Refugio, do you think I am dumb or something, you are hiding something from me. Tell me the truth, you don't have to lie to me. What in the hell happened? Where did you find the white bag with the three quails? Don't give me that bullshit tale about an old man giving them to you. Did you shoot them?"

"Listen, Paco, you are not going to believe me in a million years if I tell you what I saw and lived through in a few hours this afternoon. I prefer to show it to you in person that way you won't think I am making it up or that I was seeing mirages. Tomorrow, when we leave Las Delicias, I will take you in person, but please don't tell Pánfilo. I also want to stop by the gas station, I want to buy some chocolates for the children."

"Stop by the gas station, buying chocolates! Refugio, I believe something is wrong with you, I don't know what you are on, you have never bought a single sweet and least of all any chocolates."

On Sunday, at about eleven, after savoring a succulent breakfast, Refugio and Paco said goodbye to their friend Pánfilo and tipped Lee Chong for having treated them to such exquisite dishes and the delicious quails. Upon reaching the main road, instead of turning left toward the capital, Refugio asked his friend to turn right. After having driven a mile approximately, Refugio asked Paco:

"Stop right there, by that gravel road. Park the Jeep on the side and let's walk toward that clearing over there, close to that forest. You will admire what I experienced yesterday, it's going to leave you with your mouth open."

Paco, resigned to walk once again under the mid-day scorching sun, followed Refugio who as he walked, looked around without being able to find what he was looking at what he had seen the day before. In the distance, in the open field, they found a small mound of bricks, and on the bank of a small creek, they found an abandoned shack.

"Very well Refugio, I am not going to continue walking in this heat, going around and around, going around blindly, I am stopping right here. Let's get out of here, it's getting late, and the traffic at this time of day is horrendous. Let's stop by the gas station 'to buy your chocolates'."

Upon reaching the gas station both got out of the Jeep and went inside. As Refugio was paying for the chocolates, he asked the attendant:

"Last Friday when we came here, a middle-aged man took care of us. Is he here today? We want to ask him about an abandoned shack we found approximately half an hour north from here. Does someone live there?"

"No, I don't know who the guy was, I am the owner of this gas station, perhaps the middle-aged man was just a customer. Regarding the abandoned shack, it belonged to a crazy old man. He was always seeing hallucinations, thinking he lived in a cathedral, surrounded by slaves and servants. He had a lover, much younger than him, very beautiful indeed, but she left him a couple of years ago. He had a nephew who lived with him, but when the old man died, the nephew disappeared too, they say he left with the lover. The old man liked hunting, he also liked quails very much."

"By any chance," asked Refugio, "was the name of his lover Ana?"

"Yes, that was her name," answered the gas station owner. "Anything else?"

"No, thank you," said Refugio, taking the three chocolate bars.

Once back in the Jeep, Paco smiled and said to his friend:

"I believe, my dear friend Refugio, that you ended up worse than the old man who lived in the shack. I don't know what you have been drinking or taking that made you imagine all those things which you still have not dared to tell me. Perhaps you will share them with me on another occasion or during another 'quail hunt'."

"You will never believe me, Paco, you are a non-believer!"

Lola's Story

L os Mirones is a small town remotely located close to the border with the country of Guáimara. It is a rural community, intellectually backward, old-fashioned and ridiculed by outsiders, where the great majority of its inhabitants, in addition to meddling in other people's affairs, are engaged in agriculture and cattle breeding.

In this small town, none of its two hundred and fifty inhabitants knew for certain the origin of Dolores Altuna, or better known as *tía*[4] Lola. Some said that she was the daughter of Cipriana Altuna, a woman of dubious reputation who during her youth had shared her bedroom with a *tío*, a street hawker, of Polish origin. Others, firmly assured that she was the daughter of Don Severino Lopez, the town mayor; most argued that she had been born out of a love affair between Cipriana and Lieutenant Antonio Linares. However, the version which was closer to reality was that Lola had been abandoned by a band of gypsies who were hurriedly escaping from Los Mirones, as they were being chased by the police for having robbed a store in the nearby city of Venecia. After all, in this small town, opinions abounded and sometimes were as many as the number of its inhabitants. Often, the stories could not be counted with the fingers of one hand, each citizen would reaffirm his own version and some, to make it more credible, were ready to swear before the statue of the Holy Virgin in the Church of San Juan.

Just like Lola, Cipriana Altuna, Mayor López, and Lieutenant Linares had passed away a while back. They would have been the only ones capable of deciphering the origin of *tía* Lola, and the death that occurred at her home, which gave way to her incarceration and later to her execution.

In fact, the version that Lola had been abandoned, when she was a three-year-old girl by some gypsies was the one most accepted by the population. It was said that almost twenty-six years ago, no one in town wanted to take care of a filthy, snively little girl who wouldn't stop crying and could hardly speak a few words. Back then, only Cipriana Altuna — who notwithstanding her multiple amorous affairs, had not been able to give birth to a child — felt sorry for the

---

[4] In Spanish, the word *tío* means uncle and *tía* means aunt. It is often used to refer to a person not related to the family or respectfully to an older friend. In English, the term uncle is often given to a person, such as a regular Uncle Joe. In other occasions, the word *tío*, or *tía*, is used to refer to persons who have amorous affairs with relatives. In this story, the term *tío* or *tía* is used to refer to a person outside the family.

girl, took care of her, officially adopting and consequently giving her, her surname, Altuna.

The house of Cipriana Altuna which was located at the end of Los Mirones' main street, was surrounded by a stone and brick wall, and at its outside corner, a majestic ceiba rose up, where blue jays loudly chatted and a large number of birds chirped in a wide variety of sounds. The small adobe home was painted in washed-out yellow; its low roofline was covered with reddish tiles. A small living room was connected to a bathroom and with a room which opened into the garden. This open room functioned as the kitchen with a clay oven and a charcoal/firewood cooking place with two round openings where on iron grills water was boiled, soups cooked, meats roasted, among many other foodstuffs. Although the living quarters were rather small, the home had an ample and beautiful garden where Cipriana cultivated fruit trees bearing lemons, oranges and papayas which grew very well due to the fresh breezes and the shade provided like an umbrella by the beautiful ceiba. The fruits of these trees were very desirable to the townspeople who bought them at the local market where Cipriana usually sold them. The water extracted from the well — located in one of the corners of the garden — not only provided water for the rose bushes blooming with pink and yellow roses, the beautiful red amapolas and other floral bushes, but was also used for drinking, bathing, cooking and such. The drinking water was stored in a baked clay vase on top of a small table close to the room and the living room.

Immediately after she took in the little girl, Cipriana walked toward the house of Don Lucero Ordoñez, located next to the Church of San Juan. Don Lucero was a kind gentleman who in addition to providing apothecary services to the community, served as legal advisor, money lender, personal advisor and comforter of those left without remedy. It was Cipriana's intention for Don Lucero to thoroughly examine Lola, to make sure she didn't have infectious illnesses and to purchase from him an antiseptic bar of soap to bathe her recently adopted daughter. On her way home, she stopped at the variety store of the twin sisters, Adelaida and Lucinda Domínguez, where she purchased a pair of shoes, underwear, and a couple of second-hand dresses for the child.

After warming up a bucket of the well's water, Cipriana removed all the clothing of her new daughter, sat her on a large aluminum pan, under one of the lemon trees and started bathing the child, removing all the dirt off her small body and the soil attached to her feet and small legs. She thoroughly washed her head with the antiseptic soap to make sure that lice had not decided to adopt her head as a permanent residence. After having been bathed so thoroughly, Lola felt like a new person, and after seeing herself so clean and sweet-smelling, wearing new clothes, she thankfully embraced and kissed her new adopted mother.

Besides helping Cipriana with the house chores, Lola attended the primary school of the Sisters of Charity of the Good Venture, where she learned to read and write. In her spare time, she would swing herself on a rudimentary swing that Cipriana had hung from one of the branches of the ceiba. She also visited the Domínguez sisters at their department store and helped with the store chores. In exchange, the sisters taught her to make her own dresses.

During her school years, Lola put up with the mocking of the boys and girls who made fun of her calling her names such as: "the abandoned gypsy, the little feeble raggedy," as well as other slandering nicknames... Often kids can be crueler with their peers and classmates than adults.

When Lola turned twelve years old, she implored her mother to allow her to work full time at the Domínguez twins' shop. She was tired of the school boys and girls' harassment and mocking. The sisters, feeling sorry for Lola, offered her a job and a small salary. Lola tried to convince her adopted mother into accepting the offer since with the help of her benefactor sisters she would learn to sew and additionally she could make some money which would help pay for the maintenance of the house. Cipriana approved Lola's request.

At eighteen years old, Lola had turned into a beautiful woman. Her brown skin, black hair and dark caramel brown, bright shiny eyes accentuated her beauty. Her sensual and beautiful body had nothing to envy the body of the *Venus de Milo*. She was envied by the town's women and was the source of admiration from the male population, who spellbound gazed at her as she walked toward the market, church or as she passed by the cantina *El Ojo de Agua,* the local watering hole.

It was at that seductive age that Lola told her mother that she would move out of the house and temporarily settle in the city of Venecia where she would register at a school to learn about fashion, to refine her knowledge of textiles, modern design and haute couture. With the financial help of the Domínguez sisters, she planned to rent a room in a local boarding house and finance her fashion design studies. It was the intention of the two sisters that in the future Lola would take over their shop so they could realize their longed-for dream: to take a long vacation trip throughout America and some European countries, for which they had saved a large sum of money. However, Lola's path would veer off and take a different route than the one hoped for by the sisters.

During her stay in Venecia, Lola continued to be noticed. Just as she was besieged at Los Mirones, her beauty was the attraction of older men, younger ones as well as children who could never tire of admiring her. Some accosted her, others followed her on the streets when she went for walks on the main street. They murmured and often would say aloud: "Look at her, she's so good looking! That's Lola Altuna, there goes *tía* Lola..." Women envied her, hated her, and some went as far as falsely accusing her to the local authorities of making lewd passes at their husbands and trying to seduce their children. But no one was able to find witnesses to corroborate their accusations and prove their allegations to then to incarcerate her.

After two years, as Lola was readying to finish her studies, Venancio del Río showed up at the school.

Venancio was a good-looking middle-aged man of whitish hair, who had stayed in the capital after divorcing his wife. Venancio was a teacher by profession; however, he had dedicated a large part of his adult life to cattle breeding in a rented parcel of land. His cattle business had provided enough funds to support himself and carry on living a leisure life in the capital city.

After two years following the death of his parents, Venancio remained in Barcelona, Spain, his parent's birthplace. He had spent all this time fighting with the Spanish authorities trying to recuperate the properties inherited from his parents, a much arduous task since his parents had not left a will stipulating that Venancio and Lucila — the administrator of the school where Lola studied dressmaking — were the sole inheritors of their estate.

A large portion of the cash capital of Venancio's parents, which did not amount to much after all, was used to pay the two lawyers who represented him before the legal authorities to clarify the legal mess left by his parents. Notwithstanding all the expenses, a few thousand were still left over — but did not exceed twenty thousand pesetas — plus the sum from the sale of a house and a home in the countryside, the capital as a whole did not amount to much more than approximately one million pesetas.

In spite of the expenses incurred from the sale of the properties, taxes and such, the brothers managed to get a good sum of money which allowed Lucila to increase her savings and Venancio to purchase a small farm in the outskirts of Venecia to continue his cattle breeding business. Venancio had decided to move to Venecia to be closer to his sister of whom he hadn't seen much. He also wished to participate in the school activities and perhaps to teach a course.

It was during one of his visits to his sister while they both strolled through the school walkways that they stopped in front of one of the classrooms where Lola was modeling a beautiful and sensual dress imported from abroad. It was a tight black dress which accentuated her hips and a low-cut cleavage leaving little to the imagination of the voluptuous breasts of the young Lola. Venancio was amazed, that was the woman he had dreamed about, he couldn't stop staring at her, he ardently desired her, it was a feeling he hadn't felt since his divorce.

Becoming aware of the lewd gazes of her brother, Lucila informed him that the beautiful woman for whom he felt so passionate, was named Lola, of unknown origin and background, and at least twenty years younger than he. But Venancio was not paying attention to his sisters' warnings, not even the one about the rumor circulating around town, that one of Lola's boyfriends had mysteriously disappeared following an amorous rendezvous with her. She was accused of being a witch and of having supernatural powers. However, none of these accusations changed Venancio's mind, he had fallen for Lola's beauty, he had crazily fallen in love with the beautiful young woman of the enviable body, the young woman of shiny caramel colored eyes and brownish hair. After a brief courtship, Venancio proposed Lola to marry him. Thereafter, she telegraphed the adoptive mother of her decision to marry the good-looking gentleman and to stay in the city of Venecia. Since she was marrying a divorced man, the Catholic church would not allow a religious marriage; therefore, in a civil ceremony in front of a Judge, she married Venancio del Río.

It was a simple wedding, there weren't very many people present: just her adoptive mother, her loyal benefactors — the Domínguez sisters — Lucila del Río, the groom's sister and Leoncio Liborio, the foreman of Venancio's small ranch.

Prior to moving to her new country residence, Lola informed her new husband about the commitment made with the Domínguez sisters regarding the payment for her room and studies, to be reimbursed by offering her services in *Las Variedades*, the twins' department store, upon her return to Los Mirones. In a very generous and gentleman-like gesture, Venancio offered to settle his wife's debt plus an additional sum to cover the last six months of her schooling. However, the sisters chose not to accept such payment hoping that Lola would return and take charge of their store, so they would be able to realize their dream to travel throughout America and Europe.

However, the Domínguez sisters didn't have to wait very long for Lola to return to Los Mirones. In spite of being the object of criticism and the source of envy by a large majority of the inhabitants of both towns, Lola kept behaving herself as a simple and hardworking woman, and although she was accused of carrying out suspicious activities, including the disappearance of her boyfriend, she was not a carrier of evil omens, and much less capable of participating in illicit activities. But bad luck enveloped her life like a dark cloud as if she had been born unlucky.

As he usually did every afternoon, Venancio — mounted on his favorite mare, a Napoleonic white steady horse, went out, as usual, made the usual rounds: inspected around his property, namely his cattle, a breeding bull, six sheep and a couple of pigs. After just one month and a half after their marriage, Venancio started his habitual sweep, and late that afternoon, when he was returning home while crossing a small creek, suddenly the steed was frightened by the roar of a puma which was hidden in some bushes growing by the creek. Suddenly, the frightened horse reared straight up on its hind legs throwing Venancio backward; he, totally unable to contain the beast, fell over violently against the rocky ground, breaking the nape of his neck.

As night fell, and upon noticing that her husband was nowhere to be seen, Lola, fearing that something or someone might have hurt him, asked Liborio, the foreman, to go look for him. Lola didn't have to wait too long, about one hour and a half later, the foreman showed up pulling the reins of the Napoleonic steed with the lifeless body of her husband crossed over the saddle. Lola desperately overwhelmed by the sight, didn't know what to do or whom to call, she felt totally alone, her thoughts reviving old memories took her back to the time when she found herself alone, crying all alone after being abandoned by her mother in the outskirts of an unknown town. She thought of asking her adoptive mother for help, but Cipriana would have to travel all the way from Los Mirones. Her only refuge was Lucila, her sister in law and teacher, who immediately traveled to the country home.

Although he pretended and boasted among friends about his financial wellbeing, Venancio del Río was a man burdened with debts. As is often said: "looks are deceiving." Venancio was not a wealthy man. His creditors landed on his small ranch like vultures in search of rotting flesh. After liquidating all of her husband's debts, for which Lola had to sell everything: cattle, horses, and the ranch house, Lola found herself again without a penny to her name, poor, just as she had started her life, abandoned some twenty years back. The only things left were the Napoleonic white horse, two goats and a couple of pigs, which also she had to sell to be able to move back to the rental room and be able to finish her studies of haute couture in the city of Venecia.

When the news about Venancio del Río's tragic accident was published in the local newspapers, a large number of members of the population pointed their fingers at the young widow, blaming her for the death of her husband, accusing her of being a woman carrier of bad omens, of being a witch, who was blamed for the disappearance of one of her suitors, and now for having provoked the death of a "good man," as Venancio del Río was known around town. Some of her critics, largely those who envied her, sneakily talked about lynching her, to banish her from town, to sentence her to death for having brought so much bad luck to the entire region. Others said: "She was a bad omen, gypsy damnation!"

Just as she was about to finish her studies, Lola received a telegram from Don Lucero Ordoñez, the apothecary and consoler of the lost cases of Los Mirones, asking her to return to town as soon as possible because Cipriana, her adoptive mother, had been gravely ill with an unknown and incurable contagious decease, and most likely didn't have much longer to live.

After two years or more of being away, with the few financial resources which she had managed to save during her stay in Venecia, and after becoming a widow at such a young age, Lola returned to Los Mirones. Notwithstanding the dramatic spectacle she found in her home, with her bedridden mother about to die, her path was brightened by a shiny light that gave Lola encouraging hope. That light was the prospect of taking a job that would enable her to live a peaceful life, with a source of income to make some repairs on her house, the house of *tía* Lola, as it was already well known throughout the morbid environment of Los Mirones.

As it was to be expected, that encouraging light was the job offer from her good benefactors, the Domínguez sisters, who anxiously longed-for their protegee to take over their department store *Las Variedades*.

Upon the death of her mother, as usual, a great majority of the population blamed Lola for being the carrier of the illness that afflicted her mother which eventually caused her death. But all those accusations were nothing more than evil speculations made without supporting evidence. It was their way of taking revenge against the beautiful Lola, just because she was only a *tía*, a nobody, who had arrived in town without anyone knowing her origin.

But Lola, not giving a damn about what people's venomous tongues said about her, continued living her life as usual; she would fully apply herself to fulfilling the agreement made with the twins concerning the work at their shop.

After the mandatory nine days of mourning for her mother's death, Lola finally took over the administration of *Las Variedades*. Six months later, after she had started her new job and had introduced new clothing brought from abroad, the sales skyrocketed, thus allowing the Domínguez sisters to advance their plans for their longed-for trip. They completely trusted Lola, the new manager, and went as far as to offer her a good percentage of sales.

With her new income, Lola started to make improvements to her house. She contracted carpenters to close up the kitchen area which opened onto the patio and add a new bedroom; she hired masons to repair one of the walls in front of the house, she brought over from Venecia a portable gas stove and hired a couple of plumbers to install the necessary piping to bring potable water to the home to provide water to the bathroom and toilet to avoid relying on the well's water only.

In spite of making all the improvements to modernize her house, for unknown reasons, Lola — perhaps due to habit acquired when as a child her adoptive mother bathed under a lemon tree — used to bathe naked in the patio hidden behind the rose bushes and red amapolas. After warming up the water, she would stand under a lemon tree, would cut some of the lemon leaves and while she sang and danced, she caressed her naked body with a variety of aromatic soaps and with the lemon leaves recently trimmed. That's the way the beautiful Lola entertained herself, dancing and singing gypsy songs accompanied by her castanets, languidly caressing her naked body with long silk handkerchiefs she herself had sewn.

Although Lola believed that such baths were a private ritual that no one was supposed to witness, her early-evening routine was also the distraction of some of the town kids who, having heard her singing and the cracking of the castanets silently crawled up the low roof to witness the evenings intimate spectacle. However, their visual distraction didn't last very long. With the climbing of the boys, one of them fell in the courtyard when one of the roof tiles was dislodged. Fortunately, the boy just suffered scratches on the arms and legs, but it was enough to alert Lola that there were onlookers watching her ritual bath. Lola warned the kids, but chose not to say anything nor inform the parents and the sheriff about the boy's impertinent spying on her, she thought that after all they were just curious kids and she did not want to antagonize their parents. Least of all did she want to let the rest of the population know about her evening ritual. Lola contracted a roofer to raise the roof structure to prevent the boys or other possible curious persons from going up the roof and spy on her while she carried out her private business.

Lola mistakenly believed that she could peacefully live in Los Mirones, start a new life and perhaps marry one of her so many admirers. But the die was cast, neither the benefactor sisters would realize their trip, nor would Lola finish one year of work in *Las Variedades*.

At the start of the seventh month, while Lola was enjoying a cup of coffee in her recently remodeled kitchen the loud wailing of a siren was heard; blackish/grey smoke was covering the sky. The smoke was coming from a fire two-and-one-half blocks from her house. The department store *Las Variedades* was in flames. No one knew the cause of the sinister and vicious fire. Not even the four firemen nor the volunteers with their buckets of water were able to put out the flames and least rescue the Domínguez twins. The entire wooden structure, including the new materials, sewing machines, recently imported fabrics and all had burned to ashes, devoured by the flames in less than half an hour. The forensic doctors were unable to find the remains of the twins, the experts arriving from Venecia and the capital weren't able to identify the cause of the fire. Due to the speed of the fire which rapidly consumed the old house and due to the black clouds of smoke which partially clouded the sky, they suspected gasoline was the culprit but that was just a guess. They thought that one of the sisters had fallen asleep with a lit cigarette, but there was no way to prove such a theory. It was also unknown if anyone of the sisters was a smoker, perhaps she smoked in private as it was not proper for a lady to smoke in public.

Dressed in her robe, still with the cup of coffee in her hands, Lola peaked out of her front door. The outcome was obvious, Lola was being accused. She was the one to blame for starting the fire and for the death of the two sisters, of whom it was impossible to find the remains.

Once her presence was discovered, the onlookers and all the envious others charged against her, but as she saw them approaching her, she closed the windows and door of her house. With stones and sticks in their hands, the aggressors were ready to break and storm the door. And would have done it if it hadn't been for Don Lucero Ordoñez — the apothecary and defender of lost causes —, who intervened before the mob of aggressors. They would probably have lynched her and set her home on fire.

After such a tragic event, it was very difficult for Lola to find a job to sustain herself. She would have to depend on the sale of her garden's fruits and the rent of her newly built room which she rented to a widow who did not have negative feelings against her. Five years went by during which it was not possible to blame Lola for some of the deaths or some of the misfortunes occurred at Los Mirones. She thought, by this time, she was going to be left alone, to live in peace, to restart her life ... but she was wrong!

El Resguardo hotel, located on the outskirts of town, was not a dead-beat hotel, although it was neither a luxurious one. It was a small hotel with a central living room next to a small four table, dimly lit dining room. At the poorly stocked bar, liquor was just served after six pm, since due to the town's religious beliefs it was not allowed to serve alcohol during the day. The five rooms on the upstairs floor were rented to transients and often, on an hourly basis, to some members of the community with their respective paramours. It was rumored that the mayor was the one who most frequently used them. The hotel's entry door was surrounded by a rusting rough looking chain attached to exterior posts simulating a railing. In one of the corners of the porch — which served as a vestibule to the only entry door —, on both sides of a faded red metal table, there were two white wicker rocking chairs which just as the wall and floorboards were discolored because of the punishing summer suns.

Before lunch was served, seated on one of the rockers, smoking a cigar, was a middle-aged man, who had registered two nights before as Lotario Melalo. He was a dark-skinned thin man, very black eyes and rather short in stature. He hid the unfriendly face with a beret-type cap which covered his dark hair. Lotario's origin was unknown. He had refrained from writing it when he registered in the hotel's guest book. He barely had exchanged a few words with the receptionist and the bartender when he went to the bar the night before. His conversation was very short-spoken and antagonistic. Very cunningly he had limited himself to finding out about some of the townspeople, namely the deceased Domínguez sisters, the sheriff, the recently passed Cipriana Altuna, her daughter Lola, Venancio del Río among others.

Francisco, the waiter, approaching Lotario Melalo as discretely as he tried, couldn't avoid the creaking wooden planks of the floor with each step he took. Very courteously, Francisco asked Lotario if he wanted something to drink, a soft drink, before lunch, but Melalo, without thanking him, refused the waiter's suggestion telling him that he was going to take a walk around town to familiarize himself with its surroundings and that he would eat and drink at the nearby cantina. Both, the bartender and the waiter were very surprised about the interest of this stranger, this *tío*, in some of the town's folk, especially the Domínguez sisters who had been Lola's benefactors. They both informed the hotel's administrator, but he didn't think much of it and told them to concentrate on the hotel's chores and stop being so curious and gossiping.

The *El Ojo de Agua* cantina was a locale better stocked with alcoholic beverages than the hotel's bar, and with fewer restrictions to serve liquor. Some cowhide skins partially covered the wooden floor to muffle the frequent traffic of the clientele. Taxidermed steer heads and country decorations hung from the walls. A piece of sweetish and lazy music from the time could be heard coming from one of the adjacent rooms, perhaps from a Victrola.

As he entered the cantina, Lotario Melalo asked the young waitress, a girl no older than twenty, to bring him something to eat and a drink of rum, additionally he asked to be seated at one of the tables in the corner of the room where he could have some privacy and observe any passersby on the main street. Taking advantage of the friendly conversation of the girl, he asked her, although he already knew the answer, who lived at the corner house at the end of the street.

"That's the house of Dolores Altuna, or better known as *tía* Lola's house."

"Why is it called *tía* Lola's house?" Asked Lotario, pretending to ignore its origin.

The girl informed the guest that the house was called that, because a woman who no one knew where she came from, lived there, that she had been abandoned by some gypsies when she was three years old. People in town blamed her for many things which she had not done. She was accused of being a witch and of having supernatural powers. That her singing and the clacking sound of castanets were heard in the evenings as coming from her house.

"Lola is a good person," added the girl. "She is innocent of what she is accused of! In this town people are too envious and talk a lot, they talk just for the sake of talking."

"Does she live alone?"

"She lives with an older woman who recently became a widow."

But Lotario was not satisfied with the information provided by the girl. Upon exiting the cantina, like a wild beast, he started marauding and looking around town, asking whoever he encountered of other citizens but always ending with questions about the Domínguez twins and Lola. During the afternoon he decided to spy on Lola's house while seated on a bench close to the trunk of the leafy ceiba.

Lola already was aware of Lotario Melalo's presence in town. Suspecting she was being watched, she asked her friend Mr. Ordoñez, the apothecary, but he did not provide her with many details. He just told her that he only knew that the man was passing through Los Mirones, and not to pay too much attention to the matter.

Francisco Lugano, the hotel's waiter, was a curious and persistent man. He was not a person who was going to forget the suspicious and inquiring *tío*, Lotario Melalo. And least of all he was going to listen to the hotel's administrator admonishing him and his coworker two days before, to leave alone the only guest at the hotel.

The following morning, Francisco was surprised when he saw the sheriff entering the hotel. He ignored the motive of his visit that early in the morning. He listened unobtrusively but carefully noticing that the sheriff was asking for the room in which Lotario Melalo was staying. Very cautiously and without hesitating, not to alert the sheriff, who was already walking upstairs, he grabbed a broom and pretended to sweep the hallway. Since Lotario was the only guest it was not difficult to listen in the conversation between the two men.

"Good morning Mr. Melalo, my name is Fernando Ruiz, I am the sheriff in this city, I inconvenience you at this hour because I need to ask you a few questions."

Fernando Ruiz was a tall man, slim, boiled-lobster reddish skin, clear eyes and for this particular visit he had left the police uniform in the station's armoire, and although he was well known in Los Mirones, he chose to wear this time a civil attire. However, he was not able to fool the curious Francisco, the waiter.

"Good morning Mr. Ruiz, I see you already know my name, save your questions; I will gladly inform you who I am and the motive which has brought me to this city."

"Very well, you can start."

"Actually, I am a private investigator. For many years I worked as a detective for the capital's police central office. I have been hired by a family member of the Domínguez's sisters — but I cannot disclose his name —, to find out the cause of the fire which took their lives."

"There isn't much to investigate, the fire and the death of the twins were declared to be an accident by investigators from the capital as well as the forensic physicians. The property has been fenced to avoid intruders and curious until the mayor decides to call for an auction to sell it to the highest bidder. It was never known that the Domínguez sisters had any relatives, neither they ever mentioned to have any other family. It was always known that they were orphans. If you wish, I can open the gate for you to enter the locale and see the rubbish, but the visit will have to be supervised, I cannot allow any strangers to be roaming around that place, looking for who knows what. That property already belongs to the mayoralty."

"There is always a faraway relative wishing to inquire about the death of a family member. Besides, it is well known that the Domínguez sisters were very wealthy; they owned very valuable antique jewelry, including gold and silver coins inherited from their ancestors. It's also public knowledge that they had a substantial capital. Perhaps the person who worked for them knew it also, maybe it was she who stole their wealth and torched the shop to cover up any traces that could incriminate her."

"Are you insinuating that Lola Altuna was the perpetrator, the one who committed the crime? She was the only person who worked at the store, and, she was very much loved by the señoritas Domínguez."

"Perhaps that's what I intend to find out if you allow me and don't interfere with my investigation."

"I will not interrupt you, however, be very careful. You are stepping in quicksand and could sink deep, you could be harmed. It's said that that girl has supernatural powers. I myself don't believe anything rumored in this town. I consider Lola to be a decent woman who has been struck by bad luck."

"Thank you very much, Mr. Ruiz, my visit will be short."

"I hope so!"

Notwithstanding the sheriff authorizing Melalo, the supposed investigator, to carry out his inquiries, he was not totally convinced about the Domínguez sisters having any relatives. He suspected that the stranger, the *tío* Melalo, was not being honest; that he pretended to be an investigator, a retired detective, but in fact, he was an impostor. Ruiz suspected Melalo was a scoundrel and an opportunist in search of fortune and decided to conduct his own investigation. Upon arriving at his office, he telegraphed the police authorities in the capital. The reply was almost immediate. They had no knowledge of such Lotario Melalo. He had never worked as a detective for that jurisdiction.

After listening to the conversation between Melalo and the sheriff, as quickly as possible, Francisco, the waiter, who was Lola's friend, dropped the broom behind one of the hotel's doors, and hurriedly went looking for his childhood friend with whom, as a boy, he shared the swing hanging from one of the branches of the ceiba. Having witnessed the exchange between the two men, Francisco alerted Lola on the existence of the so-called Melalo, the pretending investigator, and the purpose of his visit in town.

Lola laughed aloud when she heard about the existence of a possible treasure, which supposedly she had stolen and hidden in her humble home: *tía* Lola's house.

"Don't worry Francisco, I don't have such a treasure, I am neither a thief nor a crazy incendiary woman. But thank you just the same for warning me. Please have a seat, may I invite you to a cup of coffee?"

"It will have to be on another occasion, I am in a hurry, I left the hotel just to warn you, thanks anyway."

That same afternoon, availing himself of the opportunity that Lola and her tenant had gone to the market, and temporarily losing sight of the sheriff — who was already trailing him —, Lotario Melalo, making sure that no one was watching him, with a picklock he forced the door lock of Lola's house.

Fearing to be found inside by Lola and her tenant, he quickly and thoroughly started to search the house. The intruder began in the living room, next he went into the bedrooms, bathroom, an armoire where Lola kept some dresses and her undergarments. While he carried out the search, he threw everything on the floor, upon finding nothing valuable and least of all the supposed treasure, he indignantly stepped on everything he found on his way. Noticing that one of the floorboards in the room creaked as he stepped on it, he thought the jewelry and the money were hidden underneath. With a hammer, he lifted the board but didn't find anything. He emptied a cupboard in the kitchen throwing all the silverware on the floor, but since he found nothing, he decided to exit to the patio thinking that perhaps Lola had buried there the valuable jewelry with the money. He grabbed a shovel and started to dig wherever he saw any recently disturbed soil.

After going through the entire garden, and looking inside the well, he noticed that among the amapolas there was an obvious square of the dirt which had been recently turned over as if someone had tried to bury or unearth something. Shovel in hand he started digging a hole; he panted, perspiring copiously, his breathing was faltering, then all of sudden, he stopped right then and there. Lotario heard that someone had entered the house, and heard screams and alarmed voices. It was Lola who couldn't believe what had happened at her house, it was as if an earthquake had thrown down the furniture. When she entered her room, she screamed horrified to see all her clothes on the floor and her underwear thrown all around, she felt violated. Alicia Romero, her tenant could not believe either what she was witnessing, her room had also been ransacked.

They both went outside to the garden, they looked among the orange and lemon trees. The place where Lola usually bathed in the evenings had been trampled over, then she walked over toward the valued amapolas and rose bushes where she had recently prepared the ground to plant a bed of lilac seeds.

It was then that she discovered the body of Lotario Melalo. He had fallen face down on the ground while grabbing his chest with both hands. The intruder had suffered a massive heart attack. Fearing to be blamed for the death of the stranger, Lola asked Alicia to go find the sheriff. While waiting for her friend to come back with the sheriff, she observed that Melalo's wallet had fallen from one of his pockets, perhaps it had fallen as he hurriedly tried to dig up the hole. When she opened it, Lola noticed an old crumpled photograph, it was the picture of a young couple and a child. In the back of the photo, Lola could see something which perhaps had been written many years back, it read:

Brother Lotario, go look for my daughter Dolores Melalo, I abandoned her many years ago in a town called Los Mirones.

Lola could not believe her eyes, she had in her hands a photo of her when she was just a child, with her mother, whom she hardly remembered, and her uncle Lotario Melalo, the intruder who lay dead at her feet, who decided to search for a nonexistent treasure instead of identifying himself with her, his blood niece. She heard steps, it was the sheriff and Leticia, she hid the photo and returned the wallet to one of Melalo's pockets.

Although Lotario had suffered a heart attack, the sheriff did not believe that that had caused his death. Even when he knew that Lola was a woman who was blamed for unheard actions of which she was incapable of doing, this time without having any proof, he blamed her for the death of the stranger; more so when, after turning the body he found a small dark brown bag hanging on a silver chain from the neck of the dead man which was full of minute blue stones and small broken bones. Immediately, the sheriff thought it was witchcraft or an amulet of a mysterious bewitching. Without wasting any time, he handcuffed Lola making her a prisoner.

During the trial, friendly testimonies in favor of *tía* Lola Altuna were heard, from Lucila del Río, her former sister-in-law, Francisco Lugano, her childhood friend, the waiter, Lucero Ordoñez, the apothecary and defender of lost causes ... But none of them succeeded in convincing the jury. The mobs demanded her execution, they asked that she be hung (this would be a legal execution) for her criminal acts, for being an impostor, a husband seducer, and a witch. The trial lasted two days, which was enough time to condemn her to death. To execute her would be the only way to permanently get rid of *tía* Lola. The only way Lola wouldn't be able to escape the law and go free.

Two days after being condemned, not even having turned

twenty-nine years of age, her lifeless body was found hanging from one of the branches of the majestic ceiba; the same tree which years before had served as silent witness of Lola Altuna or Melalo's innocence, when she as a child delighted in swinging from one of its branches. As it passed by, a sallow-eyed ravenous dog gazed indifferently at the macabre scene.

This sad event took place during the middle of July 1929.

This is how Lola's story is remembered.

Yearnings

*... memory is fiction. We select the most
brilliant and the most obscure,
ignoring what we are shameful of, and as such we knit the broad
tapestry of our life ...*
Isabel Allende

To José Aburto

Nine days after celebrating his eighty-fifth birthday, Ignacio Lopez got out bed. After washing his hands and face with his lavender soap he looked at himself in the mirror only to realize again that he had not been spared by the passing of the years. A lock of silvery thick hair fell over his brownish forehead. The eyebrows of the same color of his hair framed his clear green eyes. With a toothbrush in the right hand, he proceeded to brush his white and evenly shaped teeth, not before being reminded of the two missing back teeth on his upper jaw. He looked at himself again in the elongated mirror hanging from one of the walls that adorned his apartment, and very much satisfied, Ignacio noticed that although his body was somewhat hunched, it still maintained the tallness which had accompanied him during the good and happy years of his youth; however, despite his advanced age he had only gained very little weight which showed a slight but not so pronounced belly.

Leaning on a lathe-turned dark wooded cane, carefully measuring his steps, Ignacio slowly approached the window in his room to find out what was the commotion and noise which had awakened him at such an early hour. He wished he didn't have to get up at seven in the morning instead of at eight-thirty, as he was accustomed to and prepare a light breakfast: hot tea with sweet coconut crackers.

At the Los Robles nursing home, which two years earlier his son had chosen as permanent residence for his father, nothing of importance occurred except for the passing away of its residents and the fuss made by Mrs. Smith in the hallways who — notwithstanding her eighty-seven years — enjoyed making amorous passes at the younger men living on the fourth floor. The Los Robles house was a five-story building, which already showed signs of deterioration. The home was centrally located on the corner of Junípero and Pine in the picturesque and small-town city of Monterey, on the central coast of California. Ignacio had already fallen three times, he limped on his left leg, complained of aches in his arms ... and although the mirror in the room showed him the opposite of what he felt, he was a man with a sack-full of hardships. But what really afflicted him was the knowledge that his mind had already begun the sad and irreversible trajectory toward darkness. Yes, that implacable and vengeful trajectory which traps man after so many years of plentifully enjoying a clean and brilliant memory. Now just like the clouded glass panes of the window, his memory had begun to fog over, to become clouded. Ignacio lived a lonely life, neither his son nor the rest of his family would visit him; however, he had gotten used to his loneliness and enjoyed the few happy instances which life still gave him.

The Monterey Bay morning mist had not yet dissipated. It was early, the greenish hands of the clock over the nightstand showed seven-forty-five in the morning. With a small rag, Ignacio wiped away the moisture from one of the window panes facing the courtyard and could see how the three men, armed with picks and mauls, knocked the stones off the wall of the well in the center of the building's garden. A large dump truck loaded with fine egg-shaped stones and sandy soil entered through the rear service gate toward the middle of the yard to unload the contents of the truck's tipping box into the pit. A leveler machine finished filling the hole and leveled the ground where the well had existed since the conquest of California. It had served as a source of water and as an oasis to the first brave man, the Franciscan friar Junípero Serra and the famous Spanish explorer Gaspar de Portolá, the first settlers of the city of Monterey.

Ignacio could not believe what his eyes were witnessing. The well, his beloved well, had been totally destroyed. The time-worn circular stone wall was the only structure that distracted him and reminded him of the wonderful and happy times he had enjoyed during the thirties in Nicaragua, his home country. He remembered playing hide-and-seek with his older brother surrounded by coffee plantations and the tropical flower covered gardens of La Ceiba, his parent's, ranch. Ignacio couldn't hold back the tears that spontaneously fell from his eyes, seeing that his well had been destroyed forever. This was the second well, falling victim to progress, the first one had been taken down to give way to a highway, the Pan-American Highway.

Ignacio was so absorbed and distracted witnessing the actions of the men and trucks in the courtyard that he did not realize that Isamu Aki, the Japanese assistant and his faithful friend, assigned to the care and attention of the male patients of the fourth floor at Los Robles, had entered his room. Isamu couldn't be more than forty years old. Like a great majority of his countrymen, he combed back his straight and shiny black hair. Isamu was a young man, lean and tall, and although of Japanese origin he did not wear Japanese attire, he was already Americanized and wore jeans and a long-sleeve, dark blue shirt. After realizing that Ignacio had not noticed him entering the room, he said:

"Forgive me, Mr. Ignacio," said Isamu, "for barging in without knocking, but the door was ajar." Seeing Ignacio's cheeks moistened with tears he asked: "Why are you crying? What has caused you so much sadness?"

"They've destroyed the well!"

"It was an old well, dried up and very dangerous, someone could fall into the hole. There are many older patients strolling in the garden ... but don't you worry, instead they will build a very beautiful fountain surrounded by lots of flowers," very politely explained Isamu.

"The new fountain will not bring me the same memories that the well has brought me for all these years."

"The fountain is going to be beautiful," added the Japanese man, "they are going to plant native bushes like lantanas, daisies, and Peruvian lilies ..., that will bring hummingbirds, blue jays, and beautiful and colorful monarch butterflies, which in their migratory flight south and on their return, will settle to rest on the surrounding bushes ... I am sure you will enjoy witnessing that beautiful and colorful spectacle ..."

"I will also enjoy seeing how the deer will devour all those shrubs and flowers," skeptically answered Ignacio.

"Please don't be so pessimistic Mr. Ignacio. Tell me how the well brings you so many memories? Perhaps you should narrate them to the Los Robles residents, they could enjoy listening to you."

With a delicate white linen handkerchief, Ignacio wiped the tears from his cheeks and said to Isamu:

"My memories are of no importance; they are just mine. My memories are only a chimera; they wouldn't have a great significance for you or the residents of this place. They can barely walk and consume themselves with their ailments and pains, and wouldn't pay attention to my stories no matter how interesting they might be. Not even the few remaining contemporary inhabitants of my hometown back in my country would be interested. Everything changes Isamu, everything is forgotten, progress and technology contribute to this fateful forgetfulness."

"If they are not important to all these poor old folks," said Isamu, "they would be very valuable to me. I remember my father telling us when we were kids about how before he left Japan to come to San Francisco; he witnessed similar experiences such as the eviction of low-income and older people from their homes and transferring them to government-built houses. Worse yet, when my parents arrived in San Francisco in the mid-thirties, they suffered many hardships since in those days people discriminated against Asians. It was very hard and traumatic for them when the United States declared war on Japan. They were victims of the raids against the Japanese, and like countless Japanese families, my parents were sent out of San Francisco to concentration camps for the entire time the war lasted. Those were very difficult years for my parents, Mr. Ignacio."

"Yes Isamu, I am aware of all the vicissitudes, difficulties, abuses and discriminations suffered by your fellow countrymen in this country during that period, and I am very sorry ..."

"Mr. Ignacio, please forgive me, but it was not my intention to distract you from or minimize your grief by telling you briefly our story, my intention was only to share with you some of our experiences and perhaps revive your memory to tell me the story of your well that has so deeply affected you; however, if you prefer not to do so, I will respect your privacy, I will not insist."

"No Isamu, you are not going to force me to tell you my stories. For me it will be a great pleasure to tell you some of them, and I feel honored that you have demonstrated an interest in them, but it will have to be another day, perhaps tomorrow. This evening I am expecting company. I am waiting for Linda Smith who yesterday announced she was going to bring me a chicken stew casserole. You are very well aware of how some people take advantage of the old, and they are even more persistent if they suspect they still have some money left in the bank account. Linda, although older than some of us, is known to take advantage of the less old and believes that with her invitations to dinner she will trap us. She assumes that like fish, we widowed men by eating her food will fall, swallow the bait and get hooked. Linda does not realize that we no longer travel that road, what we are mostly interested in is her friendly company and as long as she doesn't fall asleep, perhaps share a cup of green tea or an after-dinner drink. But despite all her hullabaloo in the hallways and clamoring for attention, Linda is a good person, very attentive and affectionate. Do you know who Linda is, Isamu, I am sure you know her?"

"Of course, I perfectly know who she is!" answered Isamu. "When I started working at Los Robles, she came with her husband Bill. She was a very pretty woman, very attractive."

"In spite of her age," Ignacio added, "Linda is still attractive!"

"Yes, she still is." Said Isamu. "She is from one of Boston's most distinguished and wealthy families, her husband was Australian, and had a very successful law firm in that city. They both had fallen in love with this beautiful city of Monterey, with its panoramic views of the bay, but mainly they loved the enviable mild weather and the amazing cool and soft breezes blowing from the Pacific. Imagine, Mr. Ignacio, this city cannot be compared with the city of Boston, here it is like living in an eternal spring, like living in a sanatorium. Bill, her husband was also a handsome man, tall and slender ... he was the attraction of many of the ladies in this house. However, he was a very restless man, a hummingbird going from flower to flower. He loved golf; frequented the best and most expensive clubs in this area."

"Just like Linda nowadays," added Ignacio. "What really happened? Bill passed away?"

"Oh no, Mr. Ignacio! He left, and never came back!"

"How so? One doesn't just pick up and leaves without saying a word. There must have been a reason."

"Apparently, Bill got tired of this life. He was looking for a life full of adventures, not only of an amorous nature but for hunting, he loved to hunt, it's rumored that he returned to Australia, his country of origin. One morning one of the cleaning women saw him leaving through a back door with one of his female admirers. However, he left Linda with a substantial bank account, but he did not even leave her a note, absolutely nothing. After that, no one has heard from him. After years without knowing his whereabouts, Linda went to the judicial authorities to have her husband officially declared dead and consequently she a widow, so that she could marry again. Later, she married Mr. Anthony Smith, whom she trapped — as you would call it — with one of her famous casseroles. But three years later, Mr. Smith died of a heart attack leaving her a large inheritance. She lacks nothing; I don't understand why she puts so much effort into trying to seduce the younger male residents with her famous casseroles."

"Wow, Isamu! you know a lot about the residents in this home." Ignacio interrupted his friend. "Now I'll be more attentive to all her advances and seductive traps."

"Yes, Mr. Ignacio, it's very easy to find out what's going on at Los Robles, there is always someone who is willing to share the stories of those who live here, including a little bit of gossip. I am sorry to have taken up your time to tell you Linda's story with so much detail. But going back to *your* story, I have not forgotten that you have not told me the story and that of the notorious well, perhaps you could tell it to me on another occasion." Isamu said somehow resigned. "I am very interested in learning about the folklore of your country, and even more, I am very curious to learn about that famous well that has brought you so many memories."

Punctually, at six-thirty in the early evening, Linda Smith knocked on Ignacio's apartment door. She was carrying a fragrantly smelling delicious casserole. She hoped to stimulate not only Ignacio's appetite but also awaken his sexual desires. But both Ignacio and Linda were not in physical condition to distract themselves with activities of an amorous nature; so, after sharing the succulent and satisfying dinner, along with a glass of Porto, both were comfortably settled into separate armchairs to watch the romantic movie *Casablanca* starring the famous actress Ingrid Bergman and the gallant and mysterious Humphrey Bogart. However, neither of them was able to finish watching the film. After a short while, Linda retreated to her apartment as Ignacio's had falling asleep and was snoring loudly. She washed her casserole, put a plaid wool blanket on Ignacio's knees, gave him a kiss on his forehead and tiptoed slowly out of Ignacio's apartment, making sure the door had been closed securely.

Isamu did not return to Los Robles the following day as he had promised to Ignacio. He was away for two weeks. Although his services at the home were voluntary, on his return to Los Robles he apologized and explained to Ignacio that his absence was due to an emergency trip to San Francisco to see a nephew who had suffered an accident climbing one of the rocky and dangerous cliffs at Yosemite National Park. He added that the person he had left in charge of his laundry and tailoring business had not followed to the letter his instructions, which had given rise to complaints of some of his clients.

"I am back Mr. Ignacio!" Effusively cried Isamu, and he bowed as the Japanese usually do with both his hands together. "I am ready to spend some time with you, and listen in detail the story of the well. But first, if you allow me, I'll boil some water in the kettle, for while I was in San Francisco, I visited Chinatown and bought your favorite tea, Ceylon tea."

"Thank you, Isamu, it's my favorite tea, please add a teaspoon of honey. In the cupboard, next to the kitchen there are a few coconut cookies, bring some to accompany the tea."

"We're starting to look like those English Lords," smiled Isamu, "we just need different attires to look like those Lords, unlike what we are wearing now, you in your pajamas and I in my blue jeans. Well, Mr. Ignacio, you can begin to tell me your story," he added, serving to Ignacio a cup of the aromatic and steaming tea and then another cup for himself as they both comfortably settled on their respective chairs.

"Isamu, my good friend, please don't misunderstand me, I am not against progress, I believe that things that are eliminated or modified in our lives usually improve or modify their surroundings. But before all those scientific and technological advances, before the Pan American highway was built, everything in my hometown was so beautiful. On one side, we had the greenness of the sugar cane fields that lazily swayed to the rhythm of the breezes blowing from the south at dusk; on the other, from the porch of the hacienda house, we also admired the polychromed landscapes of the countryside and the firmament when they wear the best of their attires. All those beautiful natural paintings were enhanced by the Concepción volcano, which after spewing its last breath of smoke prepared itself to receive the nocturnal veil before retiring to rest. Those landscapes were beautiful views like the black and white photographs of the legendary photographer Ansel Adams. Those are things that I cannot forget, and I don't know how long my terrible illness will allow me to evoke those memories. Often, I remember the trips we made with our parents to visit the sugar mills of my uncles and grandparents, where we would watch the boiling juice of sugar cane turn into molasses. All of that was so beautiful."

"Maybe someday I will be able to visit your country," Isamu said, "from what you are telling me it would be a very interesting trip."

"None of that exists anymore, Isamu; everything is gone. Where my well used to be, an apartment complex was built. I am sure that none of the people living in the vicinity remember the well's existence. There was a small village called La Conquista, it was more like a hamlet but the locals called it a village, it was located about fifteen miles south of the city of Jinotepe and was one of the most picturesque villages in the province of Carazo. When we were kids, my brother and I used to play hide-and-seek around the coffee trees, at my parent's small coffee plantation called La Ceiba. We ran tirelessly all over and usually our escapades ended up around the well. Sweating and thirsty, we always managed to get that fresh and crystalline water from the well. It was a very deep well but we weren't afraid of falling. My father did not like us to get close to the edge of the well and even less drawing water from it to quench our thirst. But we were kids and at that age, we thought we could do anything, that we were invincible. We always liked to look over the edge and see how deep it was; it seemed to us that it was like the eye of the earth, like the eye of God, looking back at us without blinking as if warning us of the danger we were in.

During the coffee harvest, we helped the ranch hands cut the reddish-green fruit of the coffee trees and fill the baskets to the edges; later we scattered the beans on cement patios to prevent them from sticking together. Then we would help rake them with large wooden rakes, and once they had dried, we filled large twine bags with the raw seeds to be taken to Jinotepe and be transported by train to the markets of Granada, which is another important city in my country. That's the way we spent most of our free time, Isamu, with simple and uneventful pastimes, not like the youth of today who are distracted by cellular phones ... they have become slaves of that technology.

At that time, in the absence of paved roads and highways, almost everything was transported by *carretas* or ox-pulled carts; fruits, sugar cane, coffee, mangoes and cashew fruits, among many other things. The *carretas* would come from nearby cities such as those west of the province of Rivas which borders the province of Carazo — Rivas is another important city in my country — and from Nandaime, smaller than Rivas, but not of less importance. The well was very similar to the one they have just destroyed here. It was a place where all the *carreteros,* as the cart drivers were called, would rest overnight to fill their jugs, buckets, large decanters with water and feed the oxen, it was like a watering hole since there were few other sources of water in the nearby surrounding and the round trip to those other places sometimes lasted a few hours. But besides the water they took out of the well, the most attractive feature of the place were the mammees."

"What are mammees?" Asked Isamu. "A fruit, an animal?"

Smiling, Ignacio answered, "My dear Isamu, of course, the mammees are not animals, they are a fruit." As I said, the mammee or *Mamey* as this fruit is called in Spanish, is very delicious indeed, when it ripens the meat or reddish pulp is sweet and very tasty. In some parts of our country, it is also known as *Zapote*."

"Wow! So many names for one fruit. I have never seen a mammee."

"It is a tropical fruit," Ignacio explained. "In those days, the mammee trees served as a fence between ranches and mainly between the ranches and the roads traveled by the *carreteros*. The well, although not visible from the road — because it was hidden by the coffee trees — was very close to a barbed wire fence which served as a fence for La Ceiba. The *Mamey* trees which in the past had served as La Ceiba's fence were growing on the other side of the road, on an island formed by the road in use and the one which had been abandoned." Ignacio added.

"I understand Mr. Ignacio, thank you for your detailed explanation, you have an amazing memory."

"In my country, like in some other Central American countries, there are only two seasons; winter and summer. Winter, like here in California, is the rainy season; however, back home we experience devastating torrential rains, they cause floods, the rivers overflow, they destroy what they find in their way."

"It's the same here, the winter rains cause flooding, landslides, overflowing rivers and there is much loss of property, personal damage and even deaths," interrupted Isamu.

"True and I am aware of the damages, but the rains near the well were so devastating that little by little they were eroding the soil around the well, turning it into a small islet. As to the mammees, at the beginning of the summer season, the fruits would ripen and were attractive not only for the *carreteros* who would stock up on them but also for the locals and people from neighboring farms and cities. It was like a great party of friends and neighbors ... it was so popular in the region it came to be known as the 'Festival of the mammees.' People came from as far as nearby Rivas, Nandaime, and villages like Tola, La Conquista ... The *carreteros* brought guitars, maracas, marimbas, drums ... they sang, they danced, everything was a joy. The feast lasted three or four days. We boys used to eat all kinds of fruits, my favorites were the mangoes and jocotes, they were very tasty and sweet. From what was left, my great-aunt used to make *curbasá* — a typical Nicaraguan desert — and hers was the most famous in the whole region."

"Excuse me, Mr. Ignacio, I believe you are trying to confuse me or take advantage of my poor knowledge of the history of America and less of your country. What is *curbasá*?"

"Forgive me Isamu, whenever I talk about my country, I think that those listening know its history and culture or, more specifically, its dishes, I am always using what we call *nicaragüismos* or words, we spontaneously use, which only we Nicaraguans know. *Curbasá* is a typical desert composed of mangoes, ripe jocotes, cashew fruit, and papaya or whatever you wish to add to it. You boil this concoction slowly, adding raw brown sugar or 'panela' until obtaining a thick, delicious and palatable sauce. Usually, this dessert is consumed during the holidays of Holy Week, or when one wishes to savor it ... Those were happy times during the thirties and forties. Those are my childhood memories that "my well" brings back. Places wiped out from the face of the earth when the famous Pan-American Highway was built, which progress erased ..."

"What a beautiful story, Mr. Ignacio! I feel as if I was there sharing all those adventures and escapades with your brother, the fruit festival, the ox-driven carts, the cart drivers, and the folk's music."

"Something else I'll share with you, about the *carreteros*, Isamu, something that happened before we were even born, it's a legendary story that my father told us."

But before Ignacio could continue his account of the legendary tale, someone urgently knocked on the door. Isamu placed his tea on top of the small table next to the chair to go open the door.

"Who can it be?" Isamu wondered aloud. "It's barely ten-thirty-five in the morning; it's not the time for lunch yet."

When he opened the door, he saw Patricia, the young woman, who — as Isamu was in charge of tending to the male residents at Los Robles — was in charge with ensuring the welfare of the female occupants of the place. Usually, Patricia was abounding in energy, very active and efficient, but this time her nervousness was most visible. Her hands trembled, her face was drawn, and with a faded yellow handkerchief she wiped the tears rolling from her eyes.

"What is it, Patricia? calm down, please ..." Isamu said as he saw the woman about to collapse.

"There has been a terrible accident!" said Patricia. "Mr. Rolling, the building manager has called an emergency meeting in the conference room. He wants everyone to be present in not more than half an hour."

"I'll have to get dressed in a hurry, I cannot go to the meeting in pajamas!" Ignacio said rising from his comfortable chair and putting his half-empty cup on the table next to it. "Rolling is always calling meetings in a hurry to give us news of no significance. This must be just another one of those meetings. But we will go to listen to the bad news this man has to tell us. Are you coming too, Isamu?"

"Yes, Mr. Ignacio."

The conference room was packed; all the residents of both sexes were present. They stared at each other curiously, murmuring, speculating, whispering ... including the other two attendants, Juan Robles and Lucinda Evans. The cook and the two waiters had also been invited.

"This has to be something big," Ignacio murmured "to have invited even the cook and the two waiters; it has to be a bomb."

"It seems so," Isamu responded.

"Silence please!" said Rolling, addressing all those present. "A very unfortunate and fatal accident has occurred. A body was discovered this morning by one of the cleaning crew."

Everyone present stopped talking; the silence was sepulchral. There could be heard only the heavy breathing of Wilson; the old man suffering from angina, and the tapping of Gustavo's cane that he could not control because of his Parkinson's.

"We all know Linda Smith." Rolling continued. "We all know of her daily scurrying and her hullabaloos in the hallways, knocking on doors of the male residents younger than her, inviting them to dinner ... We have seen her leaving each apartment before dawn carrying an empty casserole in her hands. I do not know, and I do not intend to find out, where or with whom Linda spent the night; but apparently, as she descended the dark emergency stairs, she lost her balance, fell down and slammed her head into the cement floor with all her humanity and the casserole. The impact on her head was so severe that she must have lost consciousness and passed away instantly. I am very sorry for her, but I would like to take advantage of this opportunity, of this unfortunate situation to remind everyone, without exception, that the stairs are not to be used to go between floors except in an emergency. You must always use the elevator, that's what the elevator is for."

"Linda's corpse was transferred to the funeral home adjacent to the church of St. Angela," Rolling continued, "and her relatives were also notified of the tragic accident. The police were notified and today two officers were present to make sure that tragic event was an accident and not a criminal act, or rather, that nobody pushed Linda down the stairs. Soon we will inform you about the details of the wake and burial. Thank you very much!"

"I am sorry about Linda," Ignacio murmured. "Just two weeks ago I shared with her one of her famed casseroles. May she rest in peace, may God hold her in His holy bosom."

"Yes, her end was tragic" Isamu replied. "Mr. Ignacio, I would be very pleased if you would accept an invitation to lunch. They just opened a Japanese restaurant at the corner of David and Ocean, the cook is native Japanese, and supposedly prepares very tasty sushi."

"Of course, Isamu, it will be nice to share some good sushi with you."

"And a cup of Ceylon tea…" Isamu added.

It did not take long for the two friends to reach the restaurant. And as planned Isamu, who anticipated Ignacio's accepting his invitation, had previously booked a private table in the dining room adjacent to the main dining room of the restaurant.

"Very well Mr. Ignacio, as we enjoy this delicious Japanese dish, you can continue with the legendary tale that was about to begin before we received the bad news of Mrs. Smith's accident."

"The tragic death of my friend has left me puzzled and thoughtful … How easy it is to lose your life! How fragile we humans are! Today we are well and in an instant, due to a fall, we leave this world."

"Death is always lurking among us, Mr. Ignacio. It takes advantage of any moment of neglect, of distraction and fatally attacks us like a furious beast."

"But let's stop philosophizing and thinking about bad things. What I wanted to tell you is another story my father told us when we were kids; I don't know if it is a true story or just one of his tales to frighten us to be more careful when we escaped in the coffee plantation and the vicinity of the well. You know, Isamu, there are all kinds of people in life, there are good people and bad people. It was the same in the days of the *carretas*, there were good and bad *carreteros*. Travel between cities was long and arduous, not to mention risky, sometimes the oxen died, the *carretas* would break down, the *carreteros* became ill. Besides all these possible accidents they were also exposed to the thugs and thieves who took advantage of them to steal their cargo, the water or whatever little money they could carry.

Among the *carreteros,* there was a young couple of newlyweds who, with their savings, had bought a *carreta* to transport fruits, food, and other goods that they bought at wholesale prices at nearby ranches in the city of Rivas to resell them at another markets in the city of Jinotepe. All the *carreteros* admired them for their dedication but even more for their youth. Sometimes, to help them, my parents would buy some or all of their merchandise, and on rainy days they would give then shelter and let them spend the night on our ranch. Thus, the months passed until one day the young couple disappeared without leaving a trace. My father tried to find out their whereabouts from other *carreteros*, but no one knew the whereabouts of the young couple. One of the *carreteros* said that they had fallen in a ravine, but nobody had seen the *carreta*, the oxen and the young couple. Others said that they had sold their *carreta* and left the area; however, no one was certain about what really happened to them."

"What a fascinating story!" Exclaimed Isamu after taking a sip of his hot tea.

"The story gets even more mysterious," continued Ignacio. "According to my father, some of the coffee pickers, when the northern winds blow, would hear what sounded like a man's and a woman's lament. Some seemed to hear the rolling wheels of a *carreta* and the bellowing of animals like oxen. But the most significant thing in the story is that when the cutters stopped picking the coffee to determine the origin of the groans and the dragging of the chains ... the noises suddenly stopped. It was a mystery. As I mentioned, this seems to be one of those stories or legends of my country, where tales of this nature abound. Each city or town has its own stories and each person tells them in their own way, or as best as they can remember them. Some are true, others are made up, depending on who is telling the story."

"What a fascinating story, Mr. Ignacio," Isamu said. "It gives me great satisfaction that you took the time to narrate it to me in so much detail."

"It's been a pleasure for me," replied Ignacio, "not only to tell you the story of my well but to have shared with you such delicious sushi and Ceylon tea."

Isamu paused and did not immediately answer his friend. Not looking directly into his eyes, he then told the old man:

"My dear friend Ignacio, I have something to say which perhaps may surprise you. I want you to consider this lunch as a farewell lunch. Yesterday, I signed a contract to sell my dry-cleaning business. I'm leaving Monterey."

"I suspected it, Isamu," replied Ignacio, "for all the years you've served our needs in Los Robles you've never invited me to lunch. What are you going to do? Where are you going to live?"

"Mr. Ignacio, I'm going to Japan for a long time. I want to go visit the land of my parents, of my ancestors. Besides, I am about to turn forty years old and I'm not married. Maybe in Japan, I can find a wife of my own race and bring her to San Francisco. I want to start a family, have children. On my return, I want to establish a new dry-cleaning business and with the help of my wife, I am sure that I can achieve it. That is my dream. But you, Mr. Ignacio, do not worry," added Isamu, "I will write to you, I will phone you, I will keep informed of your health. I will come to visit you when I return from Japan, and I will introduce you to my wife."

Sadly, Ignacio smiled at his friend's plans and his promises to communicate with him. After a pause, he said to his friend:

"My dear friend, thank you for sharing your plans. I congratulate you and wish you the best in the country of your ancestors, in fact, your country. One never forgets one's roots, no matter how much time tries to force us to forget or how far away we are from that piece of land that witnessed our birth. I am sure that you will find a good woman who will love you, appreciate you and will give you many children, you deserve all of that; you are a very good man, a loyal friend. However, regarding your promise to write to me, to keep abreast of my well-being, and all those good intentions, I also thank you for that, but let me tell you something Isamu, it is too much of a coincidence but your plans have reminded me of a passage from Steinbeck's novel *East of Eden*. Have you read it?"

"Yes, I have read it!"

"As I said, it is too much of a coincidence because in that particular passage — I will cite it for you — Lee, the Chinese butler, Asian like you, after many years of working faithfully in the estate of Adam Trask, decides to move away and go live in San Francisco. After saying goodbye Adam asks him:

'... will you write to us?
I don't know — Lee — replied. I'll have to think about it. They say a clean cut heals soonest. There's nothing sadder to me than relationships held by nothing but the glue of a postage stamp. If you can't see or hear or touch a man, it's best to let him go ...'."

"I will reverse the dialogue, Isamu. I'm going to be Lee and you Adam and I'll tell you: if you cannot see, talk to, shake hands with a friend, and share a joke, a drink, a lunch ... it's better to let that friend go. So, go my dear friend, do what you have to do, your future is ahead of you. Forget about me, this old man who, if someday you should return, perhaps will not know who you are or perhaps will have died."

"No, Mr. Ignacio, I will not forget you!"

"Come on, Isamu, give me a hug and go in peace, don't look back. Good luck my dear friend. Thank you for your invitation to lunch."

Ignacio got up from his chair, and as he had done a few days ago, when he slowly walked toward his bedroom window to see the destruction of the well in the backyard of Los Robles, leaning on his lathe-turned dark wooded cane, slowly walked towards the door of the restaurant.

Printed in the United States
By Bookmasters